KILL OR DIE

The House of Killers

SAMANTHA LEE HOWE

One More Chapter
a division of HarperCollins*Publishers*
1 London Bridge Street
London SE1 9GF
www.harpercollins.co.uk

HarperCollins*Publishers*
1st Floor, Watermarque Building, Ringsend Road
Dublin 4, Ireland

This paperback edition 2021
First published in Great Britain in ebook format
by HarperCollins*Publishers* 2021

A catalogue record of this book is available from the British Library

ISBN: 978-0-00-844461-7

This novel is entirely a work of fiction. The names, characters and
incidents portrayed in it are the work of the author's imagination. Any
resemblance to actual persons, living or dead, events or localities is
entirely coincidental.

Printed and bound in Great Britain by
CPI Group (UK) Ltd, Croydon CR0 4YY

For David, Frazer, Andrew and Tracey – more champagne and summer nights ahead!

'*I am the way into the city of woe.*
   I am the way to a forsaken people.
   I am the way into eternal sorrow.'

— Dante Alighieri, *Inferno* (tr. by John Ciardi)

Prologue

'What was that?' says Shelley Armitage as she starts to load the food trolley.

They've been in the air for a few hours, and this is the second food service. They are en route to Shanghai with a Boeing 777 300 full of business types and tourists. It takes just under twelve hours from London.

'Just a bit of turbulence,' says Jay. 'Nothing to worry about, love.' But Jay's dark brown eyes look down the cabin and search for the nearest hatch. He stares outside at the darkening sky.

Shelley finds the gorgeous black steward's affectations a little grating and doesn't really appreciate being called 'love' by someone she hardly knows. But she lets it slide, because she wants a chance to do long-haul again and she knows this team will report on how she handles the journey, passengers and especially her interaction with the crew.

'It feels like we're turning,' Shelley says.

'I'll find out,' says Jay.

1

He calls the cockpit from the galley phone. The line rings and then the co-pilot, Carl Bennett, picks up the receiver.

'Have we changed direction?' Jay asks.

'Yeah. A slight blip,' Carl says. 'The captain says it's nothing to worry about.'

Jay hangs up. 'Everything's fine,' he tells Shelley.

But it isn't.

The in-flight manager, Angie, comes looking for them. 'You've got to keep everyone calm. Feed them, but if they ask, say we are detouring because of weather.'

'Why *are* we changing course?' asks Shelley.

Angie frowns. 'Instructions from below. It's most irregular. I'll keep you in the loop when I know more.'

Angie walks away leaving Jay and Shelley to take care of the evening meal in economy. They serve in efficient silence.

'I was just watching the flight map,' says a man in a seat over the wing, 'and we seemed to have changed direction.'

'It's nothing. Just a slight deviation. We'll be back on course shortly,' Shelley says, her face a professional mask.

She gives him his food tray and moves on to the next passenger without further explanation.

The seatbelt signs go on, followed by the pilot announcing that all crew are to take their seats.

'What's happening?' asks a woman coming out of the toilet.

'Just turbulence,' Shelley says automatically. 'Please return to your seat.'

She pushes the food trolley back to the galley and stows it. Then she sits beside Jay who is already strapped in.

'I don't like this,' he whispers.

By then Shelley's face is blanched white. She clenches her hands in her lap and stares at the partition wall between them and the cabin they are serving. She is regretting taking this flight already. It had seemed such a good idea when her supervisor rang and said that they were a crew member down. She'd never been to Shanghai and it was on her bucket list. Plus, she wanted to be offered other exciting long-haul locations. After all that's why she'd become cabin crew in the first place.

The plane plummets, free-falling through the sky as though in a vacuum. For a second Shelley thinks that the engines have failed.

Jay grabs her arm. 'What the fuck?'

Cries of fear erupt in the passenger cabin.

This is your co-pilot. Please remain calm. We are experiencing unusual turbulence…'

The plane levels out and cruises as if nothing has happened.

Shelley and Jay look at each other, knowing that this isn't true. The sudden drop in altitude is something that they have never experienced before; they are both scared. The phone beside their seat lights up and Shelley reaches for the receiver. She and Jay press their ears against it.

'What's happening?' she asks.

'You know that scenario that we all said could never happen?' Angie says.

'What?' asks Shelley.

'Someone has taken over the onboard computer.'

'It's not possible,' says Jay.

'Are we going to crash?' gasps Shelley.

3

'We are being rerouted,' Angie says. 'Hang in there. Make sure no passengers go walkabout. The pilot says keep calm, we're okay for now.'

Angie hangs up and Shelley and Jay are left feeling hopeless. The fate of all on board is in the hands of someone unknown.

'But how?' asks Jay.

'This is… Someone has hacked into the system. All they need is an iPad or an Android tablet,' Shelley says, remembering some training she'd been given when fear of hijack was at its worst.

'But that would mean the security code was compromised…' Jay says. 'It would have to be … *one of us*.'

Shelley unbuckles her seat belt. 'I have to go to the cockpit,' she says. 'Keep an eye on the passengers.'

'No. Don't…' Jay says but Shelley is already halfway through the cabin before he can unbuckle.

Shelley passes through economy and premium, ignoring the passengers who call to her for reassurance. At the end of the premium cabin, she sees two other flight attendants strapped in as the pilot had ordered. One of them looks at her, an unspoken question on the woman's face.

Shelley smiles and nods. 'We'll be back on track shortly,' she says.

Then she walks towards the business-class cabin, passes through and goes straight into first where she expects to find Angie. The passengers in this cabin are all lying flat on beds, asleep and unaware of the possible threat to their lives. Shelley finds Angie's crew seat empty.

She picks up the phone and rings the cockpit again. This time, no one answers.

What is going on? She turns to the cockpit door and picks up the interphone. She calls the cockpit but there's still no answer. She knocks on the door, breaking protocol, but she's feeling concerned that something is wrong.

'Captain?' There's no response from inside.

She turns and starts to make her way back through the cabin.

Air rushes through the plane and the oxygen masks drop down onto the sleeping business-class passengers. Shelley grabs the nearest seat and holds on. Further back down the plane, screams of fear take up again. No reassurance comes from the pilot this time. The yells continue. Shelley knows what is happening, even though this has never occurred on a flight before in all of her ten years as cabin crew. Someone has opened the middle exit door and the air is being sucked out of the plane. Shelley hooks her arm around the seat, then she pulls the nearest oxygen mask over her face. She holds on tight until the outside air fills the cabin and the pressure equalises with the outside.

'Stay in your seats!' she yells.

None of the first-class passengers move. The plane pitches left. Shelley yelps as she is almost thrown from the seat. The plane levels out again and while she catches her breath, she looks around the cabin at the sleeping passengers. Letting go of the armrests of the seat she is in, she reaches for the nearest person: a businessman that Angie had pointed out to her earlier as a regular on this flight. She shakes his shoulder roughly. His arm falls down over his arm rest, limp. He doesn't wake.

Drugged, she thinks. *Or dead.* A surge of fear rushes up inside her. The person who's opened the door in the middle of the plane is behind this. She pulls off the oxygen mask and stumbles back towards the premium economy cabin. The air is thin, but breathable. Her eyes dart over the business-class passengers, who are also silent. She's shocked that she hadn't noticed this on the way through.

She has to get to Jay and enlist his help. They need, also, to get into the cockpit and find out what the fuck is going on.

'Jay!' she yells.

Then, as she reaches the exit, she sees the door wide open. Jay and Angie are poised near it.

'For God's sake!' she yells over the noise of the rushing air. 'Who did this?'

Angie glances over her shoulder at Shelley. She is holding an android tablet and is typing something into it. On her face is a portable oxygen mask.

'Keep calm, Shell,' says Jay. 'It'll all be over soon.' There is no sign of his inflected voice. He is cold and impersonal.

Back in the premium cabin the passengers are quiet. Their screams of fear have been abruptly silenced.

'What's fucking happening?' Shelley yells. She is close to hysteria.

'You should have stayed in your seat,' Jay says.

Shelley approaches the door. She is trembling and then she notices the packs strapped around Jay and Angie's shoulders and she knows they are parachutes. Not regulation as they don't have them on board.

'You two did this...'

In the galley Shelley sees the slumped body of one of the passengers. Her eyes dart from one to the other of her colleagues; panic makes it impossible for her to think. Then Angie grabs Shelley's arm and yanks her towards the open door.

'Why?' Shelley asks.

'Because we can, love,' Jay says as Angie pushes Shelley out of the plane.

Shelley's last scream is snatched away by the howling winds as she vanishes into the clouds scudding below the crippled aircraft.

Chapter One

MICHAEL

'Come in, Mike,' says Ray.

I see that they are waiting for me. My former colleagues, Ray Martin, Bethany Cane and Leon Tchaikovsky, are sat at the briefing desk.

'Take a seat,' Ray says.

'I'll stand,' I say.

'Mike, we aren't your enemies,' Beth says. 'This is a very difficult situation for all of us.'

I've been on gardening leave for the past six months, waiting to learn my fate. Over that period I'd told them everything I knew in several debriefings. How the Network had raised me through surrogate parents and it was Ray who'd given me the final piece of the puzzle, revealing that the man I'd always known as 'Uncle Andrew' was in fact my biological father. Andrew ran the Network until he was shot, after I'd executed a sting on their assassin school. A place we now referred to as the House of Killers, or sometimes merely Kill House. As time went on, I remembered my whole sorry story. Including the brainwashing and how the Network had turned me into a sleeper agent. An agent that Andrew Beech had used as his own personal spy in MI5.

'I just don't know what more I can tell you,' I say now.

The memories, though fully returned, aren't as detailed as I had hoped. Something happened after we left the Network's house in Alderley Edge – a huge mansion disguised as a private school where they housed the abducted children whom they reared as assassins: my mind regressed. I slipped back inside myself and lost some of that gained knowledge as another piece of Beech's awful conditioning kicked in.

Archive had brought down that appalling training house of Beech's, freeing the children that had been taken and groomed. But we all knew this was just one of many such places globally and was a drop in the ocean when it came to the mechanisms of the Network.

Even so, I'd given Ray enough information that MI5 and Interpol had been able to use it to disrupt another house. Though, at the time, I wasn't privy to what they'd actually found, or how much chaos they'd wreaked on the Network, I still knew that they had halted Beech's plans for a time. The Network, for now, had been forced to cover their tracks in Europe, as well as the UK.

'The shrink you gave me says it's self-preservation,' I tell them now. 'I didn't know I was a sleeper. I don't want to remember being that person. You get that, right?'

'Sit, Mike,' Ray says again. 'We didn't call you here to give you a hard time.'

I succumb to the invitation and take the spare seat at the end of the table. They look at me. I see curiosity and something else. A mix of fear and distrust. It comes off Beth and Leon like a bad smell. From Ray ... nothing. Not even the empathy he sometimes tries to convey. For which I have at times been grateful.

'It's time to change things. This situation, the gardening leave, can't go on for ever,' Ray says.

'I guessed as much,' I say. So, this is it. I'm going to be cut loose. I'll never work in MI5 again, let alone anywhere else with security access. I can't say I blame him. It's the way of the world we inhabit and I'm a liability.

'We want you to come back to work,' Beth says. 'Naturally you won't have quite the same ... status.'

I think I've misheard her. 'What? Come *back*?'

'If you want to,' says Leon.

'I don't understand,' I say.

'Michael, you were recruited for Archive because you have a very special skill set. Your profiling is second to none. You've been a reliable agent,' explains Ray.

'But ... *Beech*? I was put here as a mole...'

'Andrew Beech had nothing to do with your recruitment here. Our finding you was purely through trusted intelligence. It just happened to be lucky for the Network. Mike, we've spent the last few months trying to bring these bastards down and we are close, but not close enough. Your assassin, Neva, she's nowhere to be found and neither is the former headteacher of the Network's kill house, Olive Redding. Both of whom could tell us a great deal.'

'However, you managed to expose another link. Janice

Brayford's Preparatory School is now closed down, though where that headmistress, Denton, scarpered off to is also anyone's guess. She was clearly involved in the disappearance of Amelie Arquette. Probably working with Simone Arquette at the time. Of course, we don't know this, it's just some of the pieces we've managed to put together,' explains Leon.

Simone Arquette was a willing recruit of the Network and many years ago she'd done a deal with Beech, gaining wealth and success for her unwitting husband, all for the price of their only child. But when Amelie was passed onto the Network to become a future assassin, they didn't know the child had a heart defect. Unbeknownst to Simone, and Beech, Amelie didn't survive the early stages of conditioning. After that another child was brought into the house to replace her. This one was later called by the codename Neva. And Neva had been the catalyst that took down Beech, revealed my sleeper status and brought my whole life into question.

'Which means,' Ray says, bringing my mind back to the present, 'the Network are still functioning despite our strikes on the properties we found connected to Beech Corp. And we haven't done nearly enough damage.'

I'm surprised at this sudden sharing of information about their investigation. Ray has been very circumspect about his findings until now. I accept it as being linked to their decision to bring me back into the fold.

'It's called the Network for a reason,' I say, dropping into my old habit of analysis. 'Someone was always going to take over from Beech.'

'True,' says Beth. 'But they are still in chaos. There've been no assassinations that we can attribute to them over the past few months. Equally we still haven't been able to solve a few previous killings. Beech was clever about that kind of paper trail at least.'

'Maybe that means we've unbalanced them enough,' Ray continues. 'But I don't think so. We've not heard the last from them. This organisation was too slick. It will be only a matter of time before we again see evidence of their movements.'

'But going back to your earlier point, I don't know about Olive Redding, but Neva didn't know much more than me. She didn't even know where the house was. I remembered and I took her there. Neva was searching for her own answers.'

'Olive should be our focus then,' Beth said, 'and you'll help us find her, won't you, Mike?'

'What can I do that you haven't already done to trace their remaining people?' I ask.

'You can give us insight,' Ray said.

'I don't know any more than I already told you. My access was limited. It was like I was two people living in one body. All the information I gained once Neva broke the conditioning is fragmented. Beech knew what he was doing on that score, though I think he was ready to share more with me.'

'The thing is,' Ray says, 'you're the closest thing we have to catching up with Beech's foot soldiers and possible replacement. All we ask is that you give it a try.'

'And my security access?'

'Limited,' says Leon. 'For now.'

I frown.

'We want you to comb over the files we found in the house. A lot of the information was redacted in the files and doesn't mean much to any of us, but we are hoping that enough is there to jog your memory,' Leon continues.

I don't comment that they are giving me grunt work. Boring information searches that a lesser operative – correction *Security Agent* (those two things are a main source of confusion for me now) – would do. I know I'll be tied to my desk, monitored and probably be viewed with general disgust and distrust. But what else can I do? My whole life was Archive and until Neva came into it, I was happy just doing my job.

'All right,' I say. 'I'll look. Does this mean I'm back on the payroll?'

Ray laughs. 'You've never been off it!'

_____

I am back in my old office. I have a new password for the computer, and limited access to files. I'm not surprised by this; I had been, after all, obtaining information that I'd then been passing onto the Network, even though I wasn't aware of doing so. I'm certain that the computer now has spyware that will monitor my every keystroke.

On my desk is a pile of folders, all of which contain information found at the Network's house in Alderley Edge. For a moment I remember the place. The school-like smell and appearance didn't detract from the fact that this building was little better than a Nazi-style camp that turned innocent children into killing machines.

I open the top folder and find it is Olive Redding's. There is a picture of Olive as a small child. She's holding the hand of someone who is not in the photograph. Olive's eyes are drained of emotion, but she is not yet the woman that I saw at the house. This depicts the early stages of conditioning that all of us had been through. A shirking of common childhood needs, and the empty void that was left was then filled with the Network's dark conditioning.

I recall the radicalisation methods. Used so often by political and religious terrorist groups. My MI5 training taught me how this was done, but I had been unaware that I had been subjected to it. We were a cult of sorts, taught ... no, *programmed* ... to obey, and fight to the death if necessary. And in my case: kill on command with no regret. But did I believe the message the Network had implanted during their subversion? No. And even during the brainwashing I never believed. That was why their work failed. They did not find 'common ground' with their young assassins. They did not persuade us that our enemy was bad and deserved what we dished out. What they taught us was fear. Fear of them, not the agencies they set us against, but of failure and the repercussions that would bring.

In the folder, Olive's training notes are nothing different from the countless others taken by the Network. I was a child of the house, though not full time, and trained to 'forget' my conditioning rather than embrace and live it. I knew them, but I didn't. I had lived my whole life – cookie-cutter parents and all – as though I were a normal person.

My psychology degree hadn't prepared me for the total mind-fuck that learning I *wasn't* 'normal' became.

I make some observations on my laptop about Olive's file. They want to find her. She knows so much that can help them bring down the network, but Olive, like Neva, was trained to hide. I'm sure this won't be easy.

I close Olive's file and stare into space. My head hurts from concentrating, but also because of the trauma of being back in Archive.

What would Neva think of this situation? Bringing her to mind creates even deeper pain. I haven't seen her since that day she helped me rescue the children and bring down the house. She had slipped away amidst the chaos, never to be heard from again. I wonder now if she found Olive and received the answers she sought. Were the two of them together, enjoying their retirement? Part of me likes to imagine this. Neva: safe, happy and no longer a killer. She deserves a life of her own: we all do.

I decide I need coffee. I stand and walk around the desk and then out into the central office where Beth is working diligently at her desk. Seeing me she drops her screen saver onto the monitor, hiding whatever it is she's working on from me. I don't question it, but I feel a jolt of sadness at the distrust. Beth and I had always worked well together. Now she looks at me with different eyes.

'I'm going for coffee; do you want one?' I ask.

Beth shakes her head. 'No thanks. I'm finishing early today. School play to go and see.'

I nod, pleased at this casual sharing of personal

information. Beth's children are growing fast and like any mother, Beth must want to be part of it.

I say nothing more as I head off to the coffee machine. Passing Ray's office on the way, I see Leon and Ray in close conference.

'It'll be fine,' Ray says. 'We'll keep a close watch on him.'

Ray sees me then and gives me a small wave. Leon looks over his shoulder, startled by my sudden appearance. Despite their 'welcome back', things are not going to be the same at Archive, and it will be unrealistic of me to expect them to be.

I fetch my coffee as Leon comes out of Ray's office. He closes the door, and walks away, back towards the main office area. He doesn't look at me.

I sit at my desk and sip the coffee. This is the most awkward I have ever felt in my work environment.

Chapter Two

NEVA

She's wearing a hard hat and a bright red jacket as she walks around the construction site, clipboard in hand. No one looks at her, and so Neva, with her newly acquired workwoman disguise, exits via the crew entrance area.

She walks down the hill, passing Michael's apartment. The work taking place nearby is a convenience she couldn't have planned but has taken advantage of. No one notices her, blatant and obvious in this gaudy coat. She's a working person. Instantly forgettable. The jacket guarantees that no one will remember her face.

She sees Michael return and watches as the obvious tail on him parks up his motorbike. Michael sees him too, though he isn't blatant in his observation as his eyes flick to the youth and then immediately away again. The tail is a total amateur. So conspicuous in his attempt to be invisible. Every well-trained spy knows how to hide in plain sight. Neva is a master of being so obvious that she isn't seen.

She's been trying to pluck up the courage to see Michael

for the past few weeks. She stayed away from London for the best part of six months. But she hasn't forgotten Michael and never will. Their origins are indelibly linked, and their past is something that neither of them can escape from.

Michael's apartment is more than likely bugged, and she shouldn't approach him there. They never leave him alone as they monitor his movements day and night, as though they expect him to run at any moment. She wouldn't blame him if he did. This is no life. Neva can see that the grip MI5 has on Michael is not that different from the sway the Network had on them both. It requires conditioned loyalty and the belief that you are doing something important.

The man on the motorbike looks around; his eyes skim over her, barely registering. Yes, a total novice. A real spy would be looking for someone who wasn't hiding. A real spy would look at her – a woman in a man's work jacket – first. But the disguise was not for a professional, it is for the general public and the useless amateur that sits bored outside Michael's apartment.

Michael goes into his building. It's unlikely that he will leave again until morning.

Making her mind up to approach him, Neva crosses the road, passing the youth on the motorbike. He's staring blatantly at the door to Michael's apartment block. He doesn't notice as Neva heads around the back of the building.

Down the alley she places the clipboard on top of a dumpster. Earlier in the day she'd tampered with the lock on the back door to the building to save herself time if she did make up her mind. She'd also checked if the stairwell was being monitored by a security camera and it wasn't. This makes her approach simple. Now she pulls it open and steps inside.

She takes the back stairs two at a time. As she begins to climb the flight to Michael's floor, she sees a figure standing by the door at the top. Michael looks down at her.

'Good disguise,' he says.

'It didn't fool you though,' she smiles.

She reaches the landing and they look at each other.

'I wondered when you'd show up,' he says. 'It's been months…'

'They watch you all the time.'

'I know.'

He reaches for her and Neva lets him take her in his arms. They hold each other for a long time. It's comforting and warm. It tells them both more about each other than words can. Neva is the first to pull away, but even then, she is hesitant.

'I'm working back at Archive. They want me to help track Olive,' he tells her.

'And how is that going?'

Michael shrugs. 'They don't trust me.'

'Naturally.'

'I can't stay here long. They monitor everything and I'm sure they know exactly how long it should take me to reach my apartment. You've taken a risk coming here right now. They'd love to get their hands on you.'

It is her turn to shrug. 'I came to warn you.'

'What about?'

'There's movement in the Network. They are rallying. New leadership has emerged.'

'And where does that leave you?' he asks. 'Are you going to work for them again?'

'I killed my handler to get away. Why would you even ask me that?'

The tension in the air has more to do with their sexual awareness of each other than the conflict his question raises. She knows why he has to ask. There will always be a question of trust between them, despite everything they have shared. How could it be otherwise?

'Michael, you have to be careful,' she warns. 'They may come for you. Beech wanted you to take over from him – they'll believe you know too much and have betrayed them. The Network are your enemy now more than ever.'

'One thing I do recall is how to deal with anyone who does come after me.' His voice is cold.

Neva doesn't enjoy his new lack of innocence. His obliviousness to the Network was always attractive, as was his apparent naivety. All of that has gone, along with his belief in his former life and childhood. She keeps her face blank and doesn't let her emotions show. She's not sure why, but his words sadden her.

'Where have you been hiding?' he asks her.

'It doesn't matter.'

'Do you know where Olive is?'

'No. I want to get my hands on her more than you do. She knows who my real parents are,' Neva says.

Michael digests this information before replying, his

voice low and carefully moderated. 'Why do you want to know who they are?'

'If they sold me to the Network, I'll kill them.'

'I understand your need for revenge,' Michael says. He places his hand on her forearm, stroking her through the thick work jacket. 'But if you find Olive, let me talk to her too. I need answers just as much as you do.'

Neva goes into his arms again. She wants to be held. The smell of him is intoxicating, male, warm, a musky scent that belongs exclusively to Michael. She squeezes her eyes shut as his arms tighten again around her.

They don't speak. There is an inexplicable bond between them that neither of them understands. Neva wants to voice it, but the intense pain chokes the words from her throat. How can she tell him seeing him brings such grief? This is why she's stayed away. This is why she hesitates to be close. She wants him in her life and she's sure he feels the same. They don't need to say anything to know this. Voicing it will only confirm the total impossibility that it could ever happen. Love, romance, relationships are not for people like them.

Michael releases her this time.

'Tell me you're safe then, wherever it is you're staying.'

'As safe as I can be,' she says. 'Safer than you.' Then on impulse she says, 'Leave here. Come with me.'

'The only thread of normality I have is my work. It's the only thing that is real.'

Neva doesn't tell him that she believes nothing is real – not even Archive in the end.

She turns then and begins walking back down the stairs.

'Goodbye, Michael,' she says, and her words sound final.

'Wait!' he says.

He joins her on the stairs, pulling her to him. They kiss for the first time in months. It's urgent and passionate but still so new to them both.

'Stop,' she says pulling away. 'We can't be together. Not unless—'

'What will it take?'

His question shocks her. How can he even think this is possible? Despite her own erratic emotions, feelings she is still struggling to process, Neva can't lie to Michael: one of them has to be that oh so distant voice of reason.

'Michael, we've never been further apart than now. Secrecy was what we had. Maybe the wrongness of "us" was what made it so attractive.'

'Are you saying it wasn't real?' he says through clenched jaws.

'No. I'm not saying that. It was real. *Is* real. But the Network haven't gone. Archive still pull your strings and...' She tapers off, unable to continue because the truth when spoken is harder to accept than when it is explored inside her mind.

Michael studies her face. 'Say it. Whatever it is. You can't hurt me more.'

'The past will always catch us up. Unless we bring the Network down once and for all. But we could run from it. Together. If you were willing.'

'Thank you,' Michael says.

'What for?'

'The reality check.'

Neva explores the ache that's growing inside her, as she anticipates what's coming next. But their story must play out, no matter what the result. She doesn't believe in destiny: she believes in her own impetus. Even so, not everything is within her control.

'I can do so much more if I have Archive resources to fight them with,' he says. 'Though nothing appeals to me more than leaving with you. But it's not possible. We'd have a lifetime of looking over our shoulders. Do either of us really want that?'

Neva sighs. She is tired. Michael has voiced their reality and now neither of them can ignore it. Her body aches and a dull sickness lurks in the pit of her stomach. She doesn't understand this new pain. It hurts almost as much as the day she broke away from the Network and sucks the life from her in the same way.

'I have to go into my flat or they'll get suspicious,' he says. 'Will I see you again?'

She turns and hurries back down the stairs without answering.

The sound of her footsteps echoes in the stairwell. She is aware of Michael watching her until she is out of sight.

Back outside, Neva retrieves the clipboard and makes her way out to the main street, striding quickly away from the man on the motorbike, who is now puffing on a vape as he continues to stare at Michael's front door.

Down the street she pauses. She's aware of the knife in her wrist holster. She glances back at the stupid youth. She could kill him, just for the hell of it. After all, she is the converse of heaven and death still means nothing to her. She feels the ebb and flow – the urge to kill – surging through her veins in a rush of adrenaline. Her blood sings in her ears, an unnameable melody that calls to the darkest, deepest depths of her being. Her never forgotten mantra plays around her consciousness, while calming her subconscious: *I am death*. And she acknowledges that, in the end, there is no escaping from this final eventuality. Why not take more down with you before the inevitable?

Her body moves of its own volition and she takes a step towards the novice as though she's being carried on an irresistible tide.

But no. She stops. She has to be smart and not draw attention to Michael, or herself.

For the moment.

Chapter Three

MICHAEL

I enter my flat with a sense of dread. Despite the warmth of the day and the heat of the apartment, stifled as it has been with the windows securely fastened throughout the day, I feel cold. But this chill is far from physical.

I open the windows now, walking through the lounge, passing on to the kitchen and ending up in my bedroom, which is the hottest room in the place. There isn't a breeze tonight and the air is slow to circulate as the evening draws in.

My apartment is in central London and I've lived here for years, never craving any other life. Until now.

I feel suffocated. My chest aches and the shallow breaths I take burn as though I'm inhaling the direct heat of the sun. But it is not the heat or the imagined chill that creates this pain. It is the dull twinge of abject sadness.

I'm miserable as I pull off my tie, and peel away the white shirt that is damp with sweat.

A shudder ripples down over my skin as I strip and

head for the bathroom and a cool, refreshing shower that should make me feel a little more comfortable. Physically anyway.

Neva is on my mind as I come back into the bedroom, and the thought of her being here in my bed again won't leave. I can smell her still, the slight scent of perfume, the aroma of salty perspiration. Delicious and clean on her skin. The taste of her mouth too still lingers on my lips. I'm not given to poetry and declarations of love. *Could I ever even say that to her?* I'm not sure what it is I feel. She's inscrutable, unattainable. Even when I'm holding her, I don't know what she's thinking. I don't believe she can ever truly be mine.

I dry my body and pull on a pair of boxers, and then I walk out of the bedroom. In the kitchen I pour myself a cold beer from the fridge, a habit that has become all too frequent since I've been home on gardening leave.

I mull over the sudden change. So, I'm back in at Archive – well, partly anyway. Is it a coincidence that Neva has returned to me now?

I try to push away the suspicion. What is the point of worrying about motive? We all have our own agendas.

My phone rings and I glance at the screen, seeing Mia's name flash up. My sister. I feel a clench of regret and guilt. I've been distant from her, trying to keep her out of this as much as possible. Mia must never know that our whole lives have been a lie.

'Hey, Sis,' I say, answering.

'I thought you were going to leave me hanging there!' Mia says. 'How you doing?'

'I'm fine. How are you?'

'I'd be better if you could find time to come and visit. See your niece. She's almost four months old and changing by the day.'

'Sorry,' I say. 'Work commitments.'

Mia sighs. 'What's happening, Mike? I thought you were on gardening leave?'

She knows a bit, a story I'd spun her about a security breach. Accusations that had put my job in jeopardy. Ray had agreed to the story to cover all of our backs and to keep Mia ignorant of the work I had done with Archive and our connection with the Network.

'She's innocent in all this,' I had told him. 'And pregnant. Why drag her in? Does she really need to know that our parents weren't who they said they were?'

Ray had agreed after a great deal of begging on my part. I think he didn't see any point in ruining her life as well. And so they'd kept Mia out of it, and she'd never know about the surveillance she was under. At least, I hoped she wouldn't.

'Well, I'm back at work,' I say. 'All is okay.'

'You've been reinstated? That's great news!'

We talk for a little longer. Mia babbles about the new baby, Freya, and about her husband, Ben, whom I've always got along with. When we hang up, she sends me several pictures of Freya. Looking at them compounds my guilt and breaks something inside me. I'm not as strong as I once was, but I'm getting better. Freya is a reminder of all I feel I have lost with the newfound knowledge of my origins.

The reason I haven't been to see her yet is that I'm afraid

to get attached to Freya. She and Mia are my true family. Just as surely as I had been trained to be a killer and spy, I was sure that Mia had been groomed as a breeder for the Network. Even though she's unaware of it. If we hadn't closed the kill house, my little niece could have ended up there in a few years' time. Unbeknownst to Mia she is only my half-sister, and not my maternal twin. We were both lied to, subjected to conditioning and sent out into the world as sleepers by the man who'd sired us. I find myself wondering if Beech had any redeeming qualities at all. Would he have really taken Freya from Mia in the future? Could he have subjected his granddaughter to the torture of the house? I'll never know the answer but suspect that he would have. He hadn't shown any remorse about doing it to me – his son – after all. Or any other child for that matter. *Bastard*.

I put down my phone on the kitchen table and look around the apartment. This place has never felt less of a haven. Within hours of my return, I'd found the surveillance that Archive had put in while they had me under lock and key (for my own safety they said) while we debriefed.

In the bathroom there is a microphone secreted along the light above the mirror. In the bedroom I'm wired for sound via a microphone placed by the window. In the living room and the kitchen, they have camera surveillance. Micro pieces of tech, no bigger than a fly, which are placed in appropriate positions. At least they have afforded me some privacy when I'm naked.

I go back into my bedroom and pull on a pair of chinos

and a T-shirt. Then, taking my wallet and keys, I leave the apartment and head towards the tube. The 'obvious' tail watches me, while he talks into his shirt. By the time I reach the station, another follower has tagged on and travels with me on the train to Soho.

My favourite sushi restaurant is here and ignoring the woman following – at least she's a bit savvier than the last one – I go inside and sit at the bar.

I reach for salmon and avocado maki rolls. My favourite king prawn tempuras soon follow along with teriyaki chicken. Hungry, in need of comfort, I eat my fill.

Outside my tail watches from across the street. I continue to ignore her. I order Asahi beer and sip it as I study the offerings that go around on the conveyor belt.

The restaurant is busy and I cast my eyes around the room, assessing whose company I'm keeping. There is a young Japanese couple sitting by the window, a family of four close by who talk too loudly to each other. Then there is a man sitting on his own in the corner. I feel a little sympathy and camaraderie with him as I eat my lonely dinner, but I'm out of sync with the world.

Eventually I have had enough. I call the waiter over and hand him the empty plates and I pay my bill. Then I leave and walk the streets for a while.

My mind won't settle on anything important, but Olive Redding's file floats behind my eyes. Information. Sentences giving detail of who and what she was. *Talking about a child as an asset. Disgusting. Vile.* The unredacted detail of the torturous process of conditioning. My stomach roils now at the thought.

The parents... Olive's parental details had been redacted, but the names had been missed on one of the pages. Her real name was Georgia Stanners and her father was Lord Stanners! I make a mental note to ask Beth tomorrow if she has seen and pursued this information. I'm kicking myself that I hadn't picked up on it earlier: maybe it wasn't there at all and I am imagining it. The shock of being back in Archive can be blamed for this, plus I haven't been working for six months, no wonder my skills are rusty.

It's after nine when I get home. I try not to think about Neva as I go to bed, determined to be in the office by eight the next morning. Besides, retiring early will end this interminable evening.

Going out has done me some good though. It's freed my mind, relieved a little tension. I'm itching now to get this investigation underway and to regain my stripes and the respect of my colleagues. However long that might take.

Chapter Four

MICHAEL

Dressed in a smart suit, new shirt and tie, I'm the first in the next day. I go straight to my office and open Olive's file. There it is: her real name, I hadn't imagined it. A quick search on the internet reveals something about little Georgia's disappearance. It's odd that this one isn't linked to other missing children of that era, and I hadn't seen her appear in the names Beth originally listed when we first started to look at these cases.

As I begin writing up a report to add to the file, it feels as though I have my mojo back. I hadn't realised quite how much I'd missed being productive during my weird hiatus. Now, I am excited and motivated as I scan the other files, looking for similar information of other children that had passed through the house.

'Hi,' says Beth from the doorway. 'You're early.'

'I remembered something,' I say as I drop back into our old working habits. 'All the real names are redacted but Olive's was missed on one page.'

'Really? Let me see,' says Beth.

When she reads the information and my notes, she shakes her head. 'Just shows you how overworked we've been. None of us saw that, Mike!'

'Someone should go and speak to Lord Stanners,' I say. 'Though he will be fairly old now. It was thirty-odd years ago when she went missing.'

'If we have this information then Olive certainly knew who she really was. Maybe we can pick up her trail through them.' Beth turns to leave then she pauses, looking back at me. 'Welcome back, Mike. We've missed you.'

Beth goes away and I consider her response to the information. Did she pretend she hadn't seen it in order to make me feel useful? I have the uncomfortable suspicion that I've just been patronised.

I try not to think about it as I take more care reading the other documents and I find three more names buried in the notes. These children are all from varying generations.

A girl referred to as 'Jewel' was formerly known as Elizabeth Denver, a young man called 'Drake' was born Dennis Proctor and a final boy with the codename 'Anchor' was originally Stefan Oliver. Jewel is the youngest of the three and is the same age as Neva. I wonder if they trained together.

I open up Beth's notes on Amelie Arquette's suspected peer group – the same that Neva was given over to. There are seven children that went missing that year under similar circumstance. Elizabeth Denver's name is not among them. I know from Ray that Amelie Arquette didn't survive the first few weeks of conditioning, and it was at this point that

Neva was brought into the house and I first met her. There are no photographs of Elizabeth Denver in the file, and I wonder if she, like Neva, was a replacement for another child. The folder doesn't mention anything, at least the unredacted parts don't. What's under those definitive blocks of black I just don't know.

I lift one of the sheets up to the light and look through it. Sometimes the redacting is insufficient to totally obscure what was beneath. But these are solid and are photocopies anyway, so any evidence of the original content is long gone.

Curious, I spend some time reading the achievements of all three of these operatives. Drake and Anchor were particularly brutal in the execution of their assignments. I make notes on this to share with the team and then I go in search of Ray to discuss my findings. There is no further mention of Jewel.

Ray, Leon and Beth are all together in Ray's office. They have a slide projected on the screen, which Beth closes down from her computer when I rap on the open door.

'Sorry if I'm disturbing you,' I say and I can't help the slight resentful tone that slips into my voice as I stare at them.

'That's okay, Mike. My door is always open to you,' Ray says.

'I'll come back later when you're free, but I wondered if you had anything else for me to look at in the meantime?'

Beth stood and went to the filing cabinet behind Ray's desk.

'The next lot are here,' she says, removing a handful of

folders from the cabinet. 'Did you find anything useful in the others? I told the guys about Olive...'

'A few more names came to light that could be leads,' I say. 'I'll add them all to my report. One in particular is interesting. No photos in the file. Same year group as Neva.'

'Great. Here are some more files we found in Beech's office.'

Feeling dismissed, I take the files back to my office. Behind me I see flickering light from the screen as Beth puts the slide back up for the three of them to discuss as I walk away.

I should be happy that I'm back at Archive but instead I feel like an outsider. I don't know if things will ever be normal again.

Chapter Five

NEVA

Neva shuts down her encrypted laptop and stares at the blank wall of her basic hotel room. She's been searching for information on a missing plane. Zen Airline flight 723 was carrying 299 passengers and 12 crew on its way to Shanghai. A Boeing 777 300. The situation resembles the disappearance of Malaysia Airlines flight 370 some years previously. In that instance it was a Boeing 777 200 bearing 227 passengers and 12 crew. While the plane was never found, several theories were bandied around about its disappearance. Neva knew what those hypotheses were because she'd taken particular interest back in 2014.

The disappearance of the Malaysia Airlines flight had been made very public, and yet, strangely, the Zen one has not. Instead, it seems to be hushed up, with very little online about it and no real information. Just a sequence of complaints and legal attempts to get the airline to assume some sort of responsibility for the disappearance of all those people. Even the press has been strangely silent on it, but

Neva knows that often those in power and with great wealth will simply buy the press's silence through their contacts with the various billionaire owners.

Neva closes the lid of the laptop and stands. She had resolved to stay away from Michael but now feels she has to approach him again. It's a concern that he has rejoined his former colleagues and returned to work at Archive, even though such a circumstance will grant him access once more to information that could help her. But would he jeopardise himself again for her sake?

She boards the tube near Michael's work and, dressed as an inspector for TFL, she inspects tickets, scans oyster cards and debit cards up and down the track. Then she waits on the platform at Michael's station until he arrives. As he boards the train, Neva enters his carriage and works her way towards him. She notes the tail – another snot-nosed youth barely out of school and keeps her back to him. She reaches Michael two stops before he's due to depart, and as she asks for proof of payment, she slips him a note. He recognises her but keeps his face straight, palming the note and pushing it into his wallet along with the card.

Neva exits at the next stop and walks away.

Chapter Six

MICHAEL

After reading Neva's note I get off the tube at my usual stop. The tail follows, but I make a quick change of direction and lose myself in the crowd that pours up and out of the station. The man following had been complacent – they are used to me doing exactly as expected. Now I cut across the road, hurry into a back street and hide behind a dumpster. I turn my phone off so that I can't be traced. From my vantage point I see the man passing the end of the alley. He glances down but can't see me. He rushes along the road, speaking into his jacket. I stay there for a long time before emerging back onto the street, then I head back to the tube and make my way to the rendezvous point.

Two hours after leaving work, I sit at a small table in a city centre bar waiting for Neva.

Nervous that I've still somehow been followed, I look around, studying the occupants of the bar. It's a Thursday evening and trade is good. By the door is a good-looking blonde girl in a skin-tight catsuit talking to the bouncer. She is enjoying the fact that the man is hitting on her, and that she keeps placing her hands on the T-shirt over his muscled chest is speaking volumes.

My eyes trail over into the dark corners of the bar. I feel anonymous and safe when I realise that no one in the place is watching me. My eyes continue around the room and then I see her – at the other end of the bar watching me in the bar mirror.

She's ditched the TFL uniform now and is wearing a simple pair of tight jeans and for once her own hair is on display. She had it tied up at our last meeting and now I can see that it has grown, almost down to her waist. She's understated and stunning.

Once she catches my eye, she moves away from the bar and away from me and I get up from my chair and follow.

Neva waits for me by the back door of the bar.

'I'm glad you came,' she says.

I try to hug her but she resists. She's not here to see me as a lover: she has another agenda and won't be distracted from it.

'What's happened?'

She is direct and to the point. 'Have your colleagues been discussing the investigation of a flight that vanished en route to Shanghai?'

'Not to my knowledge. And I haven't heard of any flight accidents on the news.'

'It's being kept out of the press.'

She tells me the flight number and the carrier. I memorise the detail.

'You know about the Malaysia Airlines flight that went off course?' she asks.

'Yes. 2014?'

Neva nods.

'There were many investigations made into that, and speculations,' I say.

'One of them was right,' she says.

'What do you know about it?'

'I wasn't involved in that job, but I had a colleague who was. She liked to talk about it. She took up a position as a crew member and then hacked into the flight computer. The plane was rerouted and eventually dropped into the Indian Ocean.'

'If that's the case, wouldn't the assassin have died too?'

'Parachute. She was on that plane for one reason only and that was to kill one of the passengers. Everyone else was just collateral damage.'

'So, you think this is the same. Someone on board was a hit?'

'I know that someone important to the Network was on board. Someone that they'd pay a hefty ransom for.'

I take a breath.

'But who would take the Network on? And what was this person doing flying to Shanghai?'

'The Network aren't the only game in town, Mike. During my time on the payroll, I discovered that often the Network's assets were hired out. We didn't just do the wet work for them, they also had us clean up the mess left by other companies.'

There is a clattering sound as someone makes their way down towards us, heading for the toilets. Neva pushes open the fire door and we exit into the narrow alley outside the bar. She checks up and down and we stand outside. I keep my foot in the door to stop it closing.

Neva fills me in on what she knows of the Network's rivals.

'Some years ago, I was sent to take out a general in Afghanistan. The Network believed him to be the spearhead of a rival faction. They are known as Almunazama. I did the job, killed the general, leaving his body to be found as a message to the conglomerate. His death threw them into chaos but there was talk before I defected that they were going to make another attempt to regain what they had lost. We were on high alert, ready to converge and go in strong against them. With the disorder in the Network this strike didn't happen. I believe that Almunazama have taken back the territories Beech and his board members stole from them. They've grown stronger. It's possible this man was going to be Beech's replacement. He may have been heading to Shanghai to secure loyalty for the Network in China, an area that Almunazama were particularly interested in.'

'This … Almunazama, do they have any political or religious views?'

'Political maybe, but not religious. Like the Network they are about power, wealth and influence. They don't see themselves as terrorists, just influencers in the global economy. That's not to say they don't fund terrorism to create unrest. Destabilising countries is something both they and the Network often deal in. It's all about money in the end. The reason no one has released the information about this new flight going down is because the powers-that-be are running scared. They don't want the public to make the connection with the Malaysia Airlines flight because this kind of attack can cause far more problems than a terrorist one.'

'They do this to terrorise those in power,' I say. 'Not the general public.'

'Exactly, and they'll use a vicious black hat hacker to do their dirty work. I mean, who wants to deal with that? It's far more insidious than a bomb planted in a mall and can do much more harm.'

'One minute you imply it's another group, then you're saying it's a hacker.'

'The hacker is the employee of the group,' Neva says. 'Think of him or her as a paid mercenary. Just like I was. Only their motives may not be perfectly in line with their employer's. And the work they were sent to do involves kidnap, not murder. But as a consequence, a whole flight of people could possibly have died so that the kidnap could occur. The word on the street is that this hacker has their own agenda and doesn't care for the Almunazama any more than the Network.'

'Have you any idea who this hacker is?'

Neva looks me in the eye and says, 'I need your help before I reveal more, Michael. I want to know what Archive have learned about the Network. I want to see what they have on me.'

I shake my head. 'I can't do that. My access is limited and your file is not among those I have been given. If I start digging around in there, they'll notice. I'm already being watched.'

I'm annoyed at her for trying to create a bargaining tool out of this information. Was the last visit a prelude of this? Was she setting me up to help her again? Does she think me that stupid?

'You can't give me anything?' she says.

'No. Maybe you can tell me something?' I say. 'Do you remember a girl in your class group called Jewel?'

Neva thinks for a moment and then she shakes her head. 'No. Who is she?'

'Just a name that's come up.'

'Michael. I need your help,' she says again. 'Please.'

I look her in the eyes and see pleading there. But I cannot help her. I hold the door with my hand and remove my foot.

'I'm sorry. I said no. I can't and won't do this. You're asking too much. I'm just getting my life back.'

I walk back into the bar and order a strong drink.

I look back down the passage and Neva is there, holding the door, looking at me.

Then she is gone and the door closes behind her.

I sit on a bar stool and down several shots of whiskey. Neva doesn't come back. She knows that when I say 'no' I mean it, but I can't help feeling some regret that she hasn't come back. It all seems to prove that she only shared what she knew so that I would give her inside information. The thought doesn't make me happy.

A few hours later I find my way home after stumbling into a taxi. My tail is waiting outside the apartment block. I ignore him as I stagger into the building. What will they report to Archive tomorrow? I went out drinking and came home pissed?

Big fucking deal.

Chapter Seven

NEVA

A s Neva walks away from the bar, she feels nauseous. Michael is angry: she shouldn't have tried to push him into helping her so soon. But his mention of Jewel threw her a curveball. Now she's remembering something she had long forgotten, when another child arrived at the house.

It was after they had taken Michael away.

Michael had been there for a month, and then Beech, headmaster's cane in hand, had passed Michael over to the people who were to raise him. What happened next Neva had not known until much later.

A few days later they brought in a new girl. Though surplus to requirements, she worked alongside Neva and the others.

She introduced herself as Lizzie, but Tracey Herod soon changed her name to Jewel.

Jewel had surpassed them all in the beginning. She

instinctively reacted as the trainers wanted, yet she was just a little girl, no different from them really, and had arrived months after the rest. It was as though she'd had a head start even so.

'There will be hot chocolate for the first of you to climb to the top of this rope,' Tracey had said. She'd been pitting them against each other a lot lately with promises of treats. But the chocolate: that was special.

Tracey took Neva to one side and spoke to her. And then the competition was on.

In the end it was a hair's breadth between Jewel and Neva as they both shimmied up the ropes. Jewel was pronounced the winner and had been taken to the kitchen and given that coveted hot chocolate that none of them had been permitted since their first night at the house, but which all remembered with a yearning for kindness and love still burning inside them, yet to be eradicated.

Back in the dorm, as Neva and the three other girls waited for Jewel to be returned to them, they had talked about her. Already jealousy was building among them and Neva, with months of conditioning behind her, had felt a strong sense of ownership where Tracey was concerned.

'It's not fair,' one of the girls said.

And the injustice of it brought about an intense feeling of rage inside Neva.

They were lying in the dark, the lights remotely switched off when Jewel returned. She came alone and unsupervised and walked to her bed beside Neva's and sat down. In the dark she began to tug off her training shoes and gym clothing and then she reached for the plain white uniform nightdress. As she pulled it over her head, Neva grabbed Jewel by the hair. She pulled her from the bed and began to kick and punch the little girl.

A fury from nowhere consumed her. She hated Jewel. Jewel was the enemy. Jewel hadn't even been to see Doctor Mendez. It wasn't right that Jewel was favoured.

As the beating continued, the other girls surrounded them cheering and whooping in feral delight. All of them wanted to hit out: Jewel was just the unlucky recipient. Then the lights went on and Neva found herself pulled away from the prone girl.

She didn't remember much after that, except that Tracey had defended her when Beech had suggested that Neva was too volatile.

'Jewel was the catalyst,' Tracey had said even though Jewel hadn't stood a chance against Neva.

Neva was put in a room alone that night while the trainers discussed her fate. When morning came, she was returned to the others, and Jewel was gone. No one ever mentioned her again.

But Tracey's final words to Neva that day were to warn her.

This was her one and only chance to be the best.

And she mustn't fail.

Chapter Eight

MIA

The room is still pitch black when Mia wakes. It's not the first time she's woken this way, anxiety pumping her blood fast and furious until she can hear every beat thudding in her ears. She glances over at Ben's sleeping form. His body is turned towards the door as though he's expecting something to happen.

Mia turns over onto her back and takes a slow breath. She's been dreaming, that's all. A frightening vision of a room. A feeling that she was small and insignificant. And then there had been this blond-haired man talking to her, and someone else...

Mia closes her eyes and tries to remember the strange abstract dream. Yes. She walked down a corridor; her mother was holding her hand and then the door had opened. Mia's anxiety levels spike again, and then the dream slips away.

Careful not to disturb Ben, Mia slips from the bed. As

she always does when she wakes like this, she makes her way down the corridor to Freya's room.

The door is slightly ajar, and there is a dim nightlight illuminating the room. Mia walks in and looks into the cot. Freya is sleeping. Mia bends forward over the side of the cot and listens to the baby's soft breathing. Reassured she sits down on the rocking chair beside the cot and closes her eyes.

Ever since Freya was born, Mia has been suffering with a claustrophobic fear. There was a deep-rooted apprehension that something would happen to her fragile child. She knows she should talk to someone about it but somehow can't find the words to broach the subject, even with the midwife on their check-ups.

Some nights, like tonight, it is worse, but always in the morning this feeling will dissipate and she will think her concerns were natural. Surely any new mother has these fears?

But then there are the dreams.

Sometimes these are more vivid than others, and on such nights, like this one, Mia experiences an intense dread that Freya is in immediate danger. The only thing she can do is come into the room and watch over her baby.

Mia glances at her watch. It's 1.50 a.m. Ben, as always, hasn't heard her leave and he doesn't come to find her. Mia wishes he would, for then she will have to reveal how scared she is and the burden won't be hers alone to carry.

With this thought firmly in her mind, Mia resolves to tell Ben first thing in the morning. She's certain that saying her concerns out loud will lessen their hold on her.

She closes her eyes, resting back into the chair and drifts into a shallow sleep where the man and the … *doctor* talk to her over and over again. They tell her something important. She has a role to play, a gift to give them. Something important for the future.

Mia jerks awake. She gets up out of the chair and stares down at Freya again.

You're mine, she thinks. *They can't have you.*

She shudders as though there is a sudden draft in the room, but the wall thermometer says the temperature is consistent.

But her thoughts have strengthened her, and feeling more in control, Mia takes one last look at her little girl and, reassured, she returns to her own room.

Ben is still sleeping as she slips back under the covers. Mia envies his ability to rest; she's never been as good at clearing her mind as he has and her awareness of this is acute.

She turns on her side, staring at the door beyond Ben's frame.

She's okay. She's safe. I'm never going to let anyone hurt her, she thinks. *Now sleep little one…*

Mia wakes to the sound of Ben showering in the ensuite. It's a workday and he'll head off soon to catch his train into London.

Mia gets up. She pulls on a light robe and goes to check on Freya. The little girl is awake and playing with her hands. The baby smiles and Mia picks her up.

'You're such a good girl,' she says.

When she's changed Freya's nappy, she brings her into the kitchen and places her into the small bouncy chair near the kitchen table. She puts the kettle on and gets two mugs from the cupboard above.

'Morning, darling,' Ben says. 'Hope I didn't wake you.'

He is dressed as usual in a suit and tie. Smart and professional. Just as anyone who works in an IT job should be. Mia loves to see him in a suit and she gives him a sultry glance, making sure he sees her do it.

'You look so lovely. I particularly like that suit... Especially removing it...'

Ben laughs. He pulls her into his arms and kisses her.

'I love you,' he says when they part. 'You can help me remove it later.'

Behind him Freya makes a cute gurgling sound.

'And how's my pretty little girl?' he says.

He picks her up from the chair and snuggles her to him as he sits down at the kitchen table.

Freya gurgles again.

'See. She's smiling at me. She knows her daddy... Yes, she does.'

Mia laughs. 'I'm sure it's just wind!'

She makes the tea and then brings the mugs over to the table.

'Toast?' she asks.

'That's okay. I'll get something later.'

Mia sits down and takes a sip of her tea.

'She slept all night again,' she says.

'Really? I thought you got up to feed her... Or was I dreaming that?'

He doesn't look at her: he's smiling at Freya and the question is casual, though Mia is looking for some sign that he knows she's anxious.

As Mia watches them both together, she experiences a rush of warmth and happiness that clashes with her fears and phobias. She'd always loved being a couple but adores being a family more.

'I'd better feed her,' Mia says.

She takes Freya from Ben's arms – though he's reluctant to let her go. Mia unstraps her top and presses the little girl to her breast. Freya begins to suckle as Ben watches. He smiles at Mia and once again she has this feeling of being safe and it reminds her that she's not alone. But the memory of her dream, and her resolve to tell Ben about it, hangs between them as she struggles to broach the subject.

'Ben... I ... *worry* a little about her,' Mia says. 'I got up to check on her. So you didn't dream it.'

'Worrying is only natural,' Ben says. He sips his tea. Then he checks his phone out of habit. He shows no real concern for Mia's revelation.

'Well, it's a little more than that...,' Mia says. 'I'm scared someone will take her from us.'

Ben looks up, frowning. 'Sweetheart?'

Mia meets his gaze. She's glad he's listening.

'I know it's irrational, but I can't help it. I've even been having these ... nightmares.'

Ben puts his hand on her knee. He strokes her leg. His hand is hot and soothing.

'I'd never let anyone hurt either of you,' he says. 'But I think this is … kind of a process all people go through. We're new to being parents and she's precious. So, when you feel scared, tell me. I'll understand. And I'll try and make you feel better. Okay?'

Mia nods.

'For what it's worth, I worry too. We love her so much and it's perfectly normal.'

He stands and kisses her on the head. She turns her face upwards to receive a kiss on her lips. Ben takes the hint and kisses her lips, lingering in a way that pleases Mia.

'Have a wonderful day,' she says.

Ben leaves for work and Mia is relieved that she's shared her apprehension. Ben always knows how to make her feel better. He is her rock and her best friend, as well as her lover, and Mia feels blessed that they have such an honest relationship. He never judges.

The fears she'd experienced in the early hours now drift away. She's more relaxed as she takes Freya back upstairs to bathe and change her.

'Should we go for a walk today?' she says. 'And isn't Daddy wonderful?'

Freya gurgles in response.

Chapter Nine

BETH

'We should let Mike cast his eyes over this,' Beth says.

Ray and Leon exchange a look. 'We need to be careful with him for the while, Beth,' Ray says.

'Look, he's still Michael. We've worked with him for years. And he's smart, Ray. That's why you brought him back. We need him.'

Ray sighs. 'This is need to know. We can't have this getting out. Can you imagine if the press get wind of this?'

'Okay,' says Beth. 'But how's he going to tell them about it? We've got him under surveillance all the time?'

'When we are certain he's not going to regress, or be triggered again, then we can move to stage two of his reintegration,' Leon says.

Beth always knew when she'd lost an argument with Leon or Ray. Before the business with Michael happened, Michael had been Ray's second. Now, Leon's temporary promotion had changed the dynamic in the group. She and

Leon had always been equal up to that point. Now she had to answer to him and he made sure she knew it. Michael had never behaved like that when he was in this role.

Ray and Leon were thick as thieves most of the time. It almost felt like they patted her on the head and sent her off to do little chores with a modicum of responsibility. A fact that was frustrating Beth more than the instability of her homelife ever did.

'When can I have access to the satellite information? I may be able to track the plane and find where it came to rest,' she says, changing the subject.

'That's being taken care of elsewhere. Even we are getting limited content,' says Ray.

'Oh. I see. So, what are *we* permitted to do?'

'For now, background checks on flight crew and then widen that to the passengers,' Leon explains.

'On it,' Beth says.

Beth returns to her office and glances in at Michael who has his head down in a pile of paperwork.

He looks a little worse for wear today, she thinks. She knows why too. She heard Leon and Ray talk about how he gave his tail the slip and went out drinking the night before. *Poor Michael, he doesn't deserve this! What a mind fuck this must be.*

Beth sits down at her desk and moves the mouse. Her screen has gone into auto-lock and she types in her password again in order to reopen it.

On her screen is a partially redacted report about the loss of a Boeing 777 300 headed for Shanghai.

She glances over at Michael's office door again before submerging herself in the document.

As part of her research Beth pulls up surveillance from the airport systems. She watches as the passengers mill around, waiting to board. An initial analysis of the flight manifest hasn't thrown up any names with a history and the travellers all appear to be behaving normally.

She turns her attention to the crew. One of their number had fallen sick and a new crew member was brought in. Shelley Armitage was the unexpected replacement. Beth looks at Shelley's employment history in an email from Leon. Shelley had been an outstanding employee for the past ten years. Nothing suspicious, but this was her first long-haul flight.

There's also a transcript of an interview with Shelley's supervisor, Maggie Hanner, who says she picked Shelley because she was 'reliable' and had 'requested' consideration for long-haul opportunities.

She reads through the names of the others. A team that had worked together for some time. Shelley was the fly in the ointment. But Shelley's family life showed nothing suspicious. A husband, a child and Shelley's parents: all of whom were calling for an investigation but had been silenced under the Official Secrets Act. Some of the other crew's families were also being hushed.

But Shelley could be a sleeper agent... Beth glances over at Michael's office again. *Anyone can be.*

There are four crew members that have no family, and no one has apparently raised an alarm to say they are missing. Beth turns her attention to Angela Carter, Chloe Bell, Jay Astor and Frank Minchin.

The security footage shows the crew going through

security with flight bags. There is no extra checked luggage from any of them, which is usual. Some of them have electronic equipment such as tablets and phones. No one has a laptop. Nothing peculiar at all. They all follow the rules to the letter and no suspicion is flagged.

She turns her attention back to Shelley. As part of her research, she finds an open Facebook account showing images of Shelley with her husband and son (who would be twelve years old at this point) on various holidays. From the statuses she sees, Shelley has no radical views, or if she does she never expresses them. She is just a normal working mum and appears to be generally happy.

She searches some of the others and finds similar pages. Chloe Bell is a petite and pretty girl. She's half Chinese and is the youngest among the crew. There are lots of pictures of her with groups of friends, drinking shots and generally partying. Her profile says she speaks fluent Mandarin. Jay Astor is openly 'out' on his page. He's black and has a male model quality that makes his slim body almost androgynous. There is a picture with him in shorts, arms around another young man who isn't tagged in the picture. Beth saves the image for a future web search. Astor, it seems, has no family members at all on his social media – merely friends or acquaintances. *Perhaps he doesn't want his family to know about his private life?* Beth thinks. She makes a note on his file: *Family may not know he's gay.*

Then she comes to Angela Carter. There is no Facebook page. No Twitter, Instagram or any other social media. But searching is hard as she shares her name with a well-known novelist. Beth recalls that this is something that is taught during induction. If you want to take a fake name, then find one which is already shared with several celebrities because it clouds the searching and makes it harder to recognise no one of that name, age and employment role exists. As most of these factors come into play with this kind of search, Beth is suspicious: Angela Carter may not exist.

'Hmmm,' Beth says.

She returns to the security footage and captures an image of Angela going through passport control. It's not a clear shot of the woman, though she can see she is tall and slender, with a neat blonde bob. Beth takes the image and does a reverse search online to see what comes up. At the same time, she searches the image in MI5 and police databases.

It is lunchtime by the time she finishes her background checks on the crew. All have thrown up something of their private lives, with the exception of Angela Carter who came out a complete blank other than a few possible email addresses. This in itself is suspicious. How best to hide? No social media, avoid being photographed. Even the screenshot Beth has managed to get isn't good enough to see what the woman really looks like. She's just such a generic sort, and her face is never full on with the camera.

She looks over at Michael's office door again, wishing she could talk this through with him. He always sees things she doesn't. Like the great work he's done already on those files. With very little effort, he'd found something that she'd missed. Though she feels she can excuse herself a little on this. She's been distracted since they became aware of the Network's assassin school. She'd been in Switzerland while it all went down following a lead that she'd hoped would take her to Neva. When she returned everything had changed at Archive.

But it isn't a good excuse for missing the original names of those operatives. Michael never goes 'information blind'; he can scan a page and the things he needs to see just stand out to him. Maybe it is a form of autism – they are all on the spectrum one way or another, and genius is a more accepted description of some people. Michael has always fallen into that category to Beth. Even so, no matter what is happening, he never lets it distract him from the task and that takes a very special kind of person in Beth's book.

Needing further information about the crew, Beth searches for the HR details from the airline. They'd been given a contact name for inquiries and a password to use so that the HR Manager would provide her with any necessary data. She picks up the phone and dials the woman now.

'Hey there, Sophia, this is Security Agent Bethany Cane, password is *domicile*. Can you give me the addresses of all of the crew that were on the missing flight, please?'

Sophia is flustered by the call, though she agrees to part with the information immediately, having been briefed that this might be a national security issue.

'Do you know anything about the personal life of the crew?' Beth asks.

'Not really,' Sophie says.

'What about next of kin?' Beth says.

'I'll look for you,' Sophia says. 'Anyone in particular to narrow the search?'

Beth gives Sophia the names of Astor, Bell, Minchin and Carter.

'Zoe Bell's grandmother is her contact,' Sophia explains. 'That's strange...'

'What is?' asks Beth.

'Carter and Astor are each other's next of kin. Details were changed on the system on the same day. When they both started working for us,' Sophia says.

'Who did they have before that?'

'I'm sorry, the file was just overwritten. We don't retain out-of-date contact details.'

Because of this revelation, Beth becomes even more interested in Jay and Angela. Beth gives Sophia her email and a few seconds after the call ends, she receives all of the information. Sophia, at least, is efficient.

She glances down the list of residences. She decides to start with Angela.

Angela has a flat in Slough, not too far from Heathrow airport, from where she has flown the Shanghai long-haul return flight for the past six months.

Beth searches the land registry database for the owner of the flat and discovers it belongs to Jake and Hilary Tate, a married couple. After a short search, she finds contact details for them both. She decides that the woman might be an easier target and she calls the mobile phone she finds listed for her.

When the call is answered, Beth goes into a well-rehearsed speech about herself.

'What can I do for you, Officer?' says Hilary Tate.

Beth doesn't correct Hilary's assumption that she is the police. It's less difficult to explain than her real line of work.

'I'm making enquiries about a tenant you have in your property in Slough. Can you tell me how long Angela Carter has lived there?' Beth asks.

This is a crucial moment. Will Hilary give her personal information on the phone, or will she be suspicious and refuse without proof of who Beth is?

'Just a minute… I'll have a look at the contract.'

Beth takes a slow breath and waits. She hears the open and closing of what sounds like a metal filing cabinet and then the rustle of paper.

'It'll be six months this Friday. She's signed up for a year, and paid the rent in advance,' Hilary explains. 'Is there something I should know about her?'

'She's been reported as a missing person. Do you have a set of keys for the apartment?'

'Yes, of course, but my tenancy agreement doesn't allow me access without her permission.'

'Don't worry about that,' Beth explains. 'Meet me at the property at four today and I'll have the necessary warrant.'

Hilary dithers a little. 'I don't know, this is all a bit sudden. I mean, what do you hope to find?'

'The thing is, Mrs Tate, Angela is missing. For all we know she could be injured and alone inside the flat.'

'Oh! Right! I see.'

'So it's very important we have your cooperation,' Beth says. 'It could mean life or death.'

'Whatever I can do, Officer. Willing to help!' Hilary says.

Beth hangs up and she sends an email to Ray requesting the warrant. A few minutes later Leon comes in.

'What did you uncover?' he asks.

'Angela Carter looks suspicious to me.' Beth explains her findings. 'I think it's crucial we search her place, see if it reveals anything more about her. She has zero social media and a search of database and online didn't find any photos of her. She took on the apartment at the exact same time that she started the airline job. Could be why she chose to live there, but I just have this gut feeling that something is amiss.'

'Let's go,' said Leon. 'We'll pick up the warrant on the way.'

Beth reaches for her coat. 'What about Michael? He could be useful.'

'We can manage this between us, Beth,' Leon says.

Beth nods.

She places her computer in standby mode and then she follows Leon out of the office.

Chapter Ten

NEVA

Her hotel room has been ransacked and her few belongings have been strewn all over the floor. Neva looks behind her, checking the corridor, and backs off rapidly. It's no accident that anything important is in the backpack she's wearing. Neva lets her knife slip down from the wrist holster into her hand as she turns and heads for the elevator. All of her senses are on full alert. She's aware of every sound, her eyes cast left and right as she prepares for an enemy to burst from one of the other rooms at any point.

At the lift, she presses the call button, then hurries to the door that leads to the stairs.

With ninja stealth she goes down the first flight to the level below. Still alert, she walks down the corridor away from the lift. On every floor there is a service elevator on a dogleg bend in the corridor.

As she moves towards this lift, she retrieves a staff pass from her pocket: she cloned the card of one of the cleaners when she checked in a few days ago, using a Proxmark 3 to scan the card and replicate it. Now she uses the card to bring the lift up to her floor and she gets inside as soon as it arrives. She presses the button for the basement and the staff parking lot.

Before the doors open, she reaches into her pocket and removes her revolver. She clicks off the safety and holds it behind her back, while securing her knife in the other hand ready for action.

The doors open. Neva tenses.

The basement is empty. Neva gets out of the lift and follows the staff route to the underground car park. If her presence has been compromised, she needs to make a quick getaway and her plan is to steal one of the cars there.

Her heartbeat is slightly elevated now, but she has a rush of adrenaline that sharpens her reactions and as she opens the door to the carpark, the hairs stand up on the back of her neck. She ducks left just as a barrage of bullet fire pounds into the wall beside the door, sending pieces of concrete flying all around her. Doing a running crouch, gun now pointing upwards, Neva throws herself behind the nearest car. The exit door to the main street isn't far away but her planned escape from the building has been anticipated. With so many options she could have taken, Neva suspects there is more than one assassin after her. The others no doubt will be covering her other possible choices.

More gunfire rains over her head as she dashes between the cars, hurling herself to the floor as bullets pummel into the nearest car. On her stomach she shuffles past another vehicle, moving closer to her escape route, which is now only one car length away. She hears the pounding of feet running towards her and pulls herself into a crouch ready to make a break for it. But first she stands and lets loose a blast of gunfire. She catches a brief glimpse of a man wearing a black suit then her pursuer throws himself aside to take cover. Neva uses this opportunity to run full pelt towards the door, hurling herself through, and out onto the street, before her assailant can recover.

Outside she carries on running even as she flicks the safety back on the gun and pushes the knife back into its holster. She keeps going, weaving in and out of the pedestrians on the busy London road, and then she dives across the chaotic street and runs towards the nearest tube station. A taxi blares its horn as she causes it to brake. Neva doesn't look at the driver as she reaches the pavement.

Her breathing is labouring a little by the time she heads down into the underground. She's not unfit but the adrenaline rush is taking its toll.

Using one of her debit cards, she passes through the barrier and hurries down the steps towards the sound of the next train.

The station is full of people, and Neva submerges herself into their throng. As the train stops and the doors open Neva boards, pushing past disgruntled commuters. Once inside the carriage she turns and studies the people boarding to see if she has been pursued. Her breath is coming fast, but she stills her beating heart, getting her breathing under control as she quells the flight adrenaline.

She stays on board as far as the line goes. This gives her time to think and assess who may have found her. Can the

Network be onto her already or is it someone else? Either way her position in central London is now untenable.

_____

Using a variety of tube lines Neva travels to Heathrow. With a different identity, she books a room on Airbnb. The room is described as a riverside retreat on the Thames. Then she orders an Uber to take her to Kingston upon Thames. She lets the driver drop her off close to the main shopping area where she buys a few essentials. As she does this, she is hyper-aware of the possibility that she still might have a silent tail.

She buys a sandwich and sits in the main pedestrian area on a bench and eats it, all the time watching everyone around her. There are no obvious tails. No one remains sitting or standing watching her. She crosses through various shops, back and forth across Kingston, all the time looking... Nothing seems awry.

After a while she purchases two new burner phones for cash, giving a false name and address when asked at the sales desk. She orders another Uber – with a different identity and card again – to take her close to the address on the river where she'll be staying.

As she waits on the kerb for the taxi, she looks around the busy Kingston streets. No one is taking any particular notice of her. Because she knows exactly what to look for, Neva wonders how she could have been so imprudent. She had not noticed she was being observed coming and going at the hotel. The Network has been disrupted, but their spies are still everywhere. *Stupid!* She feels an irrational anger that turns to frustration.

The Uber arrives and Neva gets in. As the car pulls away, she looks out of the windows again. Only then is she certain that no one is following.

The Airbnb turns out to be a quiet cabin on an island in the Thames, reached across a small walkway bridge. Neva feels she can stay here while she decides what to do over the next few days. Exits from London and surrounding stations will be watched. Perhaps Michael was tailed after all and they somehow followed her back as she left him in the bar.

Perhaps approaching him again had been a very bad idea.

She gets out of the Uber and walks across the bridge to the house. When she reaches the cabin, she sees an elderly woman waiting on a small porch that overlooks the river.

'Amanda?' the woman asks.

Neva nods.

'So, you've booked for a week. We can do a maid service every day for you but it's extra.'

'No, that's okay. I won't need it. I may need to stay longer than a week...Is it going to be available? Only the site didn't show the dates...'

'I can do a longer-term rental for you. I had it booked out on the system because I'll be away next week... But if you're staying and don't need extra services, then I don't see a problem.'

They come to terms and Neva presses cash into the woman's hand that satisfies her for the extra week's rental. Plus, the woman won't have to pay commission to the booking company so it's a win for her all round. This arrangement gives Neva some flexibility if she feels safe here. An exit strategy won't be a quick decision to make. But if she has to leave this place in a hurry it won't matter.

The woman opens the door of the cabin and walks in. Neva follows.

The cabin is small but sufficient. Neva has a double bedroom, a lounge-diner-kitchen and a small bathroom with a shower.

'I'll drop fresh bedding on the doorstep for you next week before I go away,' the woman says. 'Wi-Fi code is in the welcome book on the kitchen counter.'

She hands Neva the key then turns to go. 'Enjoy your stay!'

Neva closes the door behind the woman. She looks around at the cabin. The place is clean and functional and better than the basic room she'd had at the hotel. She goes into the bedroom and places her few new possessions on the bed.

Then she takes out one of the new phones, activates it and connects it to the Wi-Fi in the cabin.

When she's fully settled in, she notices a post-adrenaline drop in her mood. In order to relieve the fugue, she goes for a walk out along the river. Rucksack still on her back, she watches as small boats potter along the river. It's quiet. No one in sight. Neva starts to relax once more.

Chapter Eleven

BETH

There is a tall, pretty woman waiting on the doorstep of the apartment block when Beth and Leon arrive at Angela Carter's residence.

'Mrs Tate?' Beth says

'Yes. Call me Hilary. Mrs Tate makes me feel like my mother-in-law,' Hilary says.

'I'm Beth Cane. This is my colleague, Leon Tchaikovsky.'

Beth flashes her security badge and hands Hilary a card with her details on.

'We have a warrant here,' Leon says, holding out a folded piece of paper. Hilary takes it and begins reading.

'This looks okay,' she says. 'But will you wait till my husband gets here? He's on his way but got stuck in traffic.'

Leon shrugs. 'Time could be of the essence,' he says. 'But a few moments more shouldn't make much difference.'

At that moment a Mercedes convertible in brilliant red pulls up at the kerb. Jake Tate leaps out and hurries up the driveway. He presses his key fob. The car's lights flash and it makes a brief beeping sound.

Poser, Beth thinks.

Hilary introduces them and Jake studies their badges and the warrant for a lengthy time.

'Mr Tate?' Beth says. 'We really need to get inside of that apartment now.'

Tate is reluctant but can't see any reason to object.

'Aren't you bringing uniformed officers in too?' Hilary asks. Her eyes are glowing as though this is the most excitement she's had in a week.

'Hopefully they won't be needed,' Leon says. 'It'll depend on what we find.'

'What you find? What are you expecting to be in there?' asks Tate.

'Mr Tate, we aren't expecting anything. But we are hoping to have a lead on a missing person,' says Beth.

Hilary unlocks the main front door and leads Beth and Leon inside. Tate brings up the rear and closes the main door behind them.

'The building consists of four apartments: two upstairs and two down,' Hilary explains.

'Which way?' asks Beth.

'Upstairs,' Tate says. 'First door on the left.'

Leon takes the key from Hilary's hand. 'It's best you wait outside.'

'Now wait a minute. This is our property...' Tate says.

'I'm afraid you can't come into the property, Mr Tate,' Beth says. 'The fewer people go in the better because any evidence can become contaminated.'

'Come on,' says Hilary, taking Tate's arm. 'We don't want to get in trouble.'

Tate frowns but he lets his wife lead him outside. Beth closes the door behind them.

'What a friggin' nightmare *he* is,' she says, rolling her eyes.

'Yeah. Now let's get in that apartment.'

She sees then that Leon already has his Glock 17 in his hand. Beth pulls her gun free from the holster hidden beneath her jacket.

Taking the lead, Leon heads upstairs. Beth follows. When they reach the landing, Beth knocks on the door first as standard protocol: they have to give any occupant the opportunity to answer before they enter.

When no response comes Beth unlocks the door, standing to one side and not in front of it. The lock clicks, and the door springs open. Beth pushes it inwards and peeps around the door into the room.

The room beyond looks empty of people, and there are no obvious traps.

'Clear,' she says.

Leon enters first, weapon out front. Then she follows him as they begin an initial safety sweep of the place.

The door leads into a sparsely furnished living room. There is only a two-seater sofa and a small table with one chair. This serves to make the room appear larger than it is.

In the kitchen, a small galley, the surfaces are mostly bare but for a kettle and one unused coffee mug.

They move into the bedroom. A single bed, left as though newly slept in, is the only thing in the room, other than a suitcase, open, with clothing strewn half in and out as though the occupant had been searching for something.

'So, you live here for six months and don't add any furniture or possessions,' Beth says. 'This isn't normal.'

Just off the bedroom is the bathroom. Leon puts his gun away, slips on a pair of latex gloves and opens the medicine cabinet. Inside is just a tube of toothpaste and a toothbrush.

Beth stows her gun back in its holster. 'Not exactly what I expected. What do you make of this?'

'Looks to me like she knew she was here temporarily and that she wouldn't be coming back.'

Beth nods. 'Let's dust for prints and take whatever she's left behind for future analysis.'

'*Excuse me?* Hey! Is someone in there?'

Beth and Leon leave the bathroom and return to the living room to find a man standing by the front door.

'Please back out of the apartment, Sir,' says Leon.

'You're not Angela,' the man says.

'You know Angela?' Beth asks.

'She's my neighbour – I live across the landing,' he says. He looks Beth and Leon over. 'What are you doing here?'

'Official business,' Beth says. 'Why did you come over?'

'Official? I just wanted to tell Angela about the smell. She's not here then?'

'No. She's not. Smell?' asked Leon.

'Er … yeah. Who are you?'

Beth shows the man her credentials and asks his name.

'Look, I don't know anything. If she's done something…'

'Mr…?' Leon prompts.

'Kent. Bill Kent. I'm just her neighbour, like I said.'

'How well do you know Angela, Mr Kent?' Beth asks.

'We say hello now and again,' Kent explains. 'Is she okay?'

'That's what we are here to find out. You said something about a smell?' Beth says.

'Oh yeah. I think a cat must've got into her garage or something when she stowed her car. Probably dead. The stench is awful.'

Beth and Leon exchange looks. 'You can smell something from outside the garage?'

'Oh, it's a two-door double I share with her. The landlord put a partition up between her side and mine when I moved in. I use mine for tool storage and wanted security. I mean, you never know who your neighbours are or how honest they are. My tools are expensive.'

'Where is this garage?' Leon asks.

Kent explains that the garages are at the back of the apartment block.

'Show us,' says Leon.

After closing Angela's apartment door, they follow Kent downstairs.

Tate and Hilary are smoking a cigarette at the end of the drive.

'Do you have a key to the garage?'

Hilary looks startled. 'I... No. It's a padlock and we recommend each occupant buys their own.'

'Mr Kent, do you have bolt cutters?' Beth asks.

Kent nods. Then he leads Leon and Beth around the

back of the building, through a gate into a concreted area that has two large double garages on it.

Kent opens his side of the garage and Leon steps inside while Beth checks out the lock on Angela's side.

'The smell is worse over near the vent,' Kent says.

Leon goes further into the garage. The walls are filled with shelves and racks containing Kent's varied tools.

'What do you do?' asks Leon.

'Carpenter. Odd jobs. Anything I'm asked really,' Kent says.

Leon wrinkles his nose as he reaches a panel with an air vent between the two garage spaces that has been put in to avoid damp in the structure.

'When did you first notice the smell?' asks Beth.

'A few days ago. I saw Ang a week or so ago. We aren't allowed to smoke in the apartments so I was standing outside when she brought her car round and stowed it inside. She left the door open a bit while we talked, so I guess that's how the animal or whatever has died in there, snuck in.'

'You haven't seen anyone out here since?' Leon asks.

'No. Ang locked up. Then she said I wouldn't see her for a couple of weeks and not to worry. She was off flying to China or somewhere like that,' Kent says. 'I said, "Lucky you" and she complained a bit about annoying passengers on flights and said the job isn't as "glam" as it seems.'

'Those bolt cutters?' Beth prompts.

Kent fetches them from their place on the wall.

'These'll cut through anything,' he says.

Leon takes them as Beth holds out her hand. Beth resists

rolling her eyes, but barely manages to keep her face straight. Leon's macho behaviour is annoying her. She's becoming more frustrated with him every minute.

'Stay here, please,' Leon says to Kent. Then he and Beth go back to the front of the garage.

By now Hilary and Tate have come around to watch what's going on.

'I'm not sure about this,' Tate says. 'Your warrant is for the apartment.'

'This garage comes as part of the lease, right?' says Beth as she blocks him from stepping forward to interrupt Leon.

'Well ... yes. But—'

'Then it's part of the warrant,' Beth explains. 'Now back off.'

Tate goes back to the gate and talks in a low voice to Hilary. Hilary nods and walks away. Tate stands by the gate watching as Leon cuts open the padlock. The lock falls to the floor. Beth glances back at Leon, then returns her gaze to Tate.

Leon raises the garage door. It's stiff from lack of use, and he puts some effort behind it before it leaps from his hands and starts to pull back on the weighted runners.

'Beth?' Leon says.

Beth joins him at the door. They look inside the garage and see Angela Carter's car parked there as Kent had said it was.

A sickening, musty smell wafts out towards them. Beth and Leon hesitate to go inside. They already have a feeling as to what they will find: the scent of decay is far worse than a dead cat would have generated.

Hilary returns. 'I called the police,' she says. 'They are coming out.'

'That's fine,' Beth says. 'You've saved me a job.'

Leon takes a handkerchief from his pocket and places it over his nose and mouth as he enters the garage. The car is a Volvo hatchback. He glances in through the windows. One of the rear windows is cracked open an inch. The boot cover is in place and he can't see what's inside. Leon tries the doors but they are locked. Then he reaches the boot. He presses the button and the boot springs open.

The stench from within overwhelms him and Leon steps back, gagging.

'Beth, we need a forensics team here now,' he croaks, making his way back around the car and to the fresh air out front.

Beth pulls out her phone and dials a number. Then she spends a few moments giving her details to someone on the other end of the phone. She also tells them about Hilary's phone call.

'Did you get an incident number?' she asks Hilary now.

Hilary looks flustered. 'Well, no. I didn't *really* call the police. I was testing you.'

Beth shakes her head. 'Apparently it was a lie. So treat this now as the first report.'

Beth finishes the call.

'Forensics in fifteen,' she says to Leon.

Then Beth turns to Hilary and Tate. 'Don't go anywhere. They'll want to question you. And take your prints.'

'Us?' says Tate. 'Why? We don't know anything.'

'It's *not* a cat, is it?' says Kent from his side of the garage as it dawns on him that it's far worse.

'We'll need to interview you too, Mr Kent. You're the last person who saw Angela before she disappeared.'

'Oh God! Is she in *there*?' says Hilary, the colour seeping from her cheeks.

Beth glances back at Leon. Neither of them answers.

Chapter Twelve

MICHAEL

There's a small parcel in my mailbox when I get home. I'm confused because I haven't ordered anything online for months. Keeping my back to the security desk, I open the padded envelope. Inside is a burner phone: it has to be from Neva.

I'm still angry with her after last night. I think I've been used enough and don't intend to be pulled into more drama. Even so, I stuff the envelope and phone into my pocket so that it won't be seen on the cameras in my apartment.

Once I'm inside my place, I put the letters down on the kitchen counter, get myself a beer, and open them sitting at the breakfast bar as per my usual habit. Most of them are junk mail and I throw them in the recycling bin.

I take the phone out of the package but don't switch it on because of the surveillance in my flat. There's a piece of paper inside the envelope and I unfold it to find two words and a time.

Byron's. Kingston. 12 noon.

I assume she means tomorrow, which is a Saturday.

Although I'm off work, I know it will be difficult to go anywhere without being followed. I switch the phone on. Turn the sound off and type a text to the telephone number that she's stored inside.

Too risky, I say.

She doesn't answer right away. But when she does, she says, *I'll deal with your tail.*

I turn the phone off again and then I lie back on my bed.

I'm hot and tired and more than a bit pissed off that Beth and Leon had gone out on some mission I wasn't privy to. Beth didn't even come and see me to say they were going out. But then, why should she? I'm no longer her boss, Leon is. They hadn't returned by the end of day, and I'd gone to speak to Ray about my latest findings on the one case I was being given access to.

'Where is everyone?' I'd asked.

'Out on a call,' Ray said.

'Oh. Right. Anyway. No more names. So we only have a few to follow up on. Where do you want me to take this? Should I make calls and appointments with the parents?'

'Good God, no!' Ray said as though the idea of me interacting with anyone was grotesque.

I must have shown my surprise, because he then backtracked and blustered an excuse that didn't ring true.

'That wasn't how it sounded,' Ray said. 'It's just we are dealing with something that's time-sensitive and this might have to wait. For now.'

'Okay,' I said. I handed him the files along with the few

notes and observations I'd made about the contents. 'I'll call it a day then if I'm not needed.'

'Sure. That's probably for the best,' Ray had said.

I had gone back into my office and picked up my briefcase, leaving as fast as I could after that, glad it was the weekend and I'd get to be away from the team for a few days at least.

I was annoyed as I left. And more than a little embarrassed. It was difficult enough stepping back into Archive without the constant reminder that I was no longer trusted and not really one of them anymore. I was sick to the stomach.

As I travelled home, I was sad, then angry, then depressed about the last few months and how my life had been flipped upside down. I'm more upbeat, if serious, and so being miserable didn't sit well with me.

Now, lying in my apartment, I wonder if this whole 'bringing me back into the fold' is a ruse. A way of getting me to resign, and therefore letting them all off the hook. But I dismiss this thought: Ray doesn't work like that: he'd be direct and would just fire me. Besides, they could have legitimately rid themselves of my services months ago because I was compromised. Instead, Ray had put me through therapy at the agency's expense. And while I was talking about how bad the whole thing had made me feel, they'd probably been psychoanalysing me to see if I was still a danger.

After that my doctor must have reassured him that I wasn't a risk. Even so, Ray must still have doubts. Would any of us ever get beyond this?

Several years of my life had been spent at Archive. Time in which I'd honed my skills and had given my best work. But I'd also done my worst too, by feeding Beech information that the Network could use to stay one step ahead of us.

I guess it isn't much of an excuse in the end that I didn't know I was doing it.

My shrink, Doctor Sheppard, has said many times that I wasn't to blame, but deep down I didn't really believe that. I thought instead that I was weak and pathetic. That it was degrading I hadn't been able to fight the Network's control. That I hadn't been able to stop them conditioning me.

Sheppard said it was abuse in the extreme and I shouldn't be hard on myself because I was only a child. But how could I claim the stripes of 'survivor' when I'd rolled over and played along? I hadn't, of course, shared my guilt with Sheppard, but even so he'd said things that suggested he knew I felt it.

I consider calling Doctor Sheppard now in the hope he'd say some words of wisdom to ease my distress. But I didn't want the call recorded and my colleagues to learn that I was experiencing anxiety. It might make them change their minds again. I am in something of a dilemma.

I should just give up and resign, I think. But I know I can't quit. It is more important than ever to regain my colleagues' trust and start to build my life again. What else would I do, after all? My job has always been everything to me.

That means of course, no Neva.

I get up off the bed and toss the phone into the drawer by my bedside.

No. I can't meet her. It's too dangerous for both of us. Besides, I'm still not sure I can trust her. Especially after her attempt at manipulation the night before. All of which my former Network operative side recognises.

I weigh up how I feel about Neva against the risks such emotions bring to someone in my position. I am torn between a desperate curiosity and the sure knowledge that having anything more to do with her would be utter madness.

My psychology degree taught me many things about the human psyche and I would have said that I could always overrule my heart with my head. But still, I waver. And all the rational thoughts I can summon don't push away the irrational excitement I have at the thought of being with her again.

Chapter Thirteen

BETH

B eth puts on a crime scene suit over her clothing. Pulling the hood over her hair, she places a mask over her mouth and nose. It's not perfect but the filters should help to reduce the overwhelming odour of rotted flesh. She pulls latex gloves over her hands to prevent cross-contamination, then she joins Leon and the forensic pathologist as they take their initial look at the body inside Angela Carter's boot.

'Talk me through what you see,' Leon asks.

'Judging by the level of decay, I'd say she's been in here for a week or so. But I just won't know until I do the autopsy,' said the pathologist.

Beth is momentarily distracted by the fact that she doesn't recognise the pathologist's voice. She can usually identify them when they speak even when they are wearing all the gear.

'Female. Early thirties,' the man continues, talking into a recorder. 'The body is in the boot of a Volvo Estate car...'

He gives the location and describes the body. The woman in the trunk has blonde hair and could be Angela Carter's twin, except that her hair is longer. 'She is gagged. Cable ties hold her wrists, knees and ankles together...'

'She looks like she was put in there before she was dead. Why else would they bind and gag her?' Beth asks when he finishes his taped description.

'More than likely,' says the pathologist. 'But it could be they tied her up, killed her and left her like that for ease of moving the body.'

The pathologist takes several photographs as Beth and Leon wait.

'Can you hold this for me?' he says, passing Beth his recorder. 'Press record and then I'll start the second part of this examination.'

Beth does as he asks. Then the pathologist moves the woman's head, examining her neck, and cranium for injuries.

'No damage to her skull that I can see, nor does she appear to have been shot or stabbed,' he concludes. 'Let's get her bagged and back to the mortuary for more detailed study.'

'When can you let us know more?' Leon asks.

'I'll start on her tomorrow. Nine a.m. sharp. If you can stomach it, be there.'

The body is removed and then the forensics team enter the garage. By then several of them have dusted the apartment for prints and have taken all of Angela's belongings, including the toothbrush, for further scrutiny.

Beth steps away from the bustle of the forensics crew, allowing them to get on undisturbed. She's queasy: the sight of a decomposed body is something she can never quite get used to. She doesn't know how the others do it. And it annoys her that she has to hide from Leon that the whole thing sickens her. What would he think about her squeamishness, after all? Would he see that as confirmation that she was just a woman and not as efficient as he was at dealing with death? Michael never made her feel that way. He always included her in everything he did, but after such a discovery, would also confide how grossed out he was by it all. Beth isn't as bad as some of the young cops though. Especially the male ones, who go green around the gills at the mention of a corpse. Some people aren't cut out for this sort of thing. Beth often wonders if she is one of them.

'Great observation in there,' says the pathologist. He removes his mask and Beth sees he is clean-shaven, mid-forties and has very kind eyes. As she's never seen him before she assumes he is new to the department's medical team.

'Excuse me?' Beth says.

'My initial thoughts led me to believe she was alive when put in the trunk. You observed it was likely…'

'Oh yes. That's right,' says Beth.

'You have a good eye,' he says. 'Clearly not your first rodeo…'

'No. I get to do this a lot,' says Beth. 'Sadly.'

'Yeah. Hard to get used to,' he says. 'The smell is the worst part. Elliot Baker.'

Beth smiles at him.

'Beth Cane,' she says shaking Elliot's hand.

'So, are you going to join me?' Elliot asks.

'What?'

'Tomorrow morning? I think your partner will opt out,' Elliot says.

'What do you mean? This shit never fazes him.'

'Well, the pile of puke behind the garage would prove you wrong,' says Elliot.

'Seriously?' Beth says.

'Yep. Caught him as I drove up.'

Beth's smile grows wider, though she tells herself off inside her head for gloating. At least she hasn't vomited. Not even on the first outing. For the first time in months, she finds herself warming to a new face. She wonders now what her soon-to-be ex, Callum, will make of that.

'You have no idea how much better that makes me feel,' Beth says.

Elliot laughs.

'So, I'll see you again soon?' he says.

'Sure.'

Elliot turns away and gives instructions to his crew as they wheel the body, now in a black body bag, out to the waiting ambulance.

Beth glances at her watch. It's almost 7 p.m. Callum has the boys tonight and so there's no rush or pressure to get back. She never thought it would be such a relief, breaking up after all these years together. In the end Callum was unwilling to play second fiddle to her job. He'd asked her to choose: Archive, or him. It hadn't been that difficult a decision to make. The only complication was their children. Beth wants to be there for her two boys, no matter what. But Callum will need to play a very big part in their lives. She can't do it alone, not working the hours she does.

Beth is ambitious and wants to prove she can do everything that Leon can. Her career has always been foremost in her mind. Her dedication was why Ray Martin recruited her to Archive in the first place. When it all comes down to it, Beth understands she isn't cut out to just stay home and be a mother. That part of parenting has never excited her, and the reality is, she had the children for Callum. It's a hard truth to acknowledge that she would have been happier childless. But Beth has explored this scenario many times. Not that she would be without the boys now that she has them. It is just that she can't be the mother they should have and is disappointed with herself as this feels like a failure. She is perpetually remorseful.

Just like the slight flirty tone she's detected from Elliot makes her feel bad too.

It's nothing, silly, she tells herself. *He's just being friendly. Probably married or gay.*

Now Beth remembers Hilary, Tate and Kent: all waiting in Kent's apartment with a uniformed cop.

With a final glance at Elliot, she heads off back through the iron gate and around to the front of the building.

Inside the building, despite her own pep talk, she finds she's still grinning. How could someone who didn't even know her see and understand Leon's low-level misogyny and take the sting out of it? She realises that Elliot is one to watch. Smart, observant and great at his job or he wouldn't be working with MI5's pathology team.

She just remembers to remove her smile as she reaches the top of the stairs and walks up to Kent's door. It wouldn't do for the general public to see her enjoying herself; that could be misconstrued.

Chapter Fourteen

MICHAEL

To take my mind off Neva and her invitation to meet, I leave my apartment for the day and go to Covent Garden. I wander around the shops for a while, but I'm not really into shopping and the whole thing is boring. I'm aware of my tail, hanging around everywhere I go on the periphery of my vision, but I choose to ignore her. This woman is often on during the day at weekends. She stands out, though she's trying not to be noticed. But that's the point really; a good tail would blend in by being 'normal', acting as though they aren't watching, and don't mind being seen. It's always more conspicuous when someone tries not to be seen.

Twelve noon comes and goes. I get lunch at one of the cafés and swig a couple of glasses of Chardonnay, making the day stretch out as long as I can. At around three I call into a small grocery store, buy some provisions for the weekend and then head back home.

As I enter my apartment block, I'm reluctant to go

upstairs for another solitary evening. It's tempting to go and find a bar and just sit drinking, letting the bustle of people around me wash away the deep-rooted loneliness, a void that Neva had once begun to fill. I think back to our brief reunion and how easy it was to be around her, to touch her. It was like … coming home. I shake myself for having such a ridiculous and romantic notion. Especially when, on our second meeting, she asked me to betray my colleagues again.

Can I see a future for us? I shake my head. It can't be possible, not while I work for MI5.

The truth is I'd never know if she was with me because of the connection we formed or to learn what was happening in Archive.

Sleep was so slow to come the night before. The temptation to text Neva, have any form of contact, almost drove me out of my mind. I'd forced myself down, swigging brandy until two in the morning while I went through the problem in microscopic detail. Concluding in the end that this is not healthy. It's not safe. I have to cut ties with her for my own sake, for my career and sanity. Otherwise, I'll never deserve to win back the trust of my work mates.

At my front door I feel … odd. The hairs are up on the back of my neck and goosebumps shiver up my spine like the proverbial feeling of someone walking over your grave. The lock looks fine though, and the corridor is empty. All the other apartments are silent. It is still Saturday afternoon, after all, and most people are out and about doing their usual activities. Even so, I know something is amiss.

I turn the key in the door and enter the flat with caution. I'm not in the habit of carrying my gun when I'm out socially but I can handle myself even so. I step aside as I push the door open, then I see her. Neva. Sitting primly on the sofa, as though she is meant to be there, waiting for my return.

'The camera system is off,' Neva says.

'You shouldn't be here,' I say under my breath. 'There is sound surveillance as well. They will know you're here.'

'At the moment you're showering, then you'll cook something in the kitchen. Shortly after that the TV will be switched on and they'll hear you fall asleep and snore in front of it. I hacked into their systems and compiled sounds of you doing all these things into what they're listening to now.'

I'm speechless. I close the apartment door.

'How did you manage that?' I ask as I turn back to face her.

'If it's on Wi-Fi I can hack it,' she says. 'You didn't show today. I was concerned. Plus, someone found out where I was staying and I had to bolt.'

'Are you okay?' I ask.

'They tried to kill me, but I got away.' She shrugs as if this is all normal.

'How do you know you're in the clear?' I ask. 'They could be still be tailing you.'

'I did this for a living, you know.' She smiles at me.

God, she's beautiful! I feel my resolve slipping and start to steel myself against her and how her nearness makes me feel.

'I'm glad you're okay. But you need to leave. I can't do this anymore, Neva.'

'Michael, this is important. I have more news. About that flight.'

'There is no flight. Nothing has been mentioned at Archive about it,' I say. 'I think you're trying to manipulate me. And frankly I'm not up for being used by anyone anymore.'

Neva looks surprised by my words. 'I'd never do that to you.'

I sit down on the chair opposite the sofa. I flick one of the blinds aside and look down onto the busy street below.

'This is dangerous for me. I'm trying to claw back my life.'

'They are following you, monitoring your calls, watching your every move. Is that really the life you want for yourself?' she asks.

I put my head in my hands. I feel weak and confused. The strength and determination I had dissolve with her words. No, this isn't what I envisaged for myself. *But neither are my feelings for Neva.*

I don't speak for a while. This is hopeless. I'm depressed and sickened and I can't see a way forward into a normal life again.

'Maybe you're right,' I say at last. 'Maybe Archive will never truly be comfortable again. But what else will I do? Where will I go? My whole life is about this job. And I loved it a great deal … once.'

'Part of your life was. The other part made you a trained killer,' Neva says. 'Like me.'

I look at her now. She looks fragile, but I know she's anything but. She's tall, willowy, beautiful: an anomaly of perfection. And so chameleonic. Did the Network really make her this way? Or is it all so natural for her to be the killer that she is?

'Yes. I can kill,' I say. 'But it isn't a natural thing for the real me to do. Not without good cause. I remember kills I've done for the Network under Beech's influence, and though at first it felt like a dream, the guilt of it now is overwhelming. Don't you feel that?'

'No,' she says. 'It was always just a job to me. Yes, I was conditioned, but later, when I left the house and was sent out there to do their dirty work, I saw it as employment. They paid me. The rewards were designed for us to need and want to continue doing the wet work. I saw the money as a means to be free. Most didn't, they spent it, lived it up. A few of the assassins bought cars, houses, drugs. They lived as though they understood it could all be taken away. But a few years back, I had an epiphany. I saw what the future held as I took the life of one of us. Death was all that awaited us. There was no retirement except in a coffin. I no longer feared the wrath of my handler if I didn't obey. What I dreaded was the endless, pointless journey to an ultimate and extreme ending. One that no one would mourn.'

I'm overwhelmed by her candour. I hadn't thought things through the way she had. But yes, I can see how this is for her. 'Retiring' former colleagues, knowing that one day a younger, stronger assassin would come for her too, was a bleak and lonely life.

'Mortality is something we all have in common,' I say.

'But when we are young, we consider ourselves invincible. And then, you realise you aren't.'

Neva nods. I don't think we've ever had such a serious conversation before and I'm not sure where it will lead, but having this insight to her psyche gives me a sense of closeness, and a sharper understanding of who and what she is. And strangely a little understanding into what I too might have become if Beech'd had his way. She isn't what they made her, she's what she remade herself into. Can we all be reborn this way and rise from the ashes of the burnt-out flame that was once the Network?

'I was about to run. I'd planned it. But then you came into it,' she says. 'And now here I am putting myself at risk again just to see you.'

Her voice is matter-of-fact, though her words could be considered romantic. I study her face, looking for a sign of deception, but her expression is open and there's such sadness in her eyes that it pulls at my insides.

I'm on my feet and hurrying towards her before I can stop myself.

I don't say what I'm feeling, I just take her in my arms and hold her like I had on the stairwell.

Is this love? I really don't know. But we are drawn to each other. I'm a moth, ever dancing around her dangerous flame, and the fire she brings isn't easy to quell. She makes me feel weak and strong all in one go.

I take her into the bedroom and she goes willingly. I strip her clothing away and my mouth traces soft kisses over her face, neck, shoulders and breasts.

'Are you cold?' I ask when she shivers under my hands and lips.

'Not when I'm with you,' she says.

Then she opens for me, giving and responding and touching me back with the same urgency. Pulling away my clothes as I had removed hers.

I lay her on the bed, taking the lead, and she doesn't object: for control between us is something that neither of us ever worries about.

Afterwards I hold her against my chest. We fit together in comfort and it feels so right to have her here despite all my concerns and suspicions. I stop thinking. We don't talk. We sleep. And it is the best rest I've had for a long time.

When I wake, Neva has gone. But for the ruffled bedsheets, and the smell of her lingering on the cotton and on my skin, I could almost believe that our meeting was imagined. It's only then that I realise she hasn't told me what news she had about the mysterious missing flight. I'm left wondering if this was just as I'd suspected: an excuse to be around me. I decide it doesn't matter and then I turn over and drift back into sleep.

Breathing in her scent I carry her with me into my dreams.

Chapter Fifteen

BETH

It's just gone 9 a.m. on Monday when Beth parks her car and hurries inside the medical centre which holds MI5 and MI6's private mortuary.

Elliot had emailed on Friday evening explaining that the autopsy had been postponed until Monday – unavoidable but a pain, as it meant that Beth had to spend the weekend doing 'motherly' and 'householdy' things which she detested.

She shows her badge, and hands over her gun for security, before passing through the security scanner. The security guard gives her a key to her storage box so that she can retrieve the weapon before she leaves.

She takes the stairs down to the basement and walks along the corridor to the mortuary. When she arrives, she presses the bell and the daytime diener, Cyrus Fencher, comes to the door and lets her inside.

'Hi, Cyrus, I'm here for the autopsy.'

'PPE in there ready for you,' Cyrus says, pointing to a

side room where all the personal protective equipment is stored. 'You'll need some Vicks under your nose too, though she's been on ice all weekend and that helps.'

'Thanks.'

When Beth is ready, she smears the strong menthol ointment under her nose and then covers the lower half of her face with a surgical mask. She follows Cyrus into the mortuary.

'Hi, Beth. Just in time!' says Elliot. 'She's been swabbed and cleaned. Clothing sent off for analysis.'

The corpse is laid out on the examination table. It's naked but Elliot has a sheet over her, up to the shoulders. Beth likes how respectful this is, but knows that throughout the process the victim's body will slowly be revealed and the cover pulled back.

'I couldn't see this when she was foetal in the car, but it was the first thing I noticed when I cut her free from the ties.'

Beth moves closer to the body. For once her curiosity outweighs the sickness that death often makes her feel. Elliot's gloved fingers point to the woman's neck.

'You see the bruising here. Finger marks. She was semi-strangled before being dumped in the back of the car. She'll have been unconscious, but not dead.'

'How do you know?'

'No sign of cyanosis around the lips. So, we can rule out asphyxiation.'

'What killed her, then?'

'I don't know yet, but I'm hazarding a guess at

dehydration. She was locked up unconscious and basically left to die in the back of the car.'

'Jesus! How long would that have taken?' Beth asks.

'About a week. Maybe sooner because we've had such hot weather of late. The heat would have been intense inside the boot and garage, despite that small air vent. She may have lost more moisture through perspiration. She could have been conscious for some of it, probably aware she was going to die, but completely unable to raise the alarm that might have saved her life. That's the most awful and cruel thing about all this. She was so tied up, she couldn't move. There would have been pain in her limbs from the enforced positioning, headaches as she became more dehydrated. The only blessing is that she would have been unconscious through the worst of it,' Elliot says. 'Of course, when I cut her open, I may be proved wrong on all of this.'

But Elliot isn't wrong. His assessment is confirmed throughout the autopsy. The Jane Doe's stomach is empty, there are serious signs of dehydration and, in the end, it was major organ failure that finally killed her. Beth is left with the knowledge that this woman's death hadn't been easy.

'There are marks on her wrists and ankles that don't match the cable ties. It looks like long-term injuries from being restrained,' Elliot notes. 'Look here too. Stretch marks on the lower abdomen. She'd either put weight on and then lost it, or it's a sign of pregnancy. I'll know more when I examine her uterus.'

As Elliot finishes weighing and measuring the corpse's organs and samples are taken and sent away for analysis,

Beth removes the PPE, throwing it into the bin provided in the small gowning room. Then she waits in Elliot's office.

'Can I have your written report as soon as possible?' she asks when he joins her.

'I'll send over a preliminary then a final when we get the toxicology report back.'

'Thanks. I'll need to show all of your findings to my colleague who is a profiler. So, the sooner the better.'

'I need a break first, but I'll get to it and have it over this afternoon. I'm just going to take a walk to the canteen. Can I buy you a coffee?' Elliot asks.

Beth is surprised by the offer but the idea of getting to know Elliot better over coffee appeals to her. She can't deny that she finds him attractive and interesting.

'Sure,' she says. 'Maybe something more will occur to us both on the way.'

'I think we've talked enough about the body for now,' Elliot says.

Beth picks up her handbag and follows him out of the mortuary towards the canteen, which is on the ground floor of the building near the entrance.

The canteen is large and has clean, white, modern furniture scattered around the room. Like any medical facility canteen, staff are on hand, cleaning and sterilising the tables as they are vacated because this place caters for all of the medical, admin and security staff in the building. There's a long counter serving hot food, and two large fridges full of sandwiches, salads and cold drinks.

Beth glances at her watch. It is just gone 11 a.m. and she skipped breakfast, feeling that seeing a dissection on a full stomach might not be the best idea. The hot food counter is full of eggs, bacon, sausages, beans, tomatoes and stacks of toast, because it's still serving breakfast.

They join a line of medical staff as they queue.

'Something to eat?' says Elliot. 'I recommend the sausage butty.'

Beth laughs. 'Sure.'

'My treat,' Elliot says. 'Grab us a seat and I'll bring the coffee and food.'

'I should be treating you by rights,' she laughs.

'I think you deserve this. You handled all that really well.'

'Okay. Since I agree with you, I accept your kind offer.'

Beth leaves Elliot to order the food and then she walks towards the window overlooking a small garden. She chooses a table and sits down. She's pleased that the autopsy hadn't upset her. It was, in part, because Elliot was so interesting to listen to during the examination.

The facility caters for security and special agents' health needs, as well as having the 'special cases' mortuary for deaths that the secret services need to deal with themselves. Anyone working here has been through major security checks, and will also have signed the Official Secrets Act. Beth feels as much at home here as she does in the Archive office block. She is surrounded by people who, like her, work for the government.

Carrying two butties and coffees on a tray, Elliot walks over and places them down. He has brought a knife and fork for each of them, and he has plastic pouches of ketchup and brown sauce, and even small packets of sugar. Beth observes that he's covered all the bases.

Beth reaches for the brown sauce. Elliot smiles as he takes some of that too. Neither of them touch the sugar.

'You thought of everything here,' she says.

They both smear brown sauce on their sausages. Beth cuts her bap in half to make it easier to eat, but Elliot picks up the whole thing and takes a bite from it.

'When did you start here?' Beth asks. 'I hadn't seen you before the other day.'

'I transferred from Manchester two weeks ago,' Elliot says. 'After the sudden vacancy left by Doctor Lancaster.'

'Yes. I heard he left for health reasons,' Beth says. 'Hope he's going to be okay.'

'It was sudden and no one has discussed it – obviously for privacy reasons.'

'Are you here for a while then?' Beth asks.

'Well, I've just accepted a permanent role. So it's turned into a relocation!'

'That's great!' says Beth, then she blushes realising her enthusiasm might be misunderstood.

'I think so too,' Elliot says. 'So, what about you? How long have you worked for MI5?'

Beth glances out at the lawn. It's empty though she's certain it's used to allow patients to get some air at certain times of the day.

'I've been doing this job for years.'

'I was recruited at medical school, before I was halfway through,' Elliot tells her. 'I suppose they brought you in when you were at uni too?'

Beth nods. 'You know how it is. One night you're at a frat party, some hot guy gets you on your own and the next thing you know he and his uncle are putting the Official Secrets Act in front of you.'

Elliot smiles. 'They used a hot girl on me...'

They both laugh. 'Not very original then,' Beth says. 'Anyway, I was doing an intense IT course, and suddenly I'm also being added to Counter Terrorism courses and I'm not just learning about programming, I'm also being taught how to hack pretty much anything.'

Beth stops talking and her eyes flick around.

'I shouldn't really have told you any of that...'

'Believe me, you're not revealing anything I don't know about,' Elliot says. 'I had to do that Counter Terrorism course too!'

'*Really*?'

Elliot nods. He finishes his sausage bap. Then takes a swig from his coffee. 'Feeling a bit more human now after that,' he says.

'Me too. But if you'd told me at the beginning of the examination that I'd feel like eating anything – let alone a sausage sandwich – afterwards, I'd have called you insane.'

'You get used to it. And I find I need to eat afterwards. Like to remind myself I'm alive and still kicking,' he says. 'That I can still smell the coffee,' he finished, taking a deep sniff at his own cup. 'Delicious!'

'It's weird,' says Beth. 'Sometimes when I'm surrounded by the death and ghastly stuff we investigate, I find it's important to do something ordinary too. There was this case I was working on last year – I can't go into it much –

but the stuff that came up, involving kids – it knocked me sick. I had to just go home and hug my two boys. And believe me, I'm not that maternal.'

Beth is surprised at how easy Elliot is to talk to.

'So you're married then?' he asks.

'Separated. Though I haven't exactly shared that with anyone else outside our home yet…' Beth says.

'Don't worry. I won't discuss it with anyone. I'm divorced myself. This job doesn't quite work out well with relationships. My wife got fed up with me having to stay late when an emergency came in. Talking of which, sorry I had to cancel Saturday. I had to go back to Manchester because my mother took ill.'

'I'm really sorry to hear that. Is she … okay?'

'No. Not really. She has dementia. She doesn't even know who I am. She keeps asking if I know her son. It's pretty awful. Especially for my dad, who still has all his marbles,' Elliot explains.

'That must be really hard,' Beth says.

'But on a more cheerful note … I'd better get back and do that report.'

'Thanks. I really appreciate that.' Beth drinks the last of her coffee. 'Better get back to the office myself.' She stands up. 'Thank you for the brunch.'

'You're welcome. Maybe we can make it dinner sometime?'

'That would be nice,' Beth says.

She's blushing as she walks away.

Chapter Sixteen

MICHAEL

'Hi, Mike,' says Beth as she enters my office. 'How you doing?'

'All good here. Did you need me to do something?' I ask.

'I've emailed you a preliminary autopsy report. Will you look at it and give me your thoughts? Leon and I found a body on Friday.'

'Good grief. Where? How?' I ask.

Beth takes a breath. 'At the moment I can't tell you much. But she was found in the boot of a car in a suspect's garage.'

'Okay,' I say.

'I'd like you to review the photos, the pathologist's initial findings and come up with a profile for the kind of person who would ... do this to a person.'

I agree to look and Beth leaves. The moment isn't as awkward as some of the discussions I have had to have with Leon. Beth is trying hard to be normal. I open my email handler and find the report. I print the document, then flick through the photographs on the screen and compare the comments made about them. The pathologist is good, his instincts sound. I digest the information and then go into Beth's office to talk it through with her.

'I've looked, and I'll draw up an official profile but I thought I'd share my initial reaction to the information. First of all, the calluses and bruising on the wrists and ankles of the victim. Those are very interesting.'

'I thought that too,' says Beth. 'Elliot – the pathologist – suggested she could have been into bondage. There was both old and more recent scarring...'

'I'll come back to that shortly. Let's talk about the bruising on her throat, which looks like an attempted strangulation.'

'Could they have believed they'd killed her before they'd placed her in the boot?'

'I don't think so. This semi-strangulation was intentional and the perpetrator knew just how much force to use. There was, I saw, no rupture of the throat. This could buy into your pathologist's theory that the victim liked being restrained, and may have had a few other S and M fetishes. But I'm going to explode that idea now. Usually strangulation of this sort accompanies penetrative sex. But your pathologist says there was no evidence of sexual activity. Furthermore, strangulation of this sort wouldn't render the victim unconscious because you wouldn't squeeze that hard. Yet there is evidence that enough pressure was applied to do just that. She was put down, then the cable ties were used. When she was unable to resist.'

'Do you think she struggled?' Beth asks but I know she's just testing me. She already knows the answer.

'The wounds on her hands. Defensive, yes, but I reckon some of them were from her fighting for her life too. She may well have wounded her attacker. It might be why they half strangled her to regain control.'

'There was no skin under the nails,' Beth observes.

'No. There was *nothing* under the nails. The perp scraped them clean. Your pathologist says there was a chemical smell coming from her hands and they swabbed them prior to cutting the cables and washing her down. It'll be interesting to see what that chemical was. But I'm sure it will be some form of bleach. They were making sure there would be no traces of themselves on her.'

Beth is thoughtful for a minute and then she asks, 'What sort of person kills someone by starving and dehydration?'

'Someone who gets a kick out of what they do,' I say. 'This was a calculated and cruel death.'

'One of the Network's assassins?'

'Possibly,' I say.

In the past, we've discussed the way some killers disintegrate after a time and begin to enjoy what they do. I remind Beth of this as we talk more about the identity of the possible killer.

'The stretch marks were interesting. Baker observes that the uterus was swollen, consistent with a recent full-term pregnancy,' I say, continuing my observations. 'It is likely she was detained until she was full term. Maybe she was taken because she was pregnant. She gives birth. Her captor has no further use for her, but they take the kid. It's not usually the Network's MO, but things might have changed since Beech was brought down.'

Beth is about to speak but she stops herself. I can tell she knows more about this woman than she's saying.

'We might learn more if we discover where they kept her,' Beth says choosing her words carefully. 'And if Elliot's observation of stretch marks proves to have been a pregnancy, your observations are sound based on what I've been able to tell you.'

'What do you know that might help you find this place?' I ask.

Beth glances towards the door leading to the corridor and Ray's office.

'It's all right,' I say. 'I understand. Need to know basis. Though it would help with the profile if I could have some more context.'

Beth thinks for a moment. 'I agree. I'm going to go out on a limb here. We had a report of a missing person. According to her employment history Angela Carter started her new job six months ago. She also rented a flat in Slough. The woman we found matches her description. I have a theory that she is Angela. But I don't just think she was kidnapped for the child she was carrying. I believe she was imprisoned and she was replaced by someone who looked like her.'

'She had a *doppelgänger*?' I ask.

Beth nods. 'And that person has been pretending to be her for a while. Maybe months, but I'm not certain. I'm also unclear on how closely alike they were, maybe same height, colouring, build. The same hairstyle and colour, et cetera,' Beth says. 'Enough to fool a casual acquaintance.'

'But surely her family would know it wasn't her?' I say.

'That's the thing, Mike. She doesn't seem to have any. Both parents are dead. No siblings. Even stranger – there's no online presence to stalk and find friends who might recognise her, either.'

'That could be why they chose her,' I say. 'Clean slate. But it also depends on why they needed to replace her. Can you tell me what her job was?'

'Not yet. But, if this theory of replacement isn't correct, then up to two weeks ago the neighbour says he was talking to her. He's probably the only person ever close enough to recognise her. He might well have been the last to see her before whoever did this got to her.'

'That woman in the mortuary wasn't walking free two weeks ago, though,' I say.

'How do you figure that?' Beth asks.

'If what you've told me is true, then Angela Carter was replaced but that was more likely *before* she started her new job and moved into her new flat. Like you said, any *doppelgänger* will have differences and only people who didn't know her would take her at face value. People who didn't know her, or an employer that had only met her once or twice for interviews. Think about those restraint scars on her wrists and ankles... She was held a while. I think you were right with your initial theory. It *was* months.'

Beth is quiet for a moment.

'So the neighbour had never met the real Angela, only the double?'

'Yes. I suspect she was living there as if she was the original. And if I'm right on this, the replacement also imprisoned and then killed the real Angela Carter. The thing I don't understand is why she was replaced. Who was Angela Carter?'

'I can't tell you that now,' Beth says.

I don't ask where this is leading, because I think I know already: Angela Carter worked for someone important.

As I return to my office, my mind is full of questions I can't ask because I'm still on the 'not trustworthy' list.

I shouldn't really be surprised though, as I know I'm still compromised. Was Neva serious that she needed something in return for the data? Or did last night change things?

Thinking about Neva brings a bout of guilt that is difficult to disengage from. I only hope that my behaviour doesn't rouse suspicion. If they gave me a polygraph right now, I doubt I'd pass.

My computer tings then and I see an email arrive from Ray. I open it up and read the invitation to come to his office.

My face flushes with guilt. What can Ray want right now? Have they learnt that Neva tampered with their surveillance? I respond to Ray's email, saying I'm on the way.

'Come in,' says Ray when I reach his door, which has been left wide open for me.

I'm greeted by Beth and Leon, and there is another woman there whom I don't know.

'Sit down,' Ray says. 'This is Special Agent Carol Brinkman. She's been working with us on a recent and very secret problem. Michael, Beth has just shared with us your observations on part of this case. We'd now like to bring you in on it to see what else you can tell us.'

I shake hands with Agent Brinkman and sit down. I try not to let the relief show on my face.

'I'm all ears,' I say.

'A couple of weeks ago a flight went AWOL on its way to Shanghai,' says Brinkman. 'It's crucial that the news doesn't break. We are concerned that this would bring about global panic.'

Everything they say confirms what Neva previously told me.

'You see, Mike, without knowing what this was, you actually helped to analyse some crucial evidence. We are now certain that Angela Carter, a stewardess with Zen Airlines, was kidnapped and replaced some months ago,' Ray explains.

'We have no understanding of the agenda of the hacker,' Brinkman says. 'Or if the flight and its passengers are unharmed. But we believe it was hijacked.'

'Talk me through what happened,' I say.

'The flight took off from Heathrow as normal. The journey takes eleven hours and for more than half of the journey, the plane sent the expected satellite signals to confirm its whereabouts and safety. Four hours before landing, communications ceased. Then the satellite picked up an automated signal notifying us of a change of course. The plane rapidly lost altitude and disappeared completely from our radar. Needless to say, it didn't make its destination. Since then, we've had a team of experts working to retrace its movements.'

Brinkman talks me through the possible scenarios from fire to hijack. Ultimately, they suspect the plane went down somewhere.

'Maybe the pilot tried to land it because they were having engine trouble, but none of the possible courses he could have taken to bring it down safely were on the detour that it took. Obviously, this is why we think it was taken,' Brinkman says.

'What was on the route?' I ask.

Brinkman looks at me. 'We don't know. The truth is the detour was never confirmed as the information was cut off halfway through transmission. That's why we think that there may have been someone on board, hacking the system, and not only controlling the plane, but preventing any automatic distress signals as well.'

'So the only way to know what really happened is to find the plane?' I ask. 'And the flight recorder?'

'Yes,' says Ray. 'I'm going to send you all the information we have about the crew and passengers. If you notice anything, then come and discuss with me. We're looking to see if any of them fit with a possible past of hacking.'

'I take it no terrorist group has claimed responsibility?'

'No. But that might be because we've kept a lid on it. They can only claim something if it's public knowledge.'

'In view of what you've told me,' I say, 'my main observation here is the planning that went into this. As we've established, Carter must have been taken more than six months ago, before she started working for Zen Airlines – this indicates that it was a long-term covert operation. Whatever agenda these people had, they needed to establish her double as the real her to make sure she was beyond suspicion. Our main suspects in this would be the Network. But if so, this had to be set up before we disrupted their organisation.'

'That's true,' says Ray. 'We can't necessarily lay blame on them.'

'Unless communication with the Network was curtailed once the mission started as part of the double's cover,' I say. 'They may not even know that Beech is dead.'

We talk more about the possibilities then I agree to look at the full file and come back with any observations. I leave Ray's office a short time later with a folder and access codes for further information in the database.

I try not to feel excited as I walk back to my office. Adrenaline, brought on by the prospect of a new and exciting puzzle to solve, rushes through my veins, flushing my face more than the guilt had done earlier. It feels that things have made a definite move in the right direction and maybe, just maybe, I'm being accepted and trusted once more.

As I sit back down at my desk, I force my mind away from the night before and Neva. I can't deny that I'm elated at being given more responsibility again: I earned it. I deserve it. I've always loved my job. Even so, there is a palpable insecurity punctuating the excitement I'm feeling and I know it is because for the first time in months I'm starting to believe it might be possible to have my life back.

I open up the encrypted files, put in the passcodes I've been given, and begin to scan the notes that Brinkman has left here. I find my mind wandering back to Neva. What will it mean for me if our continued relationship is discovered?

My happy mood plummets.

The tentative position I have begun to build once more in Archive would be destroyed. There would be no going back after a further betrayal. *If I don't give her information, I am betraying no one*, I think. I give myself a mental shake, realising how naïve and stupid that excuse would sound if spoken aloud.

Why can't life be uncomplicated for once? Why can't I have it all?

The answer comes, but it is welcome: happiness sits between Archive and Neva, and right now never the twain shall meet. I feel like I'm in a tug of war with myself that no side can win.

Chapter Seventeen

MICHAEL

I arrive home half hoping, half dreading that Neva will be there. But as I enter my apartment, I can feel the void that confirms she hasn't turned up. In my bedroom I take the phone out of my drawer and switch it on. There I see messages from her from Saturday asking where I am. I delete the messages and send her a quick text now.

Need to hear what you know about the flight, I say.

A short time later Neva responds.

I need your help in return.

I put down the phone and curse under my breath. *Bitch!*

I turn the phone off, irritated with her for still trying this when she knows I'll be compromised. Why is she so desirable, yet so fucking annoying?

It's your own fault, I tell myself. *You've let her reel you in again. Idiot.*

I take a deep breath, my mind worrying and teasing

around her request. The Network operative side of me questions why she should give me information for free: she owes no allegiance to Archive. If they caught her, they'd imprison and interrogate her. No, she owes Archive nothing. But why doesn't she see that I can't do this? Doesn't Neva feel any loyalty at least to me?

She's a trained killer. She feels nothing. Not even for me. But even as I think this, I know that it's not true: Neva does care about me. I just don't know how much and whether she would sacrifice herself for me. Not that I'd want her to.

To distract myself I change into my joggers and go out for a run.

I leave the building and head off down the street, turning into quieter roads so that there are fewer people on the pavement that I have to swerve to avoid. Not an easy task in the centre of London. My tail is left behind, staring after me in confusion from the opposite side of the road to my building.

I jog for a half an hour before returning to my apartment. I notice that the tail is still sitting watching; bored and uninterested, he didn't attempt to follow me on my exercise excursion as he has on previous days. I give him a wave as I go back into the building. He looks startled, but then laughs and waves back.

Sweat dripping off me, but feeling more in control, I go back up to my apartment. I shower, pull some sleep shorts on then go in search of a beer.

On the coffee table in the lounge is a bottle of wine and a note that says, *peace offering*.

I switch on the burner phone again and look for further

texts, but Neva hasn't sent any.

I take the wine, stow it in the kitchen, and then help myself to a beer. I don't know how I feel about her randomly coming in when I was absent, or whether the wine is yet another trick to manipulate me.

As per my new habits I turn the television on and watch some boring game show for a short time. Then my regular phone pings as a text comes in.

Hope you enjoy the wine. I've persuaded Ray to remove the surveillance. They'll take the cameras and sound shit out tomorrow. You're back in now, Mike, don't screw it up! Beth x

I stare at the text for a long time, not quite believing what I'm reading. It had been Beth that called in! Beth that left the wine. I wonder if she had a look round while she was here.

I send her a thank you, then turn the phone off.

The adrenaline is back, an age-old excitement that can't be ignored. My earlier feelings were correct. I'm back in! Does this mean a return of full access?

The sneaky thought of using that access to learn things creeps into the back of my mind like the itch of a gnat bite. Beech would have had me using this all to full advantage. But despite Beth's reassurance that I would no longer be watched, I still know they will be keeping an eye on me because it is impossible to consider that they can forgive and forget so easily.

If the shoe was on the other foot, would I trust me? Probably not.

Chapter Eighteen

NEVA

'I can pay,' Neva says. 'But I need to know what I'm buying first.'

She sits down next to the startled man. His name is Alexi and he's Polish and by day he works as a decorator. But his other pastime is what brings Neva here. Alexi is also a hacker and has been used by the Network several times to help them gain access to classified information.

'You!' he says.

'*Me?*' Neva answers.

'If I'd known, I wouldn't have come,' Alexi says.

He starts to get up. Neva pulls him back down.

'Yes, you would, but you wouldn't have been alone.'

Alexi scowls at her. 'What do you want?'

'The information you promised me online.'

'Are you insane? They'll kill me if I tell *you* anything.'

'You can earn the fee I promised you and walk away from this, or I can... Well, you figure it out for yourself,' Neva says.

Alexi slumps in his chair. Neva knows that most hackers are essentially cowards who hide behind their keyboards because they know how to manipulate code for their own advantage. For once Alexi has been outsmarted on that score – Neva had hidden her identity well.

'What do you want?' he asks.

'What state are the Network in?'

Alexi sighs.

'There was an initial tussle for power that fed out to people like me. What I heard was that one of *yours*, codenamed Vasquez, went after the committee. In the first three months he worked his way up through the different ranks until he found out who they all were. He killed four of them before the other seven agreed to let him join them.'

'Is he in charge?' Neva asks.

'No. They have him now as their guardian and enforcer and he's responsible for bringing the others back in line,' Alexi says.

'Back in line, how?'

'There's been defections at all levels. Vasquez made an example of a few, now the others are back in play. Operatives, handlers and above. There are rumours that they are stepping up a new training programme.'

Neva lets out a breath. 'Another house?'

'I don't know about any house…' Alexi frowns.

Neva believes him. The houses have always been kept completely secret, no gossip, no leaks. No one would dare talk about it for fear of repercussions.

'You know more than most about the Network, Alexi, so

don't give me your bullshit. Who are the other seven committee members?'

'I don't know. But I have the name of someone who might,' Alexi says.

'Who?'

'Beech's former chauffeur. His name is Eldon Fracks. He went to ground when Beech's office and home were hit by MI5. Until then, no one, not even me, knew Beech was running the show,' Alexi explains.

'If Fracks has gone to ground, how will I find him?' she asks.

'I want double what I asked online. A lot of people are looking for Fracks, including Vasquez,' Alexi says. 'Just being here with you puts me at risk.'

'Give me your bank details,' Neva says, retrieving her phone from her pocket. She logs into a bank account and begins to set up the transaction as Alexi tells her his bank details. 'One click of a button and ten grand is yours. Where is Fracks?'

'He's staying in a bed and breakfast in Brighton. It's called the Seaview Guesthouse and it's opposite the pier.'

'How reliable is your information? I don't want to go on a wild goose chase,' Neva says.

'I found him because Vasquez put the word out that he wanted him. All it took was one slip-up: he used a card in a bar in Brighton. Probably because he ran out of cash. People are stupid when they drink,' Alexi says. 'I set up alerts on his name and it came up.'

'But how do you know where he's staying?' Neva asks.

'I hacked into the street cameras and tracked him,' Alexi says.

Neva studies his face and finds no sign of a lie.

'One more thing. How did Vasquez find out who the committee members were if Fracks had gone to ground?'

'I don't know. I just know he worked his way through a lot of people to glean anything he could. And most of those people didn't survive the interrogation, so they aren't telling anyone else what they know now.'

'Get out of here,' she says. 'But you better keep this morsel to yourself. I don't want to turn up and find Fracks silenced.'

Alexi stands. 'I'm talking to no one about the Network. Do you think I'm stupid? But I'll tell you what. Here's some information I'll give you for free. Vasquez put the word out and he is looking for you. He isn't looking to bring you back: it's a kill order.'

'Tell me something I don't already know,' Neva says.

Alexi and Neva both leave the bar together. They part at the door, but show no signs of having conversed or that they know each other.

Neva walks away down the street, avoiding the street cameras. She had mapped out the range of all of them before the meeting, and she's tampered with those she couldn't avoid. Opening the app on her phone that she used to hack into the system, she returns the cameras to normal service.

She crosses the road and cuts down a side street, looking at the parked cars along the way. She needs to get a ride to Brighton and fast. She doesn't trust that Alexi won't try to sell the information he has to someone else, perhaps a third party who'll pass it to Vasquez. Alexi has always been greedy. Even so, she knows he isn't stupid. If he does sell on the information, Alexi will be certain to keep himself hidden from the Network, throwing another hacker under the bus for his own safety if he has to.

Maybe I should have killed him, she thinks as she sees a car that will be easy to steal. But the thought of murdering Alexi slips away as she considers how useful he's going to be to her in the future. Yes, she knows exactly how to manipulate him for her own devices, and he won't even know she's behind it.

'Hey? What are you doing? That's my car!' says a voice behind her.

Neva turns to look at the disgruntled driver, keys in his hand.

'I was going to steal it,' Neva says. 'But now there's no need.'

'What the fuck…?' says the man.

Neva kicks him in the stomach. He doubles over, gasping for breath, and the keys to his car drop from his fingers. Neva catches them. Then she chops her hand across his neck. He stumbles to the ground, head cracking on the pavement. She doesn't want to kill him, but she needs time to make it to Brighton before the police look for the car. She drags the man down an alley. Taking cable ties from her backpack she ties him up. Then she puts gaffer tape over his mouth. He is unconscious so she feels he shouldn't be a problem for a while.

Going back to the street, she opens the car and gets in. She flips open the glove box and finds a sat nav inside.

'That's useful!'

She sets the machine to take her to the address of the guesthouse in Brighton. Then she starts the engine and drives away.

Chapter Nineteen

NEVA

Even though Brighton is only fifty-three miles from Neva's starting location, it takes almost two hours to reach the seafront. She finds a parking spot down one of the side roads, and then, using wet wipes, she cleans down the steering wheel, glove box, sat nav, door and keys. She leaves the keys in the ignition and the door unlocked: an open invitation to any thief that happens to be passing.

She walks away from the car and heads for the Seaview Guesthouse. In the window the sign is showing 'vacancies'.

Neva walks up the steps and enters. Inside, the reception area is old-fashioned and gloomy. No one is at the desk, but there is a bell push with a sign that says, 'Ring for attention.' Covering her fingers with her jacket sleeve, Neva presses the button and hears a distant ring. Then a woman comes downstairs and smiles at her. The woman is young, early twenties, which surprises Neva because the place is so dated and tired.

'I'd like a room,' Neva says.

'How many nights?' asks the woman.

'One.'

She pays cash and the woman doesn't question it. She hands her a receipt along with a key.

'First floor, left-hand side. Room 5.'

Neva hurries up the stairs. She unlocks the door and walks inside.

The room is hot and stale. She goes to the window and opens it, letting fresh air circulate. She does indeed have a 'sea view', but that is not why she's here.

Neva paces the room, determining all possible escape routes. She's on the first floor, but the guesthouse also has a basement at just below ground level. That means she's elevated by not just one storey but two. Too far to drop out and land without injury. She looks over at the next hotel. There is a blue canvas canopy over the entrance. A good place to catch her fall, but she rules this route out also because it is quite a distance from her window. If forced to leave that way she will have to slide along on a very narrow ledge that is only wide enough for her toes.

Her plan is to find Fracks, question him, then get away before anyone knows she's here. Therefore, she hopes not to need an escape plan. This place is not ideal on that score.

From her rucksack she removes her Glock and loads it, making sure the safety is on before stowing the gun in the back of her jeans. She tests the mechanism of her wrist holster; the knife slips into her hand without a sound. She pushes it back in place and then puts her rucksack under the bed.

Closing the window again, she leaves the room and

wanders down the landing, listening at the other doors. It's eight o'clock in the evening and most guests are already in their rooms. There is a couple arguing loudly over a television in room 6, a family in room 7 – she can tell this because she hears a child complaining as his mother tries to coax him to go to sleep.

In room 8 – the one directly opposite hers – she hears the sound of a television but nothing else. There may be someone in there watching it but she isn't sure. She goes up the next set of stairs to the landing above and does the same. Across the bottom of the final set of stairs leading up, there is a sign saying, 'Staff Only'. She doesn't go up as she's not interested in the employees; she wants to find Eldon Fracks.

As she passes down the right-hand side of the corridor, she hears someone climbing the stairs. She turns and walks back to the stairs as though she has just left her own room. A man approaches. Neva glances at him but he isn't familiar to her and isn't Fracks – she'd seen him when she had pulled surveillance on Beech's business premises – and so as he reaches the landing, she passes and begins her descent downwards.

She'll have to watch out for Fracks and get to him when she knows what room he's in.

There is a blur of movement and the man on the second landing throws himself down the stairs. Before Neva can pull out her knife, he catches hold of her by the throat. She cuffs him hard in the face. His eyes water but he doesn't loosen his grip as he begins to choke her. Neva kicks and punches; some land, some don't. She uses her weight to throw them both down the stairs. They roll, entwined.

At the bottom of the stairs the man cracks his head on the newel post and is momentarily stunned. They are thrown apart and Neva jumps to her feet and flicks the blade into her hand. She feels for her gun but it is missing, fallen away somewhere during the tumble.

The man is up on his feet with equal stealth. He sees her knife and laughs.

'Who are you?' she asks.

'I've wanted to meet you for some time,' the man says.

Neva holds the knife between them. She wants to locate her gun but can't take her eyes from her assailant.

'Really? Well, if you wanted a date there are better ways to approach a girl,' she says.

He laughs again, and then the man's face loses all sign of humour. A coldness sweeps over his features, a blank emotionless stare replaces the wary watchfulness. He dives at her.

Neva leaps aside, slipping away from his grasp as she anticipates his move. She backs up to her own door near the stairs, even as he throws himself at her again – obviously a favoured move.

He's a child of the house; the moves are familiar, even though his face isn't. He's a generation above hers at least. Possibly from Olive Redding's batch.

He's holding a gun now – her Glock – lost and now found by the enemy.

'We can do this easy or hard,' he says.

'I've never been a fan of easy,' she comments but there is

no wit evident on her face as she slips back into her old killer patterns. A fight is like a game of chess, after all. The winner is determined when they make the moves that the opponent doesn't anticipate.

In her mind, Neva runs through the possible scenarios of fighting an assassin with equal knowledge and skill to herself. A montage of motions and responses flicks across the back of her eyes like a film being played. This is not a skill that they taught her, but one she developed herself. Killing him is easy. In each set-up she wins the battle. She doesn't want to kill him though, and that is the challenge.

He's impatient, ready to move on her, even as she strategises. He watches her, poised like a cobra ready to strike as he moves back and forth on the balls of his feet. He wants to execute her, that's the thing. He believes himself invulnerable, more than capable of taking her – which is a dangerous confidence to have. She's seen this behaviour before: he's become a victim of his own fascination with death and his belief that he is a bringer of it. The only problem here is that this man's emotional instability makes him weak.

She smiles and pushes her knife back into her wrist holster. He gives that cold, sharp laugh, and arrogance makes him toss the Glock aside. It clatters to the wooden floor. He takes up a fighting position.

'They tell me you're the best,' he says. 'I'm going to prove them wrong.'

He moves in, they begin to fight, taekwondo moves, mixed with karate and judo. Fast and furious, but unemotional. They attack each other. He's bigger than her, and there should be a discrepancy that will make him the victor, but Neva is lighter on her feet. She moves with balletic grace.

Using his weight and impatience against him, Neva dives down as he lunges at her. She throws him over her back, chopping at his throat to incapacitate him. He anticipates this even as he's destabilised, leaping clear.

Adrenaline floods Neva's blood. Her moves speed up; she attacks before her assailant and he isn't expecting the reappearance of her knife. As soon as it drops into her hand, she buries it in his thigh, then twists to do the maximum damage before pulling it out.

The man gasps, and his leg gives under him. Neva kicks him in the face. He falls back with a dull thump. She's on his prone body in an instant. Using the hilt of the knife, she hits him hard on the temple, knocking him unconscious.

Gripping his jacket, she heaves him across the landing to room 5. Then she opens the door and drags the body inside. A brief look outside onto the landing confirms that no one has heard or seen anything, which would be something of a miracle if either of them hadn't been taught so well to fight in silence. There's a small splash of blood on the grubby reddish carpet down the centre of the corridor, but Neva knows that no one but herself will notice it against the dizzying and faded pattern.

She picks up her Glock from the floor, and then goes back into her room, closing and locking the door behind her.

Removing the cable ties from her pocket that she had prepared for Eldon Fracks, she secures the man's wrists and ankles and then splashes water on his face to bring him around.

He wakes to find himself restricted.

Neva is sitting on the edge of the bed.

'You think I'm the only one coming to look for you?' he says.

'I think you're the first to arrive, but I'll be gone before any others follow. Your arrogance was your downfall.' She tuts. 'What would your handler say about how you lost because you let emotion get in the way?'

'Fuck you!'

'That wound is deeper than it seems,' she points out.

The man looks at his leg. Blood is seeping from the wound, pooling under his thigh.

'I could make a tourniquet, give you more time to be found by your colleagues. Or I can just gag you and let you bleed out. What would you do in my shoes?'

'I'd slit your fucking throat,' he says.

'Now, now. There's no need for aggression. Such a wasted emotion,' Neva says.

She takes a sheet off the bed and begins to rip a long piece off it. Then she doubles up the strip, making it stronger.

'Part your knees and don't try anything because those cable ties cut like paper but a hell of a lot deeper,' she says.

Recognising her intention to deal with his wound, he does as instructed. She ties the strip tightly around his thigh. She looks around the room. She picks up a pen that's been left on the dresser with a satisfaction questionnaire.

She slips the pen inside the makeshift bandage and then twists it to add restriction.

'There,' she says. 'I think that should give me enough time to work on you.'

She's intrigued to see a sliver of fear cross his features.

'You're much more of a talker than they told me you were,' he says.

'Who is "they"?'

He shakes his head in instinctive refusal.

She cable-ties his calves, further restricting his ability to move.

Neva takes another strip off the sheet. She grabs the man's jacket again and pulls him into the bathroom. He tries to kick and struggle to prevent her, but the ties hold fast and he tires quickly from the effort and the blood he's already lost.

'I've always thought drowning would be a horrible way to die,' she says.

Then she pulls his body into the shower and begins wrapping the sheet around his face. He kicks and twists and protests again. Neva cuffs him until he's quiet, then she starts the shower.

His muffled cries halt her.

'Want to talk?' she asks.

She unwinds the sheet from his face.

'You piece of shit,' he spits at her.

Neva gives him a grim smile. 'Oh, that may be true. After all, I was trained by the same people as you. But the difference between us is that I don't really *enjoy* killing. Don't get me wrong – it doesn't upset me to do it. It's just a means to an end. But it's messy. And I only have limited clothing with me. So not so practical either.'

She winds the cloth back over his face. Then she holds his head under the running shower.

The assassin struggles as he begins to suffocate. She pulls him back, removes the cloth, lets him breathe again.

'Anything to say?'

He spits at her again.

She winds the wet cotton over his face again and puts him back under the shower. A few more rounds of this make the assassin more compliant.

'Who sent you?' she asks.

'The Network.'

'Don't be stupid. I already know that. Who in the Network?'

He shakes his head, 'I don't know.'

She wraps the cloth over him again. Puts him under the water. He's growing weaker now with blood loss and the torture. Neva knows she'll have to get something tangible soon or he will pass out and her time with him will end.

'Who?' she asks again.

'Vasquez…' he gasps when she releases his face again. 'He's called Vasquez.'

'What about Fracks? Is he really here or was that a set-up?'

'Not here,' he says. 'We're looking for him.'

'Where do I find Vasquez?'

'I can't. He'll kill me…'

She repeats the process of drowning him. When she

pulls him out, though, he's almost unconscious. She slaps his face, bringing him back.

'Where is Vasquez?'

'A men's club…'

'The Methuselah?' she asks.

There's a commotion outside her room in the corridor. Feet ascending the stairs from below. Neva lets go of the man. Time has run out. She stabs her blade into his throat. His windpipe ruptures. Then she slices his jugular for good measure. At least that way they won't learn what he told her.

She washes her blade and her hands, then stows it back in the holster. From her rucksack she removes a wig, a dark blonde bob and a hairnet. She stuffs her hair into the net with practised speed. Then pulls the wig on, pinning it in place.

She pulls the rucksack over her shoulders, places her Glock inside for safekeeping. Then she goes to the window.

Having previously determined this would be a difficult thing to do, Neva now has no choice. She climbs out of the window. The ledge is narrow, and she moves along on her toes like a ballerina on point, while she faces the wall of the guesthouse, gripping onto the structure as much as possible. As the ledge runs out, she glances at the hotel next door. The bright blue canopy stands proud over the door. It'll be a leap. If she misses, the fall will be substantial, and she would be lucky to merely break a limb.

She hears a loud banging on the door of the room she's just left. She looks at the canopy again. Concentrating, she works out how her body must move to reach it. Then without hesitation she throws herself backwards off the ledge, twisting like a diver. She half lands on the canopy, her chest slamming down against the frame, which buckles under her weight but breaks her fall. She's winded. Gasping for breath, she pulls her body fully onto the canvas while she regulates her breathing. Then she holds the edge of the canopy and flips herself down and off, as though she's leaving a circus net.

Above her she hears the door of her room crash open. She stands unseen under the canopy as she hears the screams and yells above.

'She must have gone out of the window!' someone calls.

Beside her under the canopy, someone has tied a small poodle to one of the railings. Neva unties it and starts to walk away. She pauses as the dog sniffs around the base of a tree.

Hide in plain sight, she thinks.

The door to the Seaview crashes open and two men emerge, shouting at each other. The dog starts to bark as though the noise terrifies him. Neva glances back as the men start looking around frantically. She picks up the dog, hushing it as any caring owner would do. One of the men runs past her.

'What's going on?' she cries after him in a Polish accent.

The man ignores her as he runs full pelt down the pavement. When both of the men have disappeared in opposite directions, Neva puts the dog back on the ground and the two of them walk away.

Chapter Twenty

NEVA

S he's calm as she ties the dog up outside another hotel. The adrenaline filters out of her blood, and the assassins who had come after her have long gone.

She'd watched one of them hurry back, passing her as she bent to pet the poodle. A coal-black people carrier with darkened windows had collected him and the car had sped off down the promenade as they did a search for anyone fitting Neva's description. Their lack of efficiency amuses her because she remained under their nose the whole time.

Fracks was never in Brighton: Alexi set me up, she thinks.

More than ever, Neva is aware that she has no one she can trust. She should have killed the hacker. He was lowlife scum who sent out mean viruses to destroy websites or to hold simple people to ransom. But Neva is not a vigilante. Although she did play her part in bringing down the Kill House, she never achieved what she'd really wanted to by that exercise. She concedes that she is happy – *is that the right word?* – that the children were found and saved.

Returned as they were to those who loved them. Even so, she failed to discover her own origins. She failed to get any real revenge, and she thirsts for that. She wonders what retribution will taste like when she at last has it.

Not chocolate.

For the first time Neva feels loneliness and understands what it is. *I have no one.*

Michael. He is someone to her. Though now she's angered him with her insistence on quid pro quo for information about the flight. Even so, her request was logical. She needs to know what Archive have on her or at least how to find Olive Redding, the only person who might have the answer.

Redding. She'd been searching for her ever since they both fled the house. But Redding was good, and Neva gained nothing from her enquiries. Redding had gone to ground, and she wasn't rearing her head. For the last month Neva had stopped looking for her. It was pointless when there were other targets she could get to and learn from.

Neva crosses the road, then walks back towards the Seaview, casually observing the arrival of police and an ambulance to take away the assassin's body. This won't please Vasquez. One of their cardinal rules was to leave no evidence behind. The door key to the room is in her pocket. The door, however, was smashed in. She doubts that Seaview Guesthouse will be needing this back.

Neva walks onto the pier and follows its long length down towards the sea. She observes a 'World Famous' fish and chip restaurant that she's never heard of, full to the brim with diners. An old gypsy booth, promising the 'honest' telling of fortunes, has some gaudy fairy lights draped outside. There is a burger stand and a sweet stall selling rock and sugar candy in a variety of shapes. The normality of a seaside town.

When she reaches the end of the pier, the sea breeze sweeps away the last sliver of tension. A casual glance ensures that she isn't being observed, before Neva throws the guesthouse key into the ocean. She watches the water move and swallow it up. She meditates on the rhythm of the waves, moderating her breathing to match its ebb and flow.

With Midsummer's Day near, the evenings are still long and light, but the night is drawing in and Neva can sense from a tang in the air a summer storm lurking off the coast.

She turns back the way she came. She sees the fortune teller locking up, a cigarette burning between old, cracked lips. Neva turns her face away from the woman: they are notoriously observant even if their communion with the dead isn't real. She does not wish to be remembered by any casual eye.

The shops begin to close in a wave as she reaches the pier entrance. The normalcy of the evening ending is in stark contrast to the drama only an hour earlier.

At the Seaview Guesthouse, the police cars remain as the ambulance departs. Neva notices that the car she stole in London is still parked on the side street, a parking ticket now attached to the windscreen. So its owner must still be trussed up and has yet to report her theft.

She passes the car. She could take it again, but you never revisit your crimes, and certainly don't use the same stolen car more than once. She turns towards the train station, pausing to open her phone and bring up the rail ticket app. She glances at her watch. It is 10.15 p.m. and the next train leaves in twenty minutes. She could just make it.

If she was searching for her right now, she'd post someone at the station. But how many did they send after her in the first place? She had killed one and seen two more, and then there was the driver of the black people carrier. So, perhaps four in all. But there could be more.

Neva turns away from the station. *Too risky*.

At this late hour, getting another hotel room will be problematic as well. She decides against it.

She walks down several streets before she notices one house in total darkness. It's a typical Victorian seaside terrace. A 'For Sale' sign is posted at the front in the small yard. Across the road she sees the flicker of light from a television in the front room of another house. The occupants sit together on a sofa – a man and a woman – watching a late-night comedy show. They don't glance outwards at her or the house.

Neva looks up and down the street. When she's certain there's no one around to observe her, she slips into the shallow garden of the house and curves around the building to the back. She looks through a window into the property. There is no furniture; the place is unoccupied.

Around the back is an even smaller garden than the front, but French windows stretch along the rear of the house. Neva looks through the dirty glass, then she retrieves her lock picks from her rucksack and begins to work on the door. The lock gives and Neva goes inside the house.

She wanders through the kitchen. It's a narrow room but the ceiling is high and so there is a feeling of space. She makes her way into the living room. At the front windows she looks out unobserved at the property opposite. Such a normal scene. She superimposes herself and Michael on them. Could they live in such domesticity? Probably not.

My brain is turning to mush.

After a few moments, she turns away and heads upstairs. There she finds three empty bedrooms and a bathroom.

She settles down in the front bedroom, curling up on the dusty carpet with the rucksack under her head. She's slept in worse places than this and it doesn't take her long to settle down.

Though she lets sleep take her, she knows that she will be awake and alert at the slightest sound. Some elements of the training never leave you.

Chapter Twenty-One

MICHAEL

Despite the run, I am restless and when I try to sleep, strange looping stress dreams hound me. I've never consciously worried about my job and yet my dream state finds me struggling to locate my office and when I do find the room, I can no longer recall how to do my work. I press buttons on the keyboard, yet everything I type comes out gibberish.

Because of my psychology degree, I understand how my subconscious is struggling to deal with my insecurities. When I wake, I try to shake the confusion and anxiety away. I explore the implicit meaning of the dreams, forcing them into my consciousness in order to deal with them. Yes, I'm anxious. I'm on the brink of rebuilding my life, but my past still poisons any idea of my future. In fact, it's a total mind fuck. Not helped by the complication of my feelings for Neva. All problems that just can't be solved overnight, if at all.

At 5 a.m. I'm looking up at the ceiling, thinking of her. I

should try and persuade her to share her knowledge with me about the flight, for the good of everyone, but I know she's stubborn. In my sleep my mind has worried at the possible outcomes of feeding her information that will help her reach her parents and learn how she was chosen for the house. In the best-case scenario, she is reunited with people who loved and missed her; in the worst, she may learn of their betrayal. I know what Neva will do in the latter situation and there will be carnage for which I'll have to take responsibility.

In the world I once thought I understood, before I learned of my own origins, recruits were picked from the gifted among soldiers and those with talents such as myself. We were enlisted through persuasive explanations of how we could protect our country and help others. We were convinced we had the same motivations as our employers and our actions were for the greater good. This too was a form of conditioning, but one that we chose to see as acceptable. In Neva's world there was no such option. She was taught to kill or die in the name of the Network and it wasn't through choice; it was through brainwashing from an early age. Although I know she broke free of her training, Neva is still not a person I can have faith in.

But then, Beech did the same thing to me. So how am I any different from Neva?

I curl up in the foetal position in my bed. The sheets still smell of her, and for a minute I'm lost in the memory of our bodies entwined under the covers.

She's like a drug and I'm addicted. I try to reason why that is. If she was just a normal woman, I would be looking at my feelings for her in a different way. I'd be considering my sexual attraction as well as my emotional attachment in order to decide if we were compatible. Though this would not be done in such a rational, cold way. It would be gradual, starting with dates and maybe holidays and ultimately being together most of the time. My feelings for her would build from the physical to a need to have her as a permanent companion because I'd be sure we worked together.

But I can't do any of this with Neva. How could we ever go on a normal date? Or book a holiday together? It just wasn't possible.

But still the strength of this attraction is there. And though I've toyed with the idea that the house is somehow responsible for this attachment I feel, I don't really want to accept it.

I sigh and try to push these thoughts away, but they won't leave me.

Unable to go back to sleep, I reach for the phone she sent me. Last night I hadn't stowed it in the drawer but left it on the bedside cabinet. For a time I'd worried that Beth might have found it, but the fact that men in black suits hadn't descended on me yet suggested that Beth had respected my privacy, despite letting herself into my flat. Now I switch the phone on and wait as it wakes up and connects to the service provider.

A text arrives.

The phoenix is rising from the ashes.

It might be a trick to reel me in again. I read the message a few times, looking for some guile, but I can't take it in any way other than face value. There is only one possible meaning: the Network are reforming and will come back stronger and harder than before if we allow it to happen.

How do you know? I reply.

Info from my attempted cleaner.

I take this information in. She's been attacked again. She must have tortured whoever it was and learnt something. This person will no doubt be dead. It's standard Network policy and she always defaults to her training.

What did you learn? I ask.

There is a long pause before she replies, *Will you help me?*

I hesitate. Anger and frustration flare up and then the Network operative in me rears its head. Of course, she has to push me into this. It's her only course of action. I'd have done the same in her shoes. And maybe by giving her something I can help the greater cause. Would that be so bad after all?

I might be able to help you, I type, being careful with my words. Nothing incriminating or that specifies it's me typing.

Neva replies with a thumbs-up emoji.

I'll be in touch, I tell her.

Be careful, she says.

I switch the phone off, plug it into the charger to get maximum charge into it before the day begins. As the Network will be stripping my apartment of surveillance, I have to take the phone with me when I leave. As an afterthought I delete all of the text messages. If it's found on me, nothing will be there to show what Neva and I have said to each other.

That is, assuming I'm talking to Neva… I'm well aware that anyone might have taken her phone and be pretending to be her in order to lure me in… But I'm trained to be careful.

I close my eyes and try to get more sleep, but I can't drift off as my mind is now too awake.

The idea of taking the phone with me to work is worrying. I have to show all electronic devices at the security portal and walk through a scanner as well.

No. I can't take the mobile with me. That could create too many awkward questions.

I could stow it in the secure box beneath my bed, but MI5 installed that initially and it would be foolish to think they wouldn't take one final peek in there to reassure themselves that I am trustworthy.

There's only one thing for it.

I get up, pull on my dressing gown and, taking a used envelope from my bin, I put the burner phone inside and stuff it into my robe pocket before walking into my living room where the cameras are still active. I pull on a pair of trainers, pick up my door keys and leave the flat to go downstairs.

In the reception area I am greeted by the security guard. He's worked here for years and is a pleasant man in his early fifties. I'm glad it's this one and not the other guard who is always a bit too chatty and friendly.

He nods and says, 'Good morning' but makes no further attempt at dialogue. All for the better as far as I'm concerned.

I go to my mailbox, blocking the guard's view of its interior with my body just in case he is curious. The mailboxes for the apartments are mini lockers with flaps that are big enough for letters and small packages. For the convenience of the owner, the door on the front opens fully with the relevant key.

The security guard is distracted as another of the residents comes downstairs. I recognise a woman from the top floor. We've crossed paths at this time of day on a few occasions in the lift. She nods to me and then chats to the guard as I open the door on my locker. After removing a letter, I stuff the envelope containing the phone into the back of the mailbox. I close the door and lock it. Then I make a show of opening the letter as I walk back to the lift.

When the elevator arrives, I step inside and turn to see the security guard holding the front door open for my neighbour. Neither of them looks at me.

Back in my apartment I throw the letter down on the coffee table. It's junk mail and wasn't worth going down for, but it's proof of what I was doing if anyone is watching on the cameras.

After that I go back into the bedroom and pull out my suit and shirt for the day. I shower, taking my time to shave away the facial bristle that's appeared overnight. Then I dress. After that I make myself coffee and toast.

I sit at the breakfast bar and drink the coffee without urgency. I'm up early, keen to the casual eye to start the new day. All the time, though, I'm praying that they won't think to check my mailbox – I have no idea if they have done this in the past or why they would want to now, but the paranoia is difficult to shake. For what will my first day back with full security see me doing? Betraying my colleagues again.

I finish the coffee and toast and place the plate and mug into my dishwasher. It hasn't been used for a few days and is now full. So, like any normal, rational human who has not a care in the world, I put in a tablet and set the thing going.

I'm hoping all of my actions appear ordinary. It is essential I don't rock the boat.

When I glance at my watch, I see that it is now a reasonable time to head off to work. I pull on my formal shoes, pick up my keys again and head out.

Archive expects me – and Neva waits.

Chapter Twenty-Two

NEVA

After her trip to Brighton, Neva is relieved to reach the cabin on the Thames once more. For the moment the place is secure. Though nowhere will ever feel safe to her. She removes the bright red wig she wore for her journey from Brighton. Having slept rough in the empty house, she feels grubby. She cleans her teeth, then showers, washing her hair.

She sits out on the porch later with her wet natural hair. It's a warm day and there's a gentle breeze coming along the riverbank. She watches the small boats and barges run along the water. They, and the sound of the water lapping against the banks, soothe her, like the movement of the sea had the night before, allowing her to think.

Michael has finally agreed to help, and this is a major leap forward. But she's concerned for him. The Network never give up on their assets unless they retire them. Now they are regrouping he will be in danger.

Leaving the porch, Neva walks to the water's edge and

looks down. A few fish swim near the surface as though they see her and expect her to throw them breadcrumbs. Neva has no desire to do this. She looks instead beyond them, down into the murky depths of the river. She focuses her mind.

The many faces of assassins she's known float in the blackness of the water as she uses it to meditate. She searches for the image of Vasquez in her memory. She's never heard the name before and cannot visualise him. Who is he? How did he learn about the committee members?

Alexi's face fills the void. She sees him now surrounded by flames. Yes, she will burn him, but how is the question.

She imagines Alexi running from his hovel on the west side of London, scared when he learns of her escape. But she won't go after him yet; that's what they'll expect, and time is on her side. Best to wait, when he won't see it coming. First, though, it's time to create problems for him.

She goes back into the cabin. Retrieving her laptop, she opens it up and creates several virtual machines using VirtualBox. Then using an app to hide her IP address, she begins to search the dark web. Her laptop is encrypted and full of applications that hide her from anyone trying to look. She moves in and out of different ones on the various virtual machines. By the time she's finished she's set up a network of profiles that begin to feed random information out. If the sources of the information are investigated, they won't appear to be connected.

She sends out anonymous data, behind tempting firewalls, that reveal Alexi (under the handle DarkRevenger) to be a hacker responsible for a viral attack on an Almunazama company in Australia. Neva knows they are offering a significant reward for information, but she doesn't want to reveal herself as the source. This will open Alexi up to cyberattacks from Almunazama's hackers and will stop him doing any of the work he does for the Network. He is probably the architect of the virus anyway.

She sits back and watches as the first wave of hackers begins to tamper with the firewall – it's strong enough to deter the inexperienced, but complex enough to challenge others, and, importantly, not impossible to crack. Perfect. This will keep him busy for weeks.

After a few hours, the code has been broken on a few of the virtual machines, and the information is now in the hands of some very interested parties. Neva pulls down the information, knowing already that the pages will have been cloned. Alexi has been dealt with for now, making him useless to Vasquez and the Network.

She goes in search online for one of his rivals. Giving the name of Eldon Fracks, she sets the other hacker the task of gleaning information for her. She promises £25,000 as a down payment if the hacker proves they have the man she's looking for. Within an hour the new hacker, who goes by the innocuous handle ElbaKitten, sends her a security camera photograph taken from outside Beech's business premises over six months ago. ElbaKitten asks for confirmation of the image. Neva confirms that this is the man she's looking for, then ElbaKitten promises to get back to her.

Neva has excellent hacking skills herself, but these things take time. Already realising she's found someone as good as Alexi, if not better, Neva is pleased to leave this new helper to the task while she concentrates on more important matters. Having obtained his details directly from him when she sent Alexi the £10,000, Neva's own task is to clear his bank account of money. She hacks into the bank system using an old trick taught to her by the Network. In Alexi's account she finds £150,000. First, she looks Alexi's family up on a genealogy site. She finds his mother's maiden name and uses it to change Alexi's personal details on the bank system. People are stupid that way – even hackers. The simplest details are always used. Once she's in, she updates the mobile number to another burner she has. After she confirms the number, she has full access to Alexi's account. She uses all the information to change his 'trusted' word. She then adds further security information that Alexi wouldn't know, blocking him from his own account. This extra precaution will only work if Alexi doesn't attempt to check his account in the next week to ten days. She hopes that the cyberattacks will keep him too busy to notice.

She sets up a series of payments, all under £10,000 and at different amounts, going to sixteen different accounts over a two-week period. The first amount, £9999, is transferred immediately.

Once she's done this, she sends ElbaKitten a down-payment link. By 4 p.m. she knows she's made a dent in

Alexi's, and therefore the Network's, insidious online dealings. For now, at least. All she can hope for is that Alexi won't pick up on the theft too soon.

That'll slow him down a bit, she thinks as she closes the laptop.

She's mentally tired when she finishes. Although she has the knowledge, hacking doesn't bring Neva any genuine excitement. She's heard that hackers feel a rush from the challenge they face, but Neva has no such passion for the pursuit: it's not a game to her. It's not an obsession. She uses what she knows to help her achieve her goals only.

She glances at her phone hoping for something from Michael, but no text has arrived. Deciding to conserve her energy, she takes a power nap while sitting on the sofa.

———

The ping of her phone wakes her a short time later. It's past six and Neva has slept longer than she intended. Even so, she's awake and alert in an instant with the phone in her hand.

Give me a few days, Michael says.

'Do you have no sense of urgency?' she says to the phone.

Neva sighs. Patience has always been a strong part of her character, but she's struggling now with the waiting.

Two days, she replies. *Then I want to know what you have.*

Chapter Twenty-Three

MICHAEL

I'd been in the office a couple of hours when Beth and Ray called me into a meeting. By then I'd made no attempt to start looking for information for Neva. I had enough to be going with anyway, just with my knowledge of who Olive Redding had once been. In the end, if I told Neva this, she might well find out where Olive was hidin and from there what she knew about Neva's history. I figure this will be enough to appease her without revealing any true secrets that Archive have, and, more, without also putting myself in a precarious position.

'I'm sending you and Beth to Scotland overnight to meet with Lord Stanners. Leon is going to remain working with Brinkman on the missing plane. Thanks so much for the report and your observations on that, Mike,' says Ray.

I nod, accepting his thanks. But all the time I'm thinking how this does throw something of a spanner in the works of me letting Neva reach Stanners first.

'I thought Olive Redding's parents weren't a priority?' I say.

'They weren't, but today we received some intel that has meant we need to step up finding Redding,' Ray explains.

'What intel?' asks Beth.

'About an hour ago one of our hackers found a trail that led to a black hat hacker we've been investigating for some time. He goes by DarkRevenger. We didn't know his real identity until this new information arrived. DarkRevenger was behind a major sting on an Australian company a couple of months ago. We've been aware of their people trying to find the culprit. A hacker with this degree of skill is likely to be used for other misdeeds. He could be behind the hacking of the missing plane and may know its whereabouts. He's certainly guilty of plenty of other activities that we can pin on him too,' Ray says.

'But how does that relate to Redding's parents?' I ask.

'Previous data we gleaned showed DarkRevenger looking for Redding. He was also known to be searching for a man named Eldon Fracks. This suggests he's working for the Network. And if they have learnt who they are, then we need to get to Redding's parents before they do.'

'Eldon Fracks was Beech's chauffeur. I remember him. You guys didn't find him at the house then?' I asked.

'Fracks got away prior to our attack on the house. He hasn't been seen since, and we've been looking for him too. That's why our people were scouring the dark web for any sign of enquiry about him and well as Redding,' Ray says.

'Makes sense,' says Beth.

'Get yourself back home and pack an overnight bag,'

Ray continues. 'Lord Stanners has agreed to meet early tomorrow morning. We need to find out as much about Redding as we can. I can't express how important it is that we find her before the Network does.'

I meet Beth at the airport a couple of hours later.

'We're flying into Glasgow, then taking a rental to Loch Lomond and the Trossachs National Park. I managed to get us rooms at the Drover's Inn. Stanners wants to meet at 8.30 a.m.,' Beth says. She hands me a ticket. 'We'll be going through a special security lane as I brought my service weapon.'

'Are you expecting trouble?' I ask.

'No. But just in case. Let's be honest, we don't know how involved Stanners is.'

'Right. I don't have one anymore,' I say.

'I have yours with me,' Beth says. 'I'll give it to you when we arrive in Scotland.'

We walk into passport control and pass through without searches and scanners and then we're taken through the terminal by two airport police staff. I've never used my MI5 status to get through passport control and security before and it's a very interesting and quick service.

All we had to do was show our security passes.

The rest of the time in the airport is like any other. We go and get a coffee and a snack. Then we wait for our gate to be called.

The flight is on time and we board it like any other

passengers taking our designated seats. An hour and twenty-five minutes later we land in Glasgow.

Because we only have our flight bag luggage, we clear the airport in record time and go to collect the car. It's a Range Rover and the hire company also give us a satnav to use. After that it isn't difficult to find our way from the airport to Loch Lomond and the Drover's Inn, which is just over an hour's drive away.

'I'm surprised that Ray didn't send Leon with you on this one,' I say as Beth pulls the car into the parking lot of the Drover's Inn.

'I'm glad he didn't,' she says. 'I'm not really getting along with him that much these days.'

'Why's that?' I ask.

'Well, he's... I shouldn't say really. It's not very professional.'

'He's being a bit of a dick?' I say.

Beth laughs. 'That's one way of putting it. Ever since you were put on gardening leave and Ray chose him to temporarily fill your shoes, he's been a bit ... arrogant.'

'A *total* dick then?' I say.

Beth laughs again. 'Yes! And I much prefer your company anyway!'

I'm pleased with Beth's words. We had always got on well, despite the fact that I had mistrusted her for a while, before I'd learned that I was the mole inside Archive.

'If it's any consolation, he's always irritated me,' I say.

'Yeah. His nose was put out of joint when you got promoted over him.' I nod. 'I hate to play the misogynist card,' Beth continues, 'but he also has this macho shit going on with me. He *has* to do all the work. I'm starting to feel like a bit of a spare part.'

'I get it,' I say. 'He's good at his job though. Which is why Ray brought him into Archive. The problem is he's a little pedantic at times. I suspect he won't even see his behaviour as misogynistic – more that he is rubbish at delegating.'

Beth looks at me. She turns the car engine off and then says, 'You always see the best in people, don't you, Mike? And yep, I see what you're saying. Again, this lack of skill at letting others do their jobs is probably the very reason why he didn't make the grade the first time for your job.'

'If it's any consolation, I think Ray was wrong to give Leon the role this time too. It should have gone to you,' I say.

She smiles at me. Then shakes her head as though she suspects the reason why she didn't get the promotion and Leon did. She says no more however and blushes a little as she opens her door and gets out of the car.

After retrieving our bags from the boot, we lock up the Range Rover and go into the hotel.

Inside we are greeted with a hallway of taxidermy. A giant bear is standing in one corner, rearing up. Beth scowls at it and then her eyes roam over the other dead things enclosed in glass cases.

'Yuck,' she says. 'Look at those awful things.'

The dead don't bother me, and I'm surprised by her reaction to the gruesome menagerie.

'Can I help you?' asks a man standing behind the reception desk. He's young, bearded and wearing a full highland kilt that falls almost to his ankles. The hotel, reception and even the receptionist all feel like something from another time.

Beth does the talking and soon we have keys to our separate single rooms.

'You should know, the hotel is haunted,' says the receptionist with a smile and an arched eyebrow. 'You enjoy your stay now.'

Beth glares at him, then taking her key she turns and walks away.

In my room, I pull out my burner phone (retrieved from my mailbox when I returned home for my overnight bag) and send Neva a text. It's 6 p.m. and I know she will be waiting to hear from me. Despite my earlier decision to tell her about Stanners, I have decided it's best that Beth and I do our interview with him first. I don't need Neva getting in the way of that, or anyone else for that matter. I agree that we need to get to Redding first if we can. Therefore, my text implies I need time.

When the text is sent, I turn the phone off and stow it back in my overnight bag.

There's a knock on the door and Beth is there.

'Can I come in?'

I step back and allow her in. She unpacks my gun from her flight bag and hands it to me with a box of ammunition clips.

'I booked us in the restaurant here tonight,' she says. 'I'm just going to phone my kids and I'll meet you back downstairs.'

'Okay,' I say. 'How is the family?'

'All fine,' she says but her voice is flat.

'Was Callum okay about you coming here tonight?' I ask.

'My mum has the kids for me. Callum and I split up a few months ago.'

'Shit, I'm sorry, Beth!' I say.

'It was for the best. He didn't enjoy playing second fiddle to the job,' she says.

She brushes off my further attempts at sympathy and goes back to her room to make her phone call.

When she's gone, I put my gun away inside my bag, check the burner again and see Neva's abrupt reply. Then I pick up my room key and head downstairs to wait for Beth.

'So, this place is haunted?' I say when she joins me.

'Yeah, right,' she says.

'They have a video on their website with actual footage,' I point out.

I open my work phone and show her the video, which ends with someone jumping out wearing a Halloween mask. Beth and I are laughing as the waiter arrives to take our food order.

'Haggis, neeps and tatties,' I say.

'What on earth is that?' asks Beth.

I explain and then she orders a 'Naked Burger' from the gluten-free menu. I don't ask her if she has intolerance or if it's a diet thing; neither question is appropriate.

The food arrives and Beth frowns at my haggis.

'Just don't know how you can eat that…' she says.

'When in Scotland,' I say.

That night there is live music on at the Inn and Beth and I share a bottle of wine while a local singer regales us with Scottish music.

When the singer breaks for a while we get onto the subject of Beth's broken marriage.

'There's no way of clawing it back?' I ask.

'Nah. Callum was too… It's the job or me. I won't be bullied like that. He knew what he was getting into when we married. He always said he understood I was a career girl. So, you can't just change your mind after making statements like that. To be honest the problems started a while back. I kept placating him, until in the end I'd had enough.'

I sympathise, even though I've never been married. A few long-term relationships hadn't ended well because of my failure to be available.

I find myself thinking about Neva again. Could we possibly be together if things were different? Would she be jealous of my job in the end? Or would I suffer from insecurity over her past? It was all just too complicated.

'Anyway, I think Ray got wind of my forthcoming divorce,' Beth says. 'But being a single mum is going to have challenges. So, I kind of get why…'

She doesn't say that she thinks this is why Leon got the promotion to my job over her, but the implication hangs in the air.

I nod, showing my understanding.

'Why not get joint custody?' I suggest. 'Not that I know

anything about these things. But that way you are both equally responsible. The pressure is not all on you.'

'I've been considering what to do,' she says. 'My mum helps a bit, but she has her own life. It's a possibility.'

It's only 9.30 but I'm tired from the early start. After a whisky from the Drover's extensive range, we both retire, because of the early-morning start.

When I return to my room, I realise it's the most company I've had in a long time, and I've really enjoyed the evening. This is a strange first day back to having full security access. Despite Beth's words that she'd rather be with me, I wonder if sending me instead of Leon was a strategy to keep me supervised and away from the office.

As I get into the comfortable bed, I push this paranoid thought away. Tomorrow I'll be back in business, interviewing someone who may or may not have sold his own child into a life of servitude as an assassin for the Network.

Chapter Twenty-Four

VASQUEZ

'Sorry to keep you waiting,' says a female voice.

An elegantly dressed woman enters the room. She is wearing a sleek black dress with a single strand of black pearls. Her silver-streaked hair is swept up into a French pleat. Vasquez hasn't met her before, but he knows he is greeting the ninth Network committee member, newly promoted by the others.

They call her Annalise, and she has moved up in the ranks. In her heyday she was a seductress whose career rivalled that of Mata Hari and before that she was top of her class, graduating with honours from the Network's French House. Where she came from when they brought her there as a child, no one knew, though it was rumoured that she was from French aristocracy. That is all Vasquez has been told and all any of the others care to know about her. The past of any assassin is irrelevant to the Network.

What is important to Vasquez is that Annalise has earned her stripes. He understands better than anyone what lengths you have to go to in order to become one of the committee members. Without Annalise's help, he wouldn't have been able to do it himself.

They'd been communicating off and on before Archive brought down the British House six months ago. After that Vasquez had put all his cards on the table and had promised if she helped him, he'd put her in an untouchable position as a member of the Network's committee.

After little coaxing Annalise had joined forces with him, using her considerable resources to feed information to Vasquez, revealing some of the names and addresses of current committee members. The taking of control from those already there was vital.

With the Network reeling from Beech's death and the compromised House, the committee were ripe for the picking. That's when Vasquez executed his plan. He forced his way into a few of their lives and killed off any resistance, until the remaining committee members offered him an associate position. Annalise had known that if he showed himself to be powerful and informed, they would have to do this. And with Annalise's intel to back up everything he did, Vasquez was strong.

'Come, Mr Vasquez,' Annalise says now, leading him into the luxurious salon of 'her' home. Though, like all of the committee members, Vasquez believed her residence was only temporary accommodation. None of them stay anywhere for long, and it is almost certain that she'll move on after this meeting.

He follows her, noting her lithe figure and the balletic

bounce of her step. 'It's been a long time coming, this meeting,' she says.

There is the trace of a beautiful accent. Vasquez is intrigued by her. She's beautiful to look at still. The idle question of her age floats through his mind. He is more partial to men, though some women do fascinate him. And Annalise has the potential to be one of them now they've finally met.

She sits on an expensive-looking upright chaise and indicates the single chair opposite. Vasquez sits.

'The next committee meeting will take place in Rome,' he tells her. 'There you will be welcomed properly into the fold.'

He reveals the location. Annalise nods. Her face is serene but unsmiling. She holds herself with dignity and reserve. Vasquez is reminded of the many icons he's seen of the Madonna, taking up such a perfect and similar pose. She looks benign and yet he knows she is dangerous.

'You've done well for me, since our communication,' Annalise says.

'We are good for each other,' Vasquez comments. 'Your information on the other committee members was very useful.'

Annalise smiles, but it doesn't reach her eyes. 'And you took full advantage of it. I had thought you would only remove two members, making room for us both. But no matter. We can move in more suitable replacements now.'

Vasquez tries to read the neutral tone of her voice. At face value, her comment would appear to be indifferent, but it could also be taken as a reproach. He doesn't care to be criticised after all he's done for her so far.

'What of Neva? Have you found her?' she asks.

Vasquez pauses before answering. 'She escaped a trap we laid for her. One of our number foolishly thought he could take her alone.'

'And where is he now?'

'In the morgue,' Vasquez says.

'Neva?'

Vasquez nods.

'She's special,' Annalise says. 'We always knew that.'

'As was Michael. But both of them have broken their conditioning,' Vasquez says.

'We all do that eventually,' Annalise says. 'Surely you know that? The important thing is to decide whether you're in or out. That decision is what can cost, or save, your life.'

'I'm a child of the House,' Vasquez says. 'I'm evolved, not broken.'

Annalise smiles again, a melancholic twist of the lips. 'Of course.'

'So tomorrow we both fly to Rome,' Vasquez says. 'The others want me to escort you. For your safety.'

Annalise raises an eyebrow at his presumption that she needs protection.

'Then you must stay here,' she says. 'Join me for dinner, keep me company and then tomorrow we'll go and meet the others.'

Vasquez agrees and, as if Annalise knew all along that he would, they are soon whisked into a magnificent dining room by a starched and formally dressed butler.

Glorious food is served, a consommé to start, followed by steak tartare. For dessert a decadent baked Alaska is brought out to them.

Annalise plies Vasquez with fine wines and she dazzles him with her wit and intelligence. His fascination with her increases. It is as if he is with a young, vibrant and beautiful woman. Which he knows she cannot be…

After dinner she persuades him to dance with her while she plays records on an old gramophone. The records are scratchy but there's something delightful and nostalgic that makes him think of wartime days he never lived through. It's charming and innocent. Vasquez is wowed by it and her. A feeling he hadn't thought himself capable of. He gives himself over to her joy. They dance and laugh and drink champagne.

Then Annalise shows him how very seductive she is. Poor Vasquez can't resist.

Several hours later he wakes in her chamber. Annalise is sleeping beside him. He is fascinated by her pure, smooth, toned body, the beautiful head of hair that, once loosed, flowed down her back. She holds the appearance of youth and yet he knows … she can't be that young. Perhaps holding back time is how she spends the wealth that her career has brought her.

Vasquez looks now around this room. A beautiful bedroom suite with a huge, extravagant four-poster bed. He knows there is a full-sized bathroom through the double doors on the left. And behind the shining silver curtains is a balcony that overlooks the glorious French landscape.

'Is it time?' she says as she wakes, feeling him stir.

'The plane is in a few hours. So yes, we need to get ready.' He gets out of the bed and stretches. Though he's naked he shows no signs of being self-conscious.

'Thank you,' she says. 'I had a wonderful evening.'

He turns to face her, 'I had…'

The bullet hits him between the eyes before he completes his sentence. Vasquez falls backwards onto the expensive carpet.

Annalise gets out of the bed, pulls on her robe and walks around to look at the now dead Vasquez.

'Beautiful. But such arrogance to think you could control us,' she says.

By her bedside she presses a call button. A short time later, the butler and two men arrive.

'Get rid of him,' she orders. Then, leaving the men to remove the body, she goes into her extravagant bathroom and runs herself a bath.

When she comes out into her bedroom once more, the body is gone, the stained carpet has been cleaned and her bed has been made. Her curtains are open and the French windows to the balcony are thrown wide, allowing the morning sun to spill into the room.

As is her habit she sits down at the mosaic table. A tray of food waits: a continental breakfast of croissants, pastries, fresh butter and delicious jams.

Annalise pours herself aromatic coffee from a cafetière into a pure china teacup that sits on a matching saucer.

Then she looks out over the immaculate gardens of her chateau. Here, in Toulouse, Annalise is happy and calm.

Long before Vasquez offered her the chance for advancement, Annalise was in line for a seat on the committee should one become vacant. But she saw his approach as an opportunity to gain a better position. After Beech's death, Annalise had drawn her plan. She had given Vasquez the names of committee members who had been an inconvenient blockage to her progression. The remainder had long seen her potential for elevation. Especially when she approached and offered to end the upstart Vasquez. They'd feared him because they knew he could reach them. They didn't know that it was Annalise who helped him do that. After this Annalise played both sides to her greatest advantage, reeling Vasquez in with the promise of this grand meeting with the other committee members. Maybe Vasquez even thought he'd take the rest – her included. But she'd never know if he was that ambitious now and it didn't matter anyway.

At sixty Annalise is long deserving of the promotion. But there would be no official welcome into the fold. Unlike the impression that Vasquez has been given, the committee rarely meet in one room. Their conferences were nearly always virtual. This was the safest option for them all as they had many enemies who would relish the opportunity to take them all out in one go. And truly, they didn't trust each other either.

Now, with Vasquez removed, Annalise's rise will be faster. She is going for the top spot, and no one will challenge her for fear of her long-reaching reprisal.

Breakfast done, Annalise dresses and goes downstairs. In her study she turns on her computer, then logs into the meeting.

Her camera switches on, and as the others join the conference. Annalise can see them all sitting in their various safe locations.

It is Marcus who speaks first. He is English and has a casual but upper-class accent. Annalise knows that in the real world he's a Lord. But they never use anyone's 'real' identity if they know it. It is safer always to retain their codenames. Marcus is in his seventies and the oldest of the committee members, promoted years back by Beech.

'Welcome to Annalise. Who is now a full committee member with all of the privileges this offers,' Marcus says.

He introduces himself and then she sees them all for the first time as the screen flicks from face to face as each of them say their codename.

Kritta; Banwick; Subra; Petters; Conor; Drake.

Annalise is recording the whole meeting for future reference. She's met a few of them in the line of duty over the years. Fleeting moments before she carried out their orders. Now she can really get to know who they are.

When the formality is completed, they begin to address the long agenda. First on the list is promotion of a new chairperson.

'I shall propose myself,' says Annalise now.

'On what grounds do you deem yourself worthy?' asks Marcus.

'Vasquez is dead,' she says. 'As I promised he would be.'

There's a ripple of noise as the committee take in the implication of this death.

'I wondered why he had not joined us today,' says Marcus.

She does not explain how she rerouted the email the committee sent, replacing it with one of her own, which was why Vasquez believed the meeting was in person in Rome.

'He was of no more use to us and posed an unstable threat. Which I have removed,' Annalise says.

This show of strength is enough for some: Subra and Kritta second and third Annalise's motion. After that the others have to follow suit. When she is unanimously approved, the business of the committee can continue. After all, few of them wanted to take over from Beech and those that do will hold their cards closer for a while longer to see how they fare under Annalise's regime.

'And next on the list,' says Marcus. 'Armin's flight never reached Shanghai.'

'Was he definitely on board?' asks Kritta in her concise German accent.

'Yes. Our sources say the flight disappeared somewhere over the Indian Ocean. For some reason the British secret service is keeping a lid on its disappearance.'

They discuss this for a time, exploring why.

'Let's find out what we can,' Annalise says. 'Do we have a mole in MI5 or 6?'

'Yes,' Subra says.

'Activate them,' says Annalise.

After the meeting Annalise reviews the footage and captures individual images of each of the committee members. So far her takeover has worked, but just in case there is any planned resistance she will learn what she can about each of them.

First off Kritta. Annalise studies the screen image taking in Kritta's appearance. Late forties. Kritta is not a natural beauty. In fact, the woman was very unattractive but not in any obvious way. It was more about her demeanour than her features. There was a humourless, bitter twist to the lips and an emptiness in the eyes. She was German House, middle generation, and Annalise had heard rumours about the warped conditioning, the brutality of this House that went above and beyond any other.

Next Annalise looks at Petters. A fifty-something former head teacher is what she sees. Though she doesn't know if this was any career that Petters had followed. He wasn't former House; Beech had recruited him from somewhere else. She takes a screenshot of him and adde it to a file with Marcus and Kritta's images.

Banwick she's met before. He'd been working in a House that Beech had sent her to inspect. He was a former trainer, and the fitness still showed on his body, such that, despite the balding pate, he behaved like someone young and vital. She is curious about his promotion, wondering when and how it had happened. Banwick wasn't the type that Beech would have deemed worthy. Yet he must have done something to qualify. She makes a note to try and find out more.

Drake had been one of the committee members that Annalise had engaged in her efforts to bring about the fall of Vasquez. Looking at him she sees a thin, twitchy man.

Nervous in the company of others, but appearances can be deceptive. Drake's kill history was intriguing and bloody. He was known to have enjoyed his work a great deal, often resorting to torture as a way to prolong the death of his kill.

Then Annalise looks closely at Subra. Israeli by birth, Subra is stunning to look at. There is an ageless quality about her. A glow that screams youth. Annalise knows about her: Subra's name has come up many times. A former assassin, Subra had been promoted by Beech and was the youngest member of the committee. She seduced and used many young men to her own advantage. Beech had been concerned by her growing power base.

Subra was certainly one to watch.

Annalise saves the screenshots of all of the committee members. Then she pulls up their images again.

Marcus – a doddering old fool – she dismisses as no threat, but the others potentially are. But one thing is for sure, no one in the Network can ever be trusted.

Chapter Twenty-Five

MICHAEL

'Stanners is an English Lord but he owns a significant estate here in Loch Lomond and the Trossachs National Park,' Beth explains as I get behind the wheel of the Range Rover. 'The place has a full staff, groundskeeper, housekeeper, cook, cleaners and even a butler. So, I'm expecting something magnificent.'

I switch the engine on and set the sat nav to take us to the estate. 'Half an hour away. We'll be in good time.'

We begin the drive further into the National Park, winding around the Loch and then turning inland. The scenery is beautiful and the roads are quiet. It reminds me of the landscape in Wales near Snowdon that I've driven through in the past with a former girlfriend.

I mention my observation to Beth to pass the time, but it doesn't take us long to reach Stanners's estate because the roads are so quiet.

We almost overshoot because the turn is set back off the road but the sat nav says we've reached our destination, so I pull to the side of the country lane. Beth gets out and takes a look to make sure we have the correct entrance to Stanners's grounds.

'This is definitely the place,' Beth says.

The name on the sign is *Hamlet's Retreat* and Beth tells me it is not a genuine Scottish castle, but is a folly built by Stanners's family back in the nineteenth century.

I turn the car down the track and within a short distance we find ourselves in front of a set of tall iron gates. At the side is an intercom system. I roll the window down and press the call button. Then I give our names and the gates open.

'Follow the main track and park in the visitors' car park, please,' says the man on the intercom.

'Thank you,' I say.

I drive through the gates and follow the long drive up towards the house and the guest parking area.

'Is there a Lady Stanners?' Beth asks.

'Ray told me she wouldn't be here. She's ill, apparently,' I tell her.

'Really?' Beth says. 'What do we know about them both?'

'Lady Stanners was thirty-five when she became pregnant with Olive. So she's probably seventy now. Stanners is older than her, by eight years,' I explain.

We reach the parking lot for the house and I pull the car into a spot that says 'Visitors'. There are signs directing us to the house, as though this is a public place where visitors need directions. But as far as I'm aware, Stanners doesn't open his house for tours. We walk down a wide footpath that runs along a row of leylandii and as we come around the tall well-pruned trees, we see the back of the house ahead.

'Looks like we have to take the servants' entrance,' Beth jokes. 'Oh, how the other half live.'

A sign directs us to the 'Estate Office' and we follow around the mansion until we reach a door at the side of the building. Here there is an extension to the property that appears to have been added as an afterthought. There's a door with the words 'Estate Reception' over it. I press the bell that's by the side of the door. Inside I can hear the echo of an old mechanism chiming within the house.

A tall man arrives, wearing a butler's uniform. We show our identification and the butler steps back from the door and invites us inside into a narrow corridor with several doors on the right-hand side. One of these is marked 'Estate Office'; another says 'Estate Staff Only'. The butler leads us down the corridor and away from these rooms and into the house proper.

We pass through an impressive hallway that has a staircase swooping up on the left-hand side to a tall balcony that leads off to multiple rooms. I glance at Beth. Her eyes are wide and she looks awestruck. She meets my gaze and mouths *Wow* to me. The house may be a folly but it does have character and is very impressive.

We pass the main front door of the house, which is locked and barred. The butler glances at me and sees me studying the door. It's twice the height and width of regular doors.

'We rarely open the front door these days,' explains the

butler. 'Most visitors come through the Estate Reception. Though there was a time when we only ever used the front for visitors. This way, please. His Lordship is waiting for you in his library.'

The butler opens another tall door and we step through a three-foot-wide arch into a magnificent library.

I try not to look around at the bookcases that line the walls, crammed with books of all types and sizes, as I focus my gaze instead on Lord Stanners.

He is standing by the large sash windows looking out over his magnificent lawns. Stanners is a tall, impressive man, with something of the Christopher Lee about him. He turns as we walk towards him and he indicates that we sit on the other side of his desk – which is spectacular: almost seven feet wide with three deep black onyx panels with white birds cut into it, running as a rim around a polished mahogany top.

'Agents Kensington and Cane,' the butler says in his lilting Scottish accent that makes us sound like a crime-fighting duo from a TV show.

'Thank you, Drew,' Stanners says. 'Can you organise some tea for our guests?'

Drew nods and walks back the way he came.

Beth and I sit down, and Stanners takes a seat behind the desk, which suits him, and doesn't dwarf him at all. Everything in this place is larger than normal, including the chairs we sit down in. I glance at Beth: she is lost in hers.

'Your boss told me that this was a matter of urgency,' Stanners says. 'So, what can I do for you?'

'As you know, we work for MI5,' I say. 'For the last year we've been investigating childhood disappearances.'

Beth goes into a practised spiel about Archive's investigations of cold cases – our default cover for the general public.

'We have news of your missing daughter,' Beth says choosing her words carefully. 'But we need to ask you some questions about her disappearance first.'

Stanners sits forward in his chair. 'You've found Georgia's body?' he says.

'When did your daughter go missing?' I ask, ignoring his question.

'It was thirty years ago this August,' Stanners says. 'She'd just turned five. She was with her nanny, on the way to a private birthday party. We lived in the London house then. It was several hours later when they should have returned that my wife rang the mother of the child whose birthday it was to see where they were. It appeared that they had never arrived. We rang the police and the nanny's car was searched for, but never found. It looked like she had abducted Georgia.'

'There were no other leads or possible explanations?' Beth asked.

'The police investigated it. Neither Georgia nor the nanny were ever found,' Stanners says.

'That must have been hard for you both,' Beth says.

'Yes.'

'I believe she was your only child?' I ask.

'My wife had had such a difficult time conceiving and after Georgia was born, because of the problems she had, the doctors recommended a hysterectomy. It didn't matter to us because we had the child we'd both always wanted.'

'Tell us about Georgia,' I say. 'What was she like as a child?'

Stanners smiles at the memory. 'Very intelligent. Gifted even. She had an instinct for languages and she was speaking fluent French with the nanny by the age of four. We'd thought it an odd thing to start teaching so young, but the nanny was French and she spoke to Georgia in both English and French from the beginning. She was reading and writing both well by the time she was five. The nanny told us all the time that she was special.'

'Can you tell us more about the nanny?' Beth asks.

'She wasn't very old, early twenties as I recall. Quite a mousey girl really. We liked her and trusted her because she was so dedicated to Georgia. We were pleased to have someone working for us who cared. My wife Sabrina often commented on how fortunate we were. I remember that particular morning, Sabrina had said, "We'll never have to worry about Nicole, she'd protect Georgia with her life."'

'How did you find Nicole?' I ask.

Stanners thought for a minute. 'It wasn't really my area, but my wife and her mother went to a recommended nanny agency. The girl had excellent references. They interviewed a few nannies and she was hired.'

Beth and I exchange a look. We are watching Stanners's reactions to our questions, and it's time to reveal our hand.

'Lord Stanners,' I say, 'we have reason to believe that Nicole worked for an organisation who kidnapped children in order to ... *radicalise* them.'

'What do you mean? Radicalising how?'

Beth takes a breath.

'It's a matter of national security and I'm afraid we can't tell you more as it may compromise you. But we believe your daughter may be alive, living under another identity,' I explain.

Stanners blinks and looks around confused. 'Alive? After all this time?'

'Yes. We also think that in the last few months she has freed herself from these people. We are certain she knows that you are her real father, and might try to contact you,' Beth explains. 'That's why we are here. If she does get in touch, we need you to let us know. We have to find her. She will have information that may help us capture these people.'

Stanners slumps back in his chair. 'She was right. It wasn't all in her head.'

'Who, Lord Stanners?' Beth says.

'My wife. She'd said she'd seen Georgia, all grown up but she recognised her.'

'When was this?' I ask.

'A few months ago,' Stanners says. 'She told me Georgia had been to see her. That she came here and was in her room.'

'Security Agent Martin told us your wife is ill,' Beth says. 'May we ask what's wrong?'

'Sabrina has Alzheimer's. It started a while ago. Then at the beginning of this year her condition worsened. She still has days when she recalls things. But mostly her mind confuses the present and the past. When she said she saw

Georgia I just thought she was remembering her and getting mixed up.'

'I need to know everything you can recall about the day Lady Stanners says Georgia visited,' I say. 'Were there any visitors, or did anything unusual happen?'

Stanners sighs. 'We had some interviews for new cleaning staff and the housekeeper was vetting them in the Estate Office. We'd had one girl move away and another was pregnant. So we were looking for two new reliable housemaids. Sabrina and I had been in London for a few weeks, and we'd arrived back the day before. Sabrina always gets a bit more confused when she's tired, and she wasn't well that day, so I'd encouraged her to stay in her room and rest. I sent food up to her, and I checked in on her regularly. By the afternoon she came running downstairs. She said, "Albert, it's wonderful, Georgia is back. She says she's going to look after me." After that I couldn't get much sense out of her. She rambled about our little girl and the nanny, and how special she was. It was a confused mess. In the end she was so excitable, I called the doctor out. He came to see her and gave her a sedative.'

I ask Stanners where Sabrina was now.

'She's in care. Her condition worsened and we couldn't contain her. We had a nurse live in for a while, but Sabrina became too much and needed twenty-four-hour care. Sometimes we'd find her wandering around the garden in the cold in only a nightdress. She was always looking for Georgia. As you can imagine it was very disturbing.'

Beth removes a wallet from her flight bag. Inside are various pictures of Olive Redding. We need Stanners to confirm that she is Georgia and so Beth places the first picture, of Olive aged five, in front of him.

'Is this your daughter?' I ask.

Stanners stares at the picture, and his eyes fill with tears as he nods.

Next Beth lays down a picture of twelve-year-old Olive. 'Could this be Georgia?'

'Yes!' Stanners says. 'She has her mother's eyes.'

The next picture is of Georgia aged fifteen and the final one is a picture that our computer system has digitally aged to show a thirty-five-year-old version of the little girl.

'Oh my God!' says Stanners. 'I know this girl! She works at the home where we put Sabrina.'

We take the details of the home and warn Stanners not to tell anyone what he's told us.

'You think she's our daughter?' he says. 'She's gone there to be near to Sabrina, hasn't she? She's taking care of her, just as my wife believed she would.'

At that moment the butler knocks on the door and brings in a tray of tea.

'That's all right,' Beth says. 'We have to leave. But please remember what we said.'

The butler leads us back through the house in silence and we exit through the door we came in by. I have an odd, prickly feeling as the butler closes the door behind us.

'Do you think the butler was eavesdropping?' I ask as we walk back to the car.

'It had occurred to me,' Beth says.

'We need to get to this home before someone warns

Olive and we lose her,' I say. 'Or before someone from the Network gets to her first.'

In the car, Beth rings Ray and tells him what has happened. I set the sat nav for the home. It's a place in Glasgow and we now have a tense journey ahead. I hope, when we arrive, that Georgia Stanners (aka Olive Redding) is oblivious to our knowledge of her.

Chapter Twenty-Six

MICHAEL

The Braemar Care Home is in a former manor house which was converted in the 1980s to become a residential care facility for the old and frail of wealthy Scottish families. As a private facility it resembles a hotel more than a care home, and as I drive into the car park, I'm reminded of the estate used in an old adaptation of *Brideshead Revisited*. The building and grounds are immense, and I can think of worse places to end up in my dotage.

I park the Range Rover and take my gun from my rucksack, stowing it in my suit jacket pocket. Beth checks her weapon too and places it in the waistband of her skirt at the small of her back for convenient access. We are both very aware that Redding is dangerous and there's no telling how she will react when she sees me.

We get out of the car and walk into the building reception.

I flash my badge to the receptionist.

'We're here to see Lady Stanners,' I say. 'I don't want you to let anyone on your staff know of our presence.'

The receptionist is young and easily intimidated and she points to the stairs, telling us which room Sabrina Stanners is in.

We climb the stairs, taking our time, and at the top I turn and follow the left-hand corridor until we find the room. Screwed to the door is a plaque with 'Sabrina' written on it.

I knock and a small voice invites us in.

Sabrina Stanners is sitting in a chair by the window. She's looking out onto the perfect lawn attached to the property.

'Hello,' says Beth as she moves into the room. 'I'm Beth. Are you Sabrina?'

Sabrina looks at us, and I see the resemblance between our aged picture of Olive and her. There is no doubt that Sabrina is her mother. However, as happens with dementia sufferers, Sabrina is overly thin and very frail for a woman only seventy years old.

Beth pulls a chair close to Sabrina and begins to talk to her. Small inconsequential snippets at first, asking how her day has been. Graduating to the weather as she tests how aware Sabrina is.

'I believe your daughter works here?' Beth slips in.

'Oh yes,' says Sabrina. 'But it's our little secret.'

Sabrina presses her finger to her lips and frowns as though she's realised that she has spoken out of turn.

'Is Georgia here today?' Beth asks.

'Who are *you*?' Sabrina says looking at me. 'Are you a friend of Albert's?'

'Yes, I am,' I answer.

'You're here for the wedding?' she says.

Beth nods her head to encourage me to go along with Sabrina's confusion.

'Yes,' I say. 'That's right.'

'Albert makes me so happy,' says Sabrina. 'It was such a whirlwind romance. Are you his best man?'

I nod, then also pull up a chair alongside her.

'That's right,' Sabrina says. 'You're *Andrew*.'

I glance at Beth.

'Albert told me you were younger than him. How did you two meet again?' Sabrina asks.

'Didn't Albert tell you?' I ask.

Sabrina frowns for a moment. 'Oh yes, of course! I remember now.'

I try to coax the answer from her but her mind is already elsewhere.

'Is Georgia working here today?' Beth asks, bringing Sabrina back to why we had come.

'Oh yes. She was here a few moments ago. Then she got a phone call and she went away.'

'Where did she go?' I ask. 'She'll be back, won't she?'

'Oh yes. She always comes back before she goes home. She's looking after me,' Sabrina says.

'I'm going to take a look around,' I tell Beth. 'Stay here in case she returns.'

Beth turns her chair to give her an advantage if Olive does come back into Sabrina's room. I slip out and walk down the corridor.

Most of the doors are open and so I'm able to glance

inside to see if anyone is there. If Olive/Georgia has taken a job here to be with her mother, then she will have other duties to attend to even if she does contrive to spend time with Sabrina.

At the end of the wing there's no sign of her and few of the residents are in their own rooms.

I walk down the north corridor and discover this is the male wing of the home. A nurse is in one of the rooms and she's giving medicine to a small, fragile old man in a wheelchair.

'Can I help you?' she asks.

She isn't Redding and I wonder if I dare risk asking her about Olive. But I don't know what name she's going by and so this gives me a dilemma.

'Lady Stanners? She's looking for someone she says is her daughter,' I say. 'I'm visiting and I'd like to thank her for being so kind.'

'Oh, you mean Sally,' she says. 'It's really sweet how Sabrina thinks she's her daughter. Sally doesn't mind either if it helps her. Poor dear.'

'Ah, that's right. Do you know where Sally is right now?'

'On a break, I think,' says the nurse. 'She'll be downstairs. The canteen is just off the reception.'

I go back downstairs and see the receptionist talking to a woman with a severe cropped haircut. The receptionist points to me as I approach.

'Excuse me,' the other woman says. 'I'm the manger here. What are you doing talking to Lady Stanners?'

'I'd prefer that you not ask me that right now,' I say. 'Where is the canteen?'

'Canteen?' asks the woman.

'Where your staff have their break?'

The receptionist points to a door behind her, around the back of the counter. I come round, walk past them both and go inside.

The room has a few nurses and carers in. Those facing me I quickly dismiss as I can see they aren't Olive. But one does have her back to me. I approach and take a seat opposite her.

Olive Redding stares at me in dumb silence. Frozen in the process of taking a bite of a sandwich.

'Hello, Sally. Or should I say Olive? I'm not here to hurt you,' I say. 'In fact, if you tell me what I want to know I'm going to go upstairs to your mother's room and give you a head start so that you can run.'

'What do you want to know?' she says.

'Where did Neva come from?'

Olive looks around the room. The manager is standing in the doorway watching us with a look of concern.

'I just wanted to spend some time with her,' Olive says. 'The nanny took me from them.'

'Nicole? What happened to her?'

'She was called Tracey Herod after that. She's dead now, as you know.'

The link between Herod, Olive and Neva is stronger than I'd suspected.

'I've always believed that Neva was Simone Arquette's daughter,' Olive says.

I sigh. 'We have all of your files from the House. We know that's not true.'

'I don't know the answer,' she says.

'Neva told me you said you knew her mother,' I say.

'So you're still helping her?' Olive says. 'She has you enthralled. The best of us can do that to men. I was never beautiful enough to have that kind of power.'

Olive's words are designed to destabilise me by implying Neva controls me. I ignore them.

'Who are her parents?' I ask again.

At that moment the manager comes over to the table.

'Excuse me,' she says. 'I really must insist—'

Olive takes advantage of the interruption and leaps from her seat. I catch hold of her arm before she gets any further.

'Go away,' I say to the manager. 'I need to speak to this woman and you are interfering with an ongoing investigation.'

The woman is shocked that I'm so rude.

'I'll speak to your superior—'

'You do that,' I say. I pull Olive around the table and force her to sit down next to me.

The manager storms away and I know I'm on borrowed time.

'Look, you left the Network, they haven't found you. When I leave here, I promise I'll give you a chance to get away. But if you don't tell me, I'm taking you in.'

'I'm telling the truth. I don't know who her parents are. But I saw her mother once. She came to the House, not long after I took over as the head there. I was told not to ask any questions. No one ever used her name, but she was with a heavy security team. I knew she was someone important to the Network because Beech had sent her to do an inspection. He did that on occasion to try and keep us on our toes.'

'How did you know she was Neva's mother?'

'At the time I didn't. But I had to give the woman a tour of the House so I spent a fair amount of time with her. She was so cold, so matter-of-fact about the training – *brainwashing*. I hated her. Then when you and Neva came to the House, and I saw her for the first time, I knew she was her daughter: she was the image of her – just younger. It all made sense.'

I take one of my cards out of my wallet and hand it to her because I believe her.

'If you remember more, then contact me,' I say. 'Now get the fuck away from here and don't come back.'

I stand and walk away. Out at the reception the manager is making a fuss. Beth comes down the stairs and sees me talking to her. She hurries over and that is when she glances through the open door and sees Olive Redding getting into her car.

'Mike! There she is!'

Pulling her gun out, Beth runs to the door and hurries into the car park. She fires a shot at the car, but Redding is already too far away.

I follow Beth and we get into the Range Rover but, with its heavy frame, it is the worst car for doing a chase in. Olive's little sports car is long gone before we are even out of the car park.

'Shit!' says Beth.

We drive up and down a few nearby roads in the hope that we can spot the car, but there's no sign of her.

'Sorry, this is all my fault. That receptionist told her manager we were here and the woman was freaking out. I'll have to go back there and sort it out before she calls in the police and we have some explaining to do.'

I turn the car back to the care home.

'You ring Ray, tell him we saw her but she got away, and I'll go and smooth things over with the manager,' I say.

I leave Beth in the Range Rover and go back inside.

I flash my security badge again to the woman and ask her to take me into her office.

'Mrs Carol,' I say. 'I do apologise for my brusque behaviour, but it was very important that I spoke to your employee Sally. You see she isn't who she told you she was.'

I spin a story about Sally. That she's a nurse we are pursuing who gets work in care homes and soon after there are suspicious deaths.

'I wasn't sure it was her, which is why I let her go. Unfortunately, it was our suspect... I think I need to see her references, and registered address.'

'References?' Mrs Carol dithers.

'You didn't just hire her? What about criminal background checks? They are required by law when working with vulnerable adults, aren't they?'

Mrs Carol looks shamefaced. 'She seemed such an honest girl and she was so good with the residents. The checks can take a while and so I took a chance and let her start...'

I smile. Then I tell her how this can be between us, as long as she doesn't talk to anyone about my behaviour.

Mrs Carol and I part with a wary agreement in place.

When I come back outside, I find Beth drawing a breath through a vape.

'I didn't know you smoked,' I said.

'I don't. *Much*. Ray gave me a bollocking. Please tell me the manager was able to give you something to help find Olive.'

'I got her address, but we both know she won't go back there.'

'And now we know about her, she won't try to see her mother again either,' Beth says. 'Fuck! Well, this has been a wasted trip.'

'Not really,' I say. 'Something is needling me. Didn't Sabrina say the best man's name was Andrew?'

'Yes, she did,' Beth says.

'She thought I was *him*.'

'She's all muddled up, Mike,' Beth says.

'But what if Albert's best man was Andrew Beech? After all, he was my father. It's not unreasonable to suppose I look like he did at my age,' I say.

'She could have meant anyone… Andrew is a fairly common name. But … the *connection*. Why was Georgia Stanners picked by the Network? We know these choices aren't random. Which might mean that Albert Stanners knows more than he's telling us,' Beth says.

'Yes. Beech gave him something he wanted, money, power – God knows what – then he took his daughter as payment,' I say. 'Redding doesn't know that part though.'

'How do you make that out?' Beth asks. She puts the vape away in her pocket.

'Because I think Redding would have killed him by now.'

'If you're right, this changes things,' Beth says. 'I'll let Ray know we are staying another night. We had better go and interview Lord Stanners again, and this time we aren't going to play nice.'

Chapter Twenty-Seven

NEVA

What's taking so long? Neva wonders when she doesn't hear from Michael all that day.

She spends the hours wandering around Kingston. She eats a burger from one of the café/restaurants on the bank of the Thames and buys some M&S ready meals that are quick and convenient to keep at the cabin. She's vigilant as always, making sure she isn't being followed anywhere, but she doubts that the Network have any idea where she is.

Back at the cabin she checks her phone for the hundredth time. There's no text.

Then at 7 p.m. the phone rings.

'Michael?'

'I'm sorry I haven't been in touch. I'm in Scotland following up on a lead. We found Olive's parents. I came here to see if she'd made contact and she had.'

He doesn't tell her who Olive's parents are, or where they are based. But he tells her almost everything else about his meeting with Olive.

'You let her get away?' Neva says. 'Why?'

'I'm not interested in punishing someone who had no say in what her life had become. When she broke away, she helped us,' he says. 'She's the same as us. Broken and trying to find some happiness.'

'But she may have known more,' Neva says.

'I left her my card. I'm hoping she will trust me and get in touch. From what she did say, your mother is someone important in the Network. Whoever she is she's being protected by them,' he says.

'She gave me to them. Like Olive's parents gave her up?'

Michael takes a breath on the other end of the phone: he hadn't told her about Albert's possible connection with the Network.

'Or weren't you going to share that you suspect him?' Neva says.

'I was, but not before I talk to him again,' he says. 'He may not be part of it. I didn't sense any guile from him this morning. He was upset and shocked to learn that his child might be alive. But that doesn't mean he wasn't lying. He could just be a good actor. After all, fooling people is a skill we were both taught, so why not Olive's father too? Beth and I will get the truth out of him tomorrow. And if he knows anything about your parents, I'll find out. I promise.'

'Do you?' she says her voice little more than a whisper.

'I said I would help you find them, and I will. No one deserves payback more than the parent who willingly sells their own child,' he says.

Neva's mouth twitches and she finds herself smiling.

'I love hearing your voice,' she says.

'I ... *needed* to hear yours,' he tells her.

She smiles again. She wonders what other lovers do in between seeing each other. Is this desire to have contact normal?

'Are you still safe?' he asks.

'I am.'

'Good.'

'When are you seeing Olive's father again?' she asks.

'Tomorrow morning. He refused to let us in today when we returned. My guess is he's sending for his lawyer,' he says.

'You'll share with me what you learn?' she says.

'I told you I would. I don't lie, Neva,' he answers.

'Thank you,' she says.

'I'll call you again tomorrow. I have to go now,' he says.

Michael hangs up and Neva is left thinking about Olive. She is surprised that Michael let her go, despite his explanation.

Still needing contact with him, she begins to write a text. She wants to use words of romance and love, and even though she's played the seductress many times without effort, the right words sound corny to her now as she types them. She deletes the text and puts the phone down. What can she tell him that deep down he doesn't already know?

Chapter Twenty-Eight

MICHAEL

I put the phone down and hide it once more in my bag. I'm not angry with Neva for pressing me. It's to be expected. Her entire life, like mine, has been based on other people's betrayal. But I have to put her from my mind and keep focused so that I can do my job.

I meet Beth in the bar and we find a quiet corner, order food, and then huddle together to talk about Stanners.

'His lawyer called and they've set up another meeting for 10 tomorrow morning. Do you think he knows we're on to him?' Beth asks, her voice dripping with irony.

'Mmmm. Just a bit,' I say, trying to feel more humour than I'm capable of.

Beth and I have a dilemma. We want to get to Stanners as soon as possible, but we don't have enough for a warrant to force our way in there. Yet. If I was doing Stanners's profile I'd want to look into his finances. I'd want to know his vices. Perhaps he's a gambler and money is the key to Beech's possible infection of his household.

'If he did hand Georgia over to the Network,' I say. 'Then his wife never knew.'

'Isn't that always the case?' says Beth. 'With the worst betrayals? God. You don't know this, but … I'm not that maternal. Even so, all of this makes me want to hug my boys. They'd freak out if I did though, because they are not used to me being soppy.'

I try not to give anything away with Beth's reveal. I'd always thought her family came first, but after years of working with her, I've learnt more about her in the last twenty-four hours than I'd previously known.

The food arrives and we eat, sharing a bottle of Merlot. Then Beth excuses herself and goes to bed early.

I stay in the bar, nursing a whisky and mulling over all that has happened so far. The world is still pear-shaped. There's something needling the back of my skull, and I'm sure I'm missing the point. But the problem isn't presenting itself to me.

It's hot inside and the bar is busy. I finish my drink, then stand.

I go outside to the front of the hotel. The night air is cool and it's a relief after the claustrophobia of the bar.

I see a young couple standing by the road smoking. The man nods to me and I return the greeting, then I walk around the building to the back of the hotel and look over the hills as the sun sets. It's a beautiful evening. In the far distance a waterfall cascades from the top of a mountainous ridge. It's too far to hear the sound of the water, but the sight of the falls cheers me.

I don't know for certain, but it feels like a lull before a coming storm.

Chapter Twenty-Nine

MICHAEL

We reach *Hamlet's Retreat* by 9.30 the next morning. As we approach the gate, we find it already open. I drive the car to the visitors' car park, and we follow the same route to the office we had previously taken.

As we draw near to the office door, we find it wide open.

'I don't like the look of this,' I say.

I pull out my Glock and remove the safety. Beth retrieves her gun and we enter the house via the Estate Reception entrance. There's a burst of adrenaline in my veins as we cross the threshold, this time not invited. I enjoy the rush and my senses go into hyperdrive.

We hurry down the corridor and into the hallway of the house. I head for the library, open the door, take a look inside and find it empty. Then we work our way through the house. The building is too quiet. There's a study on the left as we pass the stairs and a huge drawing room on the right. There's no sign or sound of movement even from the kitchen as we make our way down the main corridor to where it should be. We open the kitchen door and find the room devoid of people.

'Staff quarters?' Beth says indicating a sign that says 'Staff Only' on a door at the back of the kitchen. The door leads down a narrow corridor with rooms off it and appears to be another extension to the house, probably added to accommodate the live-in staff.

I open the first door and find it is a small suite – almost a studio apartment. I glance around the room. There's a sofa in front of a television in one corner, a kitchenette in another, and a bed over to the far left. Another room on the right is a small bathroom with toilet, sink and shower. There's someone sleeping in the bed, I'm wary as I walk over to see who it is. That's when I find the butler. He's been shot in the head twice. It's a professional hit: he probably didn't even hear his assassin enter.

Beth and I split up after that. She takes one side of the corridor to check the other rooms and I take the other. The other staff bedrooms tell a similar story. Everyone who works for Stanners has been killed in the night while they slept.

We sweep the house, looking for Stanners. Upstairs we walk through all of the ten bedrooms until we find his. There's an open suitcase, half packed, on a super-king-sized four-poster bed. But Stanners himself is nowhere to be found.

When we are sure the house is clear, I phone Ray and tell him what we've found.

'Sending a crew to you from Glasgow, they'll be there within the hour,' Ray says.

As Beth and I walk downstairs we come face to face with a small, balding man in a raincoat holding a briefcase.

'I'm here to see Lord Stanners,' he says.

'Who are you?' Beth asks.

'Edwin Hamilton. I'm his attorney,' he says.

'I'm very sorry, but Stanners is missing. Please don't touch anything,' I tell him.

We take Hamilton into the Estate Office, which appears to have been unused since the night before. More staff arrive. A gardener comes to the office to clock in. I sit him down with Hamilton. Beth stays with them and I go to the main doors of the house and open them up so that our people can park right at the front, allowing them easier access to the bodies.

As promised the forensics team arrives and the dead are examined, photographed and bagged, then they are moved into the mortuary van that turns up a short time later.

By the afternoon the local police are also on hand to take care of the employees who'd turned up to start work.

'I have other appointments,' Hamilton said. 'I really must go.'

'You're going nowhere,' Beth says. 'I suggest you ring your office and cancel all appointments. Then sit down and be quiet until we can interview you.'

Hamilton does as Beth instructs but he isn't happy. After making the phone call to his office, he spends the rest of the time on his phone texting someone.

I leave Beth with them while I coordinate the work at the crime scene. Just after one, Ray arrives with MI5's new pathologist and I meet Elliot Baker for the first time.

'Stanners hasn't been found,' I say, 'but I'm organising a search of the grounds just to be sure. That will take some time though: we've thirty acres to cover.'

'Did you check the wine cellar?' Elliot says.

'I … don't think there is a cellar … let alone a wine cellar,' I say.

'Sure there is,' Elliot says. 'All of these places have one. I'd look for concealed access. Probably from the library or even in the kitchen pantry.'

I'm not sure how to take Elliot Baker, but I know he's probably right. There *should* be a cellar.

I take Ray to the Estate Office and he interviews Hamilton while Beth and I go in search of a possible wine cellar. We check the library first, examining the bookcases to see if any of them move, but they all appear to be firmly affixed to the walls.

Back in the kitchen I explore the pantry and we don't find anything in there either.

'What about there?' says Beth.

I look over to a large meat locker. I look inside the huge refrigerator, exploring the back of it for good measure. There's hunks of meat and a full cow hanging inside but other than that it all appears to be normal. When I come out into the kitchen again, I study the outside. I see the thing that is jarring most with Beth. There's a cupboard at the side of the freezer and it doesn't match the rest of the kitchen. It looks like a tall pantry storage cupboard. Though it's wider and taller than your average cupboard.

I pull the cupboard door open to discover a full-sized cellar door behind it.

'I wonder how he knew,' I say.

'Who?' Beth says.

'The pathologist, Baker. He suggested looking for this,' I say.

Beth shrugs but she blushes a little too which I find interesting. Is there something between them?

'Good old Elliot,' she says.

I turn my attention back to the door. I try to open it but it's locked.

'Let's get someone in here and break this down,' Beth says.

'Or maybe just pick the lock,' I say.

Beth is silent as she watches me retrieve a lock-picking kit from my pocket. 'You never know when you need one of these,' I say.

It's an old mortise lock and I'm out of practice, but I manage to get us inside the cellar a short time later.

As the door springs open, Beth puts a hand on my arm. I already have my Glock in my right hand.

'What do you expect to find in there?' Beth says.

'Stanners hiding?' I say.

Beth frowns at me. 'Or dead...'

'Or maybe our killer,' I say. 'Either way, let's take no chances.'

There's a light at the top of the stairs and I switch it on before we begin to move down the stone steps into the cellar. At the bottom a sensor light clicks on, illuminating the whole of a long corridor. We follow the strip lighting to a room at the end of the corridor. Inside we find Stanners's expensive wine collection but nothing more.

'Dead end,' I say to Beth, my eyes roving over dusty bottles of vintage port, champagne and the best Malbecs and Shirazes.

'This is it? For a house this size?' Beth says.

I shrug.

As we turn to go, a waft of air drifts into the wine cellar. A strand of Beth's hair moves in the breeze. I turn to look in the direction of the draught and notice another anomaly.

'There,' I say pointing to a ridge in the brickwork.

Behind a movable rack of wine bottles, we find a hidden doorway. There is no dust and no cobwebs. I pull the rack aside, and we push on the stone. It gives easily, opening up on well-oiled hinges. We find ourselves in a small room and beyond is a thick wooden door that is wide open and leads out, up a small stone flight of steps, into the grounds.

Beth and I go through the door and out into a walled garden with low box hedges tracing out the pattern of a *fleur-de-lis*. We follow the wall around to a metal gate which leads out into the rest of the grounds. The gate is open. All of which are signs of a hurried departure.

Beyond the wall there is a large pond, and beside it is a lumpen pile of clothes.

Unlike his employees, Stanners didn't die quietly.

I find myself with Elliot Baker while he examines Stanners's body.

'Someone really hated this guy,' Elliot says. 'Look at the knife wounds here and here…'

Elliot concludes that Stanners had tried to defend himself but his killer knew what he or she was doing.

When Elliot finishes his on-site exam, the body is removed and we comb the surrounding area. I find a knife in the bushes, not dissimilar to the one that Neva carries. It *could* even be hers. My mind runs over my telephone call with her. I hadn't told her where in Scotland I was, nor even who Olive Redding's parents were. So she couldn't have found the place. Besides, the attack on Stanners is frenzied, angry. Neva's kills are always cold and concise.

'What've you found?' Elliot says behind me.

I hand over the knife.

'Interesting blade,' Elliot says. 'It looks like the murder weapon.'

When the search is over and anything even remotely interesting is taken away, I remove my gloves and wend my way back to the Range Rover.

Inside the car, and sure I am alone, I open my bag and call Neva.

'Where are you?' I ask.

'Why?'

'Olive's father is dead. Someone murdered the entire household last night,' I say.

'And you thought it was me?'

'Was it?'

'I'm sat looking at boats going up and down the Thames.' She snaps a picture and sends it to me.

'I had to ask,' I say. 'There was a knife like yours at the scene.'

'Standard Network issue,' she says. 'I'd never drop mine.'

'I'll call you later,' I say. 'Have to go before Beth comes looking for me.'

'Michael?'

'Yes?'

'I didn't ask you where Redding's parents were because if I'd known, I might well have come and questioned him. Was he tortured?' Neva asks.

'No. It was a frenzied stabbing,' I say.

'Do you think it was Olive?' she asks.

'I don't know. But someone really had a grudge.'

I hang up, turn the phone off and put it in my suit trouser pocket. This trip to Scotland hasn't worked out quite how I imagined it would. The body count sure wasn't what I'd expected.

I lock the car and head back to the house just in time to see Ray releasing Hamilton. Stanners's lawyer is red in the face as he walks past me down to the visitors' parking lot.

'Your people haven't heard the last of this,' he says.

'What's with him?' I ask Ray as I reach him.

'He didn't like being asked about the Network. Unfortunately, I couldn't take him in for proper questioning. But we're aware of him now, and I'll be taking a look into his finances. But never mind that. What a fucking mess this is,' Ray says.

'I know.'

'Talk me through what you think went down here,' Ray says.

I walk him through the house, starting with the employee quarters.

'Someone enters via the back door, which is also the staff's private entrance. See, the lock was forced. Not much finesse in that, when it could have been picked. But I think they were in a hurry. Once inside, they work their way through every room on this corridor. The killer uses a silencer so as not to alert the other occupants. He puts two shots in the head of each of them on his way through.'

'Why kill the servants?' Ray asks.

'To prevent any of them raising the alarm perhaps?'

'What next?' Ray says. We walk now into the hallway.

'At some point Stanners had started to pack his bag. He was going to run, probably before we could interview him. My guess is he comes downstairs and hears something. Look there...' I point to a cupboard under the stairs. The door isn't closed flush. I walk up and open it now.

'When the killer goes upstairs looking for him, he sneaks out of his hiding place and then goes into the kitchen. He opens the cellar door, goes in and locks it from the inside to stop them following. Then he exits into the walled garden. During this time the intruder searches Stanners's rooms, finds the half-packed case, and guesses he's running. They exit the house through the Estate Office entrance, leaving the door wide open, and go searching for him. Stanners is found as he is trying to escape. A bloody assault happens after that, in which our perp lands several deliberately painful, but not killing, blows. Ending with – and I don't know this until Baker confirms – a final sweep upwards, under the ribcage and into the heart delivering a death strike.' I pause. 'Then they drop the knife and run.'

'After being so professional up until that point, why did they drop the knife?' Ray asks.

'I have a theory. Knowing what we know of the Network, this could have been a clean-up that went wrong. Stanners was scared. He was running. If he panicked and spoke to someone at the Network maybe they thought they couldn't trust him to keep quiet about what he knew. Or maybe he tried to blackmail them. Either way, they decided to retire him. But the assassin they sent lost him in the house and Stanners got away. Then as he's escaping, thinking he's home free, Redding finds him outside. She's come to see him. Maybe she's going to reveal who she is. But Stanners knows already that she's his daughter. He thinks she's come to kill him so he begs for his life, telling her in the process what he did and why. Before then, I don't think she knew he was involved.'

'So, shocked by what he says, she loses it and kills him?' Ray says.

I nod.

'It's one scenario. And it's all I can think of that would explain the difference in the kills. Two different killers, with different motivations,' I explain. 'Also, if this was Olive it wasn't premeditated.'

'How do you figure that?' Ray asks.

'Her weapon of choice is a crossbow, not a knife. But the knife was all she had on her.'

'That's a great theory. Good work, Michael,' says Ray. 'Let's see if it matches up with any of the evidence.'

We reach the location where I found Stanners. I point to where the shape of his fallen body is marked out with tape and forensic markers and explain the circumstances to Ray, tying it all in with my concept.

'Redding, though a former killer, was broken. Having nowhere else to go she seeks out her parents. Learning of her mother's Alzheimer's, she gets work at the care home to be near her. When we blow her cover there, she sees this as the last opportunity to get to know her father before she has to disappear for good. The problem is, Stanners is the one who gave her to the Network. When she discovers her father's betrayal, it's too much. She kills him, then throws the knife because she's in a state of shock. If I'm right, she stumbled off in that direction. See the bend in the longer grass over there?' The scenario is now clearer to me.

We follow the line of the grass as it leads into a patch of woodland. The trees become denser, forming a barrier from the road with a deep dip between the trees and the road, which is designed to put off any intruders.

'The rest of this estate is walled,' I comment.

We scramble down the embankment and back up to the country lane on the other side. It's not easy to do, and would put off any casual criminal – but it's not insurmountable to someone with enough motivation.

'Something was parked here with a minor oil leak,' I say, pointing to an oil stain on the road.

'I'm inclined to agree with your reasoning,' Ray says. 'Good work, Michael, and welcome back to the team.'

Ray calls the head of the forensics team to join him back

at the house so he can walk them through the scenario that I just outlined.

We walk back to the house following the road so as not to further contaminate the route that Stanners's killer might have taken.

'Where do you think Redding will be now? Ray asks.

'Long gone. And I doubt we'll ever get such a good lead to her again,' I say. 'Remember, they are trained to disappear.'

Ray nods.

I feel a little frustrated now that I had her and let her go. But what use would Olive be to us now anyway? Stanners is dead and Olive's world has fallen apart. She won't even be able to do the only thing she wanted to – take care of her sick mother.

As we reach the estate office once more, I can't help but pity Olive. I hope she will stay out of sight and find some inner peace. More than anything I hope the Network don't find her.

Chapter Thirty

MICHAEL

Beth and I fly back from Scotland, but Ray stays behind to liaise with the local police. He arranges to have the bodies of Stanners's staff returned to their families. Stanners on the other hand is taken back to MI5's medical facility in Glasgow, where Elliot Baker will perform his autopsy. After that, Stanners's relatives will be able to claim him. I'm expecting Baker to confirm most of what I suspected, but there may be a few surprises that could give us a clearer picture.

The trip has gone a long way to normalising my relationship with Beth, and Ray was treating me like he's always done, taking my input and accepting it. I am starting to believe that we can actually get back to some normality after all and that I am welcome back on the team as Ray had said.

It's after five when we land. I say goodnight to Beth but instead of going home, I make my way back to Archive's offices to write up my report while it's still fresh in my mind. As discussed with Ray, my stance is that Olive killed Stanners, but I also believe another intruder executed everyone that had the misfortune to be in the house. Whether they were working together or not, I can't confirm, but it is unlikely, and I say so in the report. Olive's possible presence there at the same time was most likely a coincidence.

I save the report and by eight I'm heading home in a cab. On the way back I order a take-away delivery that arrives as I get out of the taxi. I pay the driver, collect my food and go upstairs.

I'm not surprised to find Neva there in my living room when I come in. I don't ask her why she's here. I merely close the door and place the food bag down on the coffee table.

Then I pick Neva up and take her into the bedroom.

She doesn't object as I take her. I'm rough, demanding and very possessive. But I can't help it. It's how I need her tonight. But no one understands this more than her.

Afterwards, sated, I hold her for a while. It is almost an apology for assuming that my behaviour was okay.

'Did I hurt you?' I ask.

'No. It was wonderful. You let go of yourself with me for the first time.'

I get out of the bed and go into the kitchen, where I open the bottle of wine that Beth had left me. Then I bring the takeaway into the bedroom. We eat the cold Chinese food out of its containers while sitting together on the bed.

'I want to tell you about the flight,' she says. 'That was the deal.'

'Okay,' I say. 'Tell me about it.'

'There's a hacker by the name of Solomon Granger that was posing as one of the flight attendants. He'd been undercover for years, waiting for his handler to place him where she needed him. He probably took over the onboard computer systems.'

'Why?'

'I told you, someone important to the Network was on the plane.'

'Who?'

'A businessman. His codename: Armin. He was taken off the plane and then it was detoured.'

I pick up a cold wonton and pop it into my mouth. 'So, you have a source that's given you this information? What do they hope to gain by telling you?'

'Solomon's handler is playing a double game. She's the one working with Almunazama. She's in over her head and doesn't know it,' she says, avoiding answering my question.

'Was this Solomon the only spy on the flight?'

'Why do you ask?' Neva says.

'We found the body of a woman. We think she was one of the flight attendants replaced by a *doppelgänger*,' I say.

'A body? She's *dead*?' Neva's face becomes guarded.

'Look, whatever you know, it could help us stop these guys.'

'I … need to make some enquiries,' she says. 'Solomon wouldn't have killed this woman. It's not his bag.'

'Well, the way it's looking, her double did it. Probably some weird Stepford moment and it was cruelly done.'

'How did she die?'

I explain the way we found the body.

'That's sick. And coming from me that's saying something,' she says. 'Though he's been radicalised by his handler for years, Solomon couldn't have done it. He was just some young IT geek when she found him. He's been warped, but he's more passive than aggressive. He wouldn't have stopped someone from killing though...'

'It sounds like you know him,' I say.

'I've had dealings with his handler ... and heard stuff about them both,' she explains.

She tries to lighten the mood again after that but I know she's disturbed by my revelation. I want to question her more about this Solomon Granger and Almunazama but I decide against it. Whatever she tells me, I can use to shape the investigation we do on the plane, but the information I tell colleagues will have to come from a provable source. I doubt that they will accept me saying I have an informant again without a complete interrogation of who that person is.

Neva moves the tray of food off the bed and pulls me to her.

'I took care of you,' she says. 'Now it's time you take care of me.'

I don't need further encouragement to make love to her again.

Chapter Thirty-One

BETH

B eth arrives home to find Callum with the boys instead of her mother.

'So you've finally showed up,' he says.

'What're you doing here?' she asks.

'Your mum had plans, or doesn't that matter to you?'

'Fuck off, Callum. This is my job and I'm done with you having a go at me about it,' she says.

'I've decided I'm going after full custody,' Callum says. 'The boys need structure in their life. When we were together, I was there for them at least.'

'You were the one who said our marriage wasn't working,' Beth says. 'I'm not quitting my job. How the hell do you expect me to keep a roof over their heads without it?'

'Please, Mum,' said Philip coming into the kitchen. 'We can't stand it when you and Dad fight.'

'Sorry, love,' Beth says. 'Look, you two go up to bed and I'll come up and tuck you in soon.'

Philip takes Callum junior's hand and leads his younger brother upstairs.

'I don't want to fight,' Beth says. 'I'm tired, Callum. Please go and I'll talk to you tomorrow.'

'I mean it, Beth. They'd be better off with me. I'll still give you visitation rights.'

'I can't do this now,' Beth says.

Callum picks his jacket up and pulls it on. Beth follows him to the door.

'How did this happen?' he says.

'What?' she answers distracted. All she wants is peace and quiet and time to herself. Something she never really has.

'Us. We were so close, then you started at Archive... I'd pull this family back together if you'd let me.'

He reaches for her, pulling her into his arms, and that's when he feels the gun stowed in a holster under her jacket.

'For fuck's sake,' he says. 'You're wearing a weapon as standard now? What the hell are you into? It's a cold case investigation team...' Callum stops talking as though the penny he couldn't catch has finally dropped and the past few years start to make sense.

'Don't ask,' she says.

'I'm not comfortable with a gun being in the house,' he says.

'I have a safe. It's in there every night.'

'A safe? Where?'

Beth lifts her eyebrows at him.

'So I have no right to know where this is? Even in my house?'

'I'm currently in the process of buying you out. So this isn't your house anymore,' she says.

'Did you have that thing and the safe when it was?'

'Goodnight, Callum,' Beth says. She puts her hand on his shoulder and encourages him to step over the threshold.

'Beth…'

'No. You don't get to criticise. You don't get to say anything to me anymore. You want to know what happened to us? You did. Your ego. You're the one who said he didn't mind his wife earning more than him. You're the one who encouraged me to keep my job after the boys were born. After all, we really needed the money then. Suddenly that's no longer acceptable. You think because you got promoted that I should just give up and stay home? You can't have it all your way, all the time. I may be a mother but I've a right to live a life I want for myself too. *Don't you get it?* I'm not housewife material. For fuck's sake, I carry a gun and I know how to use it! That should tell you all you need to know about me. Now go away, Callum. And go after the kids, that's fine with me. I never fucking wanted them anyway.'

Beth closes the door, cutting off Callum's shocked grunt as she delivers her parting blow. She turns around and sees Philip standing at the bottom of the stairs.

'Hey, baby,' she says.

Philip turns away and runs upstairs.

'No sweetheart… I didn't mean…'

But she doesn't pursue the little boy upstairs, because she can't lie to him. She did mean it and maybe they would be better off with their dad after all.

Chapter Thirty-Two

MICHAEL

W hen I get back into the office, there's an email from Ray asking me to look at Leon and Brinkman's folder on the missing aircraft.

There's a report from Beth and a list of the crew's names. Four are highlighted as suspects: Angela Carter, Chloe Bell, Jay Astor and Frank Minchin. I read the information she's gathered about Astor and Minchin. Following the link to Astor's profile page on Facebook, I look at the photographs that Beth thought genuine: Astor with various boyfriends in many different locations. There are no pictures of him with any of the other crew members, even though this team has worked together for the best part of six months.

While I read Beth's notes, I'm trying to figure out how I'm going to bring fresh evidence into what we already have without anyone knowing that I'm involved again with Neva.

Beth doesn't mention any of the crew's friends or family, so I take a look at some of the people who have left comments for Astor. I follow the trail of the accounts, and find the so-called friends are all much of a muchness with similar profile pages. I do a reverse search on the image of one young man and find the picture is actually a male model. *Tick*. It's obvious that this profile is fake. I search a few more. Some seem to be real people that Astor has befriended to fill out his lists and feed, but the majority, some thirty or more friends, I can confirm are bogus. Especially when I observe that all activity on these accounts stops the day before the flight disappeared.

I type up my observations and add it to the folder. Then I look more closely at Minchin. Minchin appears to be a real person. I see normal patterns of communication and organic threads on his newsfeed. He has a small Facebook page that has friends and a few family members. It's surprisingly transparent, a hacker's dream to be honest, because he has his 'friends list' open for anyone to see. He also puts public statuses up all the time. This man has nothing to hide or appears not to. That could be a tell – an appearance of innocence; his lack of paranoia could be misleading. A woman has posted on his feed, asking where he is. A few others have commented on it. 'Yeah, Frank... Where are you?' I click on the woman's name and check her profile page because it's also open and I see at one point she's asking publicly again if anyone has heard from Frank. There's a thread discussing the fact that no one has had any recent contact with him, and the authors of these comments express some concern.

I make a note in the folder again to contact these people and enquire about Minchin, and I glean what I can from their Facebook pages that will make it easy to search the DVLA database to find their contact details.

After that I search out the first woman. Her name is Carolyn Minchin Read, and she appears to be a relative of Minchin's. Because this is a way of ruling him out, I look for Carolyn's details first. Once they've been found, I add the information to the file. It might not be me who contacts her, but at least this piece of information might help narrow down suspicion to Astor – who is looking more and more probable to me as being the hacker Neva told me about.

I save the file and go and get myself a coffee. When I get back to my office, I find a message from Security Agent Brinkman asking me to call her.

'I just read your file additions,' she says. 'Ray told me you were good... I didn't expect you to get so much so quickly. Anyway, I want to hear what you're thinking that you didn't put in the report.'

'Well, we pretty much know that Carter was replaced by someone. I doubt she was working alone. Too big a job,' I say.

'Go on,' she says.

'I looked on social media for Astor and Minchin. As I pointed out, Minchin's is pretty average, but Astor's isn't.' I run through my thoughts, reconfirming what I've said in the report.

'Look, I know we have to deal in facts,' Brinkman says. 'But tell me what your gut is saying right now.'

'Astor was working with Carter. They were probably both *doppelgängers*. Astor's fake profile goes back three years. He's been in play for a while,' I say.

'What about Carter? Why no Facebook page?' Brinkman says. 'Surely it's suspicious that she didn't have one?'

'Carter was a late addition. They didn't have time to establish her. There probably was a Facebook page for the original Angela Carter, which they brought down. Better to have it gone, than to have to pretend to be her online with real friends and family,' I explain.

'That makes sense. It also means that no one missed her after the plane disappeared.'

'Yes. Unlike Minchin, who has been missed. I think we need to search Astor's apartment. I'm sure Leon and Beth had this on their list of to-dos before we were distracted by another case,' I say.

'Right. That happens in my department all the time too. I think you're on to something,' Brinkman says. 'Let's meet at Astor's apartment and check him out.'

After we flash our badges, the manager of the building gives us access to Astor's apartment, which is on the top floor. The first thing that strikes me as Brinkman and I enter is the solid wall of window in the open-plan space that overlooks London's docklands. Astor lived way beyond his means. And this place has the best of everything.

The space is modern, clean. It has an open-plan kitchen, large dining area and a living room with expensive furnishings. The type of place that a wealthy person would love to entertain in.

'How could he afford this?' Brinkman says.

The place looks lived in. There are the remains of milk and food in the fridge, as though Astor expected to return. And in the bedroom the wardrobe is filled with normal clothing that any man in his thirties might wear. There's nothing particularly notable about them, unlike the clothing in the photographs we've seen him in on his social media

In the living space there is a large flat-screen television hanging on the wall in front of a plush L-shaped sofa. I pick up the remote control and switch it on as Brinkman searches through his kitchen cupboards.

'Look at this,' I say. 'The programmes he records: sports, car shows, the occasional film. Looks like he's a football fan.'

I go into his bedroom and look around. The bedside table drawers have little in them, not even men's magazines. But I find one *Playboy* under the bed. I flick it open. It's full of naked women. Perhaps he was bi?

I find a laptop left open on his dresser. I switch it on, but it is password protected.

In his bathroom, his medicine cabinet has the usual toiletries you'd find in most men's: aftershave, shaving gel, deodorant.

I take the laptop with me as I leave the bedroom.

'We'll take this. See if the tech team can get into it,' I say to Brinkman as I place it on the kitchen worktop.

'Right,' says Brinkman. 'And I've sent for a forensics team. Let's lift some prints and DNA and see if this guy has a record.'

I return to the office convinced that this is the hacker Neva told me about. The only detail that casts doubt on my suspicion is the condition of the apartment: it was left as though Astor believed he was going to return. Brinkman's forensics may confirm that Astor is Granger but only if he previously had a record. I'm expecting this to draw a blank though. No one working for the Network would ever have a traceable past. They were too careful about that.

I consider using the system to look up Granger but dismiss this as it's likely Ray will be checking my work. *I would if I was him.* I can't do anything that will give away my connection with Neva or put my loyalty in any doubt. Not if I want us both to stay out of prison.

Instead, I go in search of Beth to discuss the case and to see if she has anything back from Baker. She's on the phone when I go into her office.

'No, I'm not going to fight it,' she says. 'He can have custody.'

She looks up and sees me standing by the door.

'Draw it up and I'll sign it,' she says.

I turn to leave to give her privacy.

'Wait, Mike, I'm almost done...' she says.

Then she finishes the call and hangs up.

'Sorry. My solicitor,' she says.

'I didn't mean to interrupt,' I say.

'That's okay. How can I help you?'

'Just checking to see if Baker had sent you the autopsy on Stanners yet?'

That slight flush of the cheeks again. *Interesting.*

'He's not flown back from Glasgow yet. It'll probably be tomorrow.'

Even more intriguing is that she knows Baker's whereabouts.

'I'm giving up my kids,' she says. 'I know that's weird. But I'm a terrible mother. Callum will be better for them fulltime, and I'm having them alternate weekends.'

'Beth, you're going through a divorce. That's a very emotional and stressful thing. Do you really want to make such a tough decision now?'

'I'm not wired like other women,' she says. 'I had them for Callum. The truth is they are probably the main cause of our break-up. People think it's normal to get married, have kids, and that is their idea of "happy ever after". It was ... *hell* for me. I liked us being a couple. The kids just divided us. But Callum loves them and he's a great dad. He makes up for my lack of ... empathy.'

I don't know what to say in response to this candid outburst. I sit down opposite her and offer a sympathetic ear. Which is all I can really do.

When she's let all of her thoughts out, she switches back to business as though it's never happened. I almost wish I had the luxury of telling her how I feel about things too. This verbal sharing of emotion can help you deal with it all. But I can't tell anyone about Neva, especially not Beth.

'So... I believe Brinkman took you out today to see Astor's place?' she says.

Her wording is odd, as though I need to be 'taken' places or have to be accompanied in order to do my job.

I choose not to read more into her words, and I tell her what we've learnt so far.

'It might be a lucky break,' I say. 'But I don't think Astor was gay as his social media suggests. He had a reason to pretend, which could confirm that his whole profile is fake.'

'What did we ever do without you?' Beth says, though I note the twinge of irony. 'I've been a little distracted. I should have noticed all of those things. Promise not to make it too obvious to Ray, please? I'll be much freer now I've sorted … *that*.' She glances at her mobile phone. 'I just want to concentrate on my job.'

'It's not a competition, Beth,' I say. 'We are a team. One day I won't see something you'll see.'

Beth laughs. 'Oh man! Am I hoping that day will come soon! I'm really going to rub your nose in it when it does happen.'

I find myself laughing with her but can't help thinking, *Many a true word is said in jest*. Beth's personal decision has lifted her mood though, and the tense lines that have been obvious on her face of late fall away as we laugh together.

'Hey, what's with you two?' Leon says from the doorway of his office.

This makes Beth laugh even harder. Leon, not having much sense of humour at the best of times, goes back in his office and closes the door.

Chapter Thirty-Three

SUBRA

Subra Semillon pulls a scarf up over her hair as she waits in the cool darkness of her hallway. Since the downfall of Beech, she's taken up residence in Israel: a place she often visited to do the work the Network required of her.

As a woman of wealth, she is protected from the world, and rarely ventures outside without a team of well-armed security guards. She lives in a rambling two-storey house, set in several acres of desert landscape, on the outskirts of Jerusalem. The house is surrounded by miles of electric fencing and monitored by cameras. Armed guards are posted in towers around various points of the perimeter and they watch with wary attention, both the desert and the city. To the casual eye it may seem that Subra and her household fear intruders.

As part of the Network's long-term plan to destabilise the respective governments, Subra has been working to fuel the unrest between the Palestinians and the Israelis. Such disruption ensures that the powers that be don't delve too deeply into the cover of the corporate businesses that the Network hide behind.

Subra is a vital cog within a well-oiled, corrupt and violent machine and she enjoys her role.

After the virtual meeting with the committee a few days ago, Subra prepares herself for yet another. She walks from her house and steps into a large black people carrier. Sitting in the back with her are two of her most trusted men. As the car drives out of the gates of Subra's home, a second black vehicle follows. Inside are several other guards: all armed to the teeth.

They make their way along the main road, skirting the city and driving into the wilds of the desert. After an hour they reach another perimeter fence. The vehicles follow the fence around to a guarded gate entrance. To a casual passer-by this place smacks of military. Though piled high with security, it is far from official.

In the centre of the camp both vehicles pull up beside one of the buildings. Subra and her men exit the car. She walks with confidence to the building and the three of them go inside. The men in the other vehicle get out and loiter. Some smoke, while others idly talk with the residents of the camp. They are all familiar to each other and very comfortable together.

Inside the ramshackle building, Subra finds a young man. He's wearing combats and has a gun and holster slung low over his hips. He's sitting by the door to a locked room.

'How is our guest today?' asks Subra.

'He's refusing to eat,' the young man says.

'I'll talk to him,' she says.

The young man opens the door and Subra goes in. Inside the sparse room is a military bunk bed, a table and chairs and toilet.

A man in his mid-fifties is sitting on the bunk with his back pressed to the wall. He has black hair that is greying at the temples, and other than his slightly ruffled clothing he has a sense of dignity about him. He doesn't look at Subra.

'Armin,' Subra says. 'You disappoint me. I thought you had a greater sense of survival than this. You need to eat.'

'I don't see any point. It's obvious you'll kill me when you get what you want,' Armin says in the clear British upper-class accent that he picked up after his years studying at Oxford.

They have removed his belt and shoelaces, and he's monitored twenty-four hours a day through a security camera.

'I haven't hurt you so far,' Subra says. 'I wanted you on my side. We could have taken control of the Network together. Now, because of your stubborn refusal, we have Annalise in charge.'

Armin looks at Subra now. 'Annalise? Why her?'

Subra explains Annalise's erasing of Vasquez. 'We can't ignore the support she commands in the Network. Most operatives look up to her. Some would even die for her. She's been building her own little empire within the castle walls for quite some time.'

'The idea of bringing her into the committee was to negate an attempted coup?' Armin asks.

'I'm trying to appear an ally until such time as we rid ourselves of her influence,' Subra tells him. 'We could still work together...'

'If you wanted my help, why not ask for it? You didn't need to take me from a plane. You didn't need to kill all of those people.'

Subra smiles. 'Oh, but it was such a magnificent mission. And what do you care about the death of others?'

Armin casts her a look of disdain. Subra is always about the glory. She could never be a trusted ally. She wouldn't be able to resist the drama.

'Pointless deaths are not glorious, Subra,' Armin says. 'As a deliverer of it, you should know that it is the one person that has to die that is far more magnificent. And a hard fight, not an easy one, that gives satisfaction. You on the other hand use your hackers to do all of your dirty work. If you'd come after me one to one then this would mean something.'

A frown flits over her brow, but Subra smooths it away and she gives a small smile.

'Why were you going to Shanghai?' Subra asks.

'You know why. The committee sent me. I had to make sure our business associates weren't compromised,' he says.

'By the Almunazama?' Subra says.

'Yes.'

Subra pulls the chair away from the small table and sits down. 'That's strange, because my source tells me you were secretly working for them.'

Armin doesn't answer.

'You won't deny it?' she says.

'You won't believe me, so why bother. You took the word of this source before consulting with me. Now you're holding me captive. What do you want from me?' Armin says.

'The truth,' Subra says. 'Are you working with the Almunazama?'

'No,' he says.

Subra stands and walks towards him. 'I'll ask you again. Are you working with the Almunazama?'

Armin shrugs.

'Caleb!' Subra calls.

The young man from outside now comes into the room with Subra's two guards.

'It's time we got the truth from Armin,' she says.

The two guards seize Armin. He struggles but they overpower him. They drag him to the centre of the room and tie him to the chair that Subra has now vacated.

One of Subra's guards brings in a small case.

'You know what I'm good at,' Subra says.

She lays the case on the table and opens it. Armin's eyes fall on the knives, needles and scalpels that make up her set of torture instruments.

'Coward,' Armin says. 'Fight me and we'll see who is strongest.'

Subra smirks. 'I already know the answer to that. I am. I win. Now and always.'

An hour later Subra comes out of the room. Her clothing is stained with blood.

Another young man is now sitting in Caleb's seat. Subra smiles at him.

'Solomon,' she says. 'I wondered when I'd see you.'

'Did you get what you wanted from him?' he asks.

'He doesn't know anything,' Subra says. 'Or he'd have talked.'

'Did they ever recover Angie's body?' Solomon asks. 'Either one of us could have got that dud parachute.'

'She's probably fish food,' Subra says. 'Either way, she's not talking about what went down on Zen Airlines flight 723.'

'She was a loyal operative.' He frowns. 'She wouldn't have talked. She did everything you'd asked of her.'

'It wasn't on purpose, I told you that. The man who packed the chutes has been executed for his carelessness. You better believe that will never happen again. But it's just as well you were carrying Armin. Six months of planning would have been lost in an instant.'

'Glad to know you care,' he says.

'You know I do,' Subra says. 'Come to me and I'll show you how much.'

He looks at the blood spatters on her clothing and doesn't reply.

'You're so squeamish,' Subra says. 'It's funny really.'

'Well, I wasn't brought up like you were,' he says.

'Subra!' calls Caleb from the room, 'He's awake.'

'Time for another round,' Subra says.

Solomon grimaces.

'Do I disgust you so much?' she says, her face serious now.

'It's not that you *can* torture someone,' Solomon says. 'It's that you enjoy it.'

Subra laughs and goes back into the room.

Chapter Thirty-Four

SOLOMON

Solomon Granger watches Subra go back into the room, then he takes himself out of the hut because he has no stomach to hear any more of Armin's screams. He can't help feeling disgust for what Subra does.

He walks away and back to his own small quarters, a tiny hut at the back of the camp.

He was twenty when he met Subra, a sophisticated and beautiful woman, ten years his senior at the time. Solomon was besotted with her from the start. That was fifteen years ago now, and if he'd known then what she'd turn him into, Solomon would have turned and walked away. At least he liked to believe he would.

They'd been living together for five years before he discovered the truth about her. She earned her significant salary by working for a corporation. It meant a lot of travel, and Solomon had had to cope with her frequent absences. But she always came home and showered him with love and passion and so he'd thought their relationship was perfect. Subra told him all about the prejudice she'd suffered for her race and colour. Solomon understood because his black skin had often brought him similar disdain. He became a warrior to defend her rights. He'd even started a fight with someone who he thought looked at her with contempt in a bar.

'My hero,' she'd said afterwards with a smile, as she pressed a bag of ice to his bruised and swollen eye. He didn't learn until much later that the whole racist incident had been a set-up to make sure she had him willing to do anything for her.

When she told him of her 'real' job, Solomon had laughed, taking it as some sort of silly joke. He'd never quite got her sense of humour anyway. But Subra, an assassin? It was just too impossible to consider.

She'd taken him to the House then. A place he only vaguely remembered. They showed him things, talked to him, gave him some sort of medication. Then they started training him. When he returned to her six months later, he knew she'd told him the truth and he was more than willing to do whatever she said, as long as she never sent him back to the House.

Subra continued his education after that. They'd picked him for his IT skills, and hacking was high on the list of things he was encouraged to do. Then, when she thought he was ready, she put him under cover.

For the past three years Solomon has been living in England under the name Jay Astor. Astor was a young air steward when Subra had him replaced by Solomon. At least Solomon thought that Astor must have been a real person, but he was never too sure on that score. Subra was able to summon identities out of nowhere. And as Solomon submerged himself into Astor's world – all for the love of Subra – he often wondered why no 'real' friends and acquaintances of Astor's ever came forward.

He'd been resistant to playing this role until Subra explained that he only had to 'pretend' and didn't have to have a same-sex relationship to prove himself. They set up a folder full of photographs of Jay with various men, on holidays and in clubs and bars. Jay used them randomly on the social media account they'd set up. But it was all faked, even down to most of the 'friends' that regularly interacted with him, liking and commenting on his posts. But to a certain extent he began to believe that this was who he was. He had to in order to be taken seriously.

As Jay, he started a new role with British Airways. Then, he moved over to Zen Airlines at the same time that Subra brought someone in to take over Angela Carter's life.

Solomon had accepted the woman as his colleague on the flight and they acted like old friends. As he got used to her as the real Angela's replacement, they spent the past few months doing the job like real flight attendants, and, when they were in Shanghai, hanging out, eating great local food and enjoying themselves during their rest days.

When Subra gave them the go-ahead, Jay hacked into the onboard system, and Angie (as he called her to distinguish from the real Angela he knew) had delighted in taking over the plane.

Angie, he suspected, was just like Subra deep down. She had no qualms about killing. Armin had been the target, everyone else on board was expendable but Subra had smoothed over that part of the plan. Solomon had only learned the truth when Angie shot the pilot and co-pilot, and put a fake announcement through the Tannoy system to keep the passengers calm until they had time to put them, and the crew, to sleep.

'But how did you answer as the co-pilot?' he'd asked after Shelley, another innocent to die for this cause, had called the cockpit directly.

'Voice changer,' Angie had said.

It had all been so meticulously planned, and most of it a total surprise to Solomon.

Lying on his bunk, Solomon recalls those last few moments. The terrified interference from Shelley. . . All of it was such a clusterfuck. He hadn't wanted to kill the girl, but they couldn't leave her on board in case she found a way to raise the alarm and get help. Plus, he was afraid to show that he disapproved in case it got back to Subra.

'For what it's worth,' Angie had said after she pushed Shelley out of the plane, 'no one but us and our passenger there is getting off this plane alive. So she'd have died anyway.'

Solomon had liked Angie. For the most part they'd had a casual friendship while they played their roles. They never discussed the mission until the day they were activated to do it. Each of them knew what their roles would be and talking about it hadn't been necessary. He'd been shocked by how cold and deadly Angie was in the end though. He'd thought her like himself, a hacker working for Subra and ultimately the Network. But she was so much more than that. Through Angie he learned that taking Armin had been something Subra had set up for her own agenda and the Network knew nothing about it. Through Angie he also saw what Subra really was and he realised that she wasn't the woman he fell in love with.

Solomon recalled Angie strapping Armin to him. She'd given him careful instructions.

'We're approaching the rendezvous point in the next ten minutes. Don't hesitate when I tell you to go.'

Solomon wasn't even nervous about skydiving because he'd practised every week over the last six months, even with another diver attached to him. Subra didn't take chances and she'd made sure that Solomon was up to the job and would survive the mission. He'd thought it was because she cared about him.

Then, as the time came, Angie told him the release cord had come free on her parachute.

'You have to jump without me,' she'd said.

'But what about you? Come with me! The chute can hold us all!'

'Getting Armin out is priority,' she'd said. 'You go, I'll make the plane circle round to give me time to fix it, then I'll follow.'

Solomon had jumped when instructed. He landed in the water, just off target, but Subra's men were there with a boat, dragging him and the unconscious Armin out before they could get into difficulty.

'Angie had some trouble...' he'd explained.

They waited to see the plane circle back. At the right moment Angie had leapt out, but the parachute didn't open. She plummeted fast. Solomon couldn't watch. She'd been so brave and Solomon knew that in the end she'd sacrificed herself for the mission.

Even though the boat went out to search for her, they never found her body.

The plane had been set a new course and it continued on. Solomon didn't know where she'd programmed it to come down, or if it would even reach that point. As the men rode away from the rendezvous area, he put it from his mind with thoughts of seeing Subra again. After what she'd made him do, he was no longer sure how he felt about her.

After that, he and Armin were bundled onto yet another flight and brought to this place. All he knew now was that he was somewhere in Israel. Until today, he hadn't seen Subra for a long time. Three years away from her direct influence was a long time, and Solomon had built another life until she activated him.

Now, as Solomon assesses his feelings for her, there is a knock at his cabin door. He gets up from the uncomfortable bunk. He opens the door to see Subra there. She's changed her clothes.

'Come on,' she says.

She takes him to her car. 'Get in. You're coming with me now.'

Solomon does as she says. He sees himself as a puppet and she is holding his strings. He's never been able to resist Subra or refuse to do anything she's asked. And now he really knows what she's capable of, he is also afraid of her.

Subra gets into the car beside him and so does one of the

security men. The car pulls away, leaving the camp behind them.

Solomon remains silent as they drive back towards Jerusalem but he stares out of the window, looking at the barren desert landscape as they approach Subra's home.

The SUV aircon dries the sweat-stained shirt on Solomon's back, temporarily soothing him while the car pulls into the compound and up to the house. The door beside him opens as soon as the vehicle stops, and Solomon steps out into the oven-hot air. Perspiration beads on his brow. His body begins to sweat again and he wipes his palms on his jeans.

Subra takes his sweaty hand and leads him inside the house and straight upstairs.

'Freshen up, Sol,' she says at the bedroom door. 'You've been through a lot, but you did a great job. Now take this as time to rest.'

Solomon goes inside. The air conditioning is on and he stands for a moment in the middle of the clean, fresh, cool room, enjoying the chill on his skin. He strips off his clothes and goes into the ensuite bathroom. He showers, washing away the desert dust. When he comes out, he finds clean clothing left on the bed.

Downstairs he wanders through the big house until he finds the kitchen. A bi-fold door opens onto a long wide garden: an oasis in the desert with bright green lawn, regularly watered. Solomon sees a row of orange trees to one side and a row of olive trees on the other. On a little patio under a broad parasol is a rattan sofa, and Subra is there, waiting for him.

'Feel better?' she asks.

The shower has helped to clear away his discomfort. Subra has changed again and her hair is damp. She's wearing a white cotton kaftan. He can see the dark ridge of her perfect nipples through the fabric. Solomon remembers why he's done everything she ever asked of him. He loves her and yes, there is need, a hunger for her that he had almost forgotten in his enforced separation from her.

'Come to me, my boy,' she says.

Trembling like a junkie ready to get his next fix, Solomon falls to his knees before her. She is his queen; a goddess. Her eyes are warm as she gazes into his upturned face and her welcoming lips meet his.

Chapter Thirty-Five

MICHAEL

'An interesting twist has occurred,' Ray says as we gather in his office around the conference table. He pauses for impact, making sure he has our full attention. 'We confirmed yesterday that the corpse found in the boot of her car was indeed Angela Carter.'

'How was she identified?' I ask.

'Carter was caught with cannabis when she was at university. She was given a warning but her fingerprints were on record,' Ray explains. 'With this new information, Brinkman was able to confirm that Carter's fingerprints were all over Astor's apartment.'

'Everywhere?' asks Beth before I do. 'And in the bedroom?'

'Yes,' says Ray.

What does this mean? Were Carter and Astor more than colleagues? Were they sleeping together?

'I'm going to need you to do a profile of Astor. I think it's safe to conclude that he and Carter's double *were* working together,' Ray says. 'Given that he knew the real Carter, and yet didn't "out" the double when she took over.'

I nod. 'Definitely. We need to explore what kind of relationship he had with the original Carter too. It might explain why she was picked.'

'Perhaps when we get into his laptop, we'll find out more,' says Beth.

But something is bothering me, I don't know why. Another hunch, another itch in the back of my head that I can't quite scratch. I have questions but they are not for my colleagues: I hope Neva can answer them. Then I can draw all of this together in one final conclusion that will help us find the flight or at least learn what happened to it.

'Was there any DNA on the toothbrush we found?' Beth asks.

'Yes,' says Ray. 'It belonged to real Angela. So no new lead there with our *doppelgänger*.'

'That's a shame,' says Beth.

I ask about the physical searches for the plane.

'Still no sign of it,' says Leon. 'It's like the Malaysia Airlines fiasco all over again. I doubt we'll ever know what happened.'

Back in my office, I receive Baker's autopsy report via email. Baker confirms my observations on Stanners's death. The only anomaly is that the man had pancreatic cancer. He wouldn't have been aware of any symptoms for a few more weeks, except for perhaps a drop in appetite, but Stanners was dying and he wouldn't have seen the year out. There is a poetic sort of justice in this that isn't lost on me: if Olive did kill her father, she probably saved him from worse suffering. I feel a strange kinship with the woman that was once Georgia Stanners and I hope she will get in touch with me in the future. And if she does, I doubt I'll tell her that Stanners was ill – why rub salt into the wound?

'I'm going out with Leon to search Minchin's house,' Beth tells me. 'I won't be back in today as I have plans this evening.'

With Ray sequestered with Brinkman, I'm left to wade through more paperwork and reports that may shed some light on our investigations. I find out all I can about the parents of Network assassins, ready to take this investigation forward. All the time worrying that these enquiries could lead to more death.

In the meantime, Brinkman, Ray, Leon and Beth are all taken up with the continued search for Zen Airlines Flight 723. I'm not holding out any hope of it being found. And the crew and passengers' disappearance will be forever buried in the need for secrecy.

When the day ends, I take the tube home as I'm in no rush to get back to another evening alone. After being stuck behind my desk all day, walking through the snaking passages of the tube station, and then from there to home, will at least give me some exercise as well as thinking time.

My mind is full of the mysteries we need to solve and as I always do, I mull over the reports, files and reams of information I've been looking through, trying to find anything that will give us a lead on either case.

On the tube, I find a seat and observe the pulse of life entering and leaving as the train stops at the stations. I people watch. There's a cute girl in a tartan coat, with a matching hat, holding onto the rail by one of the doors. A young couple get on with a baby in a buggy. I notice a man sitting further down the carriage engrossed in a popular paperback. Unlike myself he is not counting down the stops to his own exit. I idly consider that he'll be getting off at the end of the line and doesn't have to think about where the train is.

My stop, I think as the train pulls into the platform. I get up and walk to the doors. The train halts, the doors open and I leave. I feel the rustle of movement around me and glance backwards. The man with the paperback is leaving the train too. He's not looking at me, but he's equally not concealed: he's doing just what any good spy would do – hiding in plain sight. I pretend not to notice him as I climb the steps and head towards the tube exit.

My apartment is a good ten minutes' walk from the station. I stride at a normal pace until I reach the main road, stopping at the crossing. It's at this time that I can cast my eyes left and right, and I see him there again in my peripheral vision.

I'm definitely being followed.

But this is not one of the lackadaisical operatives that Archive have put on me before. This is a professional.

I take my phone out of my pocket and send Beth a text. *Tell Ray I'm onto the new tail. I thought I was trusted now?*

I press send, because I feel aggrieved. I haven't checked my apartment, but I'd believed they really had taken out the wires and I was no longer being watched. I'm annoyed that they have lied to me.

As I head home, I begin to worry that they know Neva is

back in touch. Maybe it was even MI5 that tried to capture her recently and not Network operatives. If this is so, then I somehow need to warn her that our tenuous relationship has been exposed.

My phone rings and it's Beth.

'What is this about, Mike?' she says.

'I'm being followed. But you know that,' I say. I describe the man to her.

'It's not us,' she says. 'I don't like the sound of this. Get home and stay inside. I'm going to ring Ray now.'

I hang up as the crossing lights turn red and I'm able to cross the road. Beth could be lying, but I thought I heard genuine concern in her voice. I don't take my usual route home, instead I take a long meandering journey, sticking to the main roads. I reach my street a little later than usual.

I speed up now, because the road is fairly empty, and I hurry into the building and head straight to the elevator. Before the doors close, I see the man passing the front of the building. He glances in at me. Then away.

Was I wrong? The doors close and then the lift comes to a stop on the very next floor. A woman gets inside with me. But I'm distracted and don't look at her.

What was that all about?

'I'm going up,' I say.

'That's all right,' she answers.

When I realise she has a gun in her hand, it's too late to reach for mine. She pulls aside my jacket and takes my Glock from the holster underneath as though she's always known it was there.

'Hello, Michael,' she says. 'You've been a very bad boy, haven't you?'

'That depends on how you view things,' I say. 'What do you want?'

I look right into her eyes and memorise her features. When I get myself out of this situation, I may be able to identify her.

She has a faint German accent. And a strange quirk of the lips that makes me think that she is mean or bitter. Mid-forties. Black hair pulled back in a severe ponytail. I search my memory for any recollection of her when I was under Beech's influence, but I find nothing.

'I've been sent to bring you back into the fold.' Without looking away, she reaches out and presses the button that takes the lift to the top floor.

The elevator reaches my floor, and because I'd pressed the button it stops and the doors open. Her eyes skitter to the landing and at that moment I take my chance, and throw myself at her, knocking the gun from her hands. It flies out of the lift and across the corridor and so does my Glock. We tussle and fight. I find the moves that the Network taught me from childhood coming back, as I respond to her, matching blow for blow. I smash her face against the side of the lift, then throw myself out as the doors start to close, blocking her inside.

Her foot is part way through the door though and so they close on it, and then start to open again. I kick her foot and move it inside the lift. She seems stunned, though is moving as though to get up. The door closes on her, blocking her from my view.

My gun is on the floor. I pick it up and take hers too, putting it in my pocket. It's likely she'll be off on the next floor and will come back down after me. I run through the fight in my mind again. She was tough and determined. If I want to get away, it's possible I'll have to kill her. The assassin in me stirs. I feel my emotions going cold. Beech's training will always be part of me and I can and will kill without remorse if the situation calls for it.

I hurry to the stairs to wait for her to come down, but as I open the door to the stairwell, I find myself looking at the man from the train who is coming up the stairs. He's no longer holding a book: he's clutching a gun. I wasn't mistaken after all.

I fire two shots at him, and he dives away, tumbling down the stairwell. I go back onto the landing, taking this as my safest option. Just then the lift returns, the doors open, and the woman comes out, gun blazing. She obviously had a backup weapon! I throw myself back through the door to the stairs, firing at her as I go.

There is a yelp on the landing from one of my neighbours. She screams that she's 'calling the police' and I hope she does. I fire a couple of shots down the stairs again to the lower floor in an attempt to pin the man down. Then I run up the next flight to the floor above, taking two steps at a time. On the next landing I bang on the nearest apartment door.

'MI5 – open up.'

No one answers and I move to the next apartment. I'm about to kick in the final door, when my pursuers reach the corridor.

The woman fires a warning shot at me: I'm trapped. Even with the best training it's hard to avoid bullets when you have nowhere to run. My training kicks in: *When is doubt, pretend to be defeated...*

'Get in the lift,' she says to me as she approaches. 'Try anything again and I'll kill you.'

The man pulls the gun out of my hands and pushes me inside. They both get in with me, guns trained for a direct hit. I know I'm not getting out of this as easily as last time but I still watch for an opportunity.

The lift travels upwards once more, and I wonder what's waiting for me on the top floor.

'I assume you're from the Network,' I say as the lift reaches its destination. 'Can I ask where you're taking me?'

'You'll know soon enough,' says the man.

The lift doors open, and they pull me out, then lead me towards the roof stairs at the far end of the corridor, past the stairs that could take me downwards.

I run it through my mind, how and when I can make my break for it. But once I pass the stairs there's no going back. I feel the gun in my back, pressed against my spine. One bullet and I'll be crippled. I have to comply.

Outside I hear sirens approaching: someone on the lower floors must have called the police. The man grabs my arm and yanks me into the stairwell; the woman brings up the rear.

It's dark on the stairs. The man flicks the light switch but nothing happens.

'Hurry,' says the woman.

I can hear a whirring sound above my head as we begin

to climb the final flight of steps to the rooftop, and I realise that this has been the plan all along. Above there's a helicopter, waiting to take me elsewhere.

I can't go back to the House. An odious panic surges up into my chest and I fight to quell this rush of weakening fear.

I decide then that I won't be controlled by the Network again. Even if they kill me.

I fall into a roll, taking the woman down with me. There's a blast of gunfire above, but it doesn't hit us. Instead, I see the man stumble and fall, as though someone has hit him from behind. He tumbles down behind us. The woman's head cracks against the concrete wall. She falls limp. My arm is grabbed again.

'Come on,' says Neva, pulling me to my feet.

We run back onto the top corridor towards the stairs, but she pulls me past them. She leads me to the last apartment on the floor. The door springs open after she taps on it.

'This is Janine,' she says.

I recognise the woman. She sometimes leaves the building early in the morning and I occasionally speak to her in the lift.

Janine closes the door behind us, blocking out the sudden burst of chaos as the police reach the top floor.

Neva grabs me and hugs me.

'So… Who…?'

'She's been keeping an eye on you,' Neva says. 'For me.'

'You'll be okay,' Janine says. She has a Russian-sounding accent. 'Go in the bedroom. I'm going to open the door and be a concerned citizen.'

Neva leads me to Janine's bedroom.

'Who is she?' I ask.

'Former KGB. I helped her get out a few years ago. She works for me on occasion.'

I sit down on the bed. 'What the fuck…?'

'When the cops have cleaned up those bastards, we can slip away. I'm getting you out of here.'

'I can't. My job,' I say.

'Michael, that was the Network. They were claiming you back and they won't stop until they have you. You have to come with me. There's no choice. You must see that.'

'MI5 will protect me,' I say.

'What, by having you followed by inadequately trained, half-arsed agents?'

I'm about to answer when Neva shushes me.

She stands at the door and we hear Janine's concerned call down the corridor. She now has a fluent English accent. 'What's going on out here?'

'It's okay, miss. We have the culprits. Please stay inside your apartment.'

A short time later, the police knock on the door and question Janine to see if she saw or heard anything. When they've gone, she comes to the bedroom.

'They're clearing out. But give yourself time,' she says to Neva.

'I'll need to get some stuff from my apartment,' I say.

'No,' Janine says. 'MI5 are in there. They'll be looking for you.'

'Give me your phone,' Neva says.

I don't ask why but I take it out of my pocket. The screen

is damaged, but I can see I have six missed calls from Beth. Neva takes it from my trembling fingers. Then she opens the window in Janine's bedroom and drops the phone out.

'If they are looking for you, they'll find that and assume you were taken when that helicopter took off. I knew there was a reason why I didn't shoot the pilot,' Neva says.

She tells me to rest for a while and she goes into the other room with Janine. But I can't rest. It doesn't make sense. Why would the Network come for me now?

I get off the bed and go into the living room, Neva and Janine are talking in whispers by the kitchen door.

'Why now?' I ask her.

'You're a risk to them if they leave you out in the cold. You know too much and you're helping MI5 with a lot of subconscious knowledge,' Neva explains.

'But they've left me alone for six months,' I say. 'So why didn't they come for me before?'

'The Network were in chaos. They're regrouping, faster now since they appointed a new chair,' Neva says.

'How do you know that?' I ask.

'I have my moles, just as they have theirs. Michael, there's something you should know. There is a spy in the ranks at MI5. Another sleeper agent. They will have told the committee something that's sparked this move to take you back,' she says.

'What could they have said? That I'm back and trusted now? Or I was before this?'

'I don't know, but I suspect you've uncovered something that they don't want you to share with your colleagues,' Neva says.

I shake my head. 'No. There's nothing. No secret that I know other than what you've told me, and I can't share that with my colleagues for obvious reasons.'

Neva thinks for a moment. 'It may be something they think you know then. Michael, have you been working on anything else, other than the flight disappearance?'

'I've been searching for information about other spies, but my colleagues know about all my findings. I've been completely transparent. What I found led us to Olive Redding's family.'

Neva says, 'It can't be that.'

Yet I'm aware that further investigation of the parents of missing children may have brought us closer to finding the Network's committee.

'What was Stanners to the Network?' I ask her now.

Neva shakes her head, 'I don't know, Michael. You know I don't. I'm trying to find out all I can but those who know keep it to themselves for fear of reprisal.'

'They didn't try to silence him for nothing,' I say.

'Well, whoever he was, it may have been someone in Archive who informed the Network you were on to him. For the moment you can't return to Archive. Not until we discover who the traitor is.'

She says this to reassure me that my life might be normal once again if this puzzle is solved. But somehow, I just can't imagine it. My work life has been turned upside down again and Neva as always is in the centre of it. Was it just a coincidence that she happened to be in the right place at the right time? I can't help suspecting her of being involved in this too.

Chapter Thirty-Six

KRITTA

Kritta had woken first in the stairwell. She had found her colleague, Stefan, on the floor beside her. He too had been knocked out. She shook him, ordering him to wake.

'We need to get to the roof!' she'd said. Stefan came round but not before Kritta heard the helicopter above take off, leaving them behind.

'Looks like we are on our own,' she had said. 'Get up! Find your gun.'

The door to the stairwell was yanked open before either of them could find their weapons.

'Freeze!' said a cop. He was armed, wearing Kevlar and even a riot mask covering his face. More armed men backed him up.

Kritta had known it wasn't worth the fight – they couldn't win. Kritta and Stefan had put their hands up. The police had swarmed around them. They were cuffed and pulled from the stairway and out onto the corridor. From there they were bundled into the lift, while some of the other officers went upstairs.

Kritta had smiled then, because the helicopter was long gone.

'I'm injured,' she had said as they pushed them both into the back of a police van. 'You have to get me a doctor.'

There were two officers with them, one driver, one accompanying.

'We don't have to get you anything,' said the older police officer.

He had slammed the back of the van shut, and then climbed into the front.

Now the van pulls away from the apartment and heads downtown to the nearest, most secure gaol.

'MI5 want a word with you,' the officer says before he bangs the partition closed between the driver's compartment and their new cage.

'This is very inconvenient,' says Kritta.

There is a sliver of drying blood on the side of her head and staining her right cheek. Her head throbs from the concussion, but she shakes away the pain because she's been through worse.

'Another double-cross, Kritta,' Stefan says. 'I thought your source said this would be easy.'

'Shut up,' says Kritta.

The van turns off the main road and takes a back route, avoiding the worst of the London traffic.

The police officer sighs to himself as they drive. He turns to the driver, 'I hate London traffic. All these back ways we have to take just to—'

At that moment all four of the van's tyres are blown out. The driver struggles with the wheel and briefly loses control. The van swerves and grazes the side of two parked cars before skidding to a halt.

There is sudden movement outside and gas grenades are thrown into the front of the van, smashing the side windows. The two officers cover their faces from the shower of glass and then start coughing as the gas takes effect.

In the back, Kritta and Stefan drop to the floor and cover their faces as best as they can. They had been expecting something like this.

The back of the van is pulled open and two men wearing gasmasks climb inside. Kritta struggles, holding her breath as much as possible as the men bodily move them out of the van and into the fresh air. Stefan is coughing and retching on the road as they are hurried to a black SUV and pushed inside.

The car speeds away, leaving the police van open and the cops now cuffed and in the back.

One of their rescuers passes Kritta a phone.

Kritta presses it to her ear and then she hears the soft exhale of Annalise. 'Well?'

'He got away,' she says. 'Neva ambushed us.'

'I see,' says Annalise. 'Now they'll run. It will be only a matter of time before one of ours spots them. In a way they are easier to find together than they are apart.'

'I thought the idea was to capture Michael,' says Kritta.

'It is. But that will be simpler when he's away from England and MI5 are no longer able to back him up.'

'What now?' says Kritta.

'I have people in all the right places, don't worry your concussed little head about it.'

Annalise hangs up and Kritta is left feeling insecure. She looks at the men sitting in the back of the car with them. She doesn't know any of them. Are they loyal to the committee? Or are they controlled only by Annalise?

The answer comes a short time later when they arrive at their destination, a nondescript house in an anonymous backstreet of North London.

'Annalise says you're both to stay here,' says one of the men.

'I'd rather get back to my own house,' she says.

'For now, this will be your home,' says the man. His tone gives no room for further discussion or negotiation.

Kritta and Stefan are taken into the house and given a bedroom each. Kritta finds bars over the windows and the door is locked behind her as she's shoved inside. She looks around at the beautifully furnished room but all she sees is a prison.

She wonders if this was Annalise's plan all along. Someone betrayed them tonight after all. Perhaps she was the one who let Neva know of the attack...

Kritta paces the room, wondering what the ultimate

game plan is and having no idea at all where this is going to end. She thought by being chosen for the committee she was safe from retirement. Beech had promised. And she'd done everything she could to back him up, follow his rules – even given up a child to the House.

There is regret and loss, and a bitter anger surges up inside her: an emotion she has denied herself for years. That bastard Beech. Why did he have to go and get himself *Getötet*? His death had left the Network in a complete mess.

Kritta sits down on the bed. She is tired and drained, and the extraction of Michael should have been easy but it was one fuck-up after another. Not helped when Stefan was observed by Michael. She should have known better than to trust him too.

The door is unlocked and opened and one of Annalise's men comes in with a food tray.

'Can't have you starving in here,' he says.

'Why am I being held?' she asks. 'You have no right. I'm a member of the committee.'

'You're not being held,' says the guard. 'You're being protected.'

'From what?' she asks.

'From doing anything foolish,' the man smiles.

Kritta runs through a scenario of how she will bring him down. She has a desire to snap his neck, but she notices then that the other guard standing by the door, gun trained in her direction.

'Thank you for the food,' she says.

When the guards leave, Kritta gets up. She begins to open drawers and cupboards, looking for anything that will help her escape. After all, the cops took her lock picks and the knife she had hidden in her boot. But the drawers are empty and the little bathroom off the room doesn't have a window, not even a mirror she can make use of to create a weapon. It seems that Annalise has thought of everything.

Chapter Thirty-Seven

MICHAEL

When Neva thinks it is safe to leave, she comes and wakes me. I'd been determined not to fall asleep, but in the end, I was exhausted, and I'd nodded off on Janine's bed.

'Time to go,' she says.

Now we leave the apartment and I discover Neva has a key for the service lift, and surmise this was her route to enter whenever she came looking for me.

We exit at the back of the building and there, under a stack of cardboard, Neva uncovers a motorbike that she'd hidden earlier. She hands me a helmet and climbs on the motorbike, turns the engine on and the Harley Davison purrs to life.

'Get on and put your arms around me. I know you want to,' she teases.

The surreal element of the moment is not lost on me. Surely in all good spy stories the man rescues the woman?

But not in our story – Neva is the one that keeps protecting me. Thank God I don't have an ego about it!

I put the helmet on and sit behind her on the bike. Within minutes we're speeding through the early morning London streets.

She drives out of the city.

'I have a temporary place here,' she explains when we reach Kingston upon Thames. 'But tomorrow we move on.'

She parks the bike up on the main road, leaves the keys in the ignition, and we dump the helmets back on top of the seat.

'Won't we need this?' I ask.

'No.'

I don't ask her plan as we walk across the bridge that crosses the Thames to arrive at a sort of lido on the other side. She leads me then to a small cabin. As I reach the door, I recognise the view from the picture she'd sent me with the boats: she'd been here all along. So that confirms that she wasn't at Stanners's estate, just as she said she wasn't. Her transparency is reassuring. Sending me a photo like this could have compromised her safety, after all. It wouldn't take much for an experienced investigator to find her location from this photograph.

'Come in,' she says.

I follow her inside and see by the signs of life within that she has been holed up here for a while.

She takes my hand and leads me to the bedroom.

'Let's get some sleep,' she says.

She strips down to her pants and pulls on a little vest top. I take it as a sign that I'm not invited to mess with her right now and sleep is all she has in mind. I feel exhausted. But I'm wired. My life has taken another weird twist, and the thought that everything I'd been working for is now lost to me pushes around the edges of my mind with paranoid insistence.

I strip to my underwear and we both get into the bed. I lie on my back, hoping she'll curl up to me, but Neva stays on her side of the bed and is asleep in seconds. I listen to her breathing as the last dregs of adrenaline leave and my racing heart begins to calm down.

Everything is completely fucked up. I'm certain that my position in Archive is no longer tenable. And with the Network determined to pull me back in, I see no choice but to go to ground with Neva. The thought of being with her permanently doesn't worry me. It's the loss of everything I've ever known that does. I turn over in the bed and look at Neva's beautiful face: the strain of the day has disappeared from her resting expression, and she looks young and sweet and innocent. I find myself daydreaming about who and what she could have been if the Network hadn't got their hands on her in the first place.

With her grace she could have been a dancer.

As I drift off to sleep, in my mind's eye I see her pirouetting. She's on a large stage and the audience are on their feet cheering and clapping as she dances to the music of their applause. I take this into my dream, and find myself standing in the wings, watching and clapping along with everyone else.

It is afternoon when Neva wakes me. She's up and dressed and I didn't hear her move.

'Come on,' she says. 'We have a flight to catch.'

I get up and shower and then find clean clothes in the bedroom, which I pull on.

'Here's your new passport,' she says.

I pick up the passport, open it and see my photograph. I'm called Richard Ellison and I'm American.

'That's my real passport photograph,' I say, rubbing my thumb over it. It's a professional job and indistinguishable to me from a real passport. 'It looks like you planned this?' I say with a frown.

'I'm always prepared,' she says.

In the living room are two suitcases and two flight bags.

'Where are we going?' I ask.

'Amsterdam,' she says. 'First.'

'Why there?'

'I have a safe house,' Neva says.

'I can't do this,' I tell her. 'I have to get in touch with Archive.'

'We've been through this. You're not safe,' Neva says.

'If there is a mole, like you say, they need to know there's a spy among them,' I say. 'Again!'

'Let's get away first, and then perhaps you can send them information. When I know more,' Neva says.

Another passport sits on top of one of the flight bags. As Neva pulls on her boots, I pick it up and take a look inside. Her picture – another identity. Neva as she really looks, not in one of her disguises. Here she is called Amanda Ellison.

'We're married?' I say.

She shrugs.

'Well? If I'm questioned, what do I say?'

'Married, two kids who are with their grandparents while we take a second honeymoon. We're doing Europe. Customs records show that we came into England a few days ago, and now we are moving on as planned.'

'How did you arrange all that?' I ask.

She raises her eyebrows at me. 'A girl doesn't give up all her secrets.'

'Seriously? You want me to trust you? Then tell me how all of this is possible?'

She zips up her second boot. 'Entry into the UK is mostly computerised. Photographs of new arrivals are taken. If it's on a computer network, it can be hacked. I have the best hackers working for me. Keep cool and we won't be questioned. They aren't interested in who's leaving, just who's arriving.'

I have a bad feeling in the pit of my stomach. The last thing I want to do is run away from my life. The thought of trying to leave the country on a false passport horrifies me, and yet I know already that these exist. It's something Archive is likely to look into if a false identity is embroiled in a case, but otherwise not our area. And here I am planning to break the law I swore to uphold.

I look at the name tags on the suitcases and find that they belong to the Ellisons too.

'What's in there?' I ask.

'Just clothes,' she says. 'You can't travel without essentials.'

I don't take her word for it. Instead, I open one of the

cases and check what's inside. It's neatly packed. Clothing, shoes, wash bag (I note that the shaving and aftershave brands I use are inside it).

I zip up the bag and then check hers. It's the same innocuous luggage, only a female version with dresses, shoes and make-up.

'What are you looking for in there?' she asks. 'Knives? Guns? Bombs?'

'Well, you're never without your knife,' I say.

'Don't worry about that,' she says. 'I have different ways of getting my weapons when I need them.'

I feel nauseous when she says this. I want to demand she tells me everything. But do I really want to know? The sheer organisation of this whole thing makes me uncomfortable. She was so *ready*. Despite my belief in her the previous evening, I'm suspicious. How did she know that the Network were gearing up to go after me?

I remind myself that if it hadn't been for Neva, I'd be in their hands right now, but it doesn't reassure me much

'I can't do this,' I say again. 'I can't just leave. What about my sister? I haven't even seen my niece yet.'

'If I were you, I'd put all of that behind me. Michael, you're on the run now, whether you like it or not.'

'No,' I say, determined to find an alternative. But for all my smarts, I can't think of any way I can go back to normal after the attempt to take me from my home.

'I don't know why you're so resistant,' she says. 'It's important that the Network never get to you. You know that. Michael, I don't want anything to happen to you.'

I hear what she says but can't shake the feeling that

something isn't right with this whole state of affairs. Less than two weeks ago, she begged me to leave with her, and even though I'd said no, she'd prepared for it anyway. Why wouldn't I be suspicious of that?

'The taxi's due to arrive soon. We need to get across the bridge with our luggage.'

'Okay. But tell me the truth. How did you know they were coming for me?'

'Janine has cameras on the landings. Yours and hers. She saw them come down from the rooftop. As it happens, I was waiting for you in your apartment. She messaged me. I went upstairs, saw the helicopter and knew what was happening. That's why I put the light out in the stairwell and waited to ambush them. I told you she works for me. I've been trying to protect you.'

Her explanation is plausible. But I feel distrustful nonetheless. It's all just so convenient and gives her what she wanted in forcing me to run. And then there is the motorbike too. Ready and waiting for our escape. Two helmets…

'As for this… I knew you'd have to leave at some point. Especially when I had news of the mole in Archive. The Network are moving in on everyone that's not towing their line. The only solution is you get out of Dodge.'

'Everyone?' I say.

'Yes. There's an assassin called Vasquez who's been chasing me down for months. My informants tell me he got to some operatives that had used Beech's death to skip away. After that the rest knew if they didn't play along…' She shrugs. 'It's kill or die right now, Michael. No one is safe. Not unless we go to ground, and I mean really lose ourselves. Now can we leave?'

'Jesus. *Mia!*'

'What?'

'My sister. If I'm not safe, then neither is she!'

Neva looks away. '*Shit.* Why couldn't this just be simple?' she says. 'Just for once.'

I take the burner phone she gave me and dial Beth's number. She answers after a couple of rings.

'Hello? Who is this?'

'Beth? It's me. The Network came after me last night. I believe they are now after Mia.'

'Where are you, Mike?' she asks.

'Safe for now. But can you put a stronger detail on Mia? You've been keeping an eye on her, haven't you?' I say.

'Mike … we … took detail off her months ago.'

I hang up. Neva takes the phone and goes through the usual process of removing the sim. I watch her do it, noting how she's almost on autopilot and isn't really thinking about what she's doing. Then she goes outside. When she comes back the phone is gone.

She picks up her suitcase and flight bag. 'You've done what you can: they know she's in trouble. They'll sort it,' she says.

'Where's my gun?' I ask.

'Michael! You can't go there! We have a flight… We are leaving *now*!'

I find my gun stowed in the bedside cabinet with my spare clip. I put it in my pocket and head for the door.

'*Shit*!' says Neva again. 'Can't we just phone and warn her? Send an email?'

'You don't understand, she doesn't know anything. She's not like … *us*. She won't know how to hide or protect herself.'

I walk out of the cabin, leaving the luggage and flight bags and the new passport. A few minutes later Neva is following me across the bridge.

The bike is still where she left it: who knew that there were so few criminals in Kingston?

I pull on the helmet and take up the driver's position. Neva reaches me as I switch the engine on. She takes the other helmet and pulls it on.

'You know how to drive this?' she asks.

'I had the same training as you did,' I say.

She climbs on the back behind me, and I turn the bike in the road, and head off in the direction of my sister's home.

Even though it's some time since I learnt to ride a motorbike, I know exactly what I'm doing. That's one good thing about the Network's conditioning, it can always be called on when I need it.

'I hope you know I'm breaking one of my own cardinal rules here,' Neva says in my ear. 'I never use the same ride twice.'

Chapter Thirty-Eight

BETH

'Michael? Mike?' Beth says before she realises he's hung up.

She tries to dial the number back but all she gets is a mailbox. The robotic voice that asks her to leave a message is not Michael's.

Ray and Leon are both out, though no one has told her where, and so Beth is in the office alone. Sending a detail to Mia Cusick's house is beyond Beth's authority. She dials Ray but also gets voicemail. Then, because the urgency she's heard in Michael's voice worries her, she dials Leon.

'Trace the phone number,' he tells her when he answers. 'Let's find him and get to the bottom of this.'

'But what about Mia?' Beth asks.

'I'll speak to Ray when I can and get back to you.'

'Where is Ray?'

'Dealing with the local plods. Michael's attackers escaped last night on the way to the police station.'

'How?' Beth asks.

'Someone jumped the police van. It was found with the driver and the officer travelling with him tied up and in the back. They are okay, other than the discomfort of the pepper gas.'

Beth tries Michael's number again from a landline, using a tracer. It goes to voicemail again and so tracing isn't possible. Then she puts the number into their system. As expected, the phone isn't registered to anyone but she can at least access service provider information. She tries to triangulate the last location from the call, but the information comes up inconclusive. Somewhere in Surrey just isn't helpful.

She sends Ray a text, asking if he's spoken to Leon. When she gets no reply, Beth looks up Mia and Ben's address. It's on the system, because they had been keeping an eye on Michael's sister, but because the Network had left them alone all this time, they'd become complacent and believed that there was no reason to continue watching them.

The night before, Beth had sent out a crew to aid Michael, as well as the local police, but Michael's disappearance had concerned Ray a great deal. That morning, Michael's security access had been revoked. Beth had fought for him, again. But it was no use.

'Why?' she had said in the end. 'If he's been taken by the Network, that's not his fault…'

'Security is our priority, Beth. Besides we don't know if the Network did take him. I have my doubts on that score,' Ray had said.

'What do you know that I don't?' Beth asked.

Ray hadn't explained himself and Beth had been annoyed that he was keeping things from her when it was likely he'd shared all of his doubts with Leon.

But now, after speaking to Michael, she knew Ray was right: Michael had gone to ground as Ray had suspected. She could hear Ray's response to this news as clearly as if he were speaking to her.

'Unless he turns himself in,' Ray would say. 'We can only assume he's gone rogue.'

Beth thought about how she would fight for Michael again, planning her speech to Ray when he got round to calling her back. She'd tell him that Michael was 'running scared' and no surprise since those bastards almost took him.

'Really? But how did he get away?' Leon would ask, always sticking the knife in and twisting just enough to cause significant damage.

Beth just wouldn't have an answer for them this time. She'd be left out in the cold again, Michael's unofficial cheerleader, because she wouldn't be able to explain Michael's escape. She could guess who was helping him though, and so could Ray and Leon.

Her phone rings again and Beth answers.

'Hi,' says Elliot.

'Oh! It's you,' she says.

'Expecting someone else?' Elliot says.

'No. It's just . . . I have an issue. Can I call you back?'

'No problem,' he says. 'Unless this is, "I enjoyed last night, but I'm going nowhere near your penis again."'

Beth laughs. 'Oh my God. I'm sorry. That did seem like I

was giving you the brush-off. But seriously, I have a work issue and I'm waiting for my boss to call me.'

'Let him call the landline,' Elliot says.

Beth finds herself smiling. Though it wasn't official, she'd started seeing Elliot a few days ago and her life was already better. Even so she feels guilty about it. While the others were responding to Michael's crisis, she'd passed the buck, claiming childcare issues. The truth was, she was in bed with Elliot, having the best time she'd had in years.

He'd invited her round to his place, made her bolognaise and then, when the trouble started, he'd pointed out to her that she was 'off duty'. Sending in the cops was the only thing she could reasonably do after notifying her superiors.

'It's not always your responsibility,' Elliot said.

He'd taken her mind off the guilt with a foot massage that worked up to her thighs and beyond. After that Beth had put Michael completely from her mind, only remembering a few hours later that he had been in danger. She'd checked in then and discovered that two perps had been arrested and Michael was missing – probably in the hands of the Network. The guilt was terrible. She felt she'd let him down, all to get laid. While Elliot slept, oblivious that she was still worried, she'd tried to call Michael's mobile. It kept ringing out, then going to voicemail.

Worried, she'd made a few more calls and set in motion the trace element on his phone. She learned that it was still at his address. The cops found it outside, smashed up. After that she couldn't go back to sleep. At that point it seemed to confirm that Michael had been abducted. Other MI5 officers had been sent in to search. His apartment was scoured, but there was no sign of him.

The duty officer told her they had caught some of those responsible, but Michael was still missing.

'What time do you finish?' Elliot asks now, bringing her mind back to him and the fun they'd had the night before.

Beth looks at her watch. 'I can leave soon. But I need to deal with this one problem first,' she says.

'Dinner?' he says.

'Sounds good,' Beth says.

Never would she have let Callum distract her from a work issue, and Beth marks the difference. Maybe she did work too hard? Perhaps she was entitled to some downtime?

'I'll text you when and where,' Elliot says.

Beth says goodbye and then hangs up. She tries Ray's phone again before calling it a night.

'Beth,' Ray says, answering at last. 'I've just authorised a team to get over to Mia's house.'

'So you think she's in real danger?'

'Whoever went after Michael meant business,' Ray says. 'I'm glad you heard from him. At least he isn't in enemy hands. But if he calls again, you have to persuade him to come in.'

'I will. I should go to Mia's too,' Beth says. 'Someone from the team—'

'Leon and I are already on the way. We'll handle this so don't worry. I'll keep you in the loop,' Ray says.

'Okay,' says Beth and for once she is relieved.

Just then, Elliot texts to say to meet him at an Italian

restaurant. She looks at her watch, and realises she just has time to go home and change. Turning her phone to mute, she locks up the office. Mia will be fine; Ray and Leon will make sure. The boys are with their dad and she has the evening to herself. Pushing Mia and Michael from her mind Beth thinks instead of the night ahead. She can't think of a better way to spend it than with Elliot.

Chapter Thirty-Nine

MIA

'I actually got back into my jeans today,' Mia says as her husband, Ben, arrives home that evening.

'Wow! Babe! Look at you!' Ben says. He kisses her and holds her, letting his hands stray on the tight denim over her bottom. 'Very nice too.'

Mia pushes him away, laughing. 'Go and get your daughter. She's in her pram in the back garden.'

Ben passes through the house and into the kitchen. At the back door he finds Freya's pram, a flynet over it to protect the baby from being bothered by insects. He looks down at his tiny little girl, then, removing the net, picks her up and brings her inside.

'I opened a beer for you,' Mia says. 'It's on the coffee table.'

'Really? What are we celebrating?' Ben asks.

'Do we need a reason?' They look at each other. Ben kisses her on the lips. They cuddle, the baby between them.

But Ben's expression tells Mia that he'd like some time alone with his wife.

'Save that thought for later,' Mia says. 'Now, go and relax, dinner won't be long and this little girl will need her feed too before she'll settle.'

Ben moves away reluctantly and Freya gives a little groan as though she too objects to the parting.

'Hey sweetie-pie,' Ben coos to her. 'Come and talk to Daddy.'

He takes the baby into the living room and, securing her in the crook of his arm, he reaches for the remote control and turns on the television.

Mia and Ben live just outside London on the outskirts of Cambridge. Their little cottage is surrounded by a few acres of farmland. They'd bought the house a few years earlier when it was a rundown, neglected former rental property. Renovations had taken up the first few years of their marriage, and just before Mia had fallen pregnant the year before, they had reached a point where almost everything was done. That was when they discovered the final bedroom had to become a nursery.

Though currently on maternity leave, Mia works in human resources for a large export firm, and she loves her job. Until Freya came along, she hadn't imagined that she'd want to just be at home and spend her time as a full-time mother.

How wonderful life is, Mia thinks. She couldn't have imagined what a wonderful father Ben would be. He'd taken paternity leave the first two weeks, and as Mia'd had to have a C-section, she'd really needed him home in those early days. When Ben had to return to work, it was hard on him not spending time with them both every day, but they'd got into a good routine, and it still felt that they shared the care of their daughter.

Every evening was lovely. Ben's return home was always wonderful as he took control of Freya while Mia made dinner. She can hear him now, chatting to their daughter as she switches on the oven and puts the tuna pasta bake she's made inside for its final cook. Half an hour and they'll be able to sit together and eat.

She's humming as she pours herself a glass of water. No wine for her until after Freya's feed. Then she picks up the glass and goes to join Ben in the living room.

'What's that?' she says. 'Outside.'

A loud droning sound can be heard outside, growing louder.

'Someone calling by?' says Ben. 'Sounds like a motorbike.'

Mia looks out of the window as the bike pulls up in front of the house. She watches as two people, a man and a woman, get off and begin to remove their helmets.

'It's Michael,' she says.

'Really? That's a surprise,' says Ben.

'That's strange, he never turns up uninvited,' Mia says. Ben notices the change of tone, the strangeness in her voice as she says this. 'Wonder what's going on?'

'Only one way to find out,' Ben says.

Mia goes into the hallway and opens the front door. She smiles at Michael as he approaches, but Michael is frowning and he looks worried.

'Hey, what's up?' she says.

'Mia, you've got to pack a bag. We're getting you out of here.'

'What are you talking about?' Mia says.

'You're in danger. You have to listen to me. All of you need to come with me right now!'

Michael stops approaching. His eyes are looking beyond her.

Mia turns. Ben is standing at the end of the hall. He's holding Freya in one hand and a gun in the other.

'*Ben*?' she says.

'You shouldn't have come here, Mike,' Ben says.

'Mia – walk out to me, slowly,' Michael says.

'What's going on? Ben, why are you…? Where did you *get* that?' Mia says.

She's trembling and in shock as she flounders in the doorway between Ben and Michael.

'Ben, I don't want to hurt you,' says Michael. 'I'm taking Mia and Freya. You can go back to your handlers, or you can come with us. You see, I don't blame you for this. I know what *their* conditioning does to people.'

'I'm sorry, Michael, I can't let you take my family. You see they are safe with me. You're the traitor. You're the poison. I can't let you contaminate them,' Ben says.

Mia walks back towards Ben. 'You're scaring me, Ben. Give me my little girl.'

'Get behind me,' Ben says.

'Stop it!' Mia says. 'He's my brother!'

'How long have you worked for them?' Michael asks.

'You shouldn't have come here,' Ben says. 'You've endangered us all.'

Mia reaches Ben. 'Give me Freya,' she says again.

He meets her eyes and Mia has never seen such coldness in them before. She's scared.

'Give me my baby, right now!' she says.

His eyes flick back to Michael and she senses a shift as Ben weighs up his chances while holding the baby.

'Please...' she says. She's crying and confused. 'Let me take her out of this...'

Freya begins to sob then as though she feels her mother's distress. Ben holds her out and lets Mia take her, but his eyes remain on Michael.

'Stand behind me. I won't let anything happen to either of you,' he says again. 'You'll go away if you know what's best for you, Michael. Because you know I won't let you take them.'

Mia backs away behind Ben. The kitchen is behind her, the garden beyond. Her first instinct is to run out the back and take Freya to safety and figure this all out later. She's torn between her brother and her husband. She thought she knew them both, but now she knows that something is seriously wrong with one or both of them.

She reaches the back door and comes face to face with Neva.

Neva presses her fingers against her lips. Mia steps back, surprised and confused. She sees the gun in Neva's hand. She pulls Freya close to her chest with trembling hands.

Neva points to the back door and indicates that Mia should leave. Mia looks at Ben, then back at Neva. She's terrified and disorientated. The bottom has just fallen out of her world. But she needs to protect her child at all costs. She hurries outside and places Freya back into the safety of her pram, then she turns around just in time to see Neva sneaking up on Ben. The woman swings the gun at him and all Mia can do is scream a warning.

Ben turns and receives a glancing blow from Neva's gun. Ben's gun fires and Neva ducks. There's a splutter of splinters as the bullet buries itself in the kitchen door frame.

Mia runs back inside towards the fight. She sees Neva take her husband down with practised ease, and Michael running inside.

Freya is crying louder now, an almost hysterical sobbing that Mia can't bear to hear.

'What is happening?' she yells. She feels like she's losing her mind as she sees her brother grabbing her husband up off the floor. Michael and Neva pull Ben into the kitchen. They throw him down onto one of the kitchen chairs and, before Mia can object, Neva cable-ties Ben's arms behind his back.

'Mia, run!' Ben says.

'It's okay,' Michael tells her. He stows his gun now that Ben has been disarmed.

'I don't understand,' Mia sobs.

'We haven't got much time,' Michael says. 'Neva, take Mia, get some essentials for her and the baby. Mia, *listen* to me… It's too much to explain but you've got to trust me.'

'Don't trust him,' Ben says. 'He's a sleeper agent. He works for a corporation called the Network. He's been activated again. I'd sworn I'd protect you… I'm sorry,' Ben says. 'Please, Mike, if there's anything of you left in there. Don't do this. Don't take them. You know what they'll do to Freya.'

'You treacherous bastard. *Me*? Give them to the Network? They came after me yesterday. I'm here to take them to safety. Don't try to confuse her with your lies,' Michael says.

'Will someone tell me what is fucking going on?' Mia screams.

They all fall silent.

'I'm MI6,' Ben says. 'A few years ago, as part of an investigation, I discovered you and Michael were somehow involved. Though until Mike was triggered, I didn't know the extent of it.'

'Liar,' says Michael. He raises his fist to strike Ben. 'I'll get the truth from you.'

'Check my pocket…' Ben says. 'It'll show you I'm telling the truth. Then you have to listen to me, Mia.'

Chapter Forty

MICHAEL

'D on't try anything,' I say to Ben, removing my gun once more from its holster. 'I will shoot you.'

'Please,' Mia says. 'There's no need for that...'

Mia reaches into Ben's jacket pocket and pulls out his wallet. Neva takes it from her and rifles through. Inside is an identity badge. It says his name and shows he works for MI6.

'What the...?' says Mia.

'*Darling*. You know now. But I couldn't tell you. I really do work for MI6.'

Mia slumps down into one of the other kitchen chairs, then turns and looks around with dull, glazed eyes. 'I don't understand any of this.'

'Start talking,' I say.

Ben looks at me. I leave him tied up. He watches me, his expression wary.

'I'd been on the Network's tail for a while. I knew you were somehow connected to Beech,' Ben explains.

'Archive only discovered what was going on six months ago. Are you telling me you married my sister to spy on *us*?'

Mia presses her hand over her mouth as she tries to stifle her sobs.

'Mia. I love you. You *know* that,' Ben says to her. She doesn't answer as she shakes her head in confusion.

'Please. Tell me what this means.' She looks at me and I feel my heart breaking for her.

'You better keep talking,' I say to Ben. 'You have a lot of explaining to do.'

'I was going after your parents. Your dad was dirty, everything about the cases he let slip through his fingers told me that,' Ben explains to Mia. 'Then as time went on, I began to notice more weird things. Beech came up on our radar, and then I realised he was your godfather. I didn't think you and Mike knew anything, innocent of your parents' deeds, but I knew they were connected to whatever Beech was doing.'

I tell her the truth about the man she thought was our Uncle Andrew – how he was our real father. I explain we aren't twins, but were born on the same day to different surrogate mothers. She stares at me with wide frightened eyes.

'When I got into trouble with Archive it's because I'd discovered the truth.'

'You *married* me...' Mia says to Ben. 'We have a child. Was that all a lie?'

'No, darling. I meant it all. I fell in love with you. That's why I married you. You know that, right? I love you, Mia. But I was investigating Beech all this time. That all ended when MI5 broke Beech's hold and Michael learned the truth. It was a relief, because I thought I'd never have to be the one to expose him and your parents. I thought it had freed us until Michael turned up today.'

'That doesn't explain you coming out armed,' Mia says. 'You pointed a gun at my brother. You had our daughter in your arms!'

'I thought he'd been triggered again. That he'd come after you and Freya. I reacted in the way I had to. I was trying to protect you. Ray Martin will confirm what I've said,' Ben says.

'Ray knew about you?' I ask.

Ben nods. The wind is taken out of my sails as I feel betrayed once more. My world forever spirals out of control.

'You can't trust anyone, Michael,' Neva says as though she's reading my thoughts.

'Who are *you*?' Mia asks looking at Neva.

'She's a former Network assassin,' Ben says.

'Jesus…' Mia says. 'You brought an assassin to my home? Put that gun away, Michael.'

I holster my weapon again as Mia walks back outside and returns holding the sobbing baby.

'It's fine, baby girl. All is fine,' she whispers, kissing the tiny creature on the head.

'It doesn't change anything,' I say. 'I still need to get you away from here. The Network is pulling back all of its assets. You're no longer safe.'

'Why would they want me?' Mia says and I take a

breath, wondering just what I can tell her that won't completely ruin her life.

'You're a sleeper too,' Neva says, making the decision for me. 'All it will take is the right combination of words and you'll be doing whatever they tell you to do. But I think only Beech knew what those triggers were for you and Michael. And he's dead. It's a silver lining, but it doesn't mean they won't pull you in and try to work it out. The baby will be tested until she's five; they'll be looking for certain signs of suitability, but it's more than likely she'd be integrated into one of the Houses.'

With this information delivered, Neva goes off to check the perimeter of the house.

'What Houses?' Mia says.

I look at Ben and he shakes his head in warning: she doesn't need to know that. At least not yet.

Neva's words ring in my head: *You can't trust anyone.* I frown at Ben.

'Approaching: several army vehicles, and a black SUV,' Neva says returning to the kitchen. 'Looks like he was lying after all.'

'No!' says Ben. 'It's Ray. He called me just before I got home. It's a combined MI5 and MI6 response team. Along with local military. They are coming to take us all in.'

'If you knew he was coming, why didn't you stall for time?' I ask. 'Instead of pulling a gun on me?'

'I don't trust you. Okay?' Ben says. 'When it comes to Mia and Freya's safety, I never will.'

'We need to leave,' says Neva.

I go and take a look at the approaching vehicles. No

sirens blazing – this could be all a trap. But I'm inclined to think it isn't. It looks like our people.

'Go before they arrive,' I say to Neva.

'Nothing's changed. You're still not safe,' she says. 'Come with me. Do as we planned.'

'I need to see this through,' I say.

Neva blinks. Her face goes cold. 'Right,' she says.

She slips away before I can say more, and I feel my chest hurting a little as I know I've upset her.

I go to the front door, open it and wait for the cars to turn into Mia and Ben's huge driveway. My heart is thudding as I see Ray and Leon climb out of the SUV. I kneel down and place my hands behind my head until they reach me.

'I came to try and protect her. Ben turned a gun on me. He's now tied up inside,' I say. 'He tells me he's MI6.'

Leon looks surprised by this news, but Ray holds out his hand to me to help me stand.

'Let's go and see him, shall we?' Ray says.

In the kitchen Mia is still holding Freya; Ben remains tied. I'm surprised she hasn't released him, until I see how my sister looks at the man she once thought she knew.

'Untie him,' Ray says. 'Are you okay?'

Ben nods. 'Misunderstandings all round,' he says.

Leon cuts the cable ties. Ben rubs his wrists and then goes to Mia.

'Don't touch me,' she says. 'You're a liar.'

'I've never lied about *us*,' Ben says.

'Save this for later, folks. We are moving you,' Ray says. 'You'll have to go into protection.'

'What does that even mean?' asks Mia.

'New life. New identity.'

She shakes her head in refusal. 'I'm not going anywhere with *him*,' she says. She glares at Ben.

'Sweetheart...' Ben says.

'Don't. Just don't,' she says.

'Look, whatever you two have got to deal with, you can't do it now,' I say. 'Go with them. Start a new life and try to put this behind you both.'

'How can you say that? We've been living a lie,' Mia says. Tears spill from her eyes again. 'I just don't believe this is happening.'

'I'm sorry,' I say. 'I never wanted you to know.'

I hold her for a while then I talk her into collecting what she needs for Freya and herself. She leaves the kitchen with Leon in tow.

'I'll join her when she's had time to calm down,' Ben says. 'This is all a total shock for her.'

'Tell me about it,' I say.

'Sorry I pulled a gun on you,' Ben says. 'I thought it was for the best.'

'The dick move was holding my niece while you did it,' I say.

'Mike, you've got to understand—'

'No, mate, I don't,' I say.

I turn away from him and for once I'm not worried what he thinks of me. I've always looked up to Ben. He was an ordinary guy, a good man, who loved my sister. Or so I thought. Now I feel the same disgust as Mia does. I don't know if she will trust him again after this, but I'm sure there will be a lot of questions first if she does take him back.

The SWAT team searches the house and surrounding land to ensure that no one untoward is lurking. I note that the bike is still there and wonder how Neva got away. She isn't found on the premises, so she's either hiding or found some other route of escape.

'Come with me,' Ray says, and I follow him, getting into the back of one of the army vehicles. 'Where were you last night?'

'Neva ambushed my attackers,' I say. 'She got me out of there and to a place of safety.'

'How come she came to your rescue?' Ray asks.

'I'm not going to lie to you about it anymore. She got in touch a couple of weeks ago. Until then, I hadn't seen her since we brought down the house in Cheshire.'

'Why did she contact you?' Ray asks.

'She said she had information about the missing plane,' I say.

I don't tell him that she strong-armed me into giving her intelligence on Olive in return.

'You should have told me she was in touch,' Ray says.

'I thought I could use her data to help our investigation. She was my informant previously, as you know,' I say.

'Okay. What did she tell you that we don't already know?'

I tell him about Solomon Granger and how I suspect he was pretending to be Jay Astor.

'Did she know what had happened to the real Astor?' Ray asks.

'No. I wanted to find out more, so I told her about Angela Carter's body being found. She was surprised that Carter was dead. She said Granger wouldn't have killed her. He's just a hacker. But she was certain he was involved with the hijack of the plane.'

'Surprised how?' Ray says.

'She dropped her guard… It was just a split second, Ray, but I knew she was genuinely shocked,' I explain.

'It seems odd that any death would upset her,' Ray says. 'Anything else?'

'The real Astor was gay, but Granger isn't. I think the real Angela Carter was having a thing with the man she thought was Astor. She probably never knew he was undercover. And, based on the suddenness of Carter's replacement, she wasn't involved with the Network either. Neva also told me that Granger had been "radicalised". Which I thought was odd because it's not a term she usually uses for the "conditioning" the Network normally does. She implied his handler was playing a double game,' I say.

'Maybe Granger tried to turn Angela Carter, but when it didn't work, they brought in a double to be her,' Ray concludes.

'I think that may be the case,' I say. 'Either way, we know Carter was being held somewhere for the past six months while the *doppelgänger* took over her life.'

Ray gave one of the soldiers instructions to take me back to 'the barracks'.

'You'll be there with Mia and Freya until we sort out what to do with you,' Ray says.

'I suppose asking to stay in Archive is out of the

question?' I say. 'But I'm more useful to you there than in hiding.'

'Is that why you didn't go with *her*?' Ray says.

'I want my life back, Ray, and I'm not letting the Network take it from me again. Running away would mean they've won.'

Ray nodded. 'Barracks for now,' he says.

A few more soldiers get in the vehicle and we drive away from Cambridge and across the border to the heart of spook central: Lincolnshire.

Chapter Forty-One

BETH

'I hate to love you and leave you,' Beth says. 'But I have to go home. The last thing I want to do is the walk of shame into work tomorrow.'

Elliot pulls her to him and kisses her on the lips. Having spent the last hour making sure she was having a very good time, he tastes of her.

'Okay. I promise not to start accusing you of using me for my body.'

Beth laughs. 'Oh, but I am. And your amazing tongue.'

They kiss again. It's deep and passionate. Beth begins to regret that she didn't have the presence of mind to bring spare clothing and a toothbrush with her, but she knows that would have been presumptuous. Most men don't like women moving their stuff in after just a few dates.

She gets up from the bed and starts to pull her clothes on. At that moment her phone rings.

'I have to take this,' she says. 'Hi, Ray.'

Beth goes out of the bedroom and into Elliot's sitting

room to take the call. Elliot gets up from the bed and pulls on his robe.

'Good to know everyone's safe,' Beth says. 'See you in the morning.'

'Work?' Elliot says.

'Yeah. Earlier problem now solved,' Beth explains.

'Come here, gorgeous,' he says pulling her into his arms again. He kisses her with small pecks until she begins to think that maybe she won't leave after all. Then Elliot releases her and makes the decision for them.

'Let me order you a taxi,' he says.

Beth pulls on her jacket and picks up her handbag, throwing the mobile phone inside.

'When can I see you again?' Elliot asks.

'I have the kids tomorrow and Saturday night this week. But I'm free Sunday.'

'Let's talk tomorrow,' he says.

He kisses her one final time and then Beth hurries out of the building and into the waiting car. Elliot remains at the door until the taxi pulls away. He gives her a final wave.

On the way home, Beth feels remorseful again. In the space of the week, she's given her ex full custody of her children, and what has she done with her newfound freedom? She's started an affair with the new pathologist. Plus, the work she gave her marriage and kids up for has become a second priority after Elliot.

What's wrong with me? she thinks. *It's like I've just discovered sex for the first time.*

Her relationship with Callum had been a little tame in that department. Her soon-to-be-ex-husband was fairly traditional in his approach to screwing. Although satisfying for the most part, it hadn't been too adventurous. In the end their sex life had fallen into a routine of only once a week – sometimes that drifted to two weeks. Beth hadn't been concerned when it had gone even longer. Callum had always instigated it after that. And although she had got something out of it whenever they did make love, the build-up to it was always a chore.

Unlike Callum, Elliot was enthusiastic, vigorous and unselfish. Beth found him addictive. He was a total distraction though, and when she wasn't with him, she worried about her lack of interest in anything else. *It's new. That's all. I'll get over this. I haven't been laid this good for years.*

Even when Ray had called to tell her that they had Mia and Michael in custody she didn't feel any particular concern or relief. She'd expected him to do his job, but normally she would have wanted to be part of that to take some of the glory. And that was why she had always loved working for MI5: the elevated feeling of success when you finally caught your bad guy, or solved a crime. Until Elliot, work had always been her passion.

She arrives home and lets herself into the quiet house. The place is a bit big for just her alone, a three-bedroom end terrace, with a small patch of garden that she'd never touched because it was Callum's department. Callum had really wanted this place back when they bought it, yet he'd been keen for her to take it over almost as soon as they broke up. As though without their marriage the bricks and mortar he'd loved so much no longer mattered. Or maybe it has too many unhappy memories for him. Beth can see that;

she had made him miserable for most of their marriage even though she hadn't intended to.

I'm selfish, she thinks. Callum had said it to her, more than once. That accusation that she didn't care about anything but herself or the job he hated. *And it is true, isn't it?*

Beth makes some hot chocolate using milk from an opened carton in the fridge. It would go off if she didn't; after all, she wasn't using as much up as she did when the boys were there.

In her bedroom, she strips off her clothes and drops them in the washing basket, before going into the bathroom and turning on the shower.

She steps in and washes, noting that she's a little sore after Elliot's athletics. At first, she was a little scared of having sex with someone else. Partly because she'd been with Callum so long. But now it was freeing. The thought that they could be together in a casual way, or if they became a couple, then that was all they needed to be. No more kids... Just great sex.

I was so comprehensively seen to, she thinks now. Then giggles at the silliness of her thoughts.

Beth has always thought she was very mature, and it is a surprise to think she is capable of such wildness. Like some heroine in a romance novel. She shakes that idea away. Romance has little to do with this. It is too soon to even consider saying the L word to Elliot. If indeed that is how she feels. Though she can't stop thinking about him, even now.

'Maybe it will work out between us,' she murmurs as

she gets out of the shower and pulls a towel around herself. Though she knows she's in no rush to get serious for now.

Patting herself dry she walks back into the bedroom, for the first time in ages not worrying that the boys will catch her naked. It's such a wonderful feeling, this sense of liberty. She decides she won't feel guilty about it after all. She's independent for the first time in over ten years. She doesn't have to answer to anyone any more in her private life.

I'm feeling guilty, because I'm used to that, she thinks. Callum compounded it. *He was always making me feel bad about one thing or another.*

Michael would explain it to her in psycho-babble, no doubt. How she's become conditioned in certain behaviour patterns. He might even say that Callum was abusive with his constant badgering.

With the added pressure of her single status mixed with a growing need to keep her finances stable without another person to fall back on, more than anything she has to keep her eye on the ball now. Work is important.

Beth drops the used towel in the washing basket.

Not as much washing to do now that the boys are gone. *Thank God.* She reminds herself how much she detests domesticity. At least she's had a cleaner for the past few years. That was one thing, working full-time, she's made sure she doesn't have to do too much of. But weekends always were about Cal and Philip. It is hard work entertaining them all the time and having to take the boys to football – which she hated as it bores her to tears.

This weekend, though, she is looking forward to seeing

them and assuaging the guilt of giving them up without a fight. She now has the urge to make it all up to them. She'll spoil them when they are together and they'll see the best of her from now on, because the time she'll spend with them won't be marred by resentment or tainted with bitter arguments. All of which were upsetting the boys, and herself, which wasn't good for any of them.

'It's for the best,' Callum had said and for once she knew he was right.

Beth pulls back the duvet. She feels like sleeping naked, something she hasn't done for years. The thought of it makes her feel decadent, but oh, the freedom to do as you please!

She turns the light off, then snuggles down into her favourite sleeping position. She feels sated and relaxed and happy. She drifts off thinking of Elliot and the fun they are both having.

A short time later, Beth jerks awake.

She's sure she's heard the distance chime of breaking glass. She switches the light back on and pulls her robe over her naked body. She looks around for her phone and remembers it is still in her handbag which she left downstairs.

She walks to the bedroom door and opens it as quietly as possible. Then she steps out onto the landing. She listens at the top of the stairs but hears nothing. Thinking she is imagining things, she returns to her bedroom. As she crosses the threshold, she experiences an odd sensation and shudders as though there is a shift of air around her.

Someone grabs her from behind.

Beth tries to kick backwards and is rewarded with a grunt as her heel meets with her attacker's shin. Then a cloth is pressed over her nose and mouth. She holds her breath, trying not to breathe in the sickly-sweet smell of the chloroform. But as she struggles against her attacker, she soon wearies from lack of air. She's forced to breathe, and then the substance takes her down and down into the blackness.

Chapter Forty-Two

RAY

'Hello, Ray,' says a smooth female voice.

'Beth? It's a bit early, isn't it? Is everything okay?'

'This is not Beth, but I do have her phone,' the woman says. 'And I do have Beth. In fact, she'll be spending some time with me until you give me Michael Kensington.'

'*Neva?*'

'How interesting that you should think I'm her,' says the woman. 'Though she was moulded from the same caste as myself. No, I'm not Neva and it is unimportant for you to know who I am. But I have Bethany Cane and she will remain with me until you give me Michael. I'll be in touch to arrange the exchange.'

The woman terminates the call and Ray is left staring at his phone.

'What's the matter?' asks his wife, Sherrie.

'Work...' Ray says getting up out of their bed.

He goes out of the bedroom and into the kitchen, where

he dials Beth's landline. The phone rings out, but no one answers.

Going back into his bedroom, he pulls on the clothes he was wearing the day before. He leaves the room and goes back downstairs, then he phones Leon.

'Meet me at Beth's and get uniform over there too,' he tells him.

'What's happened?' asks Leon.

'I'll explain when I see you,' Ray says, aware that Sherrie is in earshot.

'I'm on my way.'

Sherrie comes downstairs while he's searching for the car keys.

'I have to take this. It's an emergency,' Ray says.

'What's going on?' she asks. She's unused to Ray being called away so early, even though he's often home late.

'Nothing you need to worry about,' he says.

Sherrie frowns as she notices that Ray is wearing his gun holster again. He meets her eyes and shakes his head to try to allay her fears.

'You know I can't tell you anything.'

He exits the house via the door adjoining their garage and then he takes the small car out onto the currently quiet street.

Ray arrives at Beth's house before the police and Leon. He parks the car out front. Beth's car is there. Unused, as it is most of the time, because the tube is so much easier to get anywhere in London.

Beth's end terrace house has a small front garden and a pathway that leads around to the back. From the front, the house appears to be locked up. Ray follows the flagstone path around the side. He discovers a broken window in the back door. Pulling on some gloves he tries the door: it is unlocked. He goes inside and searches the house, room to room, calling her name.

In Beth's bedroom, the duvet is thrown back, the light is switched on, but there are no signs of struggle.

Another car pulls up on the street. Ray cracks open Beth's bedroom curtain to see a police car and a taxi arrive at the house. He goes downstairs and opens the front door. He lets in two uniformed police officers. Leon gets out of the taxi and joins them.

'Our colleague has been abducted,' Ray explains. 'We need this place thoroughly searched and dusted for prints. I'll get my team in for that but I need you to keep the street clear.'

'Yes, Sir,' says one of the constables. They go outside and take up position to ward off any spectators.

'Looks like they got in round the back,' Ray says to Leon. 'They called me from Beth's phone so we need to set up a tracker on it. See if it tells us anything.'

'I'll call in our team,' Leon says.

After he makes the call, he joins Ray inside Beth's house.

'What did they want?' asks Leon.

'To exchange her for Michael.'

'They must really want him, to have gone to such lengths,' says Leon.

'What I don't understand,' Ray says, 'is why now? Why didn't they come after him sooner? He's been a sitting duck for the last six months.'

Leon shakes his head. 'It's all weird.'

As the street wakes up, curious neighbours gather outside. The police officers do what Ray called them in for and disperse the crowd.

Elliot Baker arrives a short time later. He gets out of his car and flashes his ID to the police officer standing by the cordon.

'What's going on?' he asks

'Beth Cane has been abducted,' Ray says.

'*Beth*?' says Elliot growing pale. 'How? When?'

'I don't know,' says Ray. 'I know it's an unusual request, but I need you to go over this place and find anything you can. You've got a good eye and Michael can't be here right now. Are you okay?'

Ray studies Elliot as, trembling, the man pulls on his crime scene suit.

'For the sake for transparency. We … we're dating. I was with her last night. She left me about 10 p.m.,' Elliot says.

'Oh,' says Ray. 'That's helpful. Knowing her movements before.'

'She came home in a taxi,' Elliot says. 'My local firm. I ordered it for her.'

'Are you sure you should be involved in this?' Ray says.

'Yes. I'll do the best I can to find anything.'

Leon approaches Ray when Elliot goes into the house. 'Conflict of interest?' he says.

'Probably. But he's the best forensic specialist I've ever worked with. If there's anything to find, he'll do it.'

'I'll have my report over to you by this afternoon,' Elliot says some hours later. 'But just to confirm, the perp entered by the back door after breaking the window. Looks like Beth had left the key in the lock and it made it easier for them. She probably heard it and woke. Went to look. At some point they jumped her and she was drugged. I found a discarded handkerchief with chloroform on it. And under the bed was an empty syringe. The handkerchief was careless and probably dropped as soon as Beth was out cold. My guess is they then injected her with something to make sure she stayed asleep.'

'They were careless,' Leon says. 'Dropping two pieces of evidence.'

'Whoever phoned me was telling the truth and they have her,' Ray says. 'They left the handkerchief and syringe to prove it to us.'

'Who?' Elliot asks. 'Why have they taken her?'

'Find out what was in that syringe,' Ray says. 'I'll talk to my superiors and see if I can share more with you. Don't worry, we'll get her back.'

Elliot nods. 'Please keep me in the loop.'

Chapter Forty-Three

BETH

Beth opens her eyes. She is confused, disorientated, and can't remember anything. Her eyes dart around trying to make sense of where she is.

She's lying on a bed in what appears to be a hospital room. She tries to move and finds herself strapped down. Wrists and ankles are secured to the bed and a thick strap also wraps around her waist. She doesn't know how she got here.

A wave of nausea surges up into her throat. She squeezes her eyes shut, and swallows hard.

'Help!' she calls when the sickness subsides. But her voice cracks and breaks with the effort.

She hears movement then: someone is outside the door, as though waiting for her to wake. The door opens and a man looks inside. He's wearing a surgical mask and so she can't see his face. He's also in some kind of uniform. Scrubs? Doctor? No … a nurse.

'It's okay, Mrs Cane,' he says. 'We have you safe now.'

'Where…?' she croaks.

He comes in and pours water into a cup from a jug on a cabinet beside the bed. He adds a straw and holds it to her lips. Beth sips the tepid water. It helps to settle her stomach and soothes her dry throat.

Yes, she's in a hospital. But where and why?

'What happened?' she says.

'Don't you remember?' he asks.

She shakes her head. There's a vague recollection of being with Elliot, coming home … and then…

'Oh my God. I was attacked in my home.'

The nurse shakes his head. 'That's what the doctor said you'd say.'

'Doctor? What doctor?'

'You had an episode. A … *breakdown*. You were smashing up your house. Screaming. Saying someone had attacked you. Your neighbours called the police. I'm afraid you had to be sedated.'

'No. That's not what happened,' Beth says. 'Someone came up behind me. They…'

'It's all right. Don't upset yourself,' says the nurse.

'Where am I?'

'This is a very good hospital and we have the best doctors here,' he says. 'They'll keep you for a few days' observation and if you need help, they'll give it.'

'I … I need the bathroom,' Beth says.

'No problem. Just be calm.'

The nurse unstraps her ankles and waist first, moving to her wrists last. Then he helps Beth to sit. She feels dizzy.

'Urgh. I don't feel well,' she says.

'It's probably the sedative. They knocked you out pretty good. I believe you were hysterical.'

Beth doesn't argue, she is just relieved she has been unfastened. He helps her to her feet and walks her across the room.

'Toilet is in here. Can you manage?' he asks.

Beth nods. She goes into a small bathroom. Toilet, sink and shower all ensuite. She closes the door, leaving the nurse outside.

There's no window in the bathroom but she's observed that there are blinds in the main room that indicate a window.

Beth pees, then she washes her hands and splashes water over her face. Her memory starts to return. She was at home. There was a noise. She went to listen at the top of the stairs and then ... she was attacked. Drugged. She remembers the smell. Chloroform. She glances at the door. She's certain that she's been abducted. But by whom, and why?

'Are you okay in there?' says the nurse at the door.

'Yes,' she says. 'I'm fine.'

She checks herself over and sees the small bruise on her arm where a needle had bitten into her.

Better play along, she thinks.

She comes out of the bathroom. The nurse is standing by the door.

'How do you feel?' he asks.

'A bit better now. Can I use a phone, please? I need to let my family know where I am,' she says. 'And my work. They'll be worried if I don't show up today.'

She's finding it disconcerting that he's wearing the surgical mask.

'I'll speak to the doctor about that for you. But I believe your husband was told. He'd said he'd notify your employers.'

'My husband? I'm split from ... him.'

'Really? Well, he's listed as your next of kin. He signed for you to stay in,' the nurse explains.

'Callum did that? That doesn't make sense. He'd know...'

'Try and get some sleep. They'll bring you some food around soon, if you're hungry.'

Beth sits back down on the bed.

'You won't strap me down again?' she asks.

'Not if you're behaving okay. That's just because you were so ... violent ... I believe,' says the nurse.

'Violent? *Me*?'

'It'll probably come back to you eventually. A lot of people block the moments before a psychotic break. The doctor will talk you through it all,' the nurse says.

'Okay. What's your name?'

'I'm Joe,' he says.

'Why are you wearing a mask?' she asks.

'Rest up now. Lunch will be round in an hour.' Joe leaves and Beth gets off the bed and tries the door. She finds it locked.

'Where the fuck am I?' she whispers.

Beth sits back down on the bed. She feels unsteady. Her mind can't accept that Callum would have signed her into a place like this. But she can't dismiss the idea. Why though?

He's got everything he wanted. Full custody of the boys and her paying towards their upkeep.

Then she wonders: what if he found out about her and Elliot? Maybe he was angry and wanted to punish her. But no. Callum would just confront her. He wouldn't be behind something like this. Would he?

She thinks through possible scenarios and comes back to the same conclusion. She's been taken. This is probably a fake hospital. They'd been trained for situations like this.

But what if it isn't fake?

Then Callum might still be behind this. Beth shakes her head. She can't see him as that devious. He just isn't. What you see is always what you get with him. And, if he did arrange for someone to kidnap and place her in a mental ward, then there'll be serious repercussions. He knows she works for MI5. Her bosses won't stand for this. He'll be prosecuted for false imprisonment at the least. He'll lose everything.

No. It isn't Callum. Which means only one thing. Beth has been taken from her home by someone else. They have an agenda. She has something they want. But what?

It has to be work-related. The only consolation is that MI5 must know by now that she's missing. They'll be looking for her.

Until then, she will be the model patient.

Chapter Forty-Four

MICHAEL

When I hear from Ray about Beth's disappearance, I volunteer myself for the exchange.

'We're not doing it,' Ray says. 'But we may look as though we are.'

'The quickest way to get Beth back is to do what they ask. I'm willing. I'll get out of there again, first chance I get,' I say.

'But what if they don't want to turn you back to their side, Mike? What if they want to kill you?' Ray says.

I don't know what to say in reply but it's a risk I'm willing to take. I'm gutted that Beth has been taken like this. She doesn't deserve to suffer because of me.

'No exchange. The truth is we don't even know if Beth is still alive,' Ray says.

'Make them give you proof,' I say.

Ray hangs up and I'm left holding the phone in the Sergeant's office.

I'm in an RAF barracks in Digby. My sister Mia has been

given accommodation with Ben and their daughter. I've been given a one-room apartment in one of the other housing blocks. Though Ray has said it's for my own safety I'm worried that I am really in custody. Either way he's ordered me to stay here. There's nothing I can think of that's worse than staying here and not helping to search for Beth.

I go to see Mia in the little family apartment they've given her and Ben. When I knock, Ben answers the door. He looks dishevelled, and I notice the blanket and pillow on the sofa where he's obviously slept all night.

'Where's Mia?' I ask.

'She's feeding Freya in the bedroom,' Ben says.

'I'll wait here until she's done,' I say.

Ben knocks on the bedroom door and tells her I'm there. She comes out a short time later, the baby over her shoulder. Ben goes to her and tries to take Freya.

'Don't touch her,' she says. 'Hey, Michael. Do you want to finally hold your niece?'

I flounder a bit, not knowing anything about babies. But Mia tells me to sit down, pointing to an armchair, and I do. Then she tells me how to hold Freya.

I'm nervous: she's such a fragile little thing. A little over four months old and so damn cute. Mia places her in my arms and I look down at Freya. I'd barely given her a glance the day before because I was so focused on making sure I protected her and Mia from Ben. I feel a tremendous ache in my heart: a love I've never experienced for anyone and a huge desire to protect this precious little girl. Under no circumstances do I ever want her to turn out like me or Neva.

'You're quiet,' Mia says. 'What do you think of her?'

I look up at my sister and let her see the water that springs into my eyes.

'I'm scared for her,' I say.

'Then imagine how I feel,' Ben says.

Mia and I look at him. Mia starts to cry then and there's a torrent of emotion from all of us. She lets Ben embrace and comfort her and I hold onto Freya while they get this out of their system.

I'm over my anger at him now. It washes away as I gaze into the innocent eyes of my beautiful little niece. If Ben is who he says he is, then Mia and Freya should be safe with him. But they'll need to relocate as Ray had said. And starting a new life won't be easy for either of them. It will also mean that I'll never see Mia or Freya again. I think about that now, as I place a kiss on Freya's head. She smells … gorgeous. I'd never understood the talk about baby smell before. But there's something in it that makes me want to be her forever guardian. But that's not my job and the truth is, being around me will be more dangerous for her than not. Better that she never knows me.

I stand up, go to Ben and hand him his daughter.

'Look after them,' I say.

'What are you going to do?' Ben says.

'What I have to. But you guys don't need to be part of that,' I say.

Mia hugs me. 'I'm scared,' she says.

'I know. But you're safe here. Even the Network won't take the Air Force on.'

I kiss Mia and Freya one last time, then I turn and leave.

I exit the family barracks and take a look around. The buildings are surrounded by tall wire fences. The barracks are separate from the main base and there is a barrier between the accommodation and the base. There's also a barrier out of the accommodation into the regular village.

I walk around the building and find the car park for the families living here. I'll need a ride to get back to London and the sooner I return the better. I don't know if I can just walk off the base, or if I'll be stopped. I'm mulling over what to do when I see a young woman in the car park.

'Hello? Can I help you?' she says. She's standing by a red Picasso. 'You're new here, aren't you?'

I look at her, not knowing what to say. So far no one has spoken to me, and even when I've walked around, they haven't challenged my presence here.

'I'm Michael,' I say.

'Hi. Elsa. My husband is a mechanic on the base. Just moved in?' she says.

I nod. 'Trying to get my bearings. Would love a trip to the local village, but my car isn't here yet.'

'I'm just going into Lincoln to do some shopping. I can give you a lift,' she says. She smiles at me, flirty. I guess it can be boring being an RAF mechanic's wife. I smile back.

'I'd really appreciate that,' I say turning on the charm. 'Are you sure that's no trouble?'

'Of course not!' Elsa says.

I marvel at how trusting she is. Would any woman really just invite a total stranger into her car? Perhaps it is because she believes me trustworthy if I'm on the base to begin with?

Elsa unlocks her car using a key fob. I get into the car on the passenger side and then she drives to the barrier. The guard inside waves her through and we drive off the base without any difficulty.

I frown. *That was too easy.* Did Ray really trust me enough to stay put that no instructions were left to detain me?

Lincoln centre is about fifteen minutes from the base and Elsa drives us up to the top of Steep Hill and parks the car near Lincoln Castle. I offer to meet her later and buy her a coffee, and say I have an errand to run first. She smiles, saying 'No worries.'

And so I ditch her easily, and go off to find a way to get back to London.

My Network and MI5 training are at odds with each other. I want to jack a car and drive back, but I realise that it will be quicker if I just get a train.

At the post office I use the cash machine and draw out as much cash as possible from my bank account. Then I ask a random stranger how to find the train station. They give me directions which include walking down Steep Hill to the High Street below. I walk down as fast as I can and find a phone shop. After buying a new mobile phone for cash. I leave the high street and walk to the train station.

At Lincoln station I learn that I can get a train to Grantham and from there it is just an hour and fifteen minutes to King's Cross. I get the next train, but when I arrive at Grantham, I've just missed the London train and have to wait a further half an hour.

I've memorised Neva's mobile number and so I call her from the platform.

'I thought you'd reach out,' she says. 'Where are you?'

'Lincolnshire. Did you go to Amsterdam?' I ask.

'Not without you,' she says.

I tell her about Beth's abduction. 'That's bad, Michael,' she says. 'And worrying that they want you so badly they'd take such a risk.'

'How do I find her?' I ask.

'They'll be hiding her in plain sight,' she says. 'Especially if they are planning an exchange. You're not going to give yourself over to them, are you?'

'You mentioned someone in the Network. He was rounding up the strays – Vasquez?' I say. 'Is he behind this?'

Neva sighs. 'I followed a lead to get to Vasquez before he got to me,' she said. 'Just yesterday I heard that he's missing. I think the Network retired him. He was last seen in France.'

'What was in France?' I ask.

'I'm still trying to find out,' Neva says. 'What are you going to do?'

'I'm heading back to London. I'll be at Archive's office by this afternoon. I have to make them use me to help Beth.'

'Don't go there, the Network will be watching. If they grab you, they'll have no reason to return your colleague,' she says. 'She'll be dead within the hour.'

I agree to meet her at a hotel near King's Cross, and then I hang up. She sounds happy once we decide that I'm coming to her first. I try not to read into it but it's also good for me to know I have somewhere to go when I arrive in London.

The train is delayed by ten minutes but when it arrives it's fairly empty. I find a seat near the doors facing the direction of travel and ensuring no one is behind me. Before it moves off, I glance out of the window and see Elsa on the platform. She gets on board.

So … her helping me leave the airbase wasn't a happy accident…

I realise that Elsa's been told to tail me and not detain me. I thought the timing of meeting her and getting a lift was just too convenient. Perhaps Ray knows I'm heading straight back and may well be meeting Neva. He's set me up – though I'm not sure I blame him. I don't think I'd have trusted him to stay put either if the situation was reversed.

At Peterborough, I see Elsa hanging out of one of the doors, making sure I'm not leaving. I stay onboard. The train stops again at Stevenage. We are twenty minutes from King's Cross. I mull over slipping away here, but reason that Elsa will only be waiting for me at the other end for when I get another train into London. No, the best thing to do is lose her in the station.

When the train arrives at King's Cross. I walk along the platform as though I'm unaware of being followed, but as I reach the barriers, I slip in and out of the crowd. Elsa is way behind, trying not to be seen, but also stuck behind the commuters. I get through the barrier and then run as fast as I can towards the tube station.

Hurrying down the steps, I hope she's seen me. I go

down the escalator to the Northern Line and take the next
train.

As the doors close, I see Elsa running onto the platform.
I get off the very next stop and go outside. I join a queue at
a taxi rank. By the time I'm in a taxi to the rendezvous point
with Neva I'm sure that I've lost Elsa. She may be well
trained by MI5, but I also have skills given me by the
Network. Elsa had no chance of keeping up.

Chapter Forty-Five

SOLOMON

'Where are we going?' asks Solomon.

'Back to England,' Subra says. 'I've been called in to see Annalise.'

They are on board a private jet and have passed through security with barely any issues. No one has questioned Solomon's false passport or his reason for leaving the country. Subra had done all the talking anyway at security. Even in Israel, the rich are favoured, Solomon notes. He wonders how many working in airport security were on Subra's payroll. Probably all of them.

'How did you get all this?' he asks looking around the jet. She hadn't been able to command so much years ago.

'I came into my power once Beech died,' she says.

Subra has been telling him much more since his return. He takes this as sign that she has no intention of putting him under cover somewhere else, at least for the moment. He now knows all about Beech, and all about Annalise's takeover of the Network. As well as Subra's frustration over the coup. He hadn't understood the full extent of who and what they were until now.

'How long have you been on the committee?' Solomon asks as the plane takes off.

'A few years. It happened after we met, and after you became Jay,' she says.

'Why were you promoted?'

'Beech had promised it years ago. A reward for work I'd done for him,' she says.

'What work?' Solomon asks.

'It's not important. I'm much further up the ranks now, that's all that matters,' Subra says.

But it was important, because Solomon knows that the planting of him in the airline had been long considered, a well-constructed plan, as though Subra had always known she would need to do what she did. Solomon suspects that this is just the tip of the iceberg too: her full ambitions have yet to be realised.

He thinks about Angela again. Not the fake one – the real one. He'd liked her so much and Angie had promised she'd be freed as soon as the plane went down. He'd given Angie a number to call him when that happened. She'd said she'd pass it on to the people holding Angela, but no one had phoned, and now Solomon wonders why.

He'd liked Angela a lot. More than he was supposed to. More than Subra would have been happy with. He wasn't supposed to get involved with anyone during his absence. But Subra didn't know that he'd been sleeping with Angela. He'd kept that really quiet; he'd had to, or his cover would have been blown as a gay man.

'I can't believe you've been lying to me,' he imagined Angela would say if he ever saw her again. 'You said you loved me!'

And he did. Oh yes, he really did. It wasn't like with Subra. Oh no. She *controlled* him. She was always his superior. Angela was sweet and kind. She looked up to him and he loved her for it.

They'd met in Dubai. Solomon had been working for British Airways then, and Angela had been with United Arab Emirates. That night she was in the bar on her own. Her co-workers on that flight had been generally unsociable. But Angela had gone down to the bar to get herself a nightcap, planning to take it back to her room, but instead she'd taken a seat and stayed.

Solomon was sat on a bar stool a few seats away. He was staying at a different hotel, but had slipped away, because he was tired of playing 'Gay Jay' for the sake of his colleagues. Also, one of them, another gay man, had taken a little too much interest in him and had been hinting they spend some time together. Solomon thought maybe the guy was onto him and knew he was faking, but not why. He didn't want to get into it, and as this was his last flight on the Dubai route, he decided it was best to lie low. After that 'Gay Jay' might just disappear as he was tired of playing the role and so far, Subra had never explained to him why he had to.

When he saw Angela come into the bar though, he was glad he hadn't just merely hidden in his room but had ventured out and found this hotel instead. Here no one knew him, and he could be himself. He went into overdrive chatting her up, and Angela, bored or for whatever reason, desperately needed a bit of attention. They both drank too much and then she'd invited him upstairs. They spent the night together in her room.

He'd loved being his real self for the first time in two years. But after playing the role of 'Gay Jay' for so long, he was nervous. It all came back to him though, and it was a massive relief after two years of being celibate. The next morning, he had to slip away early, but he left her a note with his number on, telling her he lived in London and that she should call if she was there. He hadn't expected to hear from her, but it had felt like the decent thing to do.

A couple of weeks later she called and said she was going to be in town. Solomon had been pleased. He'd thought about her and their night together a lot. He agreed to meet her again and found that their connection was still there: it was dynamic.

She came and visited his docklands flat every time she flew out of, or into, London and they became close after that. It wasn't long before they were planning their meetings around their work commitments.

As time went on, and as cabin crew do, they both wanted to change airlines. Solomon received a communication from Subra telling him to apply to Zen Airlines. Angela had just completed the examination and passed the final interview already. Solomon saw this as fate that they should be together. He also knew he could finally shake the gay persona and be himself with her around. They were both moving to the same airline, for a new route to Shanghai, and he barely gave Subra's orders much thought, except that it suited him right then anyway. When he also got the job at Zen, he'd told Angela she could just stay with him, no need to get her own place. By then they were saying they loved each other. Solomon had almost forgotten that he wasn't really Jay but he was definitely no longer 'Gay Jay'.

'Really?' she'd said when she rang him, and he suggested they live together. 'That's great. I have something to tell you later.'

He'd been expecting her to arrive that day, and so when he opened the door to Angie, it had taken him a minute to realise it wasn't Angela.

'She's somewhere safe,' Angie told him. 'I'm your new friend now.'

'Where is she?' he asked.

'Do as Subra wants and you'll get your little gal-pal back,' Angie said. 'If you don't, you'll get her back in more than one piece.'

Solomon knew just what Subra was capable of. She was evil. He was terrified of her for himself and Angela. He realised he'd been stupid to believe she wouldn't know about his romance with Angela. Subra owned him and she would never let him go. Hadn't she said as much when she first sent him out into the world to play a role on her behalf?

The *doppelgänger* was good: Angie had every inflection down to a tee. She looked and sounded so much like Angela that he tried to just accept her. The first thing she did was hack into Angela's Facebook page. There she posted a status saying she'd be offline for a few months as she was doing a round-the-world trip. She waited a few days, responded to comments and well wishes and then she deleted Angela's page. As it happened Angela had no relatives, only old schoolfriends and flight crew colleagues. She hadn't been much for posting online anyway, and not that savvy when it came down to it, as she didn't realise Solomon had a page; he'd blocked her from seeing it as soon as they started to date and Angela hadn't really had the presence of mind to search for him on there anyway. This all made it so much easier for Angie to take over Angela's life.

Solomon wasn't brave enough to take Angie on, and try to make her tell him where Angela was. Occasionally he'd ask after his Angela and Angie would laugh and say, 'She's getting a little plump, she's being so well cared for.' He hoped it was true. He had to keep believing she was safe.

With Angie gone, no one had thought to tell him any more about Angela and Solomon was afraid to ask Subra because he didn't want her to know how much he cared. But on the final flight, he'd pulled Angie aside and asked her one last time how Angela was.

'They are letting her go this week,' she said. 'She won't know where she's been or that you were involved. But it's best that she never sees you again now anyway. You know you can't go back after this, don't you?'

Solomon hadn't thought about it until Angie spelt it out. No, of course he couldn't. He'd be a missing person, presumed dead. He could never see Angela again. And when she was free, she'd know that someone had taken over her identity. She'd know that he was the only person who could call out her double as a phony. She'd also know by then that he hadn't done.

'She's definitely going to be okay?' he'd asked.

'I promise,' Angie said, and she meant it. He could tell. He'd believed Angie wasn't a bad sort, despite the fact she worked for Subra.

But not seeing Angela again was his deepest regret. They'd had something special and she was nearer his own age, unlike Subra.

Back in Subra's clutches, he'd fallen into his old patterns of pandering to her every whim. He'd had autonomy for three years, but now he saw it for what it was. He'd been submerged in Subra's intrigue, and any independence he'd thought he had was just an illusion.

Even on this plane, as they fly back to the United Kingdom, Solomon understands he is a prisoner and he'll never be free of Subra, not while she still lives.

'Cat got your tongue?' Subra asks as their flight attendant puts a drink down before them.

'I was just thinking,' he says.

'About?'

'Where did Angie send the plane? We haven't heard of it being found yet,' Solomon says.

'It's never going to be found,' she says.

'Why? Why did you do any of this? All for that one man...'

'My dear Sol,' she says. 'That one man was very important to me. Especially his removal.'

'Is he dead now?'

Subra looks at him, 'Can you really stomach the answer?'

Solomon looks away.

'Did you get what you wanted from him, then?' he asks.

'Yes. I got everything. And now look. I have your safe return. My dear Solomon. My beautiful black boy,' she says. She reaches over and strokes his face. 'Do you know how much I love you?'

Solomon doesn't believe Subra capable of love. He knows that he is just her toy. He lets her touch and stroke him; starved of physical contact for the past six months, he's ripe for the picking again. But when he closes his eyes, and receives her kiss, it's Angela he thinks of. Beautiful, blonde Angela whom he will probably never see again.

Chapter Forty-Six

RAY

'Y ou wanted to see me?' says Security Agent Carol Brinkman as she walks into Ray's office.

'I'm up to my eyes in the search for my missing agent,' he explains, 'And in the midst of this I get a phone call and an anonymous letter telling me where to find the Zen Airlines flight 723.'

'Seriously?' she says.

'Yes. A woman. She said if I wanted to know where the flight was, I was to check my top drawer. I opened it up, and there this was.'

Ray holds out the letter to her. She takes it and looks at the wording.

If you want to know what happened to Zen Airlines Flight 723, go to these coordinates.

'Any idea where this came from?' Brinkman asks.

'Probably someone on the inside, involved with the job,' Ray says.

Here you'll find the Zen flight's final resting place. And all the answers you seek will be yours.

'As no country has recorded a crashed plane, we can only assume that it was sent into the ocean. But that's for your people to learn,' Ray says. 'I've enough to deal with right now.'

'I'll let you know what we find,' Brinkman says.

Ray nods. He's curious to learn where the flight went, but Brinkman will now have to deal with this alone.

As Brinkman leaves, Ray's mobile phone rings.

'I hope you have some news for me, Elsa,' Ray says.

'He ditched me. I'm in the tube security office looking at the cameras and it seems he went one stop down the Northern Line. After that I've no idea,' Elsa explains.

'I expect I'll hear from him. Michael is very loyal, and Beth was the closest to him here. I suspect he'll be heading back in after he meets with Neva. She'll help him, cover his back. It's what she does.'

'Why does she cover his back?' Elsa asks.

'I don't fully understand it. But let's put it down to their history.'

'I'm sorry,' says Elsa. 'I did everything you told me to. He was just on to me from the start, I guess.'

'I'm sorry too,' says Ray. 'I was hoping he'd lead you to her and we could bring them both in.'

Chapter Forty-Seven

MICHAEL

Neva is waiting in the reception when I reach the rendezvous point: a hotel across from Euston Station.

'I've checked us in, darling,' Neva says in an American accent as she leads me to the lifts, swiping her room key card to allow us to call it.

'Are we still Richard and Amanda Ellison, then?' I say as I get into the lift.

'Yes. The IDs are still good because they haven't been compromised. So why not?' she says.

The luggage from her bolthole in Kingston is now in the hotel room. Has she got me here to try to persuade me to leave with her? I feel awkward.

'I can't leave without making sure Beth is okay,' I say. I observe that I'm not saying I *won't* leave.

'I'm not asking you to leave,' she says. 'I have other plans.'

She draws me to her. I look down into her eyes and I'm

323

mesmerised. 'You're doing something to me. Triggering me in some way,' I say, feeling suspicious.

'There's no mystical brainwashing involved in what's between us. Just hormones,' she says.

She is the instigator most of the time for our sexual contact and I know that is because I'm often afraid to make the first move for fear of rejection.

There is no clichéd tearing off of clothing, just a slow, careful and languid removal until we are both naked. Then as she stands looking up at me, my heart hurts. It's a similar sensation to the moment I stared at my delicate little niece, except my feelings for Neva are so much more complicated. I don't feel the urge to protect – she's perfectly capable of looking after herself – but I do know that it is something akin to love. I have a flashback of the first time I saw her. A little girl, hiding under my bed, while Beech's cronies came to take me away. Did it start there? Is that why this connection is so strong?

I pull her to me now, feeling the need to take charge again, and she lets me. My kiss is intense and fierce and demanding. When we pull apart, I see a question in her eyes, but I don't understand what it is she wants to know.

I push her down on the bed. There will be no objection.

There's a slight smile on her lips as she pulls me down with her: I'm not in control, but she's letting me believe I am. I'm being manipulated even in this, but I don't mind.

Afterwards we lie together in the bed and I tell her everything that happened since we parted.

'No stranger just randomly offers you a ride,' Neva says. 'You numpty.'

I shrug. 'I needed to get out of there. It was worth the risk. Plus, she was cute.'

Neva gives me a look; it's inscrutable but I hope there is just a twinge of jealously in there. I find myself wondering how many serious relationships she's been in. *Is this a serious relationship to her?* I think.

'So what now?' she asks, changing the subject.

'I have to get to Ray,' I say. 'I need to help him get Beth back.'

'The Network will expect that. You can't give yourself over to them, no matter what.'

'Why? What will they do? Try to condition me again? I hardly think they'll be able to do that now I'm aware of it. Plus, it was only ever Beech that triggered me, you said so yourself. That and the drug I was putting in my own milk sometimes to keep me compliant. None of that can happen again,' I say but I'm not that confident inside.

'They may just want you dead. Have you considered that?' she says.

'I have, and so did Ray. But they went to a lot of trouble to capture me before, so I'm convinced they want to at least try to bring me back into the fold.'

Neva is quiet for a time and then she asks, 'Do you trust Ray?'

'With my life,' I say.

'Do you trust him with mine?' she says.

I'm not sure what to answer. *Do I?*

'What do you have in mind?'

She outlines her plan and I weigh up all the pros and cons of what could happen.

'You said there's a mole in Archive,' I say. 'Turning yourself in will put you in danger.'

'That's what I'm hoping,' Neva says. 'Then, your mole will reveal him- or herself. I can't think of a better way to draw them out.'

'I can't let you do that,' I say.

'Let's ring Ray,' she says. 'Let's see how he reacts to my suggestion.'

I don't like it but I know that expression. She's got a plan and she's going to follow it through, even if I disagree. The only thing I can do is go along with it, but be ready to help – if she needs me. And that is always a big if...

I select Ray's number on my mobile phone.

'It's me,' I say. 'We're coming in.'

'We?' says Ray.

'Neva wants to talk to you,' I say.

I hand her the phone. 'I'm looking for a job,' Neva says. 'Why don't you hire me?'

Chapter Forty-Eight

MICHAEL

The plan is simple: Neva will work for MI5 and we are the only people who'll know at first. As a former Network assassin, she will be our kryptonite against them. But we'll leak her connection with Archive at some point to draw out whoever the double agent is. This part of the plan Neva and I keep to ourselves.

We travel mostly by public transport to a meeting point.

'Not even Leon knows about this place,' Ray had said.

Ray didn't explain why he doesn't trust his right-hand man with this information. I've learned recently that Ray plays a lot of cards close to his chest – like the secret that my brother-in-law works for MI6. Did anyone else know that in Archive until then? Leon hadn't so I'm sure that Beth didn't know either.

'We were probably just as safe in Kingston,' Neva says as we come off the final train in Wimbledon. 'I've paid for it for another month.'

'Yes. I agree. But we need a place that Ray can meet up

with us that doesn't give away any bolthole we already have,' I say.

Outside Ray meets us in a small Toyota.

'My wife's car,' he says with a shrug.

We get in and he drives us to a small detached house not far from the station.

Neva looks out the back window making sure we aren't followed.

'I wasn't tailed,' Ray says. 'Leon thinks I have a dental appointment this morning as well.'

He parks on the driveway and hands me the keys to the house.

I open the door and we go inside. It's modestly furnished, two reception rooms, three bedrooms, one bathroom upstairs, a separate toilet downstairs. It's an average house. I pull the luggage in from the car and deposit it in the hallway.

'Special features you should know about,' Ray says. 'Panic room. In the back of the fitted wardrobe in the master bedroom.'

He tells us the key code to open the room.

'There's a stocked fridge with drinks and a cupboard full of tins. You could hold out in there for weeks if need be. It's steel reinforced and has its own air filter system. The room doesn't run on the electricity for the house but is isolated and reaches directly into the grid. Even if the whole of Wimbledon goes down, there will be power inside there.'

He takes us upstairs and shows us the room. It's got a standard double bed inside, a small office space with a working computer and its own personal telephone line.

'You'll be safe here until I can make the necessary arrangements to bring you into the fold,' Ray says to Neva. 'But it's all underway.'

'What about Beth?' I ask.

'They haven't been in touch yet. They are trying to make us sweat. But I'm hoping to hear soon.'

'When they do, agree to the swap,' Neva says. 'I'll be on their tail and I won't lose Michael.'

Ray removes something from his pocket. 'And just in case, you'll have this with you.'

'What is it?' I ask.

Ray hands me a container. Inside is one single pill. 'Swallow before the swap. It's a tracker. The safest way of putting one on you. They'll check your clothes, ditch your phone and anything else that's suspicious. But this is state of the art. I'll know where you are at all times for up to twenty-four hours. After that your body will break it down and expel it.'

It's a little reassuring that Ray has some form of spy gadget to keep an eye on where I am. Though each of us is trained as field operatives, our role in MI5 has often been research and investigation. Neva and I have the Network's training to back us up too. Something that in my case kicks in automatically when I need it.

'Firearms and extra rounds are in the panic room too,' Ray confirms.

He gives me back my Glock. Then he turns to Neva. They look at each other for a while.

'We've spent a lot of time investigating your work…' he says.

'My kills, you mean?'

'Yes.'

She nods to show she understands.

'I'm going out on a limb here,' Ray says.

'I know. Why do you trust me?' she says.

'I could ask you the same thing, but I know the answer: because Michael does. And, like him, I don't blame you for what you did. You didn't really have much choice. But you can use these skills now, for the greater good.'

'I don't kill to order any more,' she says. 'But I warn you, I will take out as many of the Network's people as oppose me. I want to see them destroyed.'

'I wouldn't expect otherwise,' Ray says. 'Mike, you can log into our systems through this computer. I've given you another password with full security access. Neva, for now I'd prefer you didn't have too much liberty with MI5's systems. So, Michael only.'

Neva leaves us while Ray gives me my access codes and I memorise everything out of habit.

Ray goes downstairs to debrief Neva while I log into the computer and take a look at the transcript of the phone call he'd received from Beth's abductor. This doesn't tell me anything more than I already know. I browse his notes on the missing plane and learn of the anonymous tip. In the folder, there is also an updated note from the pathologist, Elliot Baker, on Carter's autopsy. The swelling of the uterus and the remnants of placenta found in her womb were clear evidence of a full-term pregnancy. Coupled with the pregnancy hormone in her blood, it's proof that Carter had given birth a short time before her death.

I find myself wondering where the child is and if it survived. But I suspect if it did survive, the Network have it.

Now up to speed, I come downstairs just in time to hear Ray's final question to Neva. 'What do you know about Zen Airlines flight 723?'

She tells him everything she's shared with me, plus a little more.

'I did some digging after Michael told me Angela Carter was found dead. It goes against everything I know about Solomon Granger. He's not a killer. He's a mere pawn in someone else's game and that person works for the Network.'

'You've mentioned this one to me before. Last time you said that person was playing a double game.'

Neva nods. 'I'm told that her codename is Subra. She is Israeli by birth. May have even been Mossad to begin with, but it's likely she was a child of one of the Kill Houses. Subra has developed some … radical … views. The Network's conditioning "removes" personal opinion from the operatives, so I'm not sure how or why she's absorbed what she has. But she hasn't been acting in the sole interests of the Network for some time. There are rumours that she has connections with the Almunazama. Whatever she's up to, Subra always has a backup plan. For this reason, I think there were more people involved in the hijack than Carter and Granger.'

'We know that Carter was replaced and then kept imprisoned, we just aren't sure why,' says Ray. 'Why have the inconvenience of keeping her alive when you are going to kill her anyway?'

'Did you see the recent addition to the autopsy report?' I ask Ray.

'No.'

'Baker's added more. Carter gave birth before they stuffed her in the trunk of that car and left her to die.'

I'm watching Neva as I reveal this.

This revelation upsets her. She frowns and runs a hand over her brow as though to smooth it out.

'Maybe she told them she was pregnant and they thought they could use the baby,' she says. 'Was ... Granger the father?'

I look at Ray to see if I can tell her more, and he nods.

'Carter's prints were all over his place. She'd definitely spent a lot of time there. So I'd guess yes,' I say. 'Perhaps they held it over him?'

'I'm going to leave you to settle in,' says Ray. 'There are new mobiles in the panic room. Use them to contact me from now on as they are secure.'

'What about Beth?' I ask.

'I'll be in touch as soon as I hear anything. But Michael, are you sure you want to risk this?'

'Beth would do it for me,' I say.

Chapter Forty-Nine

BETH

There is no natural light coming into the room, and yet there are blinds on the left-hand side. Now Beth opens them and finds that there is not a window behind. It's a wall – white, stark painted brick. The blinds are there to give an illusion of there being a window.

This is no ordinary hospital. Or this is some strange psychological game that the doctors play on the patients.

She prowls around the room after that. Not sure what to do with herself. There isn't even a television to stave off the boredom.

Beth doesn't have a watch, but time passes. Maybe an hour or so, since the nurse released her from her bonds. Then she hears someone unlocking the door.

A tall woman, wearing a catering uniform, comes into the room. She is pushing a trolley that resembles an airline food cart. She takes a tray off and puts it down on Beth's bed.

Beth is hungry, but suspicious that the food is drugged.

333

With the door open, outside her room she hears the normal sounds she'd expect to hear in a hospital. The occasional clang of a chair being moved. The chatter of nurses talking at a station nearby that she can't see. Beth gets off the bed and starts to walk towards the open door.

'You can't go out there,' the woman says. Beth stops and looks at her. 'I left you a menu for this evening's meal. Just tick what you would like. On the tray is a tuna sandwich and some lemon drizzle cake. You want tea, coffee or water?'

'Water will be fine,' Beth says. 'Is there a common room I can go in?'

The woman looks at her. 'You're new here. You're not going to give me trouble, are you?'

'Of course not,' Beth says.

'Good. Eat up. It'll keep you strong and line your stomach for the evening meds. Okay?'

'You're very kind,' Beth says, doing her best to appear passive. 'Did they tell you anything about me? How I got here?'

'I don't have access to that, dear. I'm just a dinner lady. But don't worry. It's not that bad in here. They'll fix you up and you'll be home before you know it.'

The woman places a bottle of water down on her tray.

'Wait,' says Beth. 'Do I seem crazy to you?'

'No one is crazy, honey. Sometimes we just get sick for a while. Just do what they tell you and you'll be out of here in no time.'

The dinner lady goes and once again the door is locked.

Beth feels that being locked up like this is enough to turn anyone insane.

She looks at the sandwich. Picks it up and sniffs it. She feels lethargic, as though the original drug is still in her. She tastes the sandwich. She waits to see if there is any impact on her, and when she feels fine, she eats a bit more. Then she checks the bottled water. It's sealed, but is this just to lull her into a false sense of security? Beth isn't sure. She opens and sniffs the water, doesn't notice anything wrong, and so she sips at it.

Beth explores her options. If she was in an espionage drama, then this place would have been made to look like a real hospital, but she would know deep down that it wasn't. If it is a real hospital, then her captors have dropped her here for some other nefarious reason. And those captors may or may not have some connection with Callum.

The only thing she can do is bide her time and see how it pans out.

She walks around the room to get her energy levels back up again. Then, bored, she sits back on the bed. What the hell is anyone supposed to do with themselves in a place like this?

It feels like an age before the door is opened again and by then she is starting to get fed up.

'Hello, Mrs Cane,' says a man in a white coat, who she assumes is some kind of doctor. Or is pretending to be one. Only time will tell. 'I'm Doctor Fink. And I've come to have a chat with you.'

The nurse she saw earlier comes back in carrying a chair,

which he places down by the bed. He's still wearing a surgical mask, unlike the doctor.

'Please relax,' says Fink. 'I just want to talk through with you what you were doing prior to your little … incident.'

'I went out to dinner, with a … friend. I got home, went to bed, then woke because I heard something. I thought someone had broken into my house. I went to investigate and then, someone attacked me from behind. They chloroformed me. The next thing I know I'm in here. Which is where, incidentally?' Beth asks.

'You're in Hammersmith and Fulham Mental Health Unit,' Fink says. 'But I don't want you to worry about this. At the moment, all that counts is that you fully recover. You see, the police were called to your house. You were fighting with some invisible assailant. After that, a doctor was called in and you were medicated and brought here for assessment,' Fink explains.

'Wow! That was almost word for word what your nurse here said earlier. What doctor? Can I talk to him?' Beth says.

'Unfortunately, he was a police duty doctor. So no,' says Fink.

'I want to call someone, is that possible?' Beth asks.

'In a few days you'll be allowed,' says Fink. 'It's our policy to give you time to recover your equilibrium first.'

'I'm not hysterical, or a danger to anyone,' Beth says in her best rational voice. 'You've taken the signature of my soon-to-be-ex-husband, who is no longer my next of kin. I'd like you to call my boss, Ray Martin.'

She gives the doctor the number and he writes it down on his notepad.

'I will of course follow this up,' Fink says frowning. 'You do seem … *rational*.'

'Please. Just call Ray. He'll sort all of this out. I shouldn't be here,' Beth says.

'Of course, everyone thinks that when they first arrive,' says Fink.

Hours pass after Fink leaves and Beth is left to stew in the room. She knows the time by the arrival of the dinner lady, bringing her supper.

Then the nurse, Joe, returns, this time bringing medication.

'I don't need that,' Beth tells him.

'Everyone on this ward gets sleeping pills,' Joe says. 'Believe me, at three in the morning you'll be begging for some. And the days go quicker if you get some sleep.'

'What happens if I refuse?' Beth says.

Joe shrugs. 'Nothing, as long as you don't go off the rails. If you do, then we'd have to sedate you. I will have to tell the doctor you wouldn't take it though.'

'Why are you wearing a mask?' Beth asks again.

'I have a sore throat. I don't want to give it to patients,' Joe says.

His comment is plausible, though she can't help wondering if Joe just doesn't want to be identified when this is all over. *And now I'm sounding like a crazy paranoid person*, she thinks. *Being in a nuthouse will do that to you.*

'Did Doctor Fink call my boss?'

'He's very busy, Mrs Cane, but he'll get round to it after he's finished dealing with other patients. You sure you don't want the sleeping pills?'

Beth thinks for a minute. 'Okay. It's boring as hell in here.'

Joe laughs. 'Well, you are certainly not being difficult, Mrs Cane. I'm sure you'll be out of here soon.'

He gives her the pills and a small paper cup with water in. He watches as she swallows them. Unlike in films she's seen, he trusts her and doesn't check her mouth to see if they remain there. Joe wheels the medicine trolley out of the room and Beth sits back down on the bed.

She can't think of what else to do. If she's in a genuine facility, they'll see she isn't insane and let her go, and if she isn't, then … it's best to let her captors think she believes them. But, whatever happens, when the time comes, Beth will be ready to make her escape.

She goes to the bathroom, drops the pills she palmed into the toilet and flushes. Then she goes back to the bedroom, gets into the bed and turns over, feigning sleep.

Chapter Fifty

BEN

Ben Cusick knocks on the door of his superior's office. He shouldn't even be in London, but there's no way he's going to disappear without an explanation to Erik Steward.

He's invited in and sits by Steward's desk, waiting while his boss finishes signing a report.

'I received a rather strange note from Ray Martin at MI5 telling me you wouldn't be back at work for the foreseeable future and now you're here,' says Steward. 'Mind telling me what's going on?'

'I'm supposed to be at RAF Digby right now. My family is being relocated. Protection programme.'

Steward narrows his eyes as he frowns. It's an unattractive, somewhat predatory expression that Ben has always found hard to read.

'You took a risk coming here,' Steward says. 'Is this linked to the Network?'

'They might come after Mia. They already tried to get to

Michael. This is not information I'd care to just "phone in",' Ben says. 'But take this now as my reluctant resignation.'

Steward sits back in his chair and studies Ben. 'You're one of my best. I'd hate to lose you.'

'I love my job and it isn't what I want right now, but…'

'Did a security detail bring you in today?' Steward asks.

'Yes. Ray agreed to let me see you.'

'I appreciate that,' Steward says. 'But maybe this doesn't have to be the end of your work for MI6.'

'I'm up for keeping ties if it doesn't put Mia and Freya at risk,' Ben says.

Steward nods. 'Of course.'

Ben thinks back to how Steward had retained him, even after he had compromised himself by falling for Mia. He'd allowed their marriage, and permitted Ben to continue working behind the scenes on the case that linked his Mia to the Network, even though it was a conflict of interests. Ben thought that this wasn't because Steward was sympathetic to his situation, it was more about how it suited him to keep Ben close to a corporation whose activities he was so interested in. Ben had no doubts that he and Mia would have been thrown under the bus if it meant Steward could get the bust he'd wanted. He sometimes wondered how this would have gone down if Archive hadn't beaten MI6 to it.

Ever since Ben was recruited there had always been rivalry between MI6 and MI5 – something that Ben had never understood since they should all really be on the same side.

Now Ben stands and turns to leave Steward's office but

as he opens the door, he comes face to face with Carol Brinkman.

'Hi, Ben,' she says. 'How's things?'

'Complicated,' Ben says.

'Well, I have some news and I'd like you both to hear this. I just got off the phone with Major Craig. They've found the plane.'

'Good grief,' says Ben.

'The plane crashed on an uninhabited island. Naturally there were no survivors.'

Brinkman looks pleased as she delivers this information. It is rare for any situation like this to have a positive outcome – if finding a crashed plane with everyone dead could be deemed positive.

'We've retrieved the black box. All bodies were accounted for, with the exception of four of the stewards and one passenger,' Brinkman says. 'Anyway, the bodies are now in British Navy hands and are being returned home. We've set up a centre near the dock and I'm going there with forensics to start up the investigation.'

'That's not an outcome any of us expected,' says Ben. 'I thought the plane would have been at the bottom of the ocean.'

'Well, for once, I'm happy to have good news. Curious that four flight attendants are missing though: Carter, Astor, Armitage and Bell. Armitage and Bell didn't come up as suspicious to us. But maybe they got in the way of our hijackers?'

'I guess we'll know more when you listen to the flight recorder,' Steward says.

'Yes. I'll get a transcript of it over as soon as I do.'

Brinkman briefs them both on Ray's intel and how it led to the finding of the plane.

'When we got the coordinates, we were told there was nothing but water in the area. We thought we'd be sending divers down to retrieve bodies if we could actually find the plane. But there's an uncharted island. So micro that even the satellite maps just show it as a bit of rock protruding from the Indian Ocean.'

'Good work, Brinkman. Maybe I need to get you to work with MI5 a bit more often?' Steward says.

'*Sir*?'

'I've long wondered about Ray Martin and what they do in Archive. They often get results that none of us do. I wonder why that is?'

'Informants, I guess,' says Brinkman.

'What're your thoughts, Cusick?' Steward asks.

'How did the informant know where the plane was?' Ben says.

Steward is thoughtful. 'I'd love to know who this anonymous tipper was. See what you can find out about Martin. Have a tail put on him. Let's see who his sources are and see if we might utilise them too?'

'He won't like that if he finds out,' Brinkman says.

'Then make sure he doesn't notice he's being followed,' Steward says.

Brinkman leaves.

'Cusick?' says Steward. 'You want to remain in MI6 employment?'

'You know I do,' Ben says.

'Then use this opportunity to find out what you can about Martin. He'll have his guard down around you now, as he'll be convinced nothing matters since they will be putting you in witness protection and you won't be allowed further contact with us. But you'll keep in contact. You know how.'

Ben nods.

'So I guess you better make a show of clearing out your office, and let their detail take you back to safety,' Steward says.

Chapter Fifty-One

CAROL

Carol Brinkman returns to her office. Sometimes working for the government is like being back in a primary school yard when the boys started developing testosterone. It was a pissing contest. It was the part of the job that confused and bored her. What was it with Steward that he just had to get one up on Ray if he could? Brinkman shrugged. She'd enjoyed working with Archive – mostly. Leon was a bit of a dick, but Ray, Beth and especially Michael were all okay. Michael, from what she could see, was a great asset to the taskforce. Intuitive, gutsy, and all of it was backed up with a sound education.

Brinkman makes a phone call to set up an informal tail on Ray Martin but she feels a twinge of guilt about it. As an afterthought she instructs the team to only report directly to her. Steward's request to tail Ray is unusual. Why shouldn't Ray have his sources? She has hers, and undoubtedly Steward has his.

It comes to something when we spies start following each other, she thinks.

But even so, she's curious about Ray herself. He does have a wide range of intel, things that even MI6 didn't get to know about, and their fingers were in everyone's pies. A little insight into how he did it wouldn't hurt. It might even help inform some of her own future decisions and get her out of the rats'f nest that was MI6. To be honest, she'd prefer a placement in Archive if she could get it, but so far that looked like a closed shop: invitation only.

She sends Ray an email, letting him know that his intel led to the finding of the crash site. It didn't hurt to show her continuing cooperation. Almost immediately she receives a reply.

I was just going to contact you and ask how it went. I look forward to seeing the flight recorder transcript. It may give us a lead. Thanks for working so well with us. Must do this more. After all, we are on the same team. All the best, Ray.

She finds herself looking around her office. If only Ray knew what she had been instructed to do, then he wouldn't be quite so friendly.

Maybe she'll tell him. Maybe then she could get away from Steward. Or maybe Ray would never trust her again. You never knew how things would turn out once you played your hand in this game.

Chapter Fifty-Two

MICHAEL

After Ray leaves the safe house, Neva and I explore the kitchen. The fridge, freezer and cupboards are all fully stocked with fresh items. We won't have to venture anywhere for weeks if we don't need to. Normally in a safe house, security would be posted with the people you want to protect. But in this case, Ray knows that we can look after ourselves, and fewer comings and goings will draw less attention to our presence here.

I make us both an omelette and we sit and eat it at a small round table in the kitchen. Since meeting Neva I've spent a lot of time indoors, trying not to be seen. And now we behave just like two people that have always lived together.

'Where do you see all this ending up?' I ask her now.

'Ending? There's only one ending and it comes to us all,' she says. 'But what I think you mean is this new relationship between me and your boss. Am I correct?'

I nod.

'If I help Archive – and believe me I know a lot of things that will help you – then maybe I can have some form of normal life.'

'You'd want that?' I ask.

Neva smiles. 'Yes. But I'm realistic. I can't just run for ever. The world isn't big enough, and the Network's reach is … vast. If I'm in the employ of MI5 I may be given an identity that hides me. We'd be working together. But first we have to fix the immediate threat you face for that to be viable.'

'Ray will want to capture and question those involved in Beth's disappearance,' I say. 'How do you feel about that?'

'I've said I'll help him,' she says. 'And if capture is what he wants then it can be done. But the Network will expect retaliation. They haven't survived this long for nothing. Their people will fight and die rather than be taken. Because if they are taken and talk, then the Network will kill them anyway.'

'If they are in custody, they will be safe,' I say.

'Oh no, Michael. They'll be sitting ducks. The trick is to get information from them before they are assassinated.'

I know Neva has more insight than me, but I run the scenario of how the Network could get to our witnesses. I meet her eyes and see the truth of it. She could do it, so it's possible anyone else could too.

'I thought the Network operated by keeping most of its employees in the dark about all of their dealings. "Need to know" basis. At least that's what Beech told me. So why would they care if we have some of their people?' I ask.

'They are all pieces of a puzzle. If Vasquez was able to

put that puzzle together somehow to get to the committee, so could we. But you're right. Capture is best if we can do it. And being forewarned on security could help your people. But we still haven't discovered who the mole is. That person will be the chink in MI5's armour.'

Earlier I'd asked her why she didn't tell Ray there was a spy in Archive, but Neva hadn't answered. The truth is, I already knew the answer: she wanted to be sure she could trust Ray first. One thing we'd both learned was that anyone could be a sleeper agent. Even someone you've known for years. Time would tell if they were safe, and if we weren't, then Ray, if he was somehow compromised, would give himself away. I hoped my faith in him proved to be justified.

After lunch Neva gets her laptop out of her flight bag and opens it up. It's a heavy-duty, military-looking machine with its own Wi-Fi and I'm sure it's also encrypted.

I don't have to watch her to know what she's doing as she contacts someone on Tor websites.

'That's interesting,' Neva says. I wait for her to explain. 'Granger has made contact with my source. She and he worked together in the past. He's asked her to help him find Angela Carter.'

'He doesn't know she's dead...' I say.

'Which would confirm that he didn't kill her and thought she was safe,' Neva says. 'Unless, of course, it's a double bluff.'

'I feel for him,' I say.

'Why should you? You don't know him.'

Though it's getting easier to admit how I feel, I hesitate

before telling her, 'I went crazy not knowing if you were okay, and things are complicated with us.'

Neva looks away, her expression unreadable. I think it is because she struggles with her emotions as much as I do.

'I mean, if Granger was in love with Carter, and they were having a kid, how must that feel?' I continue.

'Yet he went back to Subra after his mission,' Neva says. 'That doesn't say love to me. Or show concern for his child.'

'If he's been conditioned...' I say.

Neva shakes her head as though what I've said is wrong.

'You obviously know more than me,' I say.

'Subra procures men,' she says. 'Young men. She's something of a cougar – though I hate that expression. Her skill has always been seduction – we all have one, as you know.'

She explains what she knows of Subra.

'She will have reeled him in, made it so that he couldn't live without her. Then, slowly she would have introduced her views, getting him on side as much as she could. But ... if Granger is wavering, then Subra's control on him isn't as strong as she'd like. She will keep him close, try to bring him back in line,' Neva concludes. 'And my source just told me he's back in England.'

'That is interesting,' I say. 'Perhaps we could ... draw him out. Give him the information he's looking for regarding Angela.'

'Tell him she's dead?' Neva says. 'If he did care for her, that will start some trouble. Good. You're thinking like a Network operative now, Michael.'

'I was thinking more along the lines of telling him that we know where she is. Get him to meet up with us.'

Neva knows exactly where my head is: if we meet with Granger, we might be able to enlist him. Especially after we tell him what really happened to Angela Carter.

Neva sends her source a message.

Tell him we know where AC is, she types. *Can arrange a meet.*

After that, it's just a waiting game.

350

Chapter Fifty-Three

SOLOMON

After finding an internet café and making some connection with old hacker contacts, Solomon returns to their hotel room bearing a gift for Subra. A latte from her favourite coffee shop and two Krispy Kreme donuts.

Solomon snuck away while she was in the shower, taking the only opportunity to ditch her he could find. She's been watching him like a hawk since his return, and he could guess why. She knew, deep down, he was no longer her stooge.

'Where have you been?' asks Subra.

'I wanted to surprise you. I had to search for these, though the coffee shop was nearby. Sorry I was so long' He kisses her and places down the donuts and coffee on the table by the window.

The hotel is in Soho, and they are waiting for news of an important meeting.

'That's thoughtful of you,' says Subra.

She sits down at the table and reaches for one of the coffees. She sips and sighs as though it's the best taste in the world. Then she takes one of the donuts out of the bag and begins to nibble on it.

Solomon watches her enjoying the treat he's brought.

'How long will it take to hear?' he says.

'Anytime soon. It's going to be an interesting day for you, Sol. You're going to learn so much about the people we work for,' she says. 'I hope you know that this shows I have great confidence in you. And that you are indeed privileged.'

Solomon nods, but inside his head he explores what he knows already. Subra has lied to him. He was about to leave the café, having set his friends up to do a discreet search for Angela, only to receive a quick response. Someone knows where she is. They also warned him to keep it from Subra... *She's not to be trusted*. They'd even used her name. This person had to have inside knowledge of Subra's precious Network. That's when he knew that they were telling the truth.

Of course, their warning wasn't needed: he would never dream of telling Subra he's been searching for Angela. After all, she is behind her being replaced on the flight. And Solomon has spent the past six months worrying where they'd taken her and if she was safe.

No one could be trusted, however. Even Angie had lied to him. And she'd been so sincere when she told him, 'Don't worry, she'll be home safe and sound before you know it.'

She'd promised they'd confirm Angela was free and he

was still waiting to hear. Why had he even trusted her when he knew she worked for Subra?

Now he has a lead, Solomon isn't sure how he can make contact again with this informant and meet as asked.

Today, as Subra had said, was a special day and he will have to accompany her; there is no way out without arousing suspicion. Disappearing for a while again is also not an option. She is distrustful of him as it is and if he wants to survive this, he has to be smart. After all he knows what Subra is capable of.

Since returning to her, she's questioned him often about what he's done while he was away. She even asked about other women. He's denied any relationships, despite the unfairness of her demands. She sent him away from her for three years! What did she expect him to do? Solomon knows that Subra would not have been faithful to him during that time. She was too sexual, and there'd always been the other young men, even when they were together. Though for some reason she expected him to remain celibate and alone during his period of absence. It just wasn't fair.

Even so, he doesn't rave at her. He just lets the anger bubble up inside him while he passively goes along with everything she asks. All the time focusing on Angela, and what he'd had with her for a brief time. It was real and equal, not anything like the relationship he has with Subra.

'I've been tasked with something very special indeed,' Subra says.

She loves to brag about her new power and Solomon doesn't mind listening because every time she speaks, he learns more. 'I'm to bring in a former sleeper turned informant. He was being groomed to take over from Beech. Now that Annalise is in charge, I think she plans to make an example of him.'

'I suppose you have other plans?' Solomon asks.

'Oh, you know me. I always have plans.' Subra finishes the last bite of her donut.

'Have the other,' Solomon says. 'I bought them for you.'

Subra smiles at him. She reaches inside the bag and at that moment her mobile phone rings.

'Hello, Annalise,' Subra says as she answers.

'Michael is coming in,' Annalise says.

'How pleasing,' Subra answers. 'What results you've had since taking over. I'm so glad I supported your application.'

'He's not to be harmed. Yet,' says Annalise. 'As discussed, I want you to do the pickup.'

'Where?' Subra says smiling.

'I'll text you the details now,' Annalise says.

When she hangs up Subra is grinning like the cat who has not only got the cream but now has access to a lifetime's supply.

'How perfect. Michael will be in my hands and Annalise will never get hers on him,' Subra says.

'Who is this Michael? Why did Beech want him in charge?' Solomon asks.

'Oh, he's no one important. A child of Beech's vanity.' Subra shrugs.

'What do you plan to do with him?' Solomon says.

'Nothing sinister, my dear boy,' she says. 'I know you're

squeamish. But I happen to have access to some information only Beech was supposed to have. You see, I was Beech's contingency plan. He always suspected Annalise would make a move if he was ever retired. Now, I'm going to take over the Network and Michael Kensington will help me do it.'

Her boast seems far-fetched and impossible, but Subra's confidence oozes from her smile. Solomon doesn't believe that 'nothing sinister' will happen. Death follows Subra like a bad smell.

'And what will you do with the Network then?' Solomon asks, indulging what he thinks is her fantasy.

'That I'll keep to myself for now,' Subra says.

Her phone pings, and Subra sees the location of the drop. Michael Kensington will be waiting for her, alone, at Richmond Park.

Chapter Fifty-Four

MICHAEL

'When they pick you up and are sure they aren't followed, I'll receive a text telling me where to find Beth,' Ray says.

'And we trust them?' Neva asks. 'What if she's already dead?'

'They sent me a recording showing me she was alive half an hour ago. We are going to have to take a chance that it was genuine. If they kill an MI5 agent, they will be opening themselves up for a whole lot of pain,' Ray explains.

'Could you tell where she was?' I ask.

'It looked like a hospital room,' Ray says. 'We're checking all of the local ones to see if she's turned up. Or at least Leon and Elsa are,' Ray says.

I make no response at the mention of Elsa; I'd already surmised that she was working for Ray. One of many field operatives that we usually never get to meet.

'Ready?' says Ray.

I nod.

We leave the safe house. Neva has another motorbike that Ray procured for her. She gets on, puts on her helmet and drives away, leaving me with Ray as previously agreed. She will be at the rendezvous before we get there.

I get into Ray's car. He holds out a bottle of water to me, and I take the tracker pill, swallowing it down with a large gulp of water.

Ray takes out his phone and opens the tracker app. He connects the device to mine and shows me; it's pulsing and static as we sit in the car unmoving. Then, he stows his phone in his pocket and we pull away.

All appears to be good.

I feel a little anxious as we enter Richmond Park and drive to the place arranged. The park is fairly quiet midweek at this time of day, and so we only see a few other cars. Ray drives slowly until he sees a park bench with a red balloon tied to it. This is the spot.

Ray pulls the car over to the side near the park bench and I get out. He looks at his phone again, checks the tracker is still working, and then he drives away.

I'm alone by the park bench now. There's no sign of Neva, yet I'm certain she's nearby. No matter what, I believe she has me in her sight.

A black stretch limousine pulls up beside me. The blacked-out window rolls down and I look inside. I see a beautiful and enigmatic woman staring back at me.

'Hello, Michael,' she says.

The driver of the limo gets out and opens the door for me.

'Please get in,' says the woman.

'I wasn't expecting this,' I say.

'There's no reason why you shouldn't return to us in style,' Subra says.

I get inside, forcing myself not to look around for Neva or Ray. As I take a seat opposite her, the chauffeur closes the door behind me.

She's not alone. There's an attractive black guy sitting beside her. He doesn't make eye contact with me but I recognise him from the photos on Jay Astor's social media: it's Solomon Granger. A circumstance that I can use to my own benefit if needed. How fortunate.

'Whom do I have the pleasure of meeting?' I ask.

The woman smiles. 'I'm Subra. Surely Mr Beech mentioned me to you.'

'No. He didn't tell me anything about anyone. So, if your plan was to get me back to stop me helping MI5, then you've wasted your time. I don't know anything that can help you,' I explain.

'Of course you don't,' Subra says. 'Can I offer you a drink?'

She indicates the limo's bar. There's a bucket with champagne on ice and a bottle of expensive whisky.

'No,' I say. 'Aren't you going to frisk me?'

'There's no need,' Subra says. 'This whole car is built like a Faraday cage. Nothing can get in and electric pulses can't get out. So, if they are tracking you, I'm afraid you'll be cut off from their tracers. And if you're carrying a weapon, then good. I may need you to use it *for me*.'

I frown at her. 'I thought you were here to collect me for

the Network. And to free my colleague. Which you will do now, since you have me.'

'Oh yes. Of course. How careless of me.' She opens the window, holds out her mobile phone and presses send. She glances at the message. Once it's away she pulls her hand back inside and then the car begins to move. She rolls the window back up. 'There, we have our privacy again.'

'Beth?' I ask.

'Don't worry, she'll be free as soon as Ray Martin reaches her. For now, I'd like to talk to you,' Subra says.

'I'm listening,' I say.

'Mr Beech wanted you to take over from him,' Subra says. 'I'm of a mind to make that still happen.'

Subra outlines her plan to me. 'No one will stop you walking in and taking over. They'll welcome it. It is, after all, your birthright. And I'd second your move. They all hate Annalise.'

'Sounds too easy,' I say. 'What's the catch?'

'You'd have to kill her. She won't go down without a fight.'

I sit back in the car. A million thoughts are running through my head. The thought of owning the Network is suddenly appealing. Yes, the other side of me, the Michael that Beech groomed, knows that everything of his should be mine. I try to push this urgent greed back down. That's not me at all. Is Subra doing something to trigger me?

'Take your inheritance,' Subra says. 'No one deserves it more.'

I see Granger turn his head to look at Subra. I focus on him. Remember what I need to tell him. Angela… She's …

dead … the child. But even though I have the opportunity I don't say the words. I don't turn him on Subra. Instead, I sit and stare, unable to do anything else.

Subra's lips move but it is as if my head is under water. I can't hear what she's saying. I feel my mouth moving too now. I'm telling her about the tracker inside me, about Neva being on our tail, and Ray's plan to send in the cavalry once she takes me to their safe house. It's as though my private thoughts can't help but tumble out. I try to focus on Granger. He can help me; I just need to say out loud the other things I know. It will break her hold. It has to.

'So you'll do it?' Subra says. 'You kill her, or you die, Michael. There will be only one opportunity. And believe me she's strong and devious. She may even suspect me of duplicity.'

I can feel the purr of the engine as the limo continues to drive away from the park.

'Don't worry about the tracker. I have something that will permanently disrupt it,' she says. 'And Neva can follow on, we'll have need of her too.'

Chapter Fifty-Five

SOLOMON

The limo pulls into an underground car park and Solomon watches as Michael follows Subra's instructions. Solomon is mesmerised by this process as she takes control of Michael.

In some form of hypnosis, Michael follows Subra from the vehicle. Solomon gets out too. He feels invisible, and surreal, as though he's left his body and is just a spectral observer of Subra's machinations.

'Search him,' Subra says, looking at Solomon.

Disconcerted, Solomon pats down Michael's coat and finds a mobile phone. He drops it into the back of the limo. He finds Michael's Glock in the holster under his jacket.

'Take it out for now,' Subra says.

'What about this tracker?' Solomon asks but Subra ignores him.

'Get in,' she says to Michael pointing to a white SUV that's parked on the left. Michael walks over, opens the back door and gets in. He sits on the back seat, quiet and passive. Solomon can't understand how Subra is making him do it. He feels uncomfortable about the whole thing but doesn't object. He wonders if she's done this sort of thing to him in the past. *Is that why she can make me do anything?*

But no, Solomon knows she hasn't hypnotised him. Seduced, persuaded, coerced with her vibrant lifestyle, she did all that. Even so, he was just as much a puppet to her as Michael is now.

Subra approaches the car and Solomon sees the Taser in her hand seconds before it shoots into Michael. Michael jerks but makes no sound. Subra tases him until he slumps.

'You had him under your control, was that really necessary?' Solomon asks. He feels sick. Her methods have never made him happy and he can't help speaking out.

'It was necessary to disrupt his ingested tracker,' Subra says. 'You drive.'

She hands Solomon the keys and then Subra gets in the back of the car with Michael. The limo pulls away and leaves the car park, turning right onto the main road.

'Go,' says Subra.

Solomon turns the ignition and pulls the car out of the parking lot.

'Left,' she says.

'Where next?' Solomon says.

'Annalise has checked into the Tower Bridge Hotel. We're going there.'

As Michael remains unconscious, Subra places a different gun in the holster under his jacket.

'When we get in, we'll say we searched him. Hand over his Glock when we arrive,' says Subra.

'But if they search him again?'

'They won't,' Subra says. 'Annalise will take my word for it even if she's wary. She knows I won't leave a weapon in the hands of a dangerous enemy.'

Solomon is not sure if he really wants to meet this Annalise in person, Subra is bad enough. But from what he's heard Annalise is even more deadly.

'He doesn't look very dangerous to me right now. What did you do to him?' Solomon says. 'He just started taking orders—'

'I spoke his trigger words,' she says. 'He'll do anything I want now.'

Solomon tries to work out what the words where that Subra used. She'd been spouting some philosophical line about how the world needed masters, then there were the strange words she'd said. They sounded … *Latin*, maybe. He wasn't sure because he couldn't remember the words or the order they fell in and he's never been good with languages.

'Take the next right,' Subra says.

Solomon turns the car down the next street. They've circled around the block and are now heading in the direction of Tower Bridge.

Solomon glances in the rear-view mirror and sees Subra looking out of the back.

'Are we being followed?' he asks.

'Undoubtedly,' Subra says. 'But we won't see her even so.'

At that moment a motorbike pulls up behind them.

'Maybe I was wrong,' Subra says.

'That's her?' Solomon asks.

Subra doesn't answer. The bike overtakes them and Solomon can see that it's not a woman but a slender man on the bike.

The rider takes the next turning and zooms away.

Solomon tries to focus on the road as they approach the hotel. They pull up in front of the door and then Subra begins to smack Michael on the cheek. He rouses. She whispers something to him again. He sits up straight: back under her control.

'What about the car?' Solomon says.

'Leave it here, we won't need it again,' she says.

Solomon follows Subra and Michael as they walk through the hotel reception. Subra goes straight to the lift and presses the call button. As they wait for the lift Solomon looks around. Wracked with guilt, he's self-conscious and paranoid.

Over by the reception desk a man in a black suit watches them. Solomon tries not to stare at him but the man is overly curious about them. He's about to mention this to Subra when the lift arrives.

'Get in,' Subra says and both Michael and Solomon obey as if they are equally under her influence.

Solomon turns and looks out on the reception. The man in the black suit is no longer standing by the desk. Solomon feels a prickle of anxiety as the lift ascends to the top floor. He doesn't know whether it was the man in reception that concerns him, or the thought of meeting Annalise for the first time. He fears she is far more dangerous than Subra.

He hates not knowing Subra's full plan. Will she really tell Michael to kill Annalise? Solomon doesn't want any part of this, but is unable to object. Since his return to her, he has grown increasingly anxious, afraid to be himself, and all because he knows deep down that she may kill him too on a whim.

There are two black-suited men waiting in the corridor as they arrive. Solomon is sure that one of them was the man from downstairs. Though he must have run up the stairs to be here as they arrived, he isn't out of breath and there isn't even a bead of perspiration on his brow.

'She's expecting you,' says one of the men and Subra smiles, confident and relaxed.

Solomon has seen Subra like this before. She is still and calm, but underneath coiled and ready for a fight. She is at her most lethal right now.

She passes the two bodyguards without acknowledging them and leads the way down the corridor, stopping at a door in the middle. The door opens, and Subra and Solomon top and tail Michael as the three of them enter.

The door opens up into a glorious sitting area. There are two plush sofas, a wide-screen television, a bar/kitchen area and a dining table with shiny black granite placemats laid out as though guests are expected for dinner.

'Sit there,' says one of the bodyguards.

The other one goes outside and closes the door behind him.

Solomon takes his lead from Subra and the three of them sit down on a plush velvet sofa. Michael says nothing.

'He's unarmed, and in my control,' she says to the guard

The guard takes the Glock as Solomon holds it out.

'And how is he so placid?' Annalise asks as she comes out of the bedroom.

She's wearing a red silk kaftan, and Solomon admires her ageless beauty and the glorious platinum hair that tumbles down over her shoulders. Other than Subra, he has never seen such mature perfection. She walks towards them with the grace of a dancer. Holding his breath, Solomon finds himself staring at her.

'Subra,' Annalise says. 'How wonderful to finally meet you in person. Only you are my equal in seductive talent.'

Subra takes Annalise's offered hand. They shake formally.

'So, this is Michael, and he's in your thrall,' Annalise says.

She ignores Solomon and his attentive gaze while she studies Michael's passive expression.

'I have complete control over him,' Subra says.

'A neat trick, one born from the school of Mr Beech, no doubt.' Annalise smiles. 'Fascinating. I always wondered who Beech used as a surrogate to carry Michael. It was you, wasn't it?'

Subra says nothing, though Solomon digests this information – was Michael her son?

'He came to me, but I said no,' continues Annalise. 'I felt no desire to be restricted by pregnancy. Kritta was the other one, I believe. I knew that, just not which child she bore.'

'We went through it together and gave birth on the same day,' Subra says. 'Mr Beech was eternally grateful to us both. And so he gave me the means to activate Michael, should I need it.'

It is Annalise's turn to wear a cold twitch of a smile.

'And this is Solomon. Your little toy,' Annalise says, turning to him.

'I'm no one's toy,' Solomon says.

'Be quiet, boy,' Subra says.

Solomon bristles at being called a 'boy'. He's tense and overwrought and is struggling to hide it.

Subra whispers something under her breath. Michael stands. He reaches into his jacket, removes the gun she put in his holster earlier, and shoots the guard between the eyes before he can react.

Annalise leaps back as Michael turns on her.

'The committee will kill you for this,' Annalise says.

'They will applaud me,' says Subra. 'Did you really think any of us would want an upstart in charge? Kill her.'

The gun levels on Annalise but as she looks down the barrel, she sees the hand holding it now trembling. Michael is fighting the kill order. Annalise narrows her eyes and a look of curiosity gives way to something else that Solomon can't fathom.

'Kill her!' shouts Subra.

Annalise uses Michael's hesitation to dive into the bedroom. She slams and locks the door behind her.

'Go after her,' Subra yells. 'Don't fail me!'

Michael doesn't give chase and Subra tries to take the

gun from his hands. She wrestles it free from his fingers and turns it on him.

'Killed ... Angela ... Subra...' Michael says.

'What's he saying?' says Solomon.

'Angela ... child ... born ... killed...'

'Shut up,' says Subra. 'Or I'll blow your fucking brains out. You're only useful to me if I own you.'

She points the gun at Michael's head.

Solomon's mind is a whirlwind of anxiety. His eyes dart from the dead guard to Subra and then to Michael. Michael knows something about Angela!

'What about Angela?' Solomon asks now. 'Where is she?'

'Killed. But ... *baby*...' Michael says.

Solomon grabs Subra's arm and tugs at her. 'Where is Angela?'

'Subra ordered kill...' Michael says.

'Shut up, damn you!' Subra says.

She shakes off Solomon and raises the gun once more. 'I'm going to enjoy this. Beech's bastard forced on me. Do you think I ever wanted to spew out any brat into this world? You're useless. I should have just aborted you,' she says.

There is a loud crack as something hard smashes down on Subra's head. Solomon swings again. He is holding one of the granite placemats and it crashes against Subra's skull a second time.

Subra's head bursts like a traumatised melon, before her legs crumple beneath her. She falls face first down on the floor.

'You had her killed, didn't you? You fucking bitch,' Solomon screams at her body. 'You murdering sick bitch.'

Solomon falls to his knees. Tears streaming down his cheeks as Michael's words all begin to make sense. Angela had told him she had something to tell him.

'A baby? Oh my God. Where's my child, you fucking cow?' He shakes Subra's body but the assassin lies unmoving and unresponsive, a red pool of blood slowly spreading over the marble-tiled floor.

Chapter Fifty-Six

MICHAEL

There's a loud pounding beside me. I come to and find myself in a hotel room. Solomon Granger is on his knees crying, Subra is unconscious on the floor or, given the amount of blood, more likely dead. I have a rush of memory as my conscious mind coalesces with my formerly triggered mind, and I realise then that I'm in peril.

There's shouting outside, and gunfire. I look over at the bedroom door and remember that Annalise ran inside. I look around the room assessing the situation. Subra took back the gun she gave me and the bodyguard is still holding mine. I take my Glock from his dead fingers. Then I walk to the door, give it a hard kick and burst inside.

The room is empty, but I see an adjoining door and realise that Annalise has escaped into a second suite. I try the door but find it locked.

Behind me I hear the door to Subra's suite caving and gather that Annalise's men are coming in. I shoot the lock on the adjoining door and run through. This suite appears to be empty also, and the main door is open onto the corridor. Annalise has made her escape. I run out and double back to the suite I was in as I hear Granger yelling. By the time I get there, two guards have him pinned up against the wall.

'She killed my lover!' he says. 'She's got my kid!'

I put two bullets into the first guard. The second lets go of Granger and turns on me, gun in hand. I shoot him in the gut, taking some pleasure in the fact that it will be painful. The gun drops from his fingers and he tumbles forward. I walk to him and shoot him once in the back of the head.

I feel cold and emotionless. I look back at Granger to see him prone. He sobs on the floor, not looking at me, with his hands covering his head. Then he starts to hit himself hard on the head and in the face as though the realisation of Angela's death tortures him more at every moment.

I look down at Subra. So, this was my mother ... or surrogate at least. I kneel down, check her pulse and, as suspected, find that Solomon did a pretty good job of bashing her conniving brains out. *Good.*

'Michael!'

I turn to see Neva at the door. The killer in me is halted by the sight of her. She is the only thing keeping me from the darkness that threatens to take me over to the Network's side. I'm relieved to see her, and my emotions slip back into play and the coldness inside me begins to thaw.

'Annalise has escaped,' I say. 'Neva... She... I *recognised* her. She was ... she had to be...'

'My mother?' Neva says.

She turns and runs down the corridor, hot on Annalise's tail. *Her* mother. I have no doubt at all that this is true. Neva was the image of her.

I don't know what to do with Granger. He hasn't looked up and acknowledged me, nor even Neva as she came into the room. I think he must be in shock.

'Solomon?' I say. 'Come on, we have to get out of here.'

'She *killed* her, didn't she? She murdered my Angela. I *loved* her.'

I feel for the man and so I kneel beside him and tell him the truth about Angela Carter. Everything I know.

I take his arm and pull him to his feet. At that moment, Ray arrives with Leon. I pass Solomon on to them.

'This is Solomon Granger. He hijacked the plane. He's all yours,' I say.

Leon takes Granger, cuffs him and leads him out. Armed police are swarming through the hotel by the time we get downstairs.

'How did you find me?' I ask Ray. 'She Tasered me and I thought that neutralised the tracker.'

'There was a tracker in your shoe,' Ray says. 'Neva put it in while you were sleeping. I was worried they'd trigger you and then get you to talk. So basically the tracker pill was a lie.'

'Subra knew the words,' I say. 'Apparently she was my incubator.'

'Your mother?' Ray says.

'I don't know. Possibly. But she carried me for Beech either way. From what she said she didn't enjoy the experience.'

'She triggered you then?' Ray says.

'Briefly. I was already fighting it when she Tased me. I think the Tasing helped me gain control. It rebooted my brain. I was playing along as we walked through the hotel and knew what I was doing when I took the guard out. Even so, it was hard to fight when Subra started speaking again and when she ordered me to kill Annalise.'

I tell him about Annalise and her resemblance to Neva.

'Can you remember the trigger words?' Ray says.

'Yes.'

'Good. We can work out how to undo their power over you,' Ray says.

I nod, and then I feel bad because I haven't asked if they got Beth.

As though he anticipates my question Ray says, 'Beth's safe. They stuck her on a psychiatric ward. Faked a doctor's sectioning.'

'Jesus. They hid her in plain sight,' I say. 'Neva said that would be the case.'

'She's with Elliot Baker. They're dating, you know.' Ray grins.

'Ha! I had my suspicions. She blushed every time he was mentioned!' I say.

For a moment this light relief makes me feel better. I'm reassured that Beth is in safe hands.

'Has Neva flown the nest?' Ray says.

I look around and then see her across the reception area talking to Elsa.

'Looks like she didn't,' I say.

'Good. She's definitely an asset. Michael, I'm going to do

everything in my power to make sure she's accepted as such.'

He casts a glance towards Leon and I wonder if words have been spoken to suggest that some people do not want her on board.

I walk towards Neva and Elsa. She looks at me and shakes her head, and I know then that Annalise has escaped. But of course, someone in her shoes would always have an exit strategy.

I nod to Elsa.

'Glad you hung around,' I say to Neva. 'But this is a long way from over.'

'It will be a steady drip, but we'll wear them down. Is that Solomon Granger?' she says.

I look towards the front door and see Leon leading a handcuffed Granger out. As if he feels his eyes on me, Granger looks up. I meet his gaze: another soul broken by the Network. But he'll have a lot to answer for even so. Hijacking the plane, and living with a false identity. Even if he was coerced, he's still guilty.

'It's her,' Granger says. 'Angie! I thought you were dead!'

I look at Neva and she glances at Granger surprised by his outburst. She and Elsa both look shocked.

'You killed her! She killed my Angela!' Solomon says and I'm sure he's looking directly at Neva.

'Get her!' Solomon shouts. 'She's in disguise but I'd know her anywhere!'

'Michael?' Neva says. 'No...'

Ray is running towards us then, gun in hand and the shit hits the fan one more time, as they come in to arrest her.

But Neva has already anticipated their move. She grabs Elsa and, holding her knife against her throat, backs towards the door.

'Neva! Wait!' I say. 'Come in and let's sort this out.'

But her eyes are cold and distant as she falls back into her assassin mode. She won't be taken alive, and she will kill as she's been conditioned to do.

I block Ray and the armed response team.

'Let her go!' I say.

'Get out of the way, Mike!' Ray says. 'She's been lying to you.'

I glance over my shoulder at Neva. She doesn't deny anything, instead she pulls Elsa out of the door with her.

The response team hurry towards the door but I'm there first and Neva pushes Elsa at me before she runs away, losing herself in a crowd of tourists.

The team flow out onto the streets after her, but I know she's already hidden.

Despite their efforts they will never find her.

'Where will she go, Mike?' Ray says beside me.

I think about the little cabin on the Thames, but I don't say a word. I shake my head as though I don't know.

'It's a misunderstanding,' I say to Ray. 'It has to be.'

'She's been playing us, Michael,' Ray says. 'She was Angie all along.'

But I'm struggling to believe it even though I know that if she wasn't guilty, she would not have run.

My mind casts back to the pictures we have from security cameras at the airport of Angela. All blurry. Face turned away for the most part. But possibly the woman was the same height and build as Neva.

Was Solomon right? Could it be her?

Chapter Fifty-Seven

MICHAEL

'You mustn't blame yourself,' Beth says as I sit in the interview room with her.

I've just briefed her on everything that's happened since her disappearance and she's recorded the conversation for Archive's files on the case.

We are looking at printouts of the only pictures they have of Angela's *doppelgänger* and the resemblance is so close I find it difficult to deny. How could I have been so wrong about Neva?

The dream of our white-sanded beach fades from my mind, worn away by the corrosive tide of doubt. A sharp and painful reality presents itself to me.

'If Granger is telling the truth then I've been a total idiot. Because of our similar backgrounds, I let my sympathy for Neva cloud my judgement. All along she was probably working for Subra,' I say.

'There still might be an explanation,' Beth says. 'This

may not be as it appears. But until we find her, we won't know.'

I don't wish her luck on the search: Neva will not be found and it's pointless to even consider telling them about her Thames bolthole. She won't have gone back there.

My only consolation is that even Ray didn't notice the similarity after meeting Neva. Or perhaps he did and just wanted to let it play out. My mind is in turmoil, and my heart hurts. It's a physical pain brought on by the shock of this revelation. She was giving up running. That's what she'd said. All to have a life with me, I'd thought. One moment my mind refuses to admit the evidence before us, the next I'm certain she's been stringing me along to get access to Archive.

'I've gone through every scenario and none of them make her look innocent,' I say to Beth. 'But thanks for the optimism.'

Beth pats my arm.

'I'm sorry they came after you,' I say. She looks tired and I think that she shouldn't be here so soon after her ordeal.

'I'm just glad my kids weren't there,' she says. 'But I was never in any danger once they dumped me on that psych ward. Eventually Doctor Fink would have called Ray and discovered the truth. But at least now we have Granger in custody and Subra is dead. Another strike against the Network.'

'Agreed,' I say.

'Want some coffee?' she asks.

I nod and Beth stands up and goes out of the room.

Alone with my own thoughts I run through my memory

of Neva's reaction to the news of Carter's death. I see again her shocked expression. For this reason, I can't believe that she was capable of killing Angela Carter in cold blood just to steal her child, yet Granger's accusation implicates Neva.

I'm not being held – my statement is voluntary – but I still stand up and prowl around the interview room like a guilty suspect. I'm a long way from being over the trauma of the last few months, and every day it feels like my life becomes more unstable, when it should be returning to normal.

The door opens and Ray comes in, carrying two coffees. He sits down in the chair Beth just vacated on the opposite side of a table from me. I remain standing, but I lean against the wall and look at him.

'What a shit show,' he says. 'She's been running rings around us all.'

'What do you mean?' I say. 'Granger could be lying…'

Ray sighs. His eyes fall on me and I see pity in them. He believes Granger. He thinks I'm Neva's stooge. I see my failure reflected in his eyes and it hurts. A flare of anger and resentment bursts inside me, though I'm not sure if it is Ray's silent judgement that makes me feel this or whether I'm annoyed at Neva for putting me once again in this position.

'Mike, it was bugging me. I wasn't sure…' Ray says.

'What was?' I ask.

'When I spoke to Neva for the first time. There was this familiarity. I don't know. The tone in the voice, the accent. I couldn't place it but I'd heard it before. Then, when I rang her and told her to put the tracker in your shoe, her voice…

It was like she was being less guarded. I recognised her then.'

'Recognised her from where?' I ask.

'I think she was the anonymous caller that told me the plane's coordinates. At the time, when I suspected it, I thought – well, great, she has resources and she's helped us. But now, it sort of confirms that Granger is telling the truth. Neva probably was Angela Carter's double and if this is so, she was on that plane.'

I'm struggling to believe this still, but I don't say anything. I see Neva in our moments alone. I recall how she gave herself to me and I want to hold onto the idea that this was real and everything they say she's done is somehow a mistake. That Granger is wrong and that Neva just resembles the girl that replaced Angela Carter.

'Granger's given me a statement,' Ray continues with the straight face of a funeral director. 'It makes interesting reading. This plan of Subra's sprang up a while ago,' he says, before outlining Subra's plan. 'Then there's Neva's part in this. Granger said he never knew her as anything other than Angie. And as Angie, it appears that she killed the flight assistant, Shelley Armitage, because she got in their way during the hijack. Granger thought she'd shot the pilot and co-pilot too. But he never saw it happen. He had believed that Angie was killed when she jumped out of the plane and her parachute didn't open. It's possible she used Chloe Bell's unconscious body to fake her own death. Chloe, as you know, was one of the other flight attendants and she's the only other body that wasn't accounted for. Other than the businessman Armin Shah, whom Granger admits to taking with him. After that it's safe to assume that Angie/Neva rerouted the plane. Probably leaping out at another rendezvous point that Subra didn't know about. To be honest this does jar with me. If she was working for Subra, why not jump at the rendezvous point and join her? It doesn't make sense really.'

'Maybe she was playing a double game with Subra,' I suggest, still searching as hard as I can for some redeeming part of her character.

'I hate to say this, Mike, but it's possible Neva was working with this Annalise, her mother, all along.'

I shake my head in denial. 'That can't be right. She was searching for her parents. She wanted revenge for being given to the House. She wanted me to help her find out who she was. I was convinced she was telling the truth.'

'I'm sorry, Mike. I know you don't want to believe it. But the evidence points to her guilt. She told you she didn't know her parents so that she could enlist your help. She used what she knew about you to gain your sympathy, to build a connection between you that you wouldn't question.'

I take a breath then let out a slow sigh. He's right. I don't want to accept it, but I can't deny it's looking more and more likely.

'Who was Armin Shah and why did they want him?' I ask. 'He came up clean on our searches. No illegal dealings and no links to the Network that we knew of.'

'Granger says he was a committee member of the Network. He believes Subra killed him, but doesn't know what information she got from him first,' Ray explains. 'For what it's worth, Granger is full of remorse and was happy to tell us everything. It doesn't excuse him though. He still went along with Subra and he's just as responsible for the deaths of everyone on that flight.'

I listen to Ray as he further outlines his theory on Neva's connection and involvement. What he says makes sense, but I still have questions. What did Subra want from Shah that was so important she would orchestrate this whole mission just to get hold of him? Planning it months, maybe years beforehand.

I don't voice this to Ray because he'll think I'm still trying to find some good in Neva, when it doesn't look like there is any. Deep down, I know I probably am, but it's hard to take after the time we've spent together. It jars with me so much that I ask Ray if I can interview Granger too.

'Let's all get some sleep and maybe he'll be able to give us more in morning. The man is in shock and it won't be economical if we wear him down further. We need him on side and willing to talk.'

'Okay,' I say despite my impatience to catch Granger out. 'Tomorrow it is.'

Ray gives me a new address to go to that night and I'm escorted by a security detail. I'm not safe in my own apartment, I can't go back to the other safe house as Neva now knows its location, and so I'm put in yet another house. This time I'm not alone, Beth is with me also because Ray is equally concerned about the kidnap. We have guards on shifts posted with us too, so that at least we can get some rest in relative safety.

As I take a shower in the new house – almost a clone of the previous safe house – I try to wash away the deep depression that the possible revelations about Neva's motivation have plummeted me into.

I had begun to trust her and, coupled with my confused emotional connection to Neva, this is all so hard to take.

I get into the strange bed and try to sleep but my broken dreams are full of anxiety and anger.

Chapter Fifty-Eight

BILL KENT

Bill Kent pulls the door down on his garage and locks in his expensive tools. It's late and he's spent the day building a bespoke bookcase for a customer in Surbiton. The shelving unit is now in the back of his van to be delivered and for the job to be finished first thing in the morning.

'I didn't think you'd still be here,' says a voice behind him.

Bill turns and finds himself face to face with Angie ... only she's no longer wearing the blonde bob wig. Now she has long red locks. Bill wonders if these are genuine because he's never had contact with her except as Angie.

'Christ! What are you doing here?' he says looking around.

'They found the body?' she says.

Bill nods. 'Yeah. Had to give a witness statement, but I said what you told me to.'

'Let's go up to your flat,' Angie says.

'Okay, but what if ... you know ... we are being watched?'

'The coast is clear,' she says.

Kent leads her away from the double garage and to the front of the apartment block. He opens the door and they both go inside. She follows him up to his apartment on the first floor.

Angie glances at the police tape covering her former apartment. Then she follows Kent to his flat across the landing.

Kent unlocks the door and they go inside.

Angie glances around as she closes the door behind them.

'It was quite hilarious,' he says now. 'Cops and MI5 in here, drinking cups of tea. Best acting job I've ever done. I was all tearful and upset.'

'Where did you keep her?' Angie asks.

Kent frowns. 'You know she was restrained in the bedroom.' He glances at the door of his bedroom.

'Did you get rid of the restraints?' Angie asks.

'Why? You fancy trying them out?'

Angie walks to the bedroom.

'Look, you've nothing to worry about. They don't suspect a thing,' Kent says. 'I was just a casual neighbour.'

Angie opens the bedroom door and walks in. She sees twin beds, one of which has a metal grilled headboard. She examines it, sees the scratches from the cuffs that had once held Angela Carter.

'What's up?' Kent says from the door.

'While I was … on the mission,' Angie says. 'What happened here?'

'What do you mean?' Kent says.

'Tell me how the end went?'

'Ah, get off on the detail, do you?' Kent says.

Angie glares at him.

'Okay. Well, I know you said we had to put her in the car and I should complain about noise and they'd come and find her. Well, when I got your note, I was a bit surprised.'

'What note?' Angie asks.

'I destroyed it, but you said, when the baby comes, to call this number and they'd take care of everything,' Kent says.

'Okay. So you got my note. How did you know it was genuine?' Angie asks.

'I get it, this is a test? It was left in the letterbox. Like usual. A brown envelope, with another envelope inside for me to leave with the reply. I kept the number and rang it when the kid was born,' Kent says.

'So the baby was born. Was it alive?' Angie asks.

'Yes. Screamed its head off – I was a bit worried we'd have complaints from the tenants below. Then I remembered that you'd taken care of that already and the place was empty.'

'Boy or girl?' Angie asks.

'Sentimental over kiddies, are you?' asks Kent.

'Answer my question,' she says.

Kent frowns.

'Boy. Your boss was pleased,' Kent says. 'Anyway, they came to get it and told me to finish her off.'

Angie nods. 'And how did you go about that?'.

'Well, I thought you wouldn't mind if I had a little fun, but then I thought about the DNA. You'd gone on about that a lot. So I strangled her a bit. Watched her eyes bulge. She was all scared… I—'

'*Liked it*?' Angie asks. She has a half smile on her lips as Kent speaks.

'Yeah…' His eyes glaze a little as though he's reliving the feeling of having his hands around Angela Carter's throat.

'You see, that's the problem with you,' she says. 'I told you to keep her alive. I told you to look after her. Not hurt her. Didn't I?' Angie says.

'Well, yeah, but once you didn't need—'

Kent's words are cut off as she grabs him by the throat. He's not a tall man and she's strong and cold and he knows she's capable of snapping his neck with barely a twitch. Kent remains still as she holds him.

She releases him suddenly. 'Where's that number?' she says.

Kent pulls his mobile phone from his pocket. Angie snatches it from him. She memorises the number and then deletes it from Kent's phone.

'I know what you did to her,' she says. 'I saw the autopsy report. I wanted her alive. I didn't authorise this and your instructions were only to come from me. You've caused me a lot of trouble, Kent.'

Her hand flicks out and the knife slices across Kent's throat. His hands fly up to his neck as the blood gushes down over his pale blue T-shirt, turning the fabric aubergine.

As he falls to the floor, unable to stop the bleeding, Kent watches her go into his bathroom. Through muffled ears he hears running water.

As Angie walks back, he sees her push the knife back up her sleeve and remove the long red wig. Underneath is strawberry blonde hair.

His eyes glaze over as she walks from the room, leaving him dying and bleeding out on his bedroom floor.

Chapter Fifty-Nine

SOLOMON

Solomon lies on top of a low bunk in a cell. He has no idea where he is. They took him from the Tower Bridge Hotel and then he spent hours telling them all about Subra's plans.

There is a cathartic relief in telling someone what Subra had forced him to do, but still, he can't sleep. It is as though the blindfold he was peeking around has at last been removed. Every detail of what has happened ever since he met Subra now repeats over and over behind his eyes, as though he is a dying man reliving the key moments of his life.

He finds his life lacking and desperate. A series of horrific mistakes. Distant from it all, he can see the experiences for what they were. He fell for the glitz of Subra, and the money, always in abundance, was a contributing factor.

That night he develops an unrealistic fear of the dark. In the cell, a box barely big enough to pace, he feels as though

389

he is already in a coffin, lying underground waiting to suffocate as claustrophobia swamps him.

The panic rises in him. He imagines Angela's ghost lurking in the corner of the room, and when he drifts to sleep, he jerks awake thinking he hears the sound of a crying baby.

When the hysteria threatens to overwhelm him, he gets off the bunk, trips over the table and chair that fill the corner nearest the door, and starts to bang on the metal, calling for help.

A duty officer comes. He opens the flap in the door and looks in. Light bursts into the space, dispelling the phantoms of Solomon's guilt.

'Please,' he begs. 'I can't sleep in the dark. Not tonight.'

They send a doctor in to sedate him. But the drug just makes him woozy, and ultimately his body fights to shake it off as his terror increases.

They've taken his watch and belt. Even the laces from his shoes, though he can't imagine what they expected him to do with those. And so the pitch blackness remains unrelenting.

'Please,' he cries again. 'Please. I can't be alone in this dark.'

The duty officer takes pity on him and leaves the flap open, letting light from the corridor drift in.

It calms him until his mind clears and he lies thinking about Angela – and Angie, whom he could never confuse with the woman he loved.

Angela is dead. He should have known, should have felt it. And above all he should have been able to stop them taking that plane. Instead, he'd used his skills to give them access to it. All those deaths were on his hands, including Angela's.

Subra would have killed me, he thinks. But it's no excuse and he rubs his palms together as though he can remove the invisible stains. *I'm a coward.*

Just past midnight, Solomon drifts off to sleep, as the doctor's sedative begins to work. He dreams of Angela, smiling and flirty in Dubai. And then he feels a tug as his body is hoisted up.

He's standing now on a precipice, teetering on the edge. His confused and drugged brain recognises danger and his mind, flushed with flight-mode adrenaline, wakes.

He's standing on the chair in his room. Something is wrapped around his throat.

He looks around. The door to the corridor is open and a female figure stands there, silhouetted. Though he can't make out her features, he knows it is her. Angela: come to take her revenge.

But no. The dead only rise in fairy tales, and Solomon reminds himself of this.

'I loved you,' he says. 'No! Not *you!*'

She looks up at him and Solomon knows then this is no ghost of the woman he loved, but the reality of a murderer.

'Angie...' he says as the chair is kicked out from under him.

His neck doesn't snap and so it's a slow death that chokes away the air, crushing his throat. His befuddled and dying brain almost sees this as poetic. He'll die as he deserves, and maybe if there's a god he will see Angela again.

The cell door closes and locks as his feet kick in an unconscious effort to flee. And then the flap is slowly drawn closed. Solomon is dropped once more into the darkness, making the fear of this cell becoming his coffin very much a reality.

Chapter Sixty

ANNALISE

Annalise sits back in her first-class seat. She's home free again and she's delighted with the outcome. She couldn't have planned it better. Subra, a thorn in her side, is now dead. And Michael is now even more in her sights. It is only a matter of time before she brings both him and Neva back into the fold and she will welcome them both with open arms.

How incredibly stupid Subra was to think that Beech had trusted her with his biggest asset. Beech had known all along that she was working with the Almunazama.

No, Subra's knowledge was only half the story, and there was Kritta who owned the other half. Mia. Oh yes, Mia: the key to Beech's empire.

She accepts a drink from the flight attendant and finds herself chuckling. Her private jet is up in the air, the Network are still under her thumb, and Subra's attempted, and failed, coup will knock back any future attempts at a takeover for a while. She is flying high in every way.

She studies the luxurious cabin of the plane. Once Beech's personal transport, it has a jacuzzi bathroom, and a bedroom at the tail end, as well as this lovely sofa relaxation area, with a personal bar.

As they climb further up into the air, Annalise's phone, attached to the onboard Wi-Fi, receives a WhatsApp call.

She glances down at the number and then answers.

'It's done,' a voice says on the other end.

'Well done. I knew I could rely on you,' Annalise says. 'You can come home to me soon, my little one.'

The call ends and Annalise sips her drink once more.

There's noise from in the bedroom, and she nods to her security guard to go and check on its occupants, trussed up and drugged. She is taking Kritta and Stefan back to her chateau. There she will have the time to get all she wants from them before she rids herself of yet another dent in the Network's armour.

The net is closing around the other committee members, but this is just the beginning. Annalise has many plans for the future as she deploys and infiltrates with her own personal, and very loyal, army.

She sips her drink. The gold locket around her neck feels heavy.

As she often does, Annalise opens it up. She looks inside at the picture of a cute five-year-old child on one side, and the lock of hair, trapped behind plastic, on the other. Strawberry blonde, the same colour her own hair was once, but now it is pure white. The picture was taken on the day that Annalise handed her over to the Network's chief procurer, Tracey Herod.

394

Neva, my child. You continue to do me proud.

Annalise closes her eyes. She gloats on her achievements. Twenty years in the planning and she is almost there. Even Subra, a tremendous strategist, did not have such foresight.

As the plane draws closer to its destination Annalise relaxes in her seat. Not long now and the Network and the Almunazama will both belong to her.

Chapter Sixty-One

MICHAEL

'Pull him down,' I say.

Elliot Baker, ever reliable, is there to do what's necessary. 'Sometime between midnight and 2 a.m.', he predicts, as the guards haul down Granger's body, found that morning hanging in his cell.

'I want all the security footage for last night,' I say.

As I walk away, leaving Elliot to do his job, Ray calls me.

'It was a busy twenty-four hours,' he says. 'Bill Kent was found dead in his apartment this morning too.'

'Who's Bill Kent?'

'He was the man who lived opposite the *doppelgänger* Angela Carter. It looks like he was more involved than we realised. Get over here, I need your observation skills, and then I want Baker here when he's done with Granger.'

Later I go to the apartment. I hadn't read the transcripts of Kent's interview about Carter, there'd been so much happening, and Leon and Beth had been dealing with him, not me, and so it was one of those things I had to catch up on.

Therefore, I'm not surprised to find both Leon and Beth at the scene.

'He didn't appear to know much,' says Beth as I reach the top of the stairs. Ray is keeping everyone outside now that forensics have taken samples and photographs, but he doesn't want to move the body until I see it.

I go inside after pulling on a crime scene suit over my clothing as we don't want any cross contamination.

'In the bedroom,' says Ray.

Kent died kneeling and then keeled over into his own blood. His throat has been cut. I examine the wound but have to take a breath as I know whose MO this is. I go into the bathroom and smell bleach, see that the sink is washed out. I note that any and all evidence has been removed.

'Mike?' says Ray from the living room door.

'It's her,' I say. 'Neva.'

'We found restraints and evidence that we think will prove Carter was being held here,' says Ray. 'In one of the drawers there were newborn nappies and clothing.'

'No sign of the child?' I ask.

'No. But we can guess who has it.'

I feel sick as I walk past Ray but I try to do my job. Pointing out everything I observe as I move through the flat. Leon and Beth remain quiet out on the landing, and I consider that both of them feel guilty for not picking up on something about Kent. I wonder if I would have felt something, had some gut reaction to Kent, if they'd allowed me to come that day. But I squash this thought, recognising it for what it is: pointless and arrogant.

Whatever Kent knew doesn't matter because he's not telling anyone now.

Afterwards I return to the safe house, depression hanging heavy on my heart. I'm haunted by the image of Neva moving through Kent's apartment.

In the kitchen I pour myself a stiff drink.

Idiot! I say to myself. *For all my education, I've been led along by my cock.*

But I know this isn't strictly true. Neva means something more to me than that. But was it all a game to her in the end? I'm still struggling to accept her betrayal after the many times she's had my back.

This is the strange place I live in. These are the dark and confused corners my mind reaches into. I try to shake away the pointless rage and push aside what I believe I know of her, focusing on the facts. She kills him. She cleans up after herself. The evidence at Kent's appears to be overwhelming.

When I weigh everything up, I can no longer deny that Neva was involved. She was probably Angie, as Granger said; why else was his silence so important? Hadn't Neva told me she could get to anyone, and if MI5 had them they were 'sitting ducks'? Which can mean only one thing: Neva lied to me. She played me. All along I've been her foil. And worst of all, she almost gained access to Archive through me. The reality of her betrayal sinks into my unwilling mind. I switch my focus from the sadness it brings. I turn on the assassin inside me, trying to freeze out the pain, but

Beech's Michael is pushed out and away as my anger rises in a way I've never experienced before.

The killer inside me analyses my fury. It has nothing to do with ego: it's not because Neva outsmarted me. It goes way deeper than that: how can I ever forgive that she made me believe in her? How can I ever forget the promise she gave of a new and fuller life? Promises that scatter now in the wind like cheap paper confetti.

To calm the rage, I make myself some promises.

I'm going to catch Neva. I'm going to end this and when I do, I'm going to make her admit every single lie she's ever told me. And in doing so, I'm going to take back the heart that I gave her. And after that, I might even kill her for her treachery.

Hell hath no fury like a man scorned.

THE END

Michael and Neva will return in *Kill a Spy*...

Acknowledgments

Huge thanks as always to my agent, Camilla Shestopal, for all of her guidance and input. She never lets me fall down and I love working with her as she totally gets me. It's a privilege and an honour!

Thank you to Colin Paul Renouf, who has been working with me on the technical accuracy of some aspects of this book. His help has been invaluable in making this a spy thriller I can really be proud of.

Also, thanks to Joshua Rainbird for his sound medical advice. Joshua has helped me now with several titles when I've needed mental health information. All of which requires accuracy and detail.

Massive thanks to my editor, Bethan Morgan, who shows such amazing understanding of everything I'm aiming for within my texts. She always delivers such insightful and positive comments that I can respond to and that help me elevate my writing to the best it can possibly be. And this book was no exception!

Thanks so much to Holly for the brilliant design of the covers for this series. I love these covers so much. They say so much about the content and if I wasn't the writer on these, I'd definitely be drawn in by them.

And finally, I'm so very proud to be part of a wonderful working partnership with One More Chapter publisher, Charlotte Ledger, and the fantastic team that work so diligently behind the scenes to help get the word out about what their authors are doing. Cheers also to Melanie Price, who does so much behind the scenes that makes sure the books get seen – we'd be lost without you! Love you guys so much!